"Brackston wonderfully blends history with the time-travel elements and a touch of romance. This series debut is a page-turner that will no doubt leave readers eager for future series installments." —*Publishers Weekly*

"Fans of Diana Gabaldon's Outlander collection will delight in Brackston's new series and eagerly await its second installment. A bewitching tale of love across centuries." —*Kirkus Reviews*

"A solid, enjoyable read with a hint of magical time travel." —*Booklist*

PRAISE FOR *THE RETURN OF THE WITCH*

"By chapter four I was cheering 'Yes! We're going back to the seventeenth century.' Dark events trigger a fascinating chase through the centuries that will appeal to fantasy and historical readers alike. Elizabeth and Tegan are back in a heart-warming tale of witchery, female power, and tantalizing time travel." —Martine Bailey, author of *A Taste for Nightshade*

"A spellbinding choice for fantasy devotees and readers happy to find a dash of magic added to English history." —*Booklist*

PRAISE FOR *THE SILVER WITCH*

"Vivid Welsh historical details, haunting surroundings, and Gothic magical elements both enchant and perplex the reader as Tilda and Dylan strive to unravel the mysteries of the past before the present danger overwhelms them. Readers who savor richly detailed paranormal fiction or have enjoyed Brackston's previous novels will want to give this one a try."   —*Library Journal*

"Paula Brackston weaves a lyrical and lovely tale . . . As ever Brackston's prose is sharp, precise, and a pleasure to encounter . . . Her world of witches and warriors, of the supernatural and divine, is one that will captivate many an unwary reader."
—*San Francisco Book Review*

PRAISE FOR *THE MIDNIGHT WITCH*

"Brackston neatly balances a vivid portrayal of 1913 London on the brink of war with fantastical necromantic set-pieces. . . . *The Midnight Witch* is a compelling read."   —*The Guardian* (UK)

"A story of sacrifice, loss, and power, this dark tapestry is sure to delight fans of both paranormal and historical fiction.
—*Shelf Awareness*

PRAISE FOR *THE WINTER WITCH*

"There's a whiff of Harry Potter in the witchy conflict—a battle between undeveloped young magical talent and old malevolence—at the heart of this sprightly tale of spells and romance, the second novel from British writer Brackston. . . . Love of landscape and lyrical writing lend charm, but it's Brackston's full-blooded storytelling that will hook the reader."
—*Kirkus Reviews*

"Brackston delivers an intimate paranormal romance that grounds its fantasy in the reality of a nineteenth-century Welsh farm."

—*Publishers Weekly*

"A sensitive, beautifully written account . . . If the Brontë sisters had penned magical realism, this would have been the result."

—*The Guardian* (UK)

PRAISE FOR *THE WITCH'S DAUGHTER*

"A riveting tale of sorcery and time travel . . . The skill with which Brackston weaves her characters through time makes this book a fascinating take on global history."   —*Marie Claire*

"Brackston's first novel offers well-crafted characters in an absorbing plot and an altogether delicious blend of historical fiction and fantasy."   —*Booklist*

"This pleasantly romantic historical fantasy debut flips lightly between the past experiences of ageless witch Elizabeth Anne Hawksmith and her present-day life in Matravers, England. . . . Bess's adventures are fascinating."   —*Publishers Weekly*

"Stretching her tale over several centuries, British-based Brackston brings energy as well as commercial savvy to her saga of innocence and the dark arts. . . . History, time travel, and fantasy combine in a solidly readable entertainment."

—*Kirkus Reviews*

THE LITTLE SHOP OF FOUND THINGS

Paula Brackston

St. Martin's Griffin
NEW YORK

Published in the United States by St. Martin's Griffin, an imprint of St. Martin's Publishing Group

THE LITTLE SHOP OF FOUND THINGS. Copyright © 2018 by Paula Brackston. All rights reserved. Printed in the United States of America. For information, address St. Martin's Publishing Group, 120 Broadway, New York, NY 10271.

www.stmartins.com

The Library of Congress has cataloged the hardcover edition as follows:

Names: Brackston, Paula, author.
Title: The little shop of found things : a novel / Paula Brackston.
Description: First edition. | New York: St. Martin's Press, 2018.
Identifiers: LCCN 2018018746 | ISBN 9781250072436 (hardcover) |
    ISBN 9781466884106 (ebook)
Subjects: LCSH: Witches—Fiction. | Fantasy fiction. | England—
    Fiction. | BISAC: FICTION / Historical. | FICTION / Fantasy /
    Historical. | FICTION / Romance / General. | GSAFD: Occult
    fiction. | Love stories. | Historical fiction.
Classification: LCC PR6102.R325 L58 2018 | DDC 823/.92—dc23
LC record available at https://lccn.loc.gov/2018018746

ISBN 978-1-250-22950-2 (trade paperback)

Our books may be purchased in bulk for promotional, educational, or business use. Please contact your local bookseller or the Macmillan Corporate and Premium Sales Department at 1-800-221-7945, extension 5442, or by email at MacmillanSpecialMarkets@macmillan.com.

First St. Martin's Griffin Edition: October 2019

10 9 8 7 6

FOR MELANIE:

CELEBRATING FIFTY YEARS OF FRIENDSHIP.

HERE'S TO ANOTHER FIFTY!

And where shall I look for thee,
When I no longer hear that voice so dear?
Where shall I seek the warmth that love
Made all things found glow bright and clear?

Look not to the heavenly stars,
Nor search the lofty spires, nor bid the choir
    sing.
I will dwell among the details of our lives;
My memory will linger in all the found things.

—DAPHNE BURTON-GORE

1

IT IS A COMMONLY HELD BELIEF THAT THE MOST LIKELY PLACE TO FIND A ghost is beneath a shadowy moon, among the ruins of a castle, or perhaps in an abandoned house where the living have fled leaving only spirits to drift from room to room. To believe so is to acknowledge but half a truth, for there is a connection with those passed over to be found much nearer home. Every soul that once trod this brutal earth leaves their imprint upon the things that mattered to them. The things that they held, the things that once echoed to the beat of their hearts. That heartbeat may yet be felt, faint but clear, transmitted through the fabric of those belongings, linking us to the dear one long gone through however many years have passed. Or at least, some may feel it. Some can hear its fluttering rhythm. Some can sense the life force that once thrummed through the golden metal, or gorgeous gem, or even the tattered remnant of a wedding gown. Some have the ability, the sensitivity, the gift to be able to connect to those lost ones through these precious objects.

Xanthe Westlake was such a person. The tall young woman with the tumble of golden curls falling about her shoulders was possessed of that special gift. She had been barely eight years old when first it had shown itself. On that particular day she held a small silver teapot, turning it over in her hands, smiling brightly.

"You like that, Xanthe?" her mother, Flora, asked.

She nodded, running her fingers over the intricate filigree pattern on the cool silver.

"It's a happy teapot," she told her.

"Really? How do you know?"

"Because I can hear it singing," she said, holding it up. "It was a present from a sailor to his daughter. He'd been away at sea for a long, long time, and when he came home he gave her this, and she made tea for them both. She loved her father very much."

"Wow," her mother said. "You got all that from the teapot?"

At the time, she must have thought such a proclamation merely the product of a youthful imagination, but later, when she inquired as to the teapot's provenance and discovered that it had originated in Spain and been part of a sea captain's estate, well, then she began to take notice of her child's opinions. From that day, she started giving Xanthe things to hold to see if they would "sing" to her. And sometimes they did. And so her daughter would accompany her on buying trips to hunt for treasures. There was never any question but that she would go into the family business.

But a family business needs a family, and this one was smashed like a porcelain platter dropped upon a flagstoned floor.

When Xanthe arrived at the little antique shop that was to be her new home, many years after that first teapot, she was not conscious of being watched. As she helped her mother from the old black taxi that was her sole possession of note, she was concerned only with assisting Flora, who had yet to master the cobbles with her crutches. Xanthe was unaware, then, of the pale eyes that were upon her. Had she raised her own to look into the dusty bow window of the shop, she would not, of course, have seen her observer. Margaret Merton, a fine, well-dressed woman in her day, no longer cast a shadow nor reflected the light, for ghosts are insubstantial things.

It was high summer. The shop had been empty for several months, closed after the passing of Mr. Morris, the collectibles left to garner cobweb shrouds, and Margaret left to wander and wait. She held hope to her breast like a tiny bird which must be grasped tightly yet with such care, lest one crush it to nothing through fear of losing it. Hope was all she had. Of late, she had become aware of a change, and her spirit has roused itself from its fitful slumber. She sensed a reason for that hope to live on, to live more brightly. On that morning, in the month of July, she watched through the small windowpanes as the girl and her mother emerged from the bulky vehicle onto the sunlit, cobbled street. The older woman was perhaps the age Mistress Merton herself had been when she had met her end. Margaret felt a tightening in her chest as she watched daughter help mother, who walked with difficulty and with the aid of sticks. How many centuries had it been since Margaret had felt the touch of her own child's hand upon hers? The pair looked up at the building, smiling, their excitement plain to see.

Flora Westlake took a key from her capacious shoulder bag and turned it in the lock. The shop door swung open, rattling into life the aged brass bell the previous owner had tolerated for a dozen years or more.

"Goodness!" Flora's nose twitched at the smell of beeswax polish, dust, and stale air. "Looks like old Mr. Morris kept the place well stocked."

"I'm not sure all of it qualifies for the word 'stock,'" Xanthe replied, picking up a battered top hat that had not gleamed for decades. "How much did you say you paid for the contents, Mum?"

"Hardly anything at all, Xanthe, love," she replied, waving one of her sticks as if to dismiss the worry.

Flora stood among her treasures and beamed. It was strange that it was not she who had the gift. Indeed, her daughter appeared largely unmoved by their new home, their new business, or the many, story-filled objects waiting for her touch. Even so, Margaret Merton saw the light that burned deep within the girl. Saw what it was and knew straight away that when the moment came, when those objects began to talk to her, Xanthe would listen. She would have no choice.

As the pair moved through the shop, Xanthe stepped so close to the ghost that her warmth seeped into that spirit. Naturally, the girl felt nothing of the specter with whom she had unwittingly elected to share her home. Xanthe's sensitivity was to substantial things, through their tactile qualities. Margaret, having no substance other than that of a spirit, was undetectable to her. And so she would remain. Until she chose otherwise. Even so, that long-buried sense that humans have allowed to atrophy through lack of use; that instinct that warns of unseen dangers, could not help but respond to such a provocation as Mistress Merton's restless soul presented. Xanthe paused, turning as if in answer to a distant calling of her name. Finding nothing, seeing no one, she shook off the sensation and resumed her inspection of the collectibles.

"There could be an awful lot of rubbish here," she warned her mother, gazing at the jumble of things that filled every shelf and cabinet or sat in unstable heaps upon the floor.

"Well, most of it will probably have to go," her mother agreed, "but there's bound to be some of it worth salvaging. And we can do a bit of work on some of the furniture." She nodded at a shabby chest of drawers which was sagging beneath bulging boxes, many filled with ancient books. "That would paint up nicely," she said. "And that chair . . . and look here." She moved forward to a box of sheet music and pulled out a selection. "There might be some material in here you could use, Xanthe, when you start singing again."

"Mum . . . I really don't want to even think about that right now."

"OK, OK, just saying. Might be worth considering." She turned to look at her daughter closely then. "You can't just *not* sing, love. It's part of you, you know that."

Xanthe feigned interest in a rusty set of scales. When she gave no reply, Flora let the matter drop.

"Ooh, look through there," Flora said, pointing with one of her crutches. "If I remember what the brochure said, Mr. Morris kept the second room just for mirrors."

They went to investigate. Moments later they were standing in a narrow, windowless room that was filled wall to wall with mirrors. They were propped up against one another, leaning at all angles, some hung properly, others wedged in a corner or resting against a wall. Xanthe switched on the light. Several of the mirrors were in simple wooden frames, others were ornate, some plaster, some painted, some gilded. The two women stood in the middle of the room and saw themselves multiplied by dozens of reflections.

Margaret Merton stood at Xanthe's shoulder, a singular presence without a single reflection.

Xanthe found the uncommon sight of herself, so repeated and replicated, an unsettling experience. These were not the distortions of a fairground hall of mirrors. The sense was more akin to Alice and her looking glass. Xanthe and her mother were truthfully mirrored, and yet, framed in so many ways, shown at so many angles, glimpsed in so many fogged and silvering surfaces, they looked oddly different. As if they were different people. They had their usual features and characteristics. There was Xanthe's mass of dark blonde corkscrew curls. And those were unmistakably her customary vintage clothes. And she remained a good six inches taller than her mother, who still had a scrap of scarf tied in her fine, fluffy brown hair. Flora had crutches, Xanthe did not. The older woman's feet were tiny and looked still smaller in her flat pumps. The black leather of Xanthe's heavy Dr. Martens boots gleamed dully in the low light. For all the similarities, those multi-Floras and multi-Xanthes were somehow, crucially, not them.

"Bit of a thing with Mr. Morris, then, mirrors," Xanthe said, rubbing a finger over one of the gilt frames. "Do you think he ever sold any or just collected them?"

"I don't know the market around here yet," Flora admitted. "But these'd sell in a week back in London."

They exchanged uncomfortable glances at the mention of the city that was now firmly a part of their past.

The doorbell rang and Xanthe raised her eyebrows. "Our first customer, d'you reckon?"

Returning to the main part of the shop, she found the driver of the moving van.

"Didn't want to risk getting stuck down that narrow street," he told her. "We're parked at the top end. Have to carry things from there."

Xanthe followed him out. It was only a short walk to the point where the cobbled lane met the high street, but even so she was glad their possessions were few. It would take a number of trips to cart them to the shop via the slender thoroughfare. She allowed herself a moment's pride that her beloved taxi with its superior design had made the tight turn required to navigate the route. The movers handed down boxes from the back of the van. There were cases of clothes and a small number of pieces of furniture taken from what had once been the family home. Flora had also demanded four boxes of stock from the auction house, despite her soon-to-be-ex-husband's loud protestations. Xanthe considered her father had been deliberately obstructive, as if he wished to make Flora's new life as difficult as possible. A point made all the more galling as it had been he who had wanted out of their marriage. Flora had been uninterested in shared household belongings, convincing herself she could replace everything when the settlement was finalized. That they were only insignificant things. That they did not matter. But Xanthe argued that they mattered a great deal, and that the reasons they were giving them up mattered, too. She admitted only to herself that not all of those reasons were the fault of her father. When it came to them having to find somewhere new and begin their lives afresh, Xanthe was painfully aware that she was, in her own way, equally to blame.

Carrying a heavy box marked KITCHEN, she made her way back down the tiny street. It was, in every respect, typical of the sort found in many English market towns, of which Marlborough was a fine example. The tarmac gave way to cobbles, smoothed under centuries of feet and hooves and wheels. The alleyway was barely 150 feet long, with small shops on either side. At the end, there was an archway under what had once been part of a coaching inn but was now apartments. It led only to some residents' parking, so there was no through traffic. The shopkeepers had taken full advantage of this, putting out their wares on the cobbles, the tea shop to the right having set up tables and chairs. The little Wiltshire town was well known for its broad high street, its beautiful old buildings, and its antiques. Which was why, fifteen years after that astonishing Spanish teapot, Xanthe and Flora had chosen this place in which to set up shop. The charming town was a popular destination for treasure hunters and shoppers, with its Georgian redbrick town houses mellowed with age, mixed among black-and-white half-timbered shops and homes that were even older, some by hundreds of years. Twice a week a bustling market set up along the wide main street, colorful and tempting, and everywhere there was a feeling of affluent, happy, provincial life.

The shop itself was built of brick the color of fox fur, with a bloom of age softening that brightness. It had a bow window, the frames painted smart white to match that of the glass door with its many small panes. The shop sign had been covered up by the estate agent's notice declaring it SOLD. Sold to Flora and Xanthe. Bought with every penny of their savings and a mortgage begged from a friendly broker. Until the divorce settlement came through they would be surviving largely on their wits, which meant the shop had to be restored, stocked, and opened as swiftly as was humanly possible. As Xanthe approached their new venture, she felt nervousness and excitement in equal measure. This was, for both of them, more than a business; it was a new life, and the modest flat above the shop was to be their new home. Xanthe recalled from the estate agent's particulars that to the rear of the house lay a fair-size garden. As she followed the movers through the front door and saw again the overflowing shelves and tables, and took in the enormity of the task ahead of them, she accepted that it would be some time before she would be concerning herself with lawns and plants. There was work to be done in the shop, and plenty of it.

What she could not have known was that the ever watchful Mistress Merton had an entirely different plan for her.

That night Xanthe slept poorly, sensitive to the unfamiliar sounds of her new home, though unaware of the silent figure who kept vigil at the foot of her bed. It was the more mundane, earthly noises that disturbed her: the creaking and sighing of the build-

ing as it cooled in the night air; the clicking of the metal gutter-
ing as it contracted; the noises of the slumbering town drifting
in through the open attic window. Both bedrooms were set into
the roof of the house, hot in summer, cold in winter. Marlborough was a genteel and respectable place, and its night sounds
were of an entirely different nature to the ceaseless thrum of
London to which she had been accustomed. Here, there was only
gentle midweek revelry, which quietened at what felt to her like
a very early hour. In the dark depths of the night, she heard
the occasional distant vehicle, the crying of a baby in another
apartment, and the barking of a dog some way off. She dreamed
no dreams as such, rather disconnected images passed through
her sleeping mind. Pictures of the town and the shop and the
mirrors with their endless reflections, seeming to offer so many
possible futures.

When the dawn light eventually fell through the faded and
flimsy curtains, she rose from her bed. Pulling the curtains open,
she sat on the windowsill that formed a dusty seat from which
to view the rooftops of Marlborough. Her room, being at the
top of the house that had no loft space, wore the slope of the
roof in its ceiling, and the window was cut in among the tiles.
From this highpoint she could see across the uneven roof-
scape of shops and houses which was punctuated with church
spires at either end of the high street, and faded into the distant, undulating countryside. Below, small birds were stirring in
the walled garden, which consisted of a long swathe of unmowed
lawn and a tangle of brambles, overgrown shrubs, and flowers.
For a moment Xanthe considered sketching what she saw. She
had always liked to draw and had developed a fair eye. It had
proved useful in the trade, noting details of objects she was
trying to authenticate, or taking down requirements from customers looking for something in particular. On that morning,

however, the challenge of finding sketch pad and pencils among the packing cases was sufficient to deter her.

The day promised to be warm, and already the sun was touching everything with a soft golden glow. The town was beginning to wake up, and she could discern the rattle of shop shutters being raised. Pulling a fluffy jumper over her nightdress she descended the stairs barefoot. She loved to feel the ground under her bare feet and could not abide heels. When she did put something on her feet it was invariably her preferred tough boots, heavy and protective. She had never owned a pair of slippers. Not wanting to disturb Flora, she moved as quietly as she was able, but every stair and floorboard seemed to want to protest loudly at her treading upon it. The narrow stairs from the attic floor led down through the rest of the flat with kitchen, bathroom, and sitting room, and then widened to descend to the ground floor. The smell of old furniture, vintage leather, and antique objects of all shapes and sizes was as natural to Xanthe as the aroma of home cooking. She had been raised among such things. She did not see them as castoffs or the belongings of the dead as some people might. To her they were mementos, relics, heirlooms. Each of them held memories of past lives and loves. Held stories. And if she was fortunate, if she found the right pieces, they would share those stories with her.

The stairs turned down into a little hallway, to the rear of which was a room with a bench and sink. It was clear this was where Mr. Morris had worked on restorations and repairs. It was possible to get to the garden through a door at the far end of the hallway. The first room on her left was the one that housed the mirrors, and then the passageway opened out into the main part of the shop. Xanthe wandered into the shop and stood at its center, trying to make sense of the muddle. In the half-light of the early morning, everything had taken on a slightly blurred look, with softened edges and muted colors. The business, contents, and building had been sold after Mr. Morris's death, and to judge by the dust, no one had touched anything since his passing. There was a sense of everything having been left just as it must have been when he was still running the shop. As Xanthe browsed through the stock, she was alert, as always, to the possibility of something special. She could not look through such a collection of antique pieces without hoping for a connection, for something with a story to tell. Her senses strained in the way a person listens hard for a familiar voice among the babble of chatter in a crowded room. There was a fair amount of china, including one or two pleasant Wedgwood plates; a good deal of "brown" furniture, mostly occasional tables, nothing spectacular; lots of boxes of old books; a cabinet of mostly Victorian jewelry; a stand of walking sticks and gentlemen's umbrellas; in short, lots of things that were nice enough, but nothing that stood out. And as yet, nothing that sang. She pulled books at random from an overstuffed box. There were one or two on local history, another entitled *Spinners*. Xanthe knew the history of crafts could be popular, so she set the books aside in a pile to keep. They could be used to show off one of the better bookcases, if nothing else. There were paper bags, tissue paper, and sticking tape on the Edwardian desk that served as a counter. There was no till. Opening one of the heavy drawers, she found a small metal box. The key was in the lock. Inside were a few five-pound notes and a handful of change. Xanthe moved her attention to the ledger underneath it. Turning to the last entry, she could see Mr. Morris had ceased trading on the second Thursday in May, a little under three months earlier. It felt like an intrusion, reading his spidery handwriting, as if she were looking over his shoulder as he wrote down the sales for that day. They were few and paltry. If the new shop was to succeed, changes would have to be made, and the first of those was surely the finding of original, tantalizing, and irresistible stock.

"Xanthe?" Flora called down the stairs. "I've got the kettle on. Come and have breakfast."

It appeared Xanthe was not alone in finding it difficult to sleep. As she left the main room of the shop to join her mother for breakfast, Margaret Merton watched her go. Out of a habit long fallen into uselessness, she smoothed the phantom fabric of her skirts with her fine, long-fingered hands. This girl's inclination to dress for comfort and her own peculiar style rather than modesty and elegance were at odds with Margaret's own preferences. As a young woman she had been beautiful and slender. A prize contested by wealthy and powerful suitors. It had been her misfortune to choose one not, ultimately, powerful enough to save her. As a married woman she had become well-respected and known for her grace and her wit. She could never have imagined wandering a house in a state of near undress, her hair disheveled, her feet bare as Xanthe's were. And yet, this wild girl, this person so lacking in the qualities Margaret had striven to install in her own dear daughter, she was to be her godsend. Her hope personified. Her daughter's salvation. For she knew now what had woken her from her incomplete sleep. She knew what it was that had caused her to stir to action, to witness the progress of the newcomer. She had seen it, clear as anything could be, that object, that thing on which a greater value had been placed than the life of her own child. It had returned to the place where it had once played such a vital part in her daughter's life. It was closer now than it had ever been to Mistress Merton, and it lay in the path of this untamed girl, waiting.

The kitchen was no less chaotic than the shop, but here the clutter was caused by packing cases rather than old stock. Xanthe found Flora digging deep in a crate, in search of mugs.

"I've found coffee but we'll have to have it black," she said. "Breakfast is over there."

Xanthe sat at the worn pine table. "Shortbread biscuits, cheese triangles, and marmalade?" she asked, examining the few edible things among the scrunched-up newspaper and piles of plates.

"You'll have to spread it with a spoon. The knives seem to have gone missing. I expect they'll turn up," she said, turning off the gas beneath the kettle.

Flora was a woman of many talents, but cooking was not listed among them. It was not that she was unable to do it, simply that she detested supermarkets and was always far too engrossed in her antiques to remember to shop for food. This had led to her becoming more of an inventor than a cook, having to create meals out of the strangest combinations of ingredients. Xanthe had been brought up to expect the unexpected when it came to dinner, and as a result could not be perturbed by the most curious concoctions. Even so, this particular combination was new.

As they ate their crumbly breakfast and sipped the bitter coffee, they made their plan for the day. Flora had arranged their arrival to coincide with a local antiques sale.

"Perfect timing," she insisted. "We can get over there early, seeing as we're both up. Have a good poke around before the auction gets underway."

"Some people might have begun by sorting out all the stock that's here before running off to buy more," Xanthe pointed out, rescuing a blob of marmalade from the front of her jumper.

"You can hardly accuse me of running anywhere," she laughed.

Xanthe grinned, as ever humbled by her mother's ability to laugh off her pain and disablement. More than eight years had passed since her diagnosis of a cruelly painful form of arthritis and still her humor, her love of life, her determination, remained undiminished.

"You know what I mean," Xanthe said. "There's a load of stuff to be gone through, never mind the unpacking and generally getting the flat organized."

"Oh, don't worry about all that. I find those sorts of things usually take care of themselves. I don't want to waste time on the flat now. We need to get the business up and running, Xanthe. That has to be our priority."

"Yes, but we do have to live here, too. You know, properly live, not just exist in heaps of craziness," Xanthe reminded her, waving at the eye-high stacks of boxes and pointedly spreading more cheese with a spoon.

"And so we shall. And it will be lovely. Just you and me. We don't need anyone else." She sounded bright enough, but Xanthe knew her too well. She could hear the catch in her voice every time she came close to mentioning her husband. Flora glanced at Xanthe, conscious of the fact that she too could be hurt by memories. After all, they both knew what it was like to be betrayed by someone they loved. "Besides," she said, steering the conversation back onto safer ground, "we've a marvelous sale to go to. By all accounts something special. Not to be missed." She fished in her bag and pulled out the catalog, waving it beneath her daughter's nose. "China, silver, jewelry, oodles of lovely things. Have a look."

The front cover declared this to be a SALE OF FINE ANTIQUES AND COLLECTIBLES taking place at the beautiful Great Chalfield Manor. Xanthe always felt a tickle of excitement when browsing through a sale catalog, but this time, as she took the glossy booklet from her mother, she felt something else. Something stronger. She was on the point of opening it, ready to scour the pages to see if she could identify what it was that she was connecting with, but she found herself hesitating. In all those years of having things sing to her, all those dozens of special objects, she had never reacted to a mere picture before. For some reason she could not quite fathom, she didn't wish to "meet" whatever it was at such a remove, seeing its captured image and a few basic lines of description. She felt compelled to wait. To come face-to-face with it. To hear it call to her. To discover it and touch it. That was the way it should be.

"Xanthe?" Flora had noticed her reluctance to open the catalog.

"Actually, I'll read it when we get there," she said, getting up from the table. "Think I'll go and see if I can get the shower to work. Wash off some of this dust."

"Well, don't be long. It's a twenty-minute drive from here. We need to get going if we are to steal a march on the other buyers. And anyway, I want to start hunting for treasure!"

Xanthe hurried to get ready, spurred on by the thought that today she would find something truly special. Or, more accurately, today something special would find her.

{ 2 }

THE DRIVE THROUGH THE WILTSHIRE COUNTRYSIDE WAS BOTH SOOTHING AND uplifting. As they left Marlborough the road climbed up onto the chalk downs that gave the area its distinctive rolling hills and far-reaching views, as well as its famous white horses. These were enormous "drawings" cut into the ground to expose the gleaming white of the chalk beneath. Some of these hill figures were centuries old, others even prehistoric. Despite their great age, the bright green of the late-summer grass that surrounded them made them stand out as if newly cut into the soft turf. On some of the hilltops, there were small copses of oak, ash, and birch trees, all fuzzy with their summer leaves. Xanthe could well imagine the way the colors of the landscape would soon change with the altering seasons, and thought how pleasing the scenery would be when spangled with a heavy frost or covered in layers of fluffy snow.

There was little traffic with which to contend. What passed for rush hour here was no more than a few private cars and de-livery vans and the occasional school bus, all periodically held up by a tractor. The roads were twisty and narrow and not good for passing another vehicle, so that traffic meandered along in a mismatched procession, forced to slow their pace. It was a reminder to Xanthe and Flora that their whole lives would now be lived to a different beat. Xanthe's black taxi drew a few curious glances, but at least out of London she was unlikely to be hailed by a would-be passenger. At last they turned up the driveway of the ancient manor house.

"Oooh!" Flora leaned forward to get a better view. "How very lovely."

And it was. Not in a grand, ostentatious way as was the habit of some big houses. Great Chalfield Manor simply stood there among its lovingly tended gardens, as solid and tangible and beautiful a link with history as you could wish to find. The style of the house was typical of the late medieval period when it had been built, although there had been later additions and improvements that gave it an asymmetrical and appealingly higgledy-piggledy layout. It was constructed of the local warm, honey-colored stone, with large, deep-set, mullioned windows and lots of tall chimneys, and even gargoyles. Every doorway was a work of art in itself, arched and broad and fitted with ancient oak doors, studded with ironwork. Xanthe followed the wooden signposts toward the graveled car park.

"Looks like you were right to get here early," she said, searching for somewhere to park in the already crowded area. There were plenty of everyday cars, but also a worrying number of four-by-fours, vans, and estate vehicles, which usually indicated the presence of dealers. Which also meant that prices could be quickly pushed up.

"Over there!" Flora pointed at a single space near the end of a row. Xanthe was just about to swing into it when an old red sports car came from the other direction and sped into the spot.

"Oy!" she yelled out of the window as a young man climbed out of the open-topped classic car. "I was going to park there," she told him. Her London habit of needing to fight for everything when it came to traffic would take a while to fade.

He grinned and gave a shrug. "Sorry. Didn't see you there. But now that I do, wow, nice wheels. Haven't seen one of these in such good nick for a long time." He started prowling around the taxi, running his hands over the bodywork and giving it a thorough inspection.

"Never mind that," she said, leaning out of the window to continue berating him. "How about finding me another space, since you've pinched mine?"

He walked around to stand at the driver's door. "She's in fantastic condition," he said, patting the bonnet. He was good-looking, tall, with closely cropped hair and an easy smile. Experience had made Xanthe wary of handsome men. She was not about to be caught off guard with a little car flattery just because he thought he was attractive enough to get away with it. He grinned but she did not return the smile. "Sorry," he said again. "Very ungentlemanly of me. Just to prove I am not a complete thug, I will indeed find you somewhere else to park."

True to his word, he threaded through the stationary vehicles and those beginning to queue up behind the taxi, seeking out a gap. At last he found one and waved Xanthe over. As she maneuvered her cab into the space, he appeared at the window again.

"There you go. Nice and shady here. Got to look after a beauty like this," he said, his gaze fixed firmly on the car.

She wound the window up, which was hard to do quickly with an old manual system.

Flora tutted. "You could have said 'thank you,' Xanthe."

"For what? He pinched my space to begin with."

Flora rolled her eyes and let the matter drop, but she had already made her daughter feel something of a shrew. It was not, after all, the young man's fault that he looked how he did. More importantly, it was not his fault that she felt about men the way she did. He was not, after all, Marcus.

It was a short walk through the gardens to the house. Flora managed the gravel skillfully on her sticks, her bag slung over her shoulder. Xanthe's heavy boots scrunched along the paths. She had chosen to wear the only thing that was not crumpled beyond use after being in a suitcase, which was a vintage tea-dress, dark green with tiny brown leaves on it. She liked the way it was so at odds with her Dr. Martens, and had shrugged on a favorite tweed jacket to keep off the morning chill. The sale was being held in the enormous barn opposite the house. Xanthe was disappointed not to be gaining entrance into the manor itself, but the ancient barn was a thing of beauty in its own right, with its hipped eaves and thick, mossy stone tiles. By the time they had followed the eager line of people in, paid for their buyer's ticket, and made their way into the central bay where most of the lots were set out, the sale was about to start. It was easy to see that this was no house clearance or small, provincial auction, but a quality sale. Flora nudged Xanthe and nodded at two antiques dealers she knew well. It was a sign of important pieces being listed that they had chosen to come to the auction in person rather than bid online or by phone as many did.

Flora had marked things in the catalog that she thought looked worth bidding on, and she began to seek them out. Xanthe let her go on, deliberately hanging back, allowing the crowd to slowly separate them. She knew there was one specific piece here that she needed to find. That she needed to hear, through all the bustle and noise of the auction room. She glanced about, looking for anything that might stand out. The abundance of lovely things was quite something, and part of her felt remiss at not paying greater attention to the matter of obtaining stock for the shop, but for now she would have to leave that to Flora. She drifted past tables of gleaming china, noticing a gorgeous Minton tea service and a good deal of Spode. One side of the area was entirely given over to eighteenth-century furniture, a lot of it French and very good. In the far corner there were rugs, half unfurled, Turkish and Persian, their colors rich and glowing, suggesting exotic countries, warm climates, and unfamiliar beauty. But she heard nothing from them. She felt nothing beyond the pull of their loveliness and the quality of their craftsmanship. Nothing that truly moved her.

And then, as she neared a low, glass-topped cabinet beneath one of the long, loophole windows, she was struck with an almost overwhelming sense of anxiety. She was so shocked by this unexpected emotion, this onslaught of fear when there was nothing remotely frightening to be seen, that she stood motionless, uncertain as to what to do next. She knew that this feeling was being brought about by something in the barn, but it was stronger than anything she had experienced before. It was not the usual gentle buzzing in her head, the dreamlike, floating sensations she experienced when she connected with a piece. This was so much more powerful. More urgent, somehow. She took a step forward. The feeling increased. She turned, searching, convinced now that what was trying to find her was in the display cabinet. And when she placed her hand upon the glass, she knew she must be close, for to her it seemed that the very glass itself was vibrating, possessed of an energy that felt easily strong enough to shatter it. She peered into the cabinet, which was low and contained two shelves of jewelry and silver. There was a charm bracelet, a snuff box, a vanity set, a collection of silver chains, and two trays of rings. And then she saw it. The second she set eyes upon it she knew, for at that moment it sang to her so clearly, so desperately, that there was no possibility of her being mistaken.

It was a chatelaine, made of lustrous silver, evidently early nineteenth century judging by the style and the items it was comprised of. A chatelaine was a belt or clip—in this case a clip—worn at the waist or hip of the lady of the house. Most, like this one, had several chains dangling from the clasp, and to the end of these chains would be attached various useful or beautiful things. Fashions and fads over the centuries had thrown up many different types of chatelaine, but this one boasted a selection of fairly common appendages, even if they were uncommonly pretty. There was a tiny coin purse made of silver mesh; a miniature scent bottle; a dear little silver notebook, still with its original pages by the look of it; and a buttonhook. There were also two chains with nothing attached to them. It was not unusual to have incomplete sets of attachments. Xanthe had seen chatelaines before and could see that this was a fine example of one, but there was nothing particularly noteworthy about it. Nothing beyond the fact that it was causing her pulse to race and setting up a high-pitched humming in her head. Even amidst the hubbub of the sale room she could hear distant whispers: the breathy voices of people no longer living. Frightened voices. Whatever its value, whatever its price, she knew she had to have it.

"So this is where you ran off to." Her mother's voice interrupted her thoughts. "What's so special that I had to come looking for you? Oh, that is pretty. A nice example, but . . ." As soon as she stopped looking at the chatelaine and looked up at Xanthe, she could see what was happening. Flora maintained that when her daughter was listening to a piece, she was visibly changed. Changed in a way she could never properly explain or describe, but it was always the same.

"Give me our buyer's card," Xanthe said, holding out her hand.

"It's going to be expensive, Xanthe, love. All that silver ..."

"Mum, I have to buy it. You know I can't leave without it. Not now that I've found it." She might more accurately have said not now that it had found *her*.

"But you won't want to sell it, will you?"

"Not straight away, no, but eventually I will be able to. It will be OK, trust me."

Flora sighed, resigned to the inevitable, and as always slightly thrilled by her daughter's gift. She had seen the same look on Xanthe's face before, heard the same note of excitement in her voice. She passed her the buyer's card. "Try not to completely blow the budget."

Xanthe glanced up at the auctioneer. He had taken his place on the platform set up at the end of the barn, and his assistant was already bringing out the first lot, a small watercolor. She checked the lot number on the chatelaine. *Six!* There was little time for her to make her case.

At that moment they were joined by a familiar, debonair figure.

"Well, well, well, Flora Westlake. Fancy bumping into you out here in the provinces. And the heavenly Xanthe, too. What a happy coincidence."

"Theo Hamilton," Flora gave him a frosty smile. There was no love lost between them. While she always admitted a grudging admiration for Theo's expertise, particularly on all things Georgian, she did not like the man and never entirely trusted him. He was a flamboyant character, well known in the trade, always to be seen in his trademark velvet jacket and silk cravat. "I never imagined you venturing beyond Chelsea," said Flora.

"Me? Oh, darling, I love a bit of the English countryside

now and again. Good for the soul, or so they tell me," he insisted.

"Something must have tempted you out," she said.

He gave a coy smile. "You know me too well, that's the trouble. I'll confess to an interest in a set of sublime Finchley dining chairs. You should see the workmanship on the carvers! Utterly divine." He paused, lost for a moment in the thrill of the chase for beauty that all true devotees of the antiques business feel. "But what about you? I hear you have a new venture starting up, somewhere nearby?" He waved his hand in a vague and dismissive way, as if anywhere between Great Chalfield and London was uncharted territory and not worth getting out of the car for.

"That's right." Flora was unruffled. "Xanthe and me, together. We're opening a shop in Marlborough."

He gave a little laugh. "How quaint! And what has caught your attention, gorgeous girl?" he asked. Xanthe did not wish to tell him. Did not wish him to see the treasure she had unearthed, fearing that he might try to bid for it himself. But his expert eye searched the cabinet for the one item of any real value and quickly found it. "Oh! A lovely little chatelaine. Quite scarce these days. Such a wonderfully *girlie* item," he declared.

"I think it's a quality piece," Xanthe said, torn between wanting to defend the thing and not wanting to raise his interest in it.

He leaned closer to the glass of the cabinet, taking out his eyeglass to study it more closely. "Yes, rather fine. But not much of a seller, sadly. The dear old general public are not renowned for their taste, I fear. You're not planning to bid on it, are you?" he asked, without looking at either of them.

Xanthe glanced at her mother. Neither of them spoke. Unfortunately, Theo read a great deal into the silence.

"Darlings, one must never buy with one's heart. That way bankruptcy lies."

As he was making this gloomy pronouncement, a sales assistant sidled through the crowd with a key. She unlocked the cabinet and removed the chatelaine. Instinctively, Xanthe reached out and touched it. The silver should have been cool, but to her it felt so hot it almost burned her fingers. The humming in her head grew louder, and the sensation of fear returned, and for a second she clearly saw a tangled woodland, dark and wildly overgrown. It was a fleeting image, but powerfully clear and vivid.

Theo Hamilton had not yet finished. "A piece of silver frippery? Dear me, what would Philip say?"

At the mention of her husband's name, Flora straightened herself up on her crutches. "You'd better go and stand somewhere the auctioneer can see you, Xanthe," she said calmly, with a stern glance at Theo.

Xanthe hurried to the front of the room and found a space to one side where she would be visible to the auctioneer but also able to watch the room for competing bidders. The earlier lots were swiftly sold, and at last the moment arrived. She could detect a buzz of excitement as the chatelaine was held up. She had to pray that this excitement did not translate into bids.

The auctioneer had a voice that sounded dependable, knowledgeable, and likeable—the perfect combination of qualities for someone selling things that came without guarantees and were worth precisely as much as he could persuade an interested person to pay.

"Lot number six, a silver chatelaine, mostly Victorian, though some parts of it thought to be earlier. It is hallmarked as being made in Bristol. A fine, quality piece, I think you'll agree. Rare to find one with so many attachments still in place. Who'll start me off at one thousand pounds? One thousand, anyone?"

Xanthe held her breath. If someone put in such a high bid at the outset, the thing would quickly go way beyond her reach.

"Come along now, ladies and gentlemen." The auctioneer continued to play his part in the game of want-it-don't-want-it that the buyers insisted upon. "Let's say eight hundred then?" He scanned the room for a twitching number card, a decisive nod, or a waving sales catalog, but found nothing. "Don't be shy now. It's a lovely piece. The clasp is engraved with oak leaves and acorns in a style typical of the day. I'm told the pages in the notebook are original, some even bearing writing, and the stopper of the scent bottle is intact and removable. Shall we say seven hundred and fifty? Who'll give me seven hundred and fifty?" There was a pause, and then, "Ah, seven hundred I have. Eight hundred anywhere? At the back, yes, eight hundred, thank you."

Xanthe's heart sank. There were two bidders in the room, and by the way in which the price was going up, they were both determined to win the lot. The price jumped up in hundreds with sickening speed and then slowed to fifties.

"Eleven hundred and fifty. Any more, sir?"

The second bidder was losing his nerve.

"Twelve hundred, anyone?"

Xanthe took a deep breath and, catching the auctioneer's eye, gave a firm nod.

"Twelve hundred I have. A new bidder. Twelve fifty . . ."

The original buyer wasn't giving up so easily. Xanthe nodded again. She could feel her mother's eyes boring into her all the way from the back of the room. She was painfully aware that she was spending a large portion of their entire budget for restocking the shop, but she had no choice. The chatelaine had hold of her and it would not let her go. The bidding went on, the price rising horribly.

"Thirteen . . . thirteen-fifty . . . fourteen. That's fourteen hundred. Another fifty from you, sir? No?"

He was backing out!

"Anyone else?"

Xanthe's heart was pounding. Fourteen hundred pounds was a high price, but she was beyond caring.

"Oh, a new bidder, on the internet. I have fifteen hundred pounds."

The whole room gasped. A fresh bidder at this point meant the price could climb much higher. Xanthe felt herself overcome by a recklessness she was powerless to control.

"Sixteen hundred pounds!" she called out, breaking with both etiquette and common sense. She heard Flora say her name. How was she going to explain this to her? How could she make her understand?

The auctioneer's voice seemed to come from far, far away. "Sixteen hundred and fifty . . . seventeen hundred . . ."

There was a terrible silence.

"Any more, ladies and gentlemen? The bid is in the room."

The internet buyer had stalled. Would he go again?

"Are you all done at seventeen hundred pounds?" He hesitated, his gavel raised, sweeping the room in a final search, then bang! He brought his hammer down with a sharp rap upon the desk. "Sold!"

Xanthe held up her number with a shaky hand. She was still shaking when Flora came to stand beside her.

"I'm sorry," Xanthe said. "I had to. I just had to."

Her mother gave a shrug and a small smile. "It sang to you."

"But, it was a lot of money. . . ."

"Xanthe, love, I understand. Now, let me get to that seat so I can put down these sticks and do some bidding of my own."

✢   ✢   ✢

At a distance of but a few miles yet also several centuries, Mistress Merton felt the connection, knew that it had been made. The girl's gift had led her to the chatelaine. The silver link to her own daughter was now linked to the one, the only one, who had the ability to use it. It remained Margaret's task to see that she did not fail.

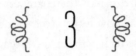

3

THEY LEFT GREAT CHALFIELD A LITTLE AFTER THREE, HAVING BOUGHT SAND-wiches from the pop-up cafe for lunch. Flora had withstood the rigors of the day well, and it was not her habit to complain, but Xanthe could see she was struggling by the time they had everything loaded into the car. She found her a bottle of water so she could take some more painkillers before setting off. If Xanthe felt bad about squandering so much of their budget on the chatelaine, she felt even worse when she thought of how most of what Flora did she did through pain. What manner of daughter was she if she failed to hold that truth in her mind? There were occasions when she wished her mother would allow herself to give in to her own frustrations, to vent her own anger and temper. There were times when her stoicism had the effect of making Xanthe feel inadequate. She was certain that, were their situations reversed, she would not be blessed with the same fortitude and patience.

"I'm sorry," Xanthe said as she steered the taxi along the twisting road toward home. "About the chatelaine, I mean." Even as she said it she knew she would buy it all over again if she had to. It was not an easy life, being pulled between her love for her mother and the overwhelming, otherworldly connection she felt to certain objects.

"It's OK. I know how much these special pieces mean to you."

"This one is different from the others."

"How different? More expensive perhaps?"

Xanthe took her eyes off the road to check her mother's expression and was relieved to see a wicked grin.

She felt herself relax, happy to have her mother's understanding yet again. "I can't explain," she told her. "It just . . ."

"—sang to you. I know, love."

"We will sell it. One day. Let me clean it up, take a good look at it. Listen to it. Find out its story." She was about to say more, but at that moment a car came tearing around the bend toward them. It was traveling at a reckless speed and the driver scarcely had control, letting it drift over the white line onto the other side of the road. Flora uttered an oath. Xanthe swerved as best she could, but the road was narrow with high hedges on either side, so that there was really nowhere to go. There was a *thud* and a smashing noise, and she felt the impact shudder through the car. Slamming on the brakes, she brought the cab to a halt.

"Idiot!" she shouted at the disappearing car. "He must know he hit us."

"Well, he's not stopping to talk about it."

He certainly was not. In seconds he was out of sight. Xanthe, shaking a little, got out of the car to check the damage. The noise had been the sound of the side mirror being hit and snapped off. She walked back and retrieved its shattered pieces from the road. "Shit," she said to herself. It was ruined beyond repair and replacement parts for old taxis were hard to come by. When she returned to the car, her mother put a hand on her arm.

"Are you OK?"

She nodded. "Bit shaken. We were lucky."

"Your poor car."

"Cars can be fixed," she said, trying to put from her mind

how close they had come to a serious accident. "Come on, let's get home. I want to see what you bought."

Flora brightened at this and chatted for the rest of the journey about the lovely pieces she had been able to get for the shop. Even so, when they drew up outside the front door she struggled to get out of her seat.

"Go on in and sit down," Xanthe told her.

"You can't unload all those things on your own."

"Yes, I can."

"I want to help."

"And I want a cup of tea. I'll fetch some milk before I come up. Now, will you go and put the kettle on? Please?"

Flora hesitated for a moment and then nodded, heading for the apartment with determined, frustrated stabs at the ground with her crutches as she went. Xanthe climbed into the back of the taxi and started to sort through the boxes. All the while, she was aware of the presence of the chatelaine and longed to take it somewhere quiet so that she might sit with it and hear what it had to tell her. She wanted to know why it had made her feel such awful fear. She always felt something, but not such a shocking sense of foreboding. First, however, there was stock to be seen to, and her mother to consider.

As she clambered among the paper-wrapped treasures, a young woman appeared in the car doorway. She was dimpled and smily, with bright red lipstick and her hair in shiny waves. She wore court shoes and tan stockings with a floral apron tied over her dress, which was pinched at the waist and had a gloriously full skirt. Xanthe was accustomed to wearing vintage clothes herself, but the woman's whole look was so authentically from another era that for a moment she thought she might have stepped out of rehearsals for a play set in the fifties.

"Hello," she said. "I've brought you a little moving-in present."

Only then did Xanthe notice she was carrying a small tray of the most delicious-looking cakes. She scrambled back out of the car.

"Wow, those look fantastic," she said, her mouth starting to water. Until that moment, she had not realized how hungry she was. "Thanks so much."

"Oh, it's nothing. I'm from over there," the young woman said, pointing back to the chintzy cafe opposite which had a bunting-strewn sign declaring it to be GERALDINE'S TEA SHOP. "That's me. Gerri to one and all," she explained, passing over the tray and holding out her hand. She laughed as the two tried to shake hands while doing the swap.

"I'm Xanthe. God, I could eat all of these right now. They smell fantastic!" She wanted nothing more than to dash upstairs and share the cakes with Flora, but felt she should at least try to be neighborly. "My mother's making tea. Why don't you come up? Oh, sorry, not much of an offer to someone who has their own cafe! And we don't even have any milk yet."

"I can't leave the tea shop. I'm on my own today. But another time, I'd love to. And I can let you have a drop of milk. Ohh!" She peered in at one of the open boxes. "What gorgeous china. I only use vintage stuff for my customers. I can see I'm going to be spending rather a lot in your shop if you're going to stock things like that."

"We can do a trade: cakes for cups."

"Now *that* I like the sound of."

When Xanthe had finished unloading and was about to move the car, Gerri reappeared with a bottle of milk. Xanthe thanked her and when she commented on the broken side mirror asked if there was a garage nearby who did repairs.

"There's Walkers at the top of the high street," she said, "but for an old car like yours you need to go and see Liam. His workshop is down by the river behind The Feathers pub. You can't miss it."

At last, tired and laden with the final box of purchases, Xanthe went inside. She was surprised to find Flora in the shop talking on the landline. She could tell by her expression that all was not well. She set down the boxes and waited. When Flora finished the call she said, "That was Roland."

"And . . . ?" It was a measure of how often she had to speak to her divorce lawyer that they were on first-name terms.

"Well, the good news is the phone is working."

"I can see that, Mum, stop stalling."

"It seems your father has decided not to accept the terms of the divorce settlement after all."

"What? But it was all agreed."

"He's changed his mind."

"Or his shiny new woman has changed it for him."

"Does it matter? The point is, he thinks the figure is too high and that I'm not entitled to half the value of the business because he owned it before we married."

"And was running it at a loss before you took the reins. I can't believe he's trying to do you out of what is rightfully yours!"

"Nothing about Philip surprises me anymore," she said, and her tone was so weary Xanthe's heart ached for her while her blood boiled at the unfairness of it all. "Looks like we'll have to get this place open and turning a profit very soon indeed because, from what Roland told me, it's going to be quite a while before we see any money from the settlement at all. Once these things are contested they can take months and months."

"Dad is being such a bastard!"

"No point getting steamed up, love. Come on, we've earned the right to tuck into those lovely cakes, I think."

"How can you be so . . . reasonable!?"

"I've wasted enough energy on your father already. I'm not going to let him get in the way of our new life, Xanthe," she said as she stick-step-sticked her way toward the stairs.

In the kitchen, they feasted upon sticky lemon-drizzle cake and chocolate-fudge brownies, which were the best Xanthe had tasted. They ate in silence until they both felt restored by the sugar and fat coursing through their systems.

"You know," Flora said, brushing crumbs from her fingers, "things are going to get better."

"I know. Sometimes it all just comes flooding back. Everything that happened. I get . . . overwhelmed."

"It's understandable. You had a dreadful experience. It takes time, getting over something like that. It was such bad timing, your father and me splitting up so soon after what Marcus did to you."

"It wasn't deliberate, Mum. He didn't mean for it to happen."

"I can't see it like that. He was the one with the drug problem. Those were his drugs that were found in your flat. He should have taken responsibility for them."

Xanthe gave a weary shrug. "We've been over this. . . . The lease was in my name. Marcus wasn't even there when they were found. The law says they were down to me."

"You've never touched drugs in your life. Marcus had plenty of time to come forward, but he didn't. He let them take you to court, to that awful prison. . . ." Even now that it was all over, all firmly in the past, Flora's eyes filled with tears when she thought about her daughter in jail. In fact, of all that he had put her through, the one thing Xanthe would never, *could* never forgive Marcus for, was seeing what it cost her mother to visit her in prison, to watch her looking at her only child, locked up, shut away, alone, and beyond her help.

Xanthe reached across the table and took hold of her mother's hand.

"New beginnings, Mum, remember?"

"Yes." She nodded with a small, brave smile.

"Stuff 'em all!" Xanthe added their little rallying cry.

Flora laughed then, the pain of the past packed away for another day. "Come along," she said, picking up the last brownie as she got to her feet, "there's work to be done."

They descended the stairs once more. Although Flora was hampered by her crutches, she had long ago developed tactics for lifting things with one arm, or filling a backpack or shoulder bag with items she wished to move, or sometimes leaning on a parcel trolley to shift heavier objects. Together, she and Xanthe put their new treasures in the room of mirrors and then began the daunting task of clearing the shop. The room would have to be emptied completely so that it could be redecorated. Xanthe suggested a system of heaps and areas: clean and keep, repair and keep, take to charity shop, and throw out. They allocated the back room for things needing repair, and it was easy to see where Flora would be spending most of her working days for many weeks to come. There was so much in the "throw out" pile that Xanthe pushed open the back door and began stacking less important items in the garden. Trips in and out at least gave her brief moments of respite from the dust. The weather continued to be warm and sunny, and she could see that the walled garden, though neglected, could be something quite lovely with a modicum of time and care spent on it. Every now and again, as they worked, she would experience a little jolt, or hear a little buzz and know that there was something else among the muddle of collectibles that was singing softly to her. It was inevitable, with so many objects, connected to so many lives lived long ago, that there should be several pieces to which she would be sensitive.

The modern name for her rare gift was psychometry. To some the term meant nothing significant, simply a label given to a fanciful, unproven ability to discern details about those who had made, owned, or held things simply by touching them. But to others, to Xanthe, it meant listening to the whispers of ghosts, to the echo of their voices, held in the fragile porcelain, or glass, or silver of something special. As they worked on, each time she felt a connection, however slight, she separated those things into a new pile, which Flora immediately called Xanthe's Stuff. The sight of so many curios wanting to speak to her made her feel dizzy, but however tempting they were she knew they would have to wait. As soon as she was free to go to it, the chatelaine would demand all of her attention.

As they worked, Margaret Merton looked on, biding her time. She had waited so very long, she was well trained in patience. God had seen fit to send the chatelaine. Soon, they could begin.

Later Xanthe and Flora had a supper of more cake and hot chocolate. In an effort to force her mother to slow down and rest, Xanthe had pushed the packing cases that were in the sitting room out of the way and cleared a path to the shabby, green-velvet sofa. The two of them flopped onto the soft, welcoming cushions and sipped in silence. This in itself was worrying, for her mother was rarely without something to say. By the time they had finished their little meal Xanthe was deeply concerned about Flora's condition, which was evidently deteriorating.

"Come on, Mum. Time to get you to your bed," she insisted, helping her from the sofa and up the second flight of stairs. She could not recall seeing her look so exhausted, and decided that the next day she would make time to go shopping. A diet of cake and biscuits would do little to help Flora's already compromised health. Once in her own room she found the sight of the unpacked cases and general chaos dispiriting, but was beyond caring sufficiently to do anything about it. She had brought the carefully wrapped chatelaine up to her room earlier, and it was all she had energy left for. In the shadowy little attic space, with only the light of a dim, bare bulb by which to study it, Xanthe folded back the layers of tissue paper and laid the silver pieces on the bed. The metal had been worn and polished by use and cleaning over many years, acquiring a particular luster that cannot be obtained any other way. The humming in her head started up immediately, though she noticed she was less fearful near the chatelaine now. There remained a tension, a sadness, but the fear and sense of doom had receded. Even so, when she touched the clasp the heat was tremendous, and again she saw a sudden image of dense woodland, of impenetrable ivy and brambles and plants twisting and climbing up the trunks of impossibly tall trees. The vision was fleeting but clear. Where was it? The hallmark on the clasp was that of a Bristol silversmith, but the chatelaine could have passed through many hands, been in the possession of a number of owners, throughout its long life.

"Who did you belong to?" she asked it gently. "Who is it who wants to tell me their story, hmm?"

Although she was no longer overwhelmed by the strong emotional vibrations connected to the piece, she was still all too aware that there was something extra special about it. Something urgent it had to tell her. But what? She felt near overcome by a tiredness she could no longer fight, and the light was so poor in her bedroom that she was unable to properly see what she was looking at. She knew that there was scant possibility of her finding a magnifying glass or loupe in the confusion of cases and boxes that surrounded her. There was nothing for it but to wait until daylight and take her new treasure out into the sunshine where she could investigate every detail, every clue that was worked into its intricate chains and attachments. She was hopeful that there might perhaps be words she could make out in the silver-backed notebook. She had at least found her sketch pad, so she made a swift drawing of the chatelaine, noting the parts she thought were older and recording which bits were hallmarked. The picture was a poor second to the real thing, but as a record it would serve.

As she fell into bed she was relieved to feel herself quickly floating toward sleep. She had spent so many nights in the past year laying wakeful and anxious, her mind churning over the events that had so changed everything. It would be bliss to sleep deeply and dreamlessly. Alas, her own past was not yet prepared to release her, it seemed, for even as her limbs grew heavy Marcus came into her mind. He had no business being there anymore, but Flora had been right about Xanthe missing her singing. It was her joy, her release, her other gift, and it was because of Marcus that she no longer sang. The two things could not be separated. It had been Marcus who had persuaded her to join the band, he who had persuaded her that she could sing well enough. Marcus who had written the words and music specifically for her voice. And when it all went wrong, when Marcus broke what they had beyond any hope of mending, he had ended everything. The two of them. Their future. The band. Xanthe's singing. And at that moment, as she toppled into an uneasy slumber, she could see no way in which she could ever hope to find her voice again.

4

THE NEXT MORNING XANTHE WOKE WITH THE DAWN, SERENADED BY THE song of garden birds. In her still-packed suitcase she found a pair of cutoff jeans and a seventies cheesecloth blouse that tied in a knot at the waist. Hastily coaxing her unruly curls into a low ponytail, she pushed her feet into her boots and took the paper-wrapped chatelaine downstairs. On her way to the garden she paused in the stock room, filling a bowl with hot, soapy water and finding some small rags for cleaning and drying. She disliked using polish on silver until it had been carefully washed, and even then hated the way some solutions clogged into carvings or engravings. Better to use liberal quantities of both water and elbow grease.

Outside the day was already bright. The garden was formed of a long rectangle of grass, edged with what would have once been flower beds but now more closely resembled mini-wildernesses. Behind these, on all three sides, were high walls of faded red brick, affording both shelter and privacy. In the far left corner there was a small stone building set into the wall and almost entirely engulfed by ivy and rampant shrubs. Xanthe was dimly aware of the sounds of Marlborough waking up, but the garden felt separate, secure, and peaceful.

Unaware that her every move was being keenly observed by Margaret Merton, she set the bowl of water down upon the flagstones of the small patio area at the house end of the unmowed lawn. The sunshine fell upon this part of the garden early, so that the stones felt warm beneath her bare knees as she knelt. With great care, she removed the chatelaine from its wrapping and immersed it in the water, making sure to keep the notebook out; the paper between its silver covers was so old and frail it would dissolve in an instant if it came into contact with the hot water. The chatelaine felt almost as though it were trembling in her hands, and despite the suds that covered it, the silver began to shine ever more brightly as she cleaned. Soon the birdsong was drowned out by the high-pitched buzzing and the jumbled whispers clamoring for attention inside her head. She strained to make out words, but the sounds were too confused. Again she had a clear sight of woodland undergrowth, and this time she saw that there were small birds among it. As she cleaned the clasp, the details of the design were better revealed, showing acorns and leaves and twining plants. Was this what was sparking the glimpses of that past? Somehow, she did not think so. She was aware of an underlying sensation of fear, but it was more controlled now. With the grime of ages removed, she could see the chatelaine's details more clearly and noticed that the silver of some of the attachments was not an exact match for the clasp and chains. The coin purse, for one, was made of a mesh that was of a harder, brighter form of the metal. The scent bottle looked simpler, almost clumsy. The notebook holder was considerably finer and more carefully worked than the main part of the piece. It was not uncommon for antiques of all kinds to be added to or altered over the years, but it made her question whether the description of the things as being mostly Victorian was accurate. The buttonhook could well have been older.

And what was missing? What had once hung from those empty chains?

She lifted the chatelaine out of the dirty water and rinsed it beneath the outside tap. A paving stone in the sunlight seemed the perfect place to set it out to dry before polishing it later. She was relieved that the reaction it provoked was no longer so intense, but at the same time she was a little confused. Why had it had such a powerful effect on her earlier? And why could she not read more from it? In the past, she had quickly been able to draw stories from pieces that had not stirred her so profoundly. It was curious. Xanthe decided that as soon as the internet connection was set up she would do some research and see if it was possible to unearth answers that way, even if that did feel a poor substitute for her more usual, visceral connection.

After taking a cup of tea to Flora she forced herself to go shopping. Her mother still looked fatigued from the day before, and Xanthe had seen what could happen if she pushed herself beyond her sensible limits. She needed hearty food, regular meals, and more painkillers. Xanthe fetched her bag. For a moment she considered putting on something less scruffy but did not, deciding that the good people of Marlborough might as well get used to her as she truly was.

In her eagerness to get on with the day she had not taken into account the early hour. The high street was slowly coming to life, but the supermarket's doors were firmly shut. She was not in the habit of wearing a watch, but the clock on top of the old town hall informed her it was half past seven. Another hour until opening time. She was on the point of returning home when she noticed the pub that Gerri had mentioned. The Feathers was a splendid example of a black-and-white timbered building, with a low, sagging stone-tiled roof, small windows, with overflowing window boxes of cheerful late summer flowers. She walked along its high street frontage until she came to the narrow lane that twisted away between the buildings. She could not see the river, but she remembered Gerri saying it was behind the inn. A walk beside gently flowing water seemed like a pleasant way to pass the time until she could do her shopping. The road followed the side of the pub and its small beer garden at the rear. Beyond that was a large stone building that resembled an old warehouse of some sort. Xanthe heard the river before she saw it. The Kennet was not a broad sweep of majestic water like the Thames, but little more than a chalk stream, shallow and perfectly clear, showing the reeds beneath the surface waving in the easeful current like mermaid hair under the sea. The water was fenced off with old metal railings, and the banks had been planted with bulbs. To the left was an antiques market, which Xanthe knew she should investigate soon. They had chosen Marlborough largely because it was a place known for its antiques, and people would travel for a day's browsing. There was definitely room for their own little shop, but they needed to make sure there was not too great an overlap in the type of things the competition stocked. To the right was a slender bridge that led to a cluster of houses on the other side of the river. It was an altogether wonderfully English and peaceful and old-fashioned part of the town. Half of Xanthe was charmed by it, while the other half felt a twinge of panic that she might have hop-skipped the rest of her youth and landed firmly in middle age if she found such a setting and such comfortable tranquility so appealing.

"Thinking about an early morning swim?"

The voice behind her was familiar, but only vaguely so. She turned to find the man who had taken her parking space at the auction the day before. He was dressed in overalls and was wiping his hands on an oily rag. Looking beyond him she could now see that the building she had passed was a workshop. The sign above it read CLASSIC SPARES AND REPAIRS. There appeared to be a small apartment on the first floor.

"Your business?" she asked, nodding past him.

"That's right. Any classic. I buy 'em, restore 'em, and sell the ones I can force myself to part with. Couldn't resist the sale at Great Chalfield yesterday. There was a cracking collection of cars going, as well as quite a hoard of parts."

"Ah. I didn't notice."

"I'm surprised, you owning such a gem of a taxi."

"I love my car," she confessed, "but that's as far as my fascination for classic vehicles goes. Actually, I was told you were the man I needed to find. Liam, is it?"

He grinned. "Good to know somebody thinks I'm useful."

"I need a new wing mirror."

"Driving too close to the hedges? Takes a while to get used to the lanes around here."

"On the driver's side," she told him firmly, not enjoying the implied criticism of her driving. "I had it removed for me by a boy racer. Can you find me another one?"

"Let me write down the make and model, and I'll see what I can do."

He led her into the tiny room that served as an office at the front of his workshop. In the larger space she could see two gleaming cars, all shiny body work and polished chrome, and another under a cover. There was a radio playing somewhere. If the workshop was orderly, the office was a chaotic collection of papers and coffee mugs. Liam found a notepad with surprising ease. The third pen he unearthed actually worked.

"Yours is an Austin Fairway, that right?" he asked.

"Yes. An FX I. 1986."

"Ooh, first to have power steering. Bet you're glad about that.

Hard work turning one of those beauties around otherwise," he added, glancing at her as if to assess her strength.

Xanthe narrowed her eyes at him. She repeated to herself her little mantra that not every good-looking man was trouble, but in truth it was still too soon for her to believe it.

"Can you get me the mirror?"

"Leave it with me, and I'll need your phone number, too."

She gave him the one for their landline, thinking her mobile number somehow too much of a personal connection. She explained about the shop and that they had only recently moved in.

"If you're in need of refreshment you could do a lot worse than The Feathers," he said, gesturing in the direction of the pub. "They do a seriously good veggie lasagna, and they have live music on Friday nights."

He could not have known how much Xanthe wished only to avoid such a thing.

"Good to know," she said, walking away. "Let me know what I owe you for the part when you find it."

"Will do," he said. She felt him watching her as she went and then he called out, "Hey, you didn't give me your name."

She paused. "It's Xanthe," she told him. "Xanthe Westlake."

"Well, Xanthe Westlake, welcome to Marlborough."

On returning to the shop Xanthe found her mother downstairs, sitting on the red brocade chaise, covered in the contents of a box of jewelry she had bought as a job lot at the auction.

"You look very regal like that," she told her. "Marie Antoinette surrounded by her jewels."

Flora laughed. "I don't think there's anything here quite in her league. Though there are some good gold chains, and one or two brooches."

"Seriously? Do people even wear brooches anymore?"

"They are coming back in, haven't you heard? Oh, and here, look at this." She held up a short rose-gold chain formed of wheat links, which were one of Xanthe's favorites. From it dangled a small locket in the same gold. It was completely plain, but instead of this rendering it dull, it left the warmth of the gold to glow. The simplicity of the oval was a joy.

"That's beautiful," she said.

"I want you to have it."

"What? No, it's worth a fair bit, and I've just splashed out all that money on the chatelaine."

"That's business. Once you've found out its story I know you will sell it. This is different, this is for you to keep."

"It's lovely, really lovely, and it would sell quickly," she protested.

"I don't care. Someone named 'the golden one' should always have a drop of gold, don't you think? Call it a moving-in present, from me to the best daughter in the world. Come here." Xanthe knelt in front of Flora so that she could fasten it around her neck. "I found it here; bit of local glamor for my girl in her new life. I couldn't do without you, you know that, don't you?"

Xanthe ran her fingers over the locket. It felt wonderfully smooth and precious. "Mum, stop. We don't have time to get sentimental," she said, giving her a hug. Flora rarely said such things, and Xanthe knew she meant them, but they were both too emotionally fragile to risk giving way to their feelings. She got to her feet, picking up the shopping bags. "Now, dig yourself out of that lot, because I am going to cook us a full English breakfast."

"Did you get brown sauce?"

"For someone who doesn't shop, you can be very picky, you

know," she told her and then grinned, pulling a bottle of her mother's favorite sauce from one of the bags.

As soon as they had eaten, Xanthe helped Flora install the computer on a small Victorian bureau in the sitting room and left her tackling the task of getting them online. Outside, the day had become noticeably hotter. Xanthe found that the sun had moved off the chatelaine, which had dried to a wonderfully gleaming finish. The decoration worked into the silver had come up better than she could have hoped. She noticed that it felt calmer in her hands this time. She wandered onto a sunnier part of the lawn, and immediately it began to sing again. This treasure was behaving unlike any Xanthe had found before. Why on earth should it react to the sunshine? To be certain, she stepped back into the shade. Sure enough, it quieted again. Holding it carefully she walked around the lawn, listening closely to when and where it became more active. At length she realized it was not the sunlight that it was reacting to, it was a certain position in the garden. It vibrated more strongly, and sang louder, when moved toward one corner. She went as far as was possible in that direction, until she was standing with the toes of her boots up against the dense brambles and ivy that covered the little stone shed. She leaned closer to peer at it, and in doing so stumbled, falling forward. Instinctively, she put out her hand to stop herself landing among the thorns. The instant she touched the leaf-clad wall of the building she experienced a swamping sense of sadness. She heard her own sob in reaction to this wave of sorrow sweeping over her, and to that was added the heart-wrenching sound of someone weeping.

Xanthe staggered back, staring at the muddle of stone and plants that made up the insignificant-looking building. "Well," she said to it, "what is so special about you, I wonder. I think I need to take a closer look."

Wrapping the chatelaine up again, she set it carefully to one side upon a low stone bench at the edge of the lawn, before fetching the garden tools they had brought with them. Armed with thick gloves, a large pair of garden clippers, and a rake, she set to work. It was tough going. The brambles were sturdy, grown thick over years, evidently left undisturbed by the previous owner and quite possibly several before him. As Xanthe hacked and chopped, she sustained countless scratches to her legs and arms, and the hot sun made sweat trickle down her back, but she was a woman entirely focused on the work at hand. There was something about that shed that she needed to discover; something that set off the chatelaine, and she was not going to stop until she found out what it was.

It took nearly an hour to uncover the building sufficiently, for it to begin to look as if it were actually made of stone rather than vegetation. To her surprise, she found the walls were rounded. Only the part where it was set into the external wall was flat. She worked hard to clear the tangle covering the door. It looked very old and extremely solid, with a tiny grilled window near the top. It even had metal bolts studded through it and a hefty lock. Why would anyone put such a lock on a garden shed? It seemed all wrong for keeping chickens or pigs in, so she decided it must have been for storage of some sort. At last she was able to get hold of the loop of metal that served as a door handle. Taking a firm grasp, she heaved and pulled and could feel movement. If the lock had ever worked, it wasn't working now. Suddenly, with a clunk and a creak, the door opened. The ground was too uneven for it to swing free, so that there was just a gap about two feet wide. Xanthe peered inside, but the windowless space was in utter darkness, save for the sliver of sunlight she was letting in through the doorway. It would have been possible for her to squeeze through, but something caused her to hesitate. The air in the shed smelled dreadful. It was damp and musty, as if it had been shut up for many, many years. Would she find a few rotting mice, perhaps? Some moldy fungus growing in the dark? She stood still and quiet, listening, but there were no sounds at all. Instead, there was something else. A sense of foreboding that instantly stirred a memory in Xanthe. A memory of a bad time, when she had been frightened and alone. More than that, she felt sorrow emanating from the inside of the building, so powerful, so heavy, it made her gasp.

Without properly considering what she was doing, she fetched the chatelaine. Unsure of what she was expecting, she knew only that she needed to move it closer to those dark, weighty stones. As she approached, holding the silver in her slightly shaking hands, she heard the weeping again, louder this time, mournful and despairing. Carefully, but with determination, Xanthe stepped through the doorway.

It was then that she felt herself falling. Her balance went, and she had the sensation she was tipping backward, yet she would later be unable to recall hitting the ground. Her eyes were open, she was certain of that, but she no longer saw the garden. Instead, the image of the dense woodland filled her vision, complete with the tiny birds among the twisting plant tendrils. Even as she was swamped by this vision, she did not feel panic, but was struck by the fact that it appeared to be night. She could see the tree trunks, vines, and brambles, but their colors were muted and dark. Why were the birds still up if it was nighttime?

All at once, she could hear the sound of someone breathing, fast and hard, as if they were running. She attempted to turn, not certain if she was in fact moving at all. Everything had taken on the quality of a lucid dream. She could now see open ground. Fields, sweeping away, flowing into the distance, and beyond them a stream. Was it she herself who was running? Was that her own labored, frightened breathing? No, she could see someone else. A girl in a long dress, tearing across the grass as if she were being chased.

"Wait!" Xanthe called. "Wait!"

But the girl kept running. Then, as if she heard her calling, she hesitated and began to turn. Xanthe then felt a curious connection. Something she could not explain. She wanted to see the girl's face, to know who she was, to speak to her.

But everything grew fainter, the sounds quickly becoming distorted and more distant, until they faded to nothing and were replaced by a deep blackness into which she fell.

{ 5 }

XANTHE WAS NOT CERTAIN IF SHE HAD LOST CONSCIOUSNESS, OR IF SHE was merely shaken by the particularly powerful vision. It had felt so very real. Why on earth was the chatelaine reacting so strongly to a forgotten building at the bottom of the garden? Shaken, she put it back in its wrapping and stepped unsteadily out of the shed. As she did so a new sensation assailed her. A cold shiver descended her spine, and she knew at once that this was not caused by what she had so recently experienced. This was quite clearly provoked by a presence, as if someone were standing directly behind her. Xanthe froze. Unlike when she had seen the girl in her vision, she had no desire to see the face of whoever it was she was convinced now stood only feet from her, silent and still in the gloom of the oppressive building. This was an entirely different manner of presence, and it carried with it real menace. She remained in the doorway of the shed, the chatelaine still clutched tightly, wanting more than anything to run but determined not to give in to the impulse. Suddenly, as quickly as it had arrived, the presence was gone. Xanthe waited for her pulse to return to a more normal rhythm and then, still with a quick glance behind her to assure herself there was nothing there, she walked briskly across the garden and into the house, slamming the back door behind her. She needed to share this with her mother, to say out loud what she had experienced if only to test that it did not sound like the ravings of a mad woman. Flora was accustomed to her daughter connecting with things, of course, but this one was different from the others. She needed her mother's calm view of what had happened. She found her at the desk in the sitting room, staring at the computer screen.

"We are connected to the world of the web," she announced, "for all the good it will do us."

It was then that Xanthe noticed the strained expression on Flora's face.

"What is it?" she asked. "Are you OK? Do you need more painkillers?"

"Sadly I don't think this can be put right with a handful of aspirin." Flora gave a sigh and rubbed her temples. "After getting us online, I tried to set up the banking for the shop. You know, move some money into the new account so we can start getting the place redecorated, buy some advertising space here and there, more stock . . ."

"And . . . ?"

"Your father has had our joint account frozen."

"You're kidding!"

"I wish. I called Roland. It's because he's contesting the settlement. All jointly held assets and accounts have been blocked until it's sorted out."

"But that could be months." Xanthe closed her eyes in an effort to bring her mind to bear on the real and the practical, pulling it back, with effort, from the very unreal events in the shed that had left her so shaken.

"Until then, we have my savings account, which I all but emptied to buy the shop, the contents of my purse, and whatever you've got stuffed under your mattress."

"Bloody hell." She shook her head. "I'm sorry, I've got about three hundred pounds."

"Snap."

"Shit."

"Exactly."

Xanthe sat next to her and put a hand on her arm. "It'll be OK," she told her, receiving a wan smile in reply. She hated to see her mother being put through more struggle. It was so unjust. She saw then that this was not the moment to burden her mother with all the frightening and inexplicable things that had happened to her in the garden. Flora had more than enough to contend with. Practical, solid, sensible, and important things. Things a mother could reasonably expect a daughter to help her with.

"We don't need decorators," Xanthe said. "I can fling some paint around."

"There is a bit more to it than that, Xanthe, love."

"And we can print our own fliers for the opening."

"Well, I suppose we can just about afford the ink."

"And there's loads of stock here. Just needs a bit of cleaning, or fixing."

She patted her hand. "You're right. Who needs money?" She picked up her crutches and pulled herself to her feet. "Right, I'll shut myself in the storeroom with the things that need cleaning or fixing. Don't let me out until I've spun straw into gold," she told her.

"And what will I be doing?"

She smiled, showing a glimmer of her more usual determination and grit. "You will be in the shop flinging paint around."

Xanthe helped her mother get set up in the storeroom and then turned her attention to the shop. It was clearly going to be some time before she could begin repainting the room; there was so much by way of preparation that had to be done first. It took the remainder of the day for her to finish emptying the space. She had to stack some boxes in the middle of the room and work round them as she commenced the task of washing and scrubbing. The filth of years of trade and indifferent housekeeping was stuck to every bit of skirting board, or window sill, or picture rail, and the old vinyl on the floor was mostly rotten, so that she had to tear it out in moldering chunks. As there was no money to hire a Dumpster, all the rubbish had to be hauled out into the garden to await sorting before she could take it to the dump. At least the taxi would be up to that job.

Each time Xanthe stepped out into the garden she felt the pull of the mystery of the tiny stone roundhouse and what she had seen there. She took a moment to photograph it on her phone so that she could try to look it up on the internet later. She reasoned that she needed clues, background information, about both it and the chatelaine itself. She could not shake off the feeling that there was an urgency to this story. As if she were being shown something that was happening now. As if somebody needed her help. At the same time, she was also unable to rid herself of the memory of that other, darker presence. She knew in her heart that she would not be able to help the first, without facing up to the second, however frightening the prospect.

By the time she had finished the windows, woodwork, and door and was rinsing off the walls of the shop space dusk was falling. She stood in the bay window, wiping her brow with the back of her hand, pleased that the glass was at least now clean enough to see through properly. A figure entered her field of vision, waving and cheerful. Even on such scant acquaintance, it was clear Gerri was the sort of friend whose company could lift a mood.

"I know you're not open yet," Gerri said, "but I saw you beavering away in here and couldn't resist a peek. Do you mind?"

"I'm glad of the excuse to stop cleaning, but there's not much to see yet, I'm afraid," Xanthe said, letting Gerri in and waving her arm to indicate the mostly empty room.

"Oh, but you've already worked wonders! I remember what this place was like when Mr. Morris had it. Lovely man, but a stranger to the vacuum cleaner. Ooh, is that a piece of Minton I see poking out of the top of that box?" She gently tugged at the wrapping paper and then lifted out a creamy tea plate decorated with exquisitely painted Lily of the Valley flowers and leaves. "So pretty!" she said, running her finger around the fluted edge. "And in such good nick, too. Is there more?"

"I think so. Dig a little deeper." Xanthe knelt beside the box and helped her pull out more and more pieces. The tea cups were turned with a small foot and double loop to the handle, giving them a charmingly delicate appearance. The glaze had not crackled despite the china being at least sixty years old, in Xanthe's opinion. She uncovered two more tea plates, three cups and saucers, and a tiny creamer.

"That's a dear little thing," Gerri murmured, turning it this way and that, holding it up to the fading light of the day. "It was what gave me the idea for my tea shop, the fact that I can't stop collecting beautiful china. I had so much of the stuff, it seemed to make sense to put it to good use."

"I'm not sure I'd risk some of these with customers," said Xanthe.

"It's surprisingly tough. Though you're right, it is hard to watch people using some of the lovelier pieces carelessly. When I first opened I was quite jittery about that, but I learned not to watch. Now I'm too busy to hover over a favorite set anyway!"

"How long have you had the cafe?"

"A couple of years. Ever since I became newly single, actually."

"Ah. I'm sorry."

"Don't be. It wasn't a happy marriage, and I'd never have thought of setting up my own business if circumstances hadn't prodded me into it."

Xanthe thought about how similar her own situation was. It was encouraging to see someone who had taken the plunge and made a success of a venture in the town.

"So what made you choose Marlborough? Had you heard it was a good place to start up a business? Did you do any market research?"

Gerri laughed at this. "Nothing so professional! My children go to the primary school here. I needed to move closer to live and work nearby. Being a single mum brings out the practical side in everyone, I suppose."

"Wow, children, too. It can't be easy, running a business and bringing up a family on your own."

"Thomas and Ellie are very easygoing. It's just normal to them now, me being busy with the tea shop, constantly baking. I think the endless supply of cakes and biscuits helped win them round to the idea."

"Well, if you need any more china, you won't have to go far, once we've got ourselves organized." Xanthe sighed, sitting back on her heels, the enormity of the task striking her once more.

Gerri smiled. "It's hardest in the first few months. Then, just about when you think you'll go mad with it all, everything falls into place. You'll see."

"I hope you're right. My mum really needs this to work. We both do."

"Marlborough's a friendly place. And it is popular for day trips and a bit of shopping. If you're going to stock such gorgeous stuff I'm sure you'll do well."

"Thanks for the tip about where to get my wing mirror fixed, by the way. Liam's finding me a replacement." She unwrapped another plate as she spoke but was still able to catch Gerri's raised eyebrow at the mention of the young mechanic.

"I expect he was only too pleased to help you," she said.

Xanthe had a feeling there was more her new neighbor would have said on the subject, judging by her smile and her sudden apparent interest. She wondered if Liam was known for being a bit of a charmer, perhaps. Or was it that Gerri herself was keen on him? It was hard to tell. Xanthe decided to steer the conversation back onto less problematic ground. She pulled out the last piece from the box, stripping it of its wrapping with a flourish.

"How about this?" she asked.

Gerri gasped. "You've got the matching teapot! Oh, it's divine. And now I have to have it. And I really shouldn't. But I can't resist!" she laughed, taking the teapot and gazing at it lovingly.

Xanthe thought about telling her she could pay in cake but stopped herself. They needed cash. Urgently.

"I can do you a good price for the whole set," Xanthe said. "It's incomplete, so it won't be mad money. And, seeing as we're neighbors . . ."

Gerri laughed again. "See? You're a natural businesswoman! You're not even open yet and you've made your first sale."

They agreed on a price and chatted easily while repacking the china. Xanthe felt some of the anxiety that had been plaguing her lessen a fraction in Gerri's company. It was cheering to think she had found a potential friend so nearby. When one of the more reliable clocks chimed the hour Gerri gasped, declaring herself late for collecting her children from their grandmother, and hurried away. Xanthe went to see how Flora was faring with the repairs and restoration jobs and found that she had all but disappeared behind a stack of small cupboards, occasional tables, umbrella stands, and assorted bric-a-brac.

"It's not all rubbish," Flora insisted, quite bright-eyed from the fun of delving into those unknown pieces. Then, noticing how tired her daughter looked, she declared work over for the day and decided they had both earned a drink at the pub.

"Oh, I don't know, Mum. . . ."

"Come on. I need beer to wash away the taste of dust. And anyway, think of it as PR—we need to make friends with the locals, and where better to do that than at our local?"

Xanthe found this reasoning hard to argue against. They went upstairs to make themselves respectable, as Flora liked to put it. This amounted to quick showers, failing to find a hairbrush, and rummaging in suitcases for the least crumpled garments that could be found. Flora emerged from her room with a different scarf knotted in her hair, a dab of pink lipstick, and a cotton summer dress she had had for a number of years.

"That thing is nearly old enough to be classed as vintage," Xanthe warned her.

"When it reaches that point you can have it." She laughed. "Come along, I've worked up quite a thirst."

Xanthe followed her out. For herself she found a long gypsy skirt that had survived being stuffed in a case for days better than anything else. This she had teamed with a clean black T-shirt which showed off her new gold locket to good effect. She had taken a moment to remove the photograph of her mother from its usual place in her wallet, trim it to fit, and then fix it inside the locket. She abandoned her attempts at taming her profusion of ringlets, settling for running her fingers through them and leaving them loose. The sun had bleached the outer layers to a gold that matched the locket.

The Feathers was bustling by the time they arrived. Inside it was all beams and brass and warm polished wood. It was not until they walked through the door that Xanthe remembered it was Friday night, and that meant live music. Flora saw the band setting up at one end of the low-ceilinged room.

"Oh, music! How lovely," she said, shepherding her daughter toward the bar.

"Can't we just get some beer from the off-license and take it home?"

"No we cannot," Flora said, nudging her way through the throng, uttering thank-yous for people who bothered to make way for her and her sticks.

There was a good-natured ambience, with a balanced mix of local residents and visitors to the town. The bar itself was manned by a huge man with a Viking beard. He was clearly good at his job, a natural host, grabbing glasses, pulling pints, flicking off bottle tops, taking money, all in an easy and familiar dance. When he spoke to the newcomers his deep voice revealed a rich Scottish burr.

"What'll ye have, ladies?" He smiled the smile of a willing landlord.

"Two pints of whatever's good," Xanthe said, looking at the array of taps.

"If it's real ale you're after, and something local, I'd say go for a drop of Henge. 'Tis a joyful thing. Not heavy at all, but full bodied."

"Sounds perfect," Flora said, handing him a ten-pound note.

The barman noticed Xanthe glance toward the band, who appeared to be almost ready to play. It was difficult to see them clearly through the crush of people.

"That's Tin Lid. Local boys. D'you like a bit of music with your beer?"

Before she could stop her, Flora piped up, "Xanthe's a singer."

"That so?" The barman raised his bushy brows. "Are ye any good, hen?"

"She's wonderful."

"Mum, please . . ."

"We've just moved here." She was unstoppable, offering her hand to the man now. "Flora and Xanthe Westlake. We're opening an antique shop down Parchment Street."

"Old Mr. Morris's place?" He shook her hand. "That's a task ye have ahead of ye. I'm from off myself, as ye might have gathered. 'Tis a friendly enough place, Marlborough. A few snooty people, but ye get them anywhere. And there's history and stories around every corner. I've made something of a study of the area. Annie"—he nodded toward the woman at the other end of the bar—"she thought it would help us fit in." He laughed a little at this idea. It was true, he was far from the manner of middle-Englander one might expect, with his burly arms and tattoos and beard rings and Scottishness. "Anyway, I hope to see more of both ye ladies in here, now that we're neighbors, so to speak."

"Oh, I'm sure you will," Flora told him. She had spied two seats in the window at the back of the room and headed toward them.

Xanthe picked up the drinks and followed. When they sat down she tutted at her. "You can't keep doing that, Mum."

"Doing what?"

"Trying to get me gigs."

She shrugged. "You're a singer. You need to find places you can sing."

"I *was* a singer."

"It doesn't go away, a talent like yours. You need to get out there again, love," she insisted, lifting the foaming beer to her mouth.

Xanthe drank in silence. It seemed to her she had more than enough to think about without trying to resurrect her career as a singer. As she sipped her drink she peered through the crowd for a better view of the musicians, and there, on lead guitar, was the man from the garage. Liam. He appeared relaxed and even more handsome than before. He looked up at that moment and noticed her. To her embarrassment, and Flora's amusement, he gave a grin and a quick wave. Ridiculously, Xanthe found herself blushing, but she was spared any questions from her mother as the band finished their sound check and began to play.

That night, once they had returned home and Xanthe had helped Flora to her bed, she sat in her own room at the open window. Below, the garden was in darkness save for the faint glow of nearby streetlights, but the moon was bright enough to cast shadows and throw down patches of silvery light. While she waited for her mother to get to sleep, she searched for round stone buildings on the internet. A quick look revealed all manner of things— theaters, livestock markets, silos—none of them right. None of them a match for her own curious shed. She narrowed her search to English rural areas, particularly small towns or large villages, and then specifically Wiltshire. Suddenly she was finding images of many similar buildings. Small, humble constructions, always in heavy stone, often with slate- or stone-tiled roofs, with no windows, and a single, sturdy door. The captions read: *Lock-ups or ancient jails, sometimes called "blind houses" due to their lack of windows or light. Used to hold offenders awaiting transportation to larger towns where there were law courts and proper jailhouses.*

A jail! All at once Xanthe's strong reaction to the place made perfect sense. Somehow, something in her had known it was a place of suffering, a place of despair. She closed her eyes against a painful flashback to her own time of incarceration. She would never forget her first night in the women's prison in north

London. She had had a cell to herself, which she later discovered was unusual. She did not know if this had made things better or worse, but when that door clanged shut, when the lock turned and she was in there, trapped, removed from everyone she loved and everything she knew, at that moment she knew what it was to despair. The sentence she had been given was three years, and it was not until she had been there four long months that her appeal was heard and she was released. On that first night she had been facing the prospect of being locked up for at least two years. Even now, years later, she could still feel the panic welling up inside her, still taste the bile in her mouth as she was sick again and again, reacting to the unjust horror, fighting a scream that she dare not start for fear she might never be able to stop.

And now it transpired she and Flora had bought a jail. At the bottom of the garden of what must have originally been a private house. It still seemed unlikely, though it would explain, perhaps, the vibration of sadness and fear she had felt emanating from it. But what could it possibly have to do with the chatelaine? And why had she also experienced that other, deeply disturbing presence? Had there, perhaps, been a murderer locked up in the place once long ago? Someone violent and vengeful?

Xanthe kicked off her boots, picked up the chatelaine, and went downstairs, doing her utmost to avoid stepping on any treads that creaked. After the clamor and noise of the pub, and the stuffiness of her attic room, the garden was wonderfully quiet and the night air fresh. She could hear sounds of the weekend nightlife of the town continuing, but they were muffled and hardly raucous. Cautiously, more than a little nervously, she made her way over to the stone shed, or what she might well have to start thinking of as the jail, even if that made it harder to approach. She tried to give herself a talking to, tried to muster courage, tried to be rational: this was just an old building, and she was not a convicted criminal anymore. There was no reason for her to be frightened of the place. Even so, her whole body was tense. She did her best to concentrate on the grounding, gentle feel of the unkempt grass of the lawn, soft and stalky under her bare feet. As she approached the newly exposed walls of the building she felt the chatelaine begin to grow warmer. Even through the paper she could feel its increasing heat. When she unwrapped it and the silver touched her skin she was immediately struck by the now-familiar connection, powerful and urgent. She had left the shed door open to let out the old, stale air in the shed and let in some new. Where the moonlight fell through the doorway she could see that the floor inside was dusty but quite dry, there being a layer of cobbles just visible. She needed to go in, but was reluctant to take the next step. At that moment she experienced another vision, but not of the running girl or the tangled woods. This was from her own memory, her own past. She felt the dull pull of dread in her stomach as she saw again the narrow cell into which she had been led. The walls painted institutional cream. The high, mesh-covered window that afforded no view. The low, hard bed. The dismal sparsity of the furnishings that spoke of lack and loss and lonely weeks, months, years to come.

Xanthe shook her head, refusing to let her own experiences hold her back. She was not here for herself. Someone was calling her. Someone else was trapped and afraid. Aside from her own memories, she could feel another level of anxiety. One that was connected to the antique silver in her hands. Was the fear she was experiencing that of whomever had owned the chatelaine, or her own nervousness at what might be shown to her? At what she might be made to feel and to experience? Or at her reluctance to meet again that malevolent presence that had so scared her the time before? And then, as she hesitated, she heard a voice, as clearly as if someone had been standing right in front of her. It was a young woman's voice, and it was taut with emotion.

"Help me!" she begged. "Oh, please, help me!"

Xanthe knew then that she could not hold back, could not turn away, for those words did not feel like a random snippet of the past, something merely transmitted through the silverware. Nor did they feel like a simple echo of an event lost in time that only some people have the ability to hear. They felt personal. Carefully selected specifically for her, as if that plea, that cry for assistance, was spoken directly to her and no one else. And she knew how it felt to be shut up, locked in, separated from those she loved. She could not turn away.

Taking a steadying breath, she stepped across the threshold.

She was deeply relieved not to encounter the earlier sinister presence she had so dreaded meeting again. She had but a moment to take stock, however, before she was assailed by a violent sense of movement, as if she were being shaken and then thrown, though without ever hitting the ground. There was a moment of blackness, of airlessness, where she thought she might suffocate, and then abruptly she was able to see and to breathe again. To take great gulping breaths.

But what she saw was not the inside of the shed, nor the little garden. She was standing on an old road, which was rough and stoney. It had been raining, and she could feel watery mud beneath her bare feet. Once again she felt she was having a lucid dream that was shockingly real. It seemed to be dusk. The track was set among sweeping farmland, with no fences. On one side there was a deep ditch and beyond that some trees. The road turned a corner behind her, so that the distance she could see in that direction was short. Ahead, the landscape swooped on down and then up, and at the limit of her vision she could make out stone gate pillars and what looked to be the beginning of a grand driveway. It was then that she started to both hear and feel the rumble and clatter of galloping horses. Seconds later she could see them, pulling fast out of the driveway, steering hard right and charging along the road toward her. The covered carriage was large and fine and pulled by four white horses, the driver atop urging them on with whip and voice.

Would he see her? What would he do if he did? Xanthe looked for a place to hide, but the trees were too far for her to reach. Dream or not, she could not allow herself to be mowed down by the hurtling carriage. She ran for the verge and then jumped down into the ditch. It was filled with weeds and dirty water that came up to her knees, soaking her long skirt. She crouched low so that she could not easily be seen, though she need not have worried about the driver noticing her, as he was far too taken up with controlling the galloping horses. Xanthe raised her head as the carriage passed. It was so close she felt the air disturbed as it swept by. It was plain in style, but expensive-looking, with glass windows, and a groom standing on the back, holding tight as the conveyance lurched and bumped along the uneven road.

And then she saw her.

It was little more than a glimpse, but it was sufficient to catch the expression of fear on the face of the girl at the window. She could have been no more than sixteen, her eyes tear-filled, her brown hair escaping from its pins and her simple cream cap. She wore a brown woolen dress with a pinafore over it, and as Xanthe watched she was convinced, beyond any doubt, that the girl saw her. She raised her hand and pressed it against the glass in a gesture of silent despair. Xanthe reached toward her, and as she did so she stumbled, falling onto the muddy ground. As she pushed herself up on her knees she realized the clasp of the chain around her neck had wrenched undone and the locket lay on the gritty earth. She snatched it up, fearful of losing something so personal, something that reminded her so much of her mother.

And as suddenly as it had started, the hallucination was over. Xanthe was back in the garden, laying on the ground, half in and half out of the stone shed, the chatelaine beside her. She clambered unsteadily to her feet and staggered out onto the lawn. Her pulse was racing, and her breathing labored as if she had been running. For a while she stood and waited, wanting to allow her disturbed senses, her shocked body, her confused mind to return to a steadier state before moving again. And as it did she stood there and became aware of two things. The first was that she could still hear the sounds of galloping hooves and the rattling of the carriage wheels as they faded into the distance.

The second was that her bare feet, her legs, and the lower half of her long skirt were soaked through with muddy ditch water.

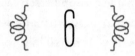

{ 6 }

AN HOUR LATER SHE WAS STILL STARING AT THAT MUDDY HEM. IN HER bedroom, she had undressed but could not bring herself to take the skirt downstairs and put it in the washing machine. Somehow, hanging it up so that she could sit and look at it forced her to think the unthinkable. Dreams might be scarily vivid, could feel frighteningly real, that much she knew, but however bright the colors, however clear the sounds and everything else about them, dreams did not send you back to the waking world covered in ditch water and mud. Wherever it was she had gone while she was in that shed, it had been somewhere real. Xanthe dearly wished that she had bought some beer or wine while she had been shopping. For a moment she even contemplated waking her mother so that she might talk to her, but how would that conversation have sounded? How could she explain that she believed she had just traveled through time? Would Flora think her only child was taking leave of her senses?

She started to pace around the room, the notion of getting any sleep being laughable. The more she tried to piece things together the more she came to a single conclusion, and it was not a reassuring one: when she had taken the chatelaine into the blind house she had been transported to somewhere and some time other than her own time and place. She had, in point of fact, time traveled.

"Ha!" She was unable to stop herself laughing aloud at having even thought such a thing with any seriousness. "Xanthe Westlake, you are losing your mind!" she told herself. Was it the stress of the events of the last year? Being betrayed by Marcus, ending up unjustly accused and prosecuted for something she had not done, spending time in jail, giving up on her singing career, and seeing her parents' marriage disintegrate? It was, to be fair, enough to tip any reasonable person over some sort of edge. Was this what a nervous breakdown looked like? Did such things truly drive a person to madness?

She sat down heavily on the edge of the bed and stared at the saturated skirt. There were two options, it seemed. Either she had traveled back in time, temporarily, or she was going mad, possibly permanently.

"Great choices," she said to the room.

To stop herself feeling as if she were losing control of her mind she focused on what exactly it was that she had seen. On what precisely any of it meant. There was a place that was unfamiliar to her, though it looked like any small slice of rural Britain, with its rolling greenery, the usual trees, and the easily recognizable damp climate. And the voice she had heard had been speaking English. There were still leaves on the trees, but they had started to turn, she remembered, so that meant autumn. Not summer, like it was in her real, feet-on-the-ground, sensible existence. She took a deep breath and listed what else she might dare to call facts. A girl in a carriage, scared out of her wits, apparently being taken at speed somewhere she did not wish to go. And she had looked at Xanthe. Right at her. Had *seen* her. That was one of the few things she felt completely certain about. Not that it made her feel any better. Why her? What did the chatelaine have to do with the girl? And why did the little jail trigger such a thing? Xanthe had connected with found treasures before, certainly, but nothing like this. It had to be the combination of the piece of antique silver and the jail. Was the place haunted? There was certainly what felt like a presence there. Something besides the panicking girl. Could it be that there were well-known ghost stories about the town, or even the shop itself?

At last, exhaustion began to get the better of her. She clambered into bed and closed her eyes, hoping against hope that she might sleep without dreaming. It was all too big to face all in one go. She decided she would do some research regarding local legends and stories, as well as investigating the origins of the building itself. If she was not to consider herself falling into madness she had to find a way of making sense of what had happened to her.

The next morning life continued with surprising normality. Xanthe's head might have been full of impossible things, but for the rest of the world it was simply business as usual. It was almost shocking to find herself getting on with everyday, mundane life while her mind struggled to come to terms with the enormity of what was at the bottom of their ordinary-looking garden. After a few fitful hours of sleep she had risen and pulled on jeans, a T-shirt, and boots. She shared a quick breakfast with Flora and then persuaded her to go with her to the high street to buy paint for the shop.

Outside, the little cobbled street looked particularly pretty in the morning sunshine. Hanging baskets and window boxes of pansies and geraniums with trailing ivy softened the ancient brick walls of the shops. Flora gamely struck out across the rounded stones on her crutches, and not for the first time Xanthe admired her mother's dexterity.

"The going is easier in the high street, Mum. Do you want me to take your bag for you?"

Flora ignored the offer. "All I need is some new rubber ferrules for my sticks. There must be an outdoorsy shop here where I can buy some. Only a few more yards." She hobbled on, her expression giving away the effort the short journey was costing her.

The smoother paving stones that bordered the high street were far simpler for her mother to navigate. What neither of them had anticipated was the bustle of shoppers so early in the day.

"Wow," said Xanthe. "They take Market Day a bit seriously around here."

The high street being so unusually broad allowed room for the market stalls to be set up down the middle of it. Traffic was light and slow moving, giving way to pedestrians, whether stall holders or shoppers, so that the loudest sounds were the shouts of the traders as they advertised their wares. The stalls themselves were open-sided with red- or blue-striped canvas roofs and awnings, giving the place the feel of a carnival. The three dozen or so traders offered a tempting range of produce, crafts, and general supplies. Xanthe could see someone selling homemade cider, another stall boasting artisan beer brewed from local hops, two bakers, a butcher, a particularly colorful stall selling hand-dyed wool, a florist and garden plant supplier, a display of patchwork materials and quilts, some pottery, three fruit and veg stalls, one offering freshly made smoothies. It was an almost bewildering selection.

"Hmm, now this is my kind of shopping." Flora was smiling. "This could take a little longer than expected." So saying, she stick-step-sticked her way to the nearest stall, no doubt lured by the aroma of freshly made pies.

"Mum, the paint?"

"I'll leave that to you, love," she called over her shoulder. "I'll see if I can pick up a few interesting things here. Meet you back at the shop later, OK?" And with that she disappeared into the throng.

Xanthe felt the tension in her shoulders ease a fraction. Seeing her mother cheered up by the market, happy in her new hometown, her pain forgotten for the moment, was a welcome relief from the perpetual worry she carried about her. Turning up the street, Xanthe headed in the direction of the hardware stall she could see near the top of the hill. She had every intention of buying the paint quickly and returning to the shop to start decorating. She could not, however, shake away thoughts of what had happened to her only a matter of hours ago. She had to search for answers, to try to find facts on which to at least build a theory.

With this in mind, she stepped into a corner shop that sold maps and guidebooks on the area. She thumbed through lists of best pubs, finest views, wonderful walks, and so on, and even found a book entirely about local ghost stories. It was while she was reading this that a familiar Scottish voice interrupted her.

"You'll be giving yourself nightmares with that, hen," said Harley. He looked even larger and like more of a biker now that she saw him out from behind the bar. He nodded at the book in her hand. "Is it the ghosts ye're interested in or the local history?" he asked.

"Oh, both. Neither, possibly," she said, sliding the book back onto the shelf. "Just trying to find out . . . stuff." Harley gave her a look, clearly picking up on her reluctance to be more specific. She chose another book and flicked through it. "You know, local stories. History of the houses. That kind of thing."

He nodded. "Aye, it's good to learn about your new home. And there's plenty to discover around here, if it's history you're after. Or the unexplained."

"Sorry?"

He took the book from her and held it up, pointing to the title she had not read. "*Ley Lines of Wiltshire.* Fascinating stuff."

"Seriously?"

"Oh, aye. Ancient lines of incredible power and strange occurrences, particularly at points of convergence. If you've a mind to believe that kinda thing. This place is riddled with them."

"Strange occurrences?"

He put the book back on the shelf. "Come away back with me to The Feathers. I'll show ye a map of the things."

"I really ought to get back at the shop. . . ."

"Tsk, ye've time for a cup of coffee with your new neighbor now, surely to God?" he said, taking a newspaper, waving it at the shopkeeper, and holding the door open for her.

Xanthe had never been in a pub at breakfast time before. It was surprisingly clean and fresh smelling after the busy Friday night. Sunshine was streaming in through the low, small-squared windows, picking out the gleaming brasses hanging around the fireplace. The heavy black beams and broad floor-boards gave an impression that the inn had changed little in centuries. Harley left her sitting at the bar while he disappeared to fetch the promised coffee and map. She glanced at the clock above the mantelpiece. Already she had been gone half an hour and not purchased the paint. She told herself that her mother would still be happily browsing the market stalls. She considered texting her to make sure she was OK, but Harley reappeared quickly.

"Here we are," he said, setting down a tray of coffee and taking a rolled map from beneath his arm. He unfurled it on the bar and weighted down the corners with bottles of brown ale. It was a map of the whole county of Wiltshire, showing the major towns, some of the smaller villages, and landmarks, but no roads or railways. Instead it had perfectly straight lines drawn upon it in red.

"Now, ye can see just how many ley lines crisscross the county. Right from Old Sarum, with its Iron Age hill fort, up and along through Stonehenge, of course, the mother of all ancient energy sources, right through the middle of the Preshute White Horse up here . . ." His enthusiasm for what they were looking at was infectious.

"There certainly are lots," she agreed. "And you say they have . . . special energy?"

"So it is believed, aye."

"But, who put them there? I mean, what are they for?"

"Nobody rightly knows. They are very, very old. You see, people long ago identified these lines and then built important places upon them. They believed they could tap into that unseen power, and that it would be a positive influence on whatever stood upon it. That's why there are so many churches and cathedrals connected by Ley lines. See? Here, and . . . here."

Xanthe peered closer. "Are there any that go through Marlborough itself?" she asked.

"Indeed there are, two beauties. This one is one of the longest known, from west to east, plum through the center of the town"—he ran a finger along it—"and the other is north-south, d'you see? And the two cross one another right . . . here." He followed the second one with the index finger of his other hand until the two met. "Well, will ye look at that," he said brightly. "I'd not noticed that before. The point of convergence is right about where old Mr. Morris's shop is. Or I should say, where your shop is. Yup, right about there. You, hen, have an ancient point of convergence in your very back garden!"

She left The Feathers with two books Harley had been happy to lend her. One was on ley lines, and the other was entitled *Mysterious Buildings of Wiltshire*. She hurried to the hardware store and bought quantities of white emulsion, before heading back to the shop. She was quite breathless from rushing by the time she arrived, and her head was racing, working on all manner of possible answers to impossible questions regarding the little jail. The whole concept of ley lines was new to her, but already she could see that the position of the old stone building was as significant as its original purpose, if not more so.

The bell clanked as she entered the shop, where she found Flora and, to her surprise, Liam.

"There you are," her mother said. "I was just about to send out a search party. Look, you have a visitor."

Liam grinned and held up a small, brown parcel. "Your wing mirror came," he said. "Thought I'd pop it over. Can't have you dicing with the crazy Wiltshire traffic without it."

"Maybe I should fit bars on the front, too," said Xanthe, putting down her paint and books. If Flora noticed the titles she didn't say so, but she saw Liam frown at the one on ley lines. Did all local people know about those sorts of things? He had told her that he had grown up in the town, and for a moment she contemplated asking him about the jailhouse, but where could that conversation go? How could she start to talk about her bizarre experiences with someone she had only just met? Then again, in some ways it might be easier than discussing such things with her mother.

"You've been busy," Liam said, looking at the emptied shop.

"Painting next," Flora told him. "And then fitting everything back in, getting the displays right . . . there's lots to be done."

Xanthe went to take the side mirror from him. "Thanks for getting this," she said. "How much do I owe you?"

He held on to it. "I'll fit it for you."

"I can do it myself," she said, a little more sharply than she had intended. How long would it take for her instinct to defend herself to become less sharp, she wondered?

Liam did not react as some might have, did not become defensive himself. He simply gave another broad grin and said, "I bet you can do just about everything and anything to that lovely taxi that she needs. She's a fine car, very fine. Tell you what, I'll fit your mirror if you take me out for a spin in her. I'd love to see how she runs. I could give you a quick tour of the area, take you to see one of the famous white horses. The view from the top of the downs is quite something. You can see the whole town spread out before you."

"Oh, I don't know. . . ." She glanced at Flora. "We've so much to do here." She was surprised to find that in fact she wanted to go with him. But then, she knew it was not Liam who interested her. It was what he could tell her about the mysterious place that she now called her home. And what she might discover by seeing it from another perspective.

Seeing her hesitate he said, "When we get back I could give you a hand with the decorating. Two of us would get it done in no time at all, I reckon. What do you say, Mrs. Westlake"—he turned to her mother—"can Xanthe have a bit of time off for good behavior?"

Xanthe flinched. He could not have known what the common reference to a prison term, so lightly and casually used, could have meant to them. She wondered how her mother would react. She saw Flora take a breath, and then, as if she decided that her daughter needed to be allowed to take time away from all the things they had to do, all the things in life that had to be dealt with, she smiled.

"I don't see why not," Flora said, "especially if it means I get an extra worker for a few hours later on."

"Great!" said Liam. "I like you antique people, you know how to strike a deal."

Flora laughed. "Mind who you're calling 'antique'!"

"Do I get a say in this?" Xanthe asked, secretly glad to have had the decision made for her.

Flora waved them toward the door. "No. Now go on, off with you, before I change my mind and have you polishing the tarnish off all that silver plate we found."

Liam quickly fitted the new side mirror, and they took the road north and west out of town. It was good to have the windows down and breathe in the scents of the countryside: the cut hay, silage, and overflowing hedgerows. The weather was still warm, but not as scorchingly hot as it had been. The landscape was washed in a golden glow of summer sun, the beginnings of a drought tinging the grass, the breeze that had picked up whipping up a little dust. Liam made easy conversation as they went, commenting on the car or points of interest along the route. Xanthe found it a relief to be away from the shop, from the inexplicable occurrences in the garden, and from the pressures of the new life she and Flora were struggling to manage. The car purred along the largely empty roads, and with every mile she felt herself relax a little more.

"This is a treat. Thanks for agreeing to a run out, Xanthe."

"You're doing me a favor. I didn't realize how much I needed some time out from the shop. We've only been there five minutes, but, well, it's been pretty full on since we arrived. Lucky for me you're not working today."

"I keep the workshop closed on Saturdays. It means I can go to auctions and recover from any gigs I might have done."

"We enjoyed the band last night," she told him, and meant it. "You were good."

"Thanks. I hear you're something of a singer yourself."

"Good grief, word gets around quickly in these parts!"

"In a town this size everyone knows everyone else's business. Especially if you're local. Harley told me."

"He's certainly a man with a lot of local knowledge." She hesitated and then added, "He's been opening my eyes to the wonders of ley lines."

"Ah, one of his favorite topics."

"Apparently, according to him, we've got a 'powerful point of convergence' in our back garden."

"Lucky you! Be careful, or Harley will have you opening it to the public and selling tickets. Can you imagine the weirdos that would queue up for that?"

"Especially, as it turns out there's an old jailhouse built on the exact same spot," she said, testing his reaction to the information.

"A blind house? Cool."

"You know about them?"

He waved his hand vaguely. "There are quite a few around here. Good one in Labrook, and a famous one built into the bridge in Bradford. Oh, take a left at the next junction."

The car shifted down a gear to tackle the steepness of the hill as they wound their way up toward a high point in the landscape. Liam directed Xanthe to a small car park among some ancient oak and ash trees. They locked up the cab and followed a narrow path out of the copse and onto the open farmland.

Xanthe was enjoying the opportunity to lose herself a little in the exertion of walking. She kept wanting to stop and take in the view, but Liam insisted she not look until they reached the best vantage point. After another fifteen minutes walking, they crested the hill. The path continued on, but an offshoot led to a grassy area where people could pause to catch their breath, or to have a picnic, or simply to stand and stare at the spectacular scenery.

"There you go," Liam said, grinning, as if what he was showing her was all down to him. "Best view in Wiltshire."

Xanthe would have found it difficult to disagree. It felt as if the whole of England was spread out before her. As far as she could see in any direction the fields and hills rolled away, a hundred shades of green and gold. Small clusters of trees punctuated the swaths of grass and crops. To one side there were wide fields dotted with plump sheep. Far below she could make out tractors working to cut and turn more hay. There weren't many houses save for the occasional farm or hamlet of cottages, with, at the limit of the view, the rooftops of Marlborough just visible. Above it all was the wide, wide sky, powder blue with wisps of cotton-white cloud whipped into feathery shapes by the summer wind. And there, to her right, on the facing hill, was the most magnificent chalk horse she had yet seen. It was hard to judge its size precisely, but she guessed it to be at least sixty feet long. There was something timeless and powerful about its simplicity and the way it seemed to stand sentinel, proud and fearless, over the landscape around it.

"He's quite something, isn't he?" Liam said, nodding at the horse. "I like to come up here and clear my head. Take in the view and spend some time in his company. Don't want to sound like Harley and his ley lines, but, well, the old horse has a powerful presence, don't you think?"

She nodded. "He does. I never expected this place to be so

filled with things that can't properly be explained. To be honest, I feel like I've moved to a whole new world. And it's a pretty darn mysterious one. Particularly our new home."

He looked at her. "Old man Morris still hanging around the shop, is he?"

"As a ghost, you mean?" She shook her head, dismissing the idea along with a chill that came with the memory of whatever it was that lingered in the blind house. "No, not a ghost. Not that."

"But . . . something?"

The warm breeze kicked up a miniature whirlwind at their feet, whisking dust and leaves into a brief flurry. Xanthe found she was avoiding Liam's gaze. It was a complicated subject to tackle without feeling at least in the smallest measure insane. She pushed her messy hair out of her face and attempted a nonchalant tone. "Do you know of any stories about a local girl, someone who lived here, oh, I don't know, maybe a couple of hundred years ago? Someone who might have been accused of something and locked up in a jail in the area, possibly even the one in our garden?"

"Not that I can think of. Have you asked Harley?"

"Not yet. I don't have anything much to go on, really. Just a feeling. And a . . . dream. Something about that jail connects to a piece of silver I bought at the auction, and to this girl, only I don't know how."

"Wow. Sounds like you've had a lot going on in the short time you've been here."

She shrugged, feeling suddenly foolish. "It's probably nothing. They say moving to a new house is one of the most stressful things you can do. Then there's the business to set up, and Mum's not been great lately."

"Did she have an accident?" he asked.

"It's arthritis," she explained. "She gets her days. Sometimes she overdoes things and then pays the price."

"It must be hard for you too, having to be the one to look after her."

"Trust me, most of the time it's the other way around."

"If you say so," he said in a way that suggested he did not entirely believe that this was an accurate description of the way things were. Perhaps he was right. He was quick on the uptake, having already sensed there was something she was trying, and largely failing, to talk about. That it was something beyond the normal getting-to-know-you pleasantries and small talk. But how could she tell him she had traveled back through time? What kind of a lunatic would she sound like? She did not know him well enough for that manner of confidence. She was simply going to have to fathom things out by herself.

She put on her brightest smile. "Thank you, for bringing me here, for showing me this. It is wonderful. I can see I'll be coming here whenever I need a bit of time-out, a bit of a breather. But, well, there's a room waiting to be painted. . . ."

"Say no more." He rubbed his hands together in a show of eagerness for the job. "A deal is a deal. Let's get at those brushes and rollers, and we'll have the job done in good time for a pie and a pint at The Feathers."

"The pub two nights running? What kind of wild living goes on around here?" She smiled.

"Maybe Harley can book you up for a gig. I'd like to hear you sing."

Xanthe suddenly felt the weight of her own past catching up with her as she turned to go. "Oh, I think I've got enough to do right now without singing, don't you?" She tried to keep her voice light but knew there was a note in it that more than likely gave something away, particularly as Liam had turned out to be a good deal more perceptive than most people. Even so, he did not question her further, and they walked back to the cab in an easy silence. He could not have known that as soon as they headed for home Xanthe's mind was focused once more on what she had experienced the night before. She knew about the ley lines now, but beyond that she was still at a loss to work out what she was being shown in the jail. Still she did not know who the terrified girl was. All she did know, beyond any doubt, was that she had not succeeded in helping the girl. And that the only way she might do so was to return to the blind house, to allow the girl to connect with her again. Xanthe also knew that this meant risking being taken back in time as she had been before. The thought terrified her. What if she was in danger there, where nobody knew her and nobody would come to her aid? What if she was not able to return to the present? If she had so little control over what happened to her when she stepped inside the jail, how could she be sure she would come back? It was a truly dreadful thing to face. In trying to help the desperate girl who was reaching out to her across time, she might become lost, cut off forever from home, from her own time, from her mother. Never able to return. She shook her head at the thought of it. *Never* was simply too enormous a thing to contemplate. She could not risk it. Not for herself and especially not for Flora. However much she wanted to help, she had to stay away, stay out of the jail, turn her back on the poor girl. She had no real choice in the matter.

Xanthe could not have known that at the very moment she was coming to this conclusion, Margaret Merton was standing in the garden, waiting. Waiting for her. For Margaret knew enough of the workings of young women, of the frailties of the human spirit, of the many conflicting demands life could make upon a person. She had seen the fear in Xanthe's eyes. She would not be surprised by the girl's reluctance to revisit the blind house. She had anticipated such a reaction. Anticipated it, considered it, and arrived at a manner in which to overcome it. For Xanthe was her daughter's only chance of deliverance, and for this salvation to come about, the girl must return to the blind house. And, however reluctantly, she must also return to the past.

{ 7 }

TRUE TO HIS WORD, LIAM HELPED XANTHE PAINT THE SHOP. THEY APPLIED A coat of emulsion in no time at all and even succeeded in glossing the woodwork. He offered to come back the next day to finish the task, but Xanthe told her she could manage. It had been agreeable having his company, having his help. It surprised her that she liked it, indeed, but she had no wish to become beholden to him. Nor did she want him entertaining ideas that she might be interested in him. Which was why she also turned down his suggestion of supper at The Feathers. Later, when she and Flora sat down to pasta, garlic bread, and locally made pesto that Flora had bought in the market, she found herself reluctant to talk about her trip out.

"It was nice," Xanthe said, tearing off some garlic bread.

"Nice? Is that all I'm going to get out of you?"

"Liam knows a load of stuff about the area. He made a good guide. And it did me good to get out in the fresh air and blow away the cobwebs. Better?"

Flora ate thoughtfully for a moment. Xanthe could see she was considering talking about all manner of things she herself would sooner avoid, so she attempted to turn her attention back to the business.

"The shop's shaping up, don't you think? Have you decided on an opening date yet?"

"Well, there's still a mountain of stock to be prepared. I don't want us to rush it and let people see us before we are at our best. But—" she paused to take a swig of bottled beer "—we do need to be selling stuff as soon as we possibly can."

"So, two weeks' time, d'you reckon?"

"Before the August bank holiday and all those lovely tourists and holiday makers desperate to spend money? Would be ideal. It's possible, if we push on with everything. Time to get adverts in the local paper, put up some fliers."

"Book the mayor to cut a ribbon?" Xanthe teased.

"Very funny. Think we'll just go with offering an opening day discount. Maybe we could get cakes from across the road, too."

Xanthe agreed she would ask Gerri and sent her mother to bed dreaming of the perfect launch event for her new baby. Because it was her passion, in truth. While Xanthe was happy to be a part of it, and considered herself lucky to be given the opportunity with her own life and plans in such a state of disintegration, the shop would always be Flora's. She was glad that her mother had something on which to pin her hopes. Something other than her father. Something more than just Xanthe herself.

Once the house was dark and quiet Xanthe sat on her bed and began examining the chatelaine again. She turned it over in her hands, letting its warmth throb into her fingers, paying no heed to the buzzing noise it set up in her head. It was, she was certain, only a part of the puzzle, and, surprisingly, the less frightening part. It was the stone building that had tipped her from the present and sent her tumbling into the past, even if it had done so because of the chatelaine. Laying the intricate silver piece on her lap, Xanthe snatched up her sketchbook, not for drawings this time, but for notes. Perhaps setting things down plainly on paper would make them less ludicrous and more manageable. Firstly, the stone shed was, according to definitions of the things in the slim volume she had found entitled *Historic Buildings of Wiltshire*, definitely an old jail. It seemed strange to her at first that it had lain undiscovered for so long. Even an enthusiast such as Harley did not know of its existence. Then, after more reading, she came across a photograph of Marlborough's famously wide high street, taken in 1910, and there was another little jail, right in the middle of it. At some point, this second blind house had been built and was used more and more until the first one fell into disrepair and had become forgotten.

Then there were the ley lines. There were two that intersected in the garden, at the precise spot where the jail stood. Had the person who chose the site for it known about these mysterious things? It seemed possible, though she was still uncertain as to when precisely the jail had been built, let alone by whom. If wisdom on the subject of these curious lines was to be believed, such a convergence meant a tremendously powerful location.

The chatelaine was an important factor in what had happened to her, but it was proving a difficult piece of the puzzle to understand. More difficult than it should be. After all, antiques were the thing Xanthe felt she knew something about. If she was unable to solve all of the silver piece's mysteries, what hope did she have with the rest of it? The auctioneer had described the silver as Victorian, with some parts thought to be earlier. In fact, she was certain the most significant part of it was at least a century older, if not more. The clasp and some of the chains were definitely from an earlier century. The weight of the silver, its luster, the way the carvings were worked, all pointed to an era of slower, simpler craftsmanship than the Victorian parts of it. And besides, whenever it was she had visited in the past, whenever the story had its origins, it wasn't the nineteenth century, of this much she was certain. The carriage and the way the girl was dressed, even the way she wore her hair, and the landscape itself all pointed to a much earlier time in English history. There were no fences or hedges, so it could have been before the time when people started farming in fields. That was an easy fact to fix in time, something that could be investigated and pinpointed. But plain clothes, with a pinafore like that, and few buttons or decorations? That was far trickier. A servant girl, probably, and a county one, but her clothes could have been anything from mid-fifteenth century to late eighteenth. Xanthe had barely had more than a glimpse of what the girl was wearing, after all.

If she was going to get anywhere with discovering her story, with helping her in any way she could, she knew that she would have to at least make herself receptive to another vision. She needed to see more of the girl, of where she was, and *when* she was! She still had so little to go on. On top of that, she had no idea how the girl thought that she could actually, practically, do anything to help her. Xanthe failed to see how she could have any influence over something that had happened centuries ago. She rubbed her temples against a burgeoning headache. If only she could see her, hear her, talk to her, without risking traveling back in time. Might there be a way to use the blind house safely? To use it to communicate with the girl without ever leaving her own time? She was a long way from having answers to those sorts of questions. Nothing felt as if it were under her control. She knew that taking the chatelaine into the jailhouse was what had triggered her traveling, but the thing itself had not made the journey with her. She had not been holding it when she arrived on that muddy road in the path of those galloping horses. Would it help if she wore it, perhaps? Would that keep her somehow anchored to the present?

And then there was the menacing presence she had felt inside the jail. What did that have to do with the girl? Was it dangerous to herself or to the girl? Were the two things even connected?

"Xanthe Westlake," she muttered aloud, "what are you getting yourself into?"

Downstairs, one of Mr. Morris's several ormolu clocks struck twelve. She made her decision and got to her feet, unwrapping the beautiful treasure from its paper. This time she clipped the clasp onto the waistband of her jeans. The chains hung down her leg, the attachments swinging a little as she moved. It looked incongruous, having been designed to sit upon full skirts, so that the buttonhook, notebook, scent bottle, and purse would not have swung to and fro quite so much, but would have sat more comfortably. Before she had time to lose her nerve, Xanthe hurried downstairs again.

Outside the night was cloudy for the first time since they had moved in, so that she fumbled her way across the garden, wishing she had taken a moment to fetch a flashlight. At the door of the jail she hesitated. The chatelaine was singing louder than ever, and now she could hear a chorus of whispers. The breathy voices were many and muffled, but she was certain they were urging her on, pressing her to step over the threshold. She took hold of the iron ring that was the door handle and pulled hard, preferring to have the door as fully open as possible. That way, perhaps, she might be able to talk to the girl, or experience another vision, without having to step into the jail itself. The enormity of what might happen if she took that extra step struck her anew. To truly leave her own time and journey into the past, it was both astonishing and terrifying. She put her hand on the warm, worn wood of the door, trying to let in more light, but the cloudy night was unhelpfully gloomy, the moon too shy to show its face.

"Hello?" The tremor in her own voice did nothing to steady her nerves. She was too frightened to feel ridiculous about talking to herself, so she tried again. "Hello? Can you hear me? I'm here. I'm listening. What is it you want to tell me?"

Inside the jail, standing in the darkness, Margaret Merton willed Xanthe to move forward further, just a little further. It would be so much easier, so much better for all concerned, if the girl were to go to Alice's aid all of her own accord. A willing savior must surely have the best chance of success.

Xanthe, squinting into the gloom of the interior, didn't know what it was she expected to see. She half-wished there to be nothing, no sound, no vision, so that she could tell herself she tried but got nowhere. Still, guilt and curiosity, combined with a desire not to fail, caused her to lean in through the doorway.

And then, her eyes adjusting to the darkness, she did see something. She could make out a figure, shadowy but definite. But it was the form of a woman, not a girl, and Xanthe knew at once that this was not who had called her, not the one she had glimpsed running, not the girl who had pressed her hand and face to the carriage window pleading for help. This was somebody altogether different. In this woman she had found the source of the sense of dread and menace that had so overpowered her once before. Here was the very center of that threat, of that danger. Xanthe was torn between wanting to flee and being too frightened to move. Her left palm was still against the door, and for a moment she contemplated grabbing at the handle and heaving the thing shut. But what would be the point? She knew with unshakeable certainty that whoever, whatever it was that stood before her could not be kept anywhere by something so basic, so simple, so earthbound as a heavy wooden door.

"Who are you?" she found herself asking. "What do you want?"

As she watched, transfixed, the figure took a step toward her. And then another. At last the distance between them was less than a stride. As the woman moved from the dark of the interior to the thinner cover of the urban night that washed over the garden, she was revealed in more than sufficient detail to cause Xanthe to gasp. Her age was hard to define with any degree of accuracy, partly because of the lack of light, and not least because one side of her face was badly disfigured, the skin taut with scar tissue. Her throat also bore a broad scar, the skin raised and puckered around it. She wore a plain, ankle-length woolen dress beneath a filthy white pinafore, both of which were ragged at the hem. Her cotton mob cap was tattered and stained and not equal to the task of containing her coarse hair, which hung in gray hanks about her face. As if conscious of her appearance, the woman pushed at the hair and tugged at the cap, ineffectually attempting to neaten and tidy herself. When the apparition opened her mouth to speak, Xanthe held her breath.

"My name is Margaret Merton," she said, her voice dry, insubstantial, an echo of a whisper. "I have waited so very long."

"Waited?" Xanthe did not allow herself time to ponder the madness of talking with a ghost. "Waited for what?"

Margaret tilted her head a little, and the faintest hint of a smile visited her lopsided features as she breathed a reply that made Xanthe's stomach turn over. "For you," she said. "For you."

"But, I don't know you. How could you have known I was coming here? Coming to live here?" Xanthe asked, taking a step back.

"I knew that someone would come, one day. Someone who could help me. Someone with a gift such as yours."

"A gift?"

"The chatelaine found you," said Margaret, lifting a painfully thin hand to point to the silver at Xanthe's waist. "It sang to you. You found it because of the shop. And now you are here." She paused to gesture at the jail. "Now we can begin."

Xanthe could not find the courage to ask what it was the specter wanted to begin. At that moment she was struggling to make sense of what was happening. First the powerful connection with the chatelaine, then the fact that she had traveled back through time, and now, now she was talking to a ghost. A ghost who, it seemed, had plans for her. Instinctively, she began to back away, but each step she took Margaret Merton matched.

"Leave me alone!" Xanthe gasped.

The ghost suddenly circled round her, moving with unnatural speed, coming to stand behind Xanthe. Between her and the garden, effectively trapping her in the doorway of the jail. While reason told Xanthe she could have run straight through the apparition, she could not bring herself to do it.

"I have not waited these many, slow years to step aside," Margaret said coolly. "I have need of your assistance. Alice has need of you."

"The . . . the girl in my vision? The one I saw? That's Alice?" Xanthe tried to move past Margaret as she spoke, but the phantom moved silently and swiftly, pressing forward again.

"Alice is alone," the ghost told her, her own voice trembling as she spoke. "I cannot go to her. It has been my lot to linger, to drift in this purgatory, waiting, hoping. Now that hope is to be fulfilled. You can go in my stead. You can help her!"

Xanthe began a shout of protest, but it was too late. Margaret Merton jumped forward, causing her to leap to one side as a reflex. So sudden was the movement, and so unsteady was Xanthe on her feet for fear of what was happening to her that she lost her balance. She fell. And as she fell, as she twisted and put her hands out to break that fall, she saw at once what was inevitable. She was falling across the threshold of the jail, and even as it happened, in that giddy instant, she knew she would not reach the cobbled floor. Would not feel the grit and dirt of ages hard and real against her palms, her knees, her shoulder. For she had already begun another more profound descent as she plummeted down through the steep, deep centuries once more.

THIS TIME THE TRANSITION WAS FAR MORE SWIFTLY ACHIEVED. WHETHER or not it was because she was actually wearing the chatelaine, Xanthe could not be certain. When she had stepped into the jail it was to the accompaniment of Margaret Merton's voice urging her on, beseeching her to find Alice, to go to her aid. There was a sense of pressure against her ears and in her head, and then it was done. She was standing, gasping for breath, no longer in the jail, but in a large, airy room, with wood-paneled walls and deep, wide windows. She was perplexed to find that the chatelaine had yet again failed to travel with her. Or at least, most of it had. Why? Why did it not stay on her like her clothes, mercifully, did? A quick check showed her that the parts that had not traveled were the older ones, which meant all of the chains bar two, the clasp, the key, scent bottle, and buttonhook. She was just left holding the notebook and coin purse. She quickly tucked them into her pocket.

The room was unfamiliar to her, though it looked like the interior of many a grand manor house she had visited in the course of her work. The heavy carved wood of the chairs, the tapestry bolsters and cushions, and the style of the paintings suggested a time at least three hundred years before her own. No electricity, not even gaslights. Instead there were sconces for candles on the walls as well as candelabra on the tables and mantelpiece. She was relieved to note that there was no sign of the ghost, nor of her oppressive presence. She could detect a faint smell of woodsmoke, although the fire in the wide hearth was out. She struggled to take in the enormity of what was happening. She had traveled through time again, and again she had emerged into a place other than where she had started. The ghost of Margaret Merton had meant her to go there, had been determined she would. Xanthe knew as soon as she had entered the blind house she had been powerless to stop herself falling back though the centuries. How would she get home? If she had no control over traveling through time, how could she return to her own time again? A cold wave of dread swept over her.

"Don't panic," she told herself. "Think, girl. Just think it through." She rubbed her arms as she paced the room, trying to keep out both the cold of the day and the chill of fear she knew was no friend to rational thought. She quickly told herself that she *had* returned home after her last brief journey to the past, even if she did not know how she had done it. Therefore, it was possible. And then there was Margaret Merton. The ghost wanted her to help Alice and knew all about her connection with the chatelaine, knew that she had a special gift with certain things that found her. The ghost had made sure that she went back into the blind house, so she must have known that this was the door through to earlier times. "OK, so if I do what she wants, why wouldn't she let me go home again? She would have no more reason to keep me here." Saying it aloud did not, unfortunately, make Xanthe's logic sound any more convincing. That she was putting her trust in a terrifying phantom, that this might be her only route home, was a far from comforting thought.

There was no time to think further, as at that moment she

heard a commotion outside. Creeping over to the window, taking care to peer out from behind one of the folded-back shutters so that she could not easily be seen, she observed the scene taking place. A plump man and a taller woman were standing on the driveway, and a carriage was being brought up. Xanthe leaned forward so that she might see more. There she was! The girl she had seen before. The girl she now understood to be Alice. She was held firmly by a rough-looking man, who began to drag her toward the carriage. He was speaking to her gruffly, and Xanthe could hear her shouts of protest.

"No! Mistress, please! I have spoken only the truth! Master Lovewell, I beg you, do not let them take me!" The girl was crying as she spoke, but the couple did not answer her and made no move to stop what was being done. Xanthe could see there was another woman standing with them too, younger, dressed more elaborately than the others, and holding a small dog in her arms. The manner in which they all watched Alice's distress, so dispassionately, so apparently without caring, was chilling.

"Please, Mistress!" Again she tried to appeal to them, but the older woman merely looked away, stepping back a little from the man who must have been her husband. It was then that Xanthe saw the chatelaine hanging from the woman's waist. Even from that distance she was certain it was the same one, not just because of the attachments—there were two keys, the buttonhook, and the scent bottle, and another chain still missing an attachment—but because of the clasp, with its distinctive curved shape. There was no mistaking it. This was the same chatelaine, minus its Victorian additions. When the woman moved again it did not rattle about like it had when Xanthe had worn it. Instead it just lay neatly against the fine wool of her skirts, glinting in the low sunshine.

At that moment, the struggling servant girl managed to break away from the man who was trying to bundle her into the carriage. He gave a shout as she hitched up her skirts and ran. The small dog, stirred up by the drama and giving way to its instinct to chase anything that moved, jumped from his mistress's arms and tore away after the girl, yapping as he went. The middle-aged couple still did not move, but the carriage driver joined the other man in running after Alice. Xanthe willed her to get away. Her youth and fear were giving her an edge over the men, so that soon the gap between them widened.

Xanthe felt rather than heard someone enter the room. Turning, she found a boy of about twelve standing behind her, his mouth open as he took in the sight of this curiously dressed stranger. He stood as if frozen for a moment. There was no chance for her to hide. There was nothing for it but to speak to him, to grab the chance to find out what she could. The idea that if she succeeded in helping the girl then Margaret Merton would somehow let her return home was all she had to work with.

She took a step toward the boy. "Hello," she said gently, "can you help me? Can you tell me if that is Alice, the girl they are trying to send away? What is it that she's done?"

He was so shocked when she spoke, and so apparently amazed at what came out of her mouth, that he turned on his heel and fled. Xanthe cursed herself for being an idiot. Of course she not only looked odd, she must have sounded like someone from a foreign land, too. The clothes people were wearing, the interior of the house, all seemed to point toward her being in a year somewhere in the fifteen or sixteen hundreds. Merely forming this thought sent a tremor of fresh excitement and fear through her. It was all so very real that it was easy to forget the impossibility of what she was doing. It was likely the boy would return with someone else to show them the bizarrely dressed woman spouting nonsense. What would they do with her? She had no prepared story to tell people, which suddenly seemed a serious oversight. She would be of no use to anyone locked up as a lunatic. Quickly and quietly she left the room, peering into the hallway to make sure it was empty before hurrying toward a passageway that looked as if it might lead to a door at the rear of the house. It was then that she realized where she was. This was Great Chalfield Manor, where the auction had been held. Where she had found the chatelaine. Of course it had changed in many ways, but the core of the building was still easily recognizable. As she reached the dark oak door, she could hear more shouting coming from the front of the house. Whatever the girl had been accused of, it sounded as if it mattered very much to the lady of the house that the girl be dealt with. Xanthe was sure it was the lady's voice she could hear raised and strident, issuing orders and despairing at how incompetent everyone appeared to be. Her husband's voice was little more than a soothing murmur. He was having scant success in calming her down, by the sound of it, which gave Xanthe hope that the girl might have gotten away.

Cautiously she lifted the heavy iron latch. The door opened onto a beautifully tended herb garden, all low box hedges clipped into loops encircling bushes of rosemary, thyme, lavender, and a wide variety of useful-looking plants. Beyond this was a rose arbor and she could just make out an orchard. Hearing footsteps to her right, she turned left and ran along the back of the house. She risked sprinting across the curve of the driveway that passed between the wall of the house and the stables opposite and was fortunate not to be noticed as she dashed in through the main door of the barn, trusting to luck that everyone would now be too taken up with catching the runaway to see her. The interior of the stable block was divided into stalls at one end. Three slightly startled horses turned to look at her briefly before going back to the feed in their mangers. Xanthe made her way to the other end of the building. Here there was a large cart as well as a small, one-horse gig parked up. Through the open door she could see three people still standing at the main entrance to the house, and away in the distance, at the edge of the parkland where the pasture dipped down toward a deep-set stream, she could just make out the fleeing girl and her pursuers.

"There she is!" This shout was not about the fleeing servant, it was about Xanthe. She wheeled around to see the boy from the house pointing a trembling finger at her. A tall, rustically dressed, elderly man stood beside him.

She held up her hands. "Please," she began, choosing her words with care, "I mean no harm."

"She was asking about Alice," the boy said.

"What business have you here?" the man asked, taking a step toward her.

Her mind was racing. As she searched for a plausible reply, the man looked her up and down. He frowned.

"You one of the players staying in town?"

"Oh," she said cautiously, "the players . . ."

"I heard the mummers were up for the harvest fair. Be you one of them?"

Mummers and players? A traveling theater, perhaps? He thought her clothes were some sort of costume. She nodded. "I am," she said, not daring to elaborate.

He seemed about to question her further, but the sound of voices coming nearer stopped him. She looked about for somewhere to hide. She had to trust that she might be able to win the cooperation of the servants if she trod carefully, but she would surely be on more dangerous ground with the master and mistress of the house. In desperation, she flung herself into a pile of hay, burying herself as deeply as she was able. She heard the boy gasp and knew that he and the man could give her away if they chose to.

"Willis? Willis, fetch my husband's horse this minute!" The woman had a tone of voice and a manner of speaking that did not invite argument.

Xanthe held her breath. She was completely at the mercy of the old man and the boy. They had no reason to help her beyond the wish not to get someone else into trouble. After what seemed like an eternity the old man answered.

"Right away, Mistress. Shall you be wanting to ride out, too?"

"Certainly not. Master Lovewell must go after that wretched girl, as it seems the sheriff is incapable of doing his job without assistance. I shall wait in the house upon their return," she said. As she strode out Xanthe had a clear view of the chatelaine, and could hear the high ringing in her head of it calling to her again. At least she now knew that she had indeed found the girl Margaret Merton had begged her to help, and that she had found the girl the chatelaine was leading to, and that there was no mistaking the fact that they were one and the same. What she did not yet know was how on earth she, a powerless outsider from another time, was to do anything to save her.

She stayed hidden in the stables as the drama unfolded outside. Had she traveled back in time just to be a helpless bystander? Would the chatelaine allow her to return home if she proved ineffectual at saving Alice? Would the ghost stop her from getting home if she failed? However frustrating the situation was, she knew that to rush in and act without thinking would not help Alice, and would almost certainly end badly for herself. Willis took out a saddled horse for his master, but by then word reached them that the girl had been captured. All Xanthe could do was watch as Alice was dragged back to the carriage and taken away. The sun was dropping toward the far western hill, lengthening the shadows of the tall trees and casting a warm light that would soon turn to dusk. She had no option other than to bide her time, hoping that she might find a way to reach the girl under cover of darkness.

She emerged from her hiding place, dusting hay from her clothes, and put on her friendliest face for her unlikely allies. Willis, she discovered, was the groom, in charge of the horses. His own family had worked for the Lovewell family for two generations. He was a man of few words but told Xanthe that she could stay in the stables for a short while as long as she kept hidden. It would not do for him to be found harboring a stranger. It was a selfless act, the simple wish of a person who knew what it was to be nobody and to want to help another, and she was humbled by it. The young boy's name was Peter. He was officially a stableboy, but it sounded to Xanthe as if he was in truth more of a general lackey. He complained that he was forever being asked to carry out duties that took him away from Willis and their beloved horses. He came to sit beside her on the hay.

"Do theater players have fine horses?" he asked.

"Some do," she said cautiously. "But we are a very small . . . troupe."

"If we see to our duties well, the mistress allows us to go to the harvest fair market. Last year I wished very much to watch the mummers, but Willis dragged me away. Said I was too young and their story too bawdy." He threw a frown at the older man. It was the typical scowl of youth thwarted by the older generation, yet filled with affection. Xanthe marveled at how little some things change over the centuries. Peter looked at her suddenly, a new thought lifting his features. "Might you perform some story for us?" he asked.

"Now, Peter . . ." Willis tutted at him.

"Only a short piece," he pleaded. "Something of knights. Or dragons!"

With his floppy brown hair, pale blue eyes, and eager expression, he was a hard person to say no to, but if Xanthe attempted any acting she would be found out in a minute. "Well, actually, I'm more of a singer."

"A minstrel?"

"Yes. A minstrel. I don't take a part, I . . . sing," she explained, feeling a little relieved. If she were called upon to sing, at least she could do so convincingly, although already she was frantically trying to bring to mind a song that would fit the times.

Before the boy could request something, Willis stepped in. "Peter, you have duties to attend to."

"But . . ."

"If you please," Willis said. There was a steely note to the old man's request, and the boy got to his feet without further complaint.

"I shall return later," he whispered to her.

Willis put a hand on Peter's arm as he passed. "Not a word to anyone, mind. Else there will be trouble for all of us." When Peter nodded he let him go and then turned to Xanthe. "Now then, maid. If you are to stay here I shall have answers from you." He looked at the ground before her feet as if avoiding staring at what he must have considered immodest clothes.

"I'm grateful for your kindness," she told him, trying hard to use language that might not sound jarringly modern or even completely incomprehensible to him.

"I ask again, how came you here?"

She wanted to be truthful, but that was not a sensible option. Instead she attempted to remain focused on her reason for being there.

"I want to help Alice," she said, and seeing the interest this sparked in his expression went on, "You don't believe she has done anything to deserve being taken away by the sheriff, do you?"

"I do not. She is an honest girl. Hardworking. With a quiet mind. She has known hardships in her life and overcome them."

"And she was happy here?"

"Happy as one can be who has lost their family and their position in life. But then, if you know Alice, you will know her history."

"I know she needs a friend now. Someone to prove her innocence."

"And that someone is you?"

"I want to help, but I need to know more of what has happened here." Xanthe worried that he might ask how she came to know her, where they had met, or why she thought it was her business to defend the girl. These questions might have been in his mind, but he did not ask them. Perhaps he was waiting to see what she had to offer. Waiting to see if her actions would speak for themselves.

"Something of value went missing from the house. Something belonging to Mistress Lovewell."

"And Alice is accused of stealing it?"

"The maid is no thief," he said again.

"Then why did Mistress Lovewell accuse her? Why does she think Alice would steal something, risking her position, her home, her liberty, maybe her very life?"

He hesitated then, as if answering might be dangerous. As if he might unintentionally reveal something of his own opinion of his employer. And reveal it to a stranger at that. Xanthe needed to gain his trust. To show him that she was truly on Alice's side and that he had nothing to fear from her. There was something she was becoming increasingly sure of, but still lacked proof. To voice her thoughts was to take a risk, but she could see no other way.

"The thing that was stolen," she said, lowering her voice a little, "it was part of the mistress's chatelaine, wasn't it?"

His eyes widened. Clearly this was not common knowledge, and yet she, someone from outside the household, knew of it.

"The needle case and scissors were precious to the mistress," he explained. "And they were of the finest silver. Valuable."

Xanthe took an informed guess as to what might be the girl's position in the house. "And Alice was accused of stealing them because she is the mistress's maid? As such she helps care for her pieces of silver and her jewels, doesn't she?"

"The mistress was certain she was the only one who could have taken it. Mistress Lovewell wears the chatelaine every day, so it is only ever from her sight at night. Alice is the only servant permitted to enter the mistress's bedchamber."

"But even if she *could* have taken it, why *would* she?"

"It seems the mistress did not concern herself with the girl's intentions."

"And did they find the thing in her possession?"

"They did not. It remains lost."

"Then surely they cannot keep her locked up. They have no proof."

Willis regarded her as if she were simple. "The word of a servant is a flimsy, weightless thing when put against the word of a great lady," he said flatly.

He was right of course. Where was the need of proof in such a society? Mistress Lovewell was clearly a woman of power and influence. Alice's life was in her hands. It came to her then that the missing chatelaine attachments could be the key to her freedom. If she could find them, could return them, then there would be no case against Alice. Which meant she should not go after the girl, but should stay at the house, for wasn't it most likely that they were there somewhere still? So long as it had not been removed by someone else. This was a worrying possibility.

"Have there been any visitors to the house, Mr. Willis? Anyone else you might suspect of taking the silver?"

"The family are social enough when they've a mind, but there have not been functions or gatherings of late. And no hawkers or traders have called." He narrowed his eyes at Xanthe again. "Save for yourself."

"Mr. Willis, I believe you have a theory. . . . Won't you share it with me?" she asked, holding his gaze.

"Talking out of turn can get a person into a great deal of trouble," he said.

"I know. And I know it is asking a lot of you to trust someone who is a stranger to you. But I am here only to help Alice, truly I am. Anything you can tell me that might save her . . ."

He considered this for a moment and then said, "The mistress had her doubts about the maid. 'Twas Master Lovewell who took her in, against his wife's wishes."

"Didn't she trust her? Or was it just that she didn't like her?"

"She liked her well enough, for Alice is a likeable child. No, it was her background that did not sit well with the mistress. Her husband held that Alice's past should not be a bar to her future, but the mistress was not comfortable with showing herself to be in sympathy to a person whose family were executed as traitors."

Xanthe opened her mouth to start on a whole heap of questions that instantly formed in her mind. *Traitors!* But Willis held up his hand.

"I'll speak no more on the matter. You may stay the night, but be gone before the master is about in the morning. I wish you well with your task, but I can do nothing further. To do so would put Peter in peril too, and that I will not risk. Not for anyone."

"I understand."

He pointed at a stack of horse rugs. "Sleep there," he said.

"Oh, I'm very comfortable in the hay, thank you."

"That's as may be, but my horses don't want their breakfast tainted. The blankets will do for you."

"Of course," she said, stepping away from his precious hay. "I wasn't thinking. . . ." But she was now talking to herself, as Willis was busy sweeping the cobbles between the stalls and muttering soothing words to the horses. She had been dismissed.

Later, as she lay awake, breathing in the warm, fuzzy fumes of the horses and listening to the sounds of them contentedly chomping, she wondered how long she would be compelled to stay in the past. How much time would move on at home? When would her mother notice her absence? The thought of how frantic she would be to find her daughter simply vanished caused a tightening in Xanthe's chest. It was while she was being tormented with such thoughts that young Peter returned with a chunk of bread and a piece of cheese.

"There's this, too," he said, passing her a small jug of beer.

"You are a kind boy, but you must be careful. If someone caught you taking food from the pantry . . ."

"Oh, they won't catch me." He laughed lightly. "I'm like a shadow in the house. I come and go as I please. I know where the candle stubs are to be found. No one has ever seen me, nor will they." He sat and watched her eat, staring at her as if she were the strangest sight he had ever seen. Which quite possibly she was.

"Tell me, Peter, how long have you been here at Great Chalfield?"

"I came two years since," he said. "My ma died when I were born, and my pa had to go away to find work. Master Lovewell took me on to help Mister Willis."

"And you are happy here?"

She could tell by his expression this question struck him as odd. Of course, the value put upon happiness, upon the importance of the individual, is such a modern idea. Peter knew his

place, and it was a lowly one. His personal happiness was in all
likelihood not something anyone had ever bothered to ask him
about before. She tried another approach.

"Do they treat you well, the family?"

"I have my own bed in the hayloft." He pointed up above.
"And two sets of clothes. I get half a day off a month, as well as
time for church twice on Sundays. And at Christmas last year
the master gave me a crown!"

Xanthe had her answer. "They certainly sound like good employers. I mean, good people to work for. But I thought, and I
might be wrong about this, but, well, Mistress Lovewell seems
the type that might be a bit . . . sharp sometimes?"

He nodded. "You don't want to go getting her riled. Our mistress is a great lady of the area, you have to understand," he said,
and she heard Willis's instruction being repeated for her benefit,
"great ladies have a lot to consider. They have responsibilities. Often times they appear sharp when in truth they be so busy, so
taken up with all they must do and all the people they must care
for, why, 'tis only natural they should be short of good temper."

"Well, I think she's very lucky to have you, Peter. You are
clearly a good worker and very loyal." A thought struck her. "You
are clever too, I can tell. I bet you know what month it is."

He laughed. "A fool could tell you 'tis October."

"And can you name our king?"

"Certainly! James the First, and I his loyal subject!" he told
her with laudable sincerity.

"And the year is?"

"Sixteen hundred and five, and I shall turn twelve on Christmas Eve."

"Excellent! I can see why the mistress keeps you here. It's a
pity she took against Alice so, isn't it?"

This time he shook his head. "Alice never stole nothing, but the mistress never had a day's peace since Alice came into this house."

"Why ever not?"

He looked at the ground, picking up a piece of straw to poke at the dust, not quite daring to meet her eye any longer. When he spoke his voice was little more than a whisper, but she heard his words quite clearly.

"Mistress Lovewell might be a great lady," he said, "but everybody's the same underneath. Everybody looks out for themselves when they are afraid."

"Mistress Lovewell, afraid? She doesn't look like she'd scare easily."

He turned his face back to her then, his eyes showing that he too knew about the fear his mistress felt. "She's not frightened of ordinary things, not like me being afraid of the dark," he said, glancing up at the hayloft. "But, oh yes. The mistress is frightened all right. They all are."

"But what are they frightened of?"

Peter would have answered but Willis's gruff voice called to him from the stable doorway.

"Peter! Stop your jabbering now. Get to your bed. 'Twill be morning soon enough."

The boy scuttled away without another word, leaving Xanthe to wonder what on earth it could be that had the whole family scared, and what that had to do with Mistress Lovewell wanting to get rid of Alice.

{ 9 }

XANTHE SNATCHED A FEW HOURS OF SLEEP BUT WAS TOO KEYED UP TO rest properly. Every time a horse sneezed or a dog barked or a door slammed somewhere, she sat up, listening, waiting, not quite knowing where she was. She could not cease worrying about home and Flora. How long had she been away now? What would happen if her mother had a bad night and went looking for her, only to find her bed empty? She forced herself to put her mind to what needed doing. She must find the missing needle case and scissors. She must begin her search, without being seen, as soon as possible. And the obvious place to start was inside the house.

She rose stiffly from her bed of horse blankets and crept over to the window. A misty autumn dawn was rising, giving a blurry edge to the trees and buildings as they were slowly revealed, drawn out of the receding night. She had a good view of the house itself, and of the grounds sweeping away toward the steam in the distance. She wondered how far Alice had gotten before they caught her. Had she raced away in that direction for a reason, or just run blindly anywhere to escape? Xanthe was about to risk making her way inside the house when the main door to the stables opened and Willis appeared. She should not have been surprised to find him up with first light.

"You'd best be off," he said. "Master Lovewell will be breaking his fast soon and then be about his business. He is a man of many ideas and connections and has not time to lie long in his bed. If you are discovered, there will be questions."

"I will go soon, I promise, but I need to get back into the house."

"'Twill serve no purpose, and I say you will be found out."

"I will be quick. I want only to find the needle case. How else can I prove Alice's innocence?"

"It could be anyplace. Could be hidden."

"But if you are certain Alice did not take it, who would hide it? One of the other servants?"

"You cannot accuse folk!"

"I won't, I promise, but if you say none here could have stolen it, then it must be merely misplaced, an accident. . . ."

"The mistress does nothing without purpose!" he snapped.

"What do you mean? Do you think she has framed Alice to get rid of her? I mean, you suspect a trick by your mistress?"

"I will say no more." Willis had become agitated. He strode to the small door that led out the back of the stable block. "You must leave now. If you follow the footpath to the bridge over the river you can be beyond sight before anyone is about." When she hesitated, he added, "It will not go well for Peter if it is discovered he helped himself to food for you."

It seemed Peter was right. Everyone was afraid, even Willis.

She had no alternative but to go. As she left she turned and said, "Thank you. For not giving me away. I am grateful." He merely nodded in reply and closed the door after her. She set off walking, knowing he was likely watching. Only when she had reached the cover of a small copse of birch trees did she risk stepping off the path and hiding. From there she watched the house and waited. She decided that as soon as she saw any of the family leave the house she would creep back, seize the moment, and search for the scissors and needle case. If Willis's suspicions were correct she need only search one room: Mistress Lovewell's bedchamber.

An hour later, just as she was beginning to think her plan hopeless, she saw Willis take the best carriage to the front of the house. Moments later, the mistress and the girl Xanthe surmised must be the mistress's daughter, still carrying her little dog, came out of the front door. Master Lovewell waved them off and went back inside. Xanthe hurried back, relying on the fact that Willis, and the rest of the household, would be too busy with their chores to notice her. She had reached a small outhouse that served as the dairy when she heard carriage wheels again. This time she was able to watch through a small, glassless window. The carriage was drawn by two handsome bay horses, and looked expensive, but not as grand or as elaborate as the mistress's. The driver reined in the horses, and three men got out. The first was middle-aged but with the stride and purpose of a younger man, wearing a sweeping cape and a matching green felt hat. Behind him came a young man with a swagger in his step, and then another man who also looked to be in his twenties. He had a serious face, slightly stern, with black hair that fell forward to partially obscure his eyes. Even at a distance she could see he had about him a restless energy.

The front door opened, and Master Lovewell came hurrying out again. He greeted his visitors warmly and seemed particularly delighted when the older man handed him what looked like a rolled-up map or set of drawings. They all made their way into the house. When he reached the door the darkest of the young men paused, as if sensing he was being watched. He turned, looking around him, until he was looking directly at Xanthe. She gasped and quickly stepped back into the shadows.

He stared toward the window for a moment longer and then followed the others inside.

Her heart was racing. What would she have done if she had been discovered? What did she think she was going to do, simply walk into the house, trot up the stairs, and start searching the private quarters of the lady of the house? Suddenly it all seemed desperate and impossible. She felt almost overwhelmed by fatigue and worry, and by the thought of how very far she was from home. She found that she was holding her locket, stroking the smooth, worn gold, which was warm from lying against her skin. She held it in front of her and opened it. It helped to see her mother's cheerful face smiling back at her. And then, as Xanthe looked at the photo, as she felt the pull of home and of all that she knew and loved, everything began to fade. She glanced anxiously about and saw the light of the day itself was dimming, darkening, blackening.

"No!" She could not stop herself shouting. "No, not now! Not yet!"

But she was powerless to prevent what was happening to her. She had the sensation she was falling backward, tipping, plummeting, being engulfed by a weighty darkness, and then suddenly all was blackness again as the centuries flew past her.

It took several bleary moments to shake off a curious feeling of dislocation and confusion when Xanthe arrived back in the jail. She was short of breath, as if she had been running fast and hard, and her head pounded. Every time she opened her eyes she was almost overcome by a dizziness and a highly unpleasant bout of nausea to go with it. She sat upon the gritty floor, trying to steady her breathing and calm her ragged nerves. She was surprised to discover that it was dark. Nighttime. But which

night? The one when she had left, or the following one? She had
spent a whole night in the stables, but had time moved at the
same rate in her own era during her absence? A sudden surge of
fear drove her to her unsteady feet. Was the ghost waiting for
her? What would she do now that she had returned and, more
importantly, returned before she had a chance to help Alice? She
tensed, listening, searching for that cold presence. To her relief,
she could detect nothing. She searched the floor blindly, feeling
for the rest of the chatelaine. As soon as she had found it she
hurried from the jail and crept back into the house, tiptoeing
up the stairs and into her room. She checked her phone. Ten
minutes past twelve. And the date was the same as the day she
had left. She distinctly remembered the clocks downstairs in the
shop striking twelve, which meant all the time she had spent in
the past had only amounted to a matter of minutes back home.
Roughly ten hours in the seventeenth century equaled ten minutes in the present day. She had no way of fathoming a why or
a how for this, so that it was simply something else to make her
head swim.

"Xanthe? Xanthe, are you awake?" Her mother's voice broke
into her muddled thoughts and she hurried to her room. Flora
only ever called out at night if she was in serious difficulty.

"Mum? You OK?" Xanthe could see at once that she was not.

"Oh, Xanthe, love . . . my back is really bad tonight. I need
to take my medication, but I can't sit up on my own. My silly
hands . . ." She struggled to push herself up, but her fingers were
bent over, locked firmly and useless. Xanthe had seen them do
this before and knew that only painful manipulation would
straighten them again.

"Here, let me help you."

She slipped her arms under her mother's and counted before
lifting. As she moved her carefully up and back, an action in

which they were both well practiced, she thought how awful it would have been if her mother had called and found no one there. What would she have done? She would have had no way of finding her daughter. The terrifying thought of being stuck in the past struck Xanthe anew, but there was no time to dwell upon it. Flora was in a great deal of pain.

"Ow!" she cried out as Xanthe tried to set her back on the pillows.

"Sorry, Mum," she said.

"Not your fault," Flora gasped.

"There. That OK?"

Flora nodded, eyes shut tight against the pain. Xanthe fetched fresh water and passed her the arthritis tablets. Her mother fumbled with them awkwardly, her hands rendered little more than painful claws. It was all Xanthe could do to resist putting the pills into Flora's mouth herself to spare her the struggle, but she knew better than to try. Her mother still had her pride.

"And the painkillers," she said.

She handed her two. Flora took them clumsily, trembling, swallowing them quickly.

"Another one," she said.

"You sure? They're pretty strong. Doctor Jones said—"

"Doctor Jones isn't the one in agony!" she snapped, and then made a tremendous effort to speak more gently. "It's fine, Xanthe. I know what I'm doing." She took the extra tablet and closed her eyes. Carefully, Xanthe sat on the edge of the bed. Together they waited for the pain to subside. Xanthe knew from past experience that there was nothing more she could do. Slowly she reached out and took hold of her mother's hand. Flora's skin was clammy, making Xanthe wonder how long she had held out before calling for help. After ten minutes or so she opened her eyes again and gave a weak smile.

"Sorry," Flora said.

"Don't you dare apologize."

She frowned. "You're dressed. Why are you dressed? It's the middle of the night."

Xanthe looked down at her clothes. It was impossible to pass them off as nightwear. There were even bits of hay stuck to her from her time in the stables. She shrugged as casually as she could.

"Couldn't sleep," she said. "Thought I'd go and . . . tidy up a bit in the garden."

"In the dark?"

"There's a moon. And streetlights."

"Our neighbors will think we are bonkers."

"Hopefully."

Flora smiled at this, a better smile this time. A true, heartfelt smile. She was too wrung out from the pain and the medication to talk more, so the two sat holding hands until she drifted off to sleep.

Back in her room Xanthe peeled off her grubby clothes and clambered, exhausted, into her own bed. She might only have been up for a couple of hours after her night in the stables, but she felt weary to her bones. It was as if her journey back and fore through the centuries had left her suffering from an extreme version of jet lag. The suddenness of the way in which she had returned still felt like one of the biggest shocks. Why had it happened when it did? What had caused her to be flung forward across time like that? She tried to remember exactly where she had been and what she had been doing. She had been in the dairy, looking out of the window, worrying about being discovered. She had been excessively tired, weary, and feeling homesick, and had taken hold of her locket. She remembered that clearly, the feel of the old gold in her fingers, recalled looking at her mother's picture inside it and thinking of her. Was that what it took to bring her back? To focus on something from the present, something found where she lived, given to her in her home, by the person who mattered most to her in the world? The idea certainly did not seem the most unlikely thing that had recently happened to her. Once again she found herself trying to make sense of the impossible. She realized that one of the most incredible things was how quickly she had begun thinking about such astonishing events as normal. Such as the fact that she had just traveled back in time. Again. And the fact that she had spoken with people who lived their lives centuries ago. Such as the fact that she had been sent back by a ghost on a mission to help her daughter. Thinking about the girl, Xanthe found it hard to put from her mind the desperation on her face and the despair in her voice as she was being taken away. She could not rid herself of the thought of how terrible it would be for her, locked up in a damp, cold, dark jail that would have made the one she herself had once inhabited seem luxurious by comparison.

At last sleep claimed her, profound and heavy, so that she remained unaware of the figure sitting on the end of her bed. Margaret Merton frowned as she watched Xanthe sleep. She knew the girl had failed her. Had failed Alice. She had returned too soon, and her daughter was still captive, locked away, awaiting her lonely, violent fate. It occurred to Mistress Merton that she might have done better to more clearly instruct Xanthe, to impress upon her the fact that she must succeed at all costs. That she should not return until Alice was safe. She had pleaded with her, had revealed her own despair, but that, it seemed, had not been enough. If Margaret had still possessed a heart, it would have been heavy with sadness at the realization that altruism, doing what is right, acting out of Christian charity and goodness, these things had proved insufficient. The girl would have to be compelled to go to Alice's aid. And it was up to Margaret to find a way to compel her.

Xanthe was in such a deep sleep it took some time to realize that the hammering she could hear was not part of a dream, but someone at the door. Blearily, she grabbed the nearest garment, which was her tea-dress, from the hanger on the back of the door and hurried barefoot down the stairs.

"OK, I'm coming!" she called to the insistent visitor. Peering through the glass, she recognized the stout, velvet-jacketed figure at once. Theo Hamilton. What on earth had induced him to make the journey so far out of London twice in one week?

"Xanthe! Lovely girl, I thought for one awful moment I had the wrong address and would find myself alone and adrift in the Wiltshire wilderness," he said, sweeping past her and into the shop.

"Theo? A bit early for a visit, isn't it?" she said, dragging her fingers through her ringlets in a futile attempt to look less as if she had just that moment staggered out of bed.

"I always imagined country types were up with the lark," he said. "Or the cockerel, possibly. Really, darling, this is quite a respectable hour, even by Chelsea standards."

Xanthe glanced at the ormolu clock. *Ten thirty!* How long would she have slept if Theo had not arrived, she wondered.

"Would you like tea?" she asked, trying to pull herself together and wake up sufficiently to deal with someone she did not entirely trust.

"I would die for tea, but later, lovely girl. First, lead me to the mirrors!"

"The mirrors?"

"Your mother has me in a positive froth of excitement over

them. I know, I know, I should feign boredom and lack of interest to stop you girls hiking the prices, but oh, what's the point? We're all in the same business. You know if they're worth something and so do I, so no charades needed. Now, lead on, *do*." He flapped his hands at her.

The mirrors. At last Xanthe began to make sense of why Theo had dragged himself from the city. Flora must have offered him the mirrors as a job lot. And without consulting her. Xanthe felt a stab of hurt that her mother should have made such a decision alone. Or at all. It was certainly a quick way to make money, but Theo would offer only a fraction of their value if he was buying all of them. While she knew they were precariously short of money she could not help but be resistant to the notion of passing them on to a dealer for a pittance and letting him make a handsome profit. It was bad business, and it rankled her. She could not help feeling it was the sort of desperate bit of selling her father would expect of them. It was amateurish. As she led Theo through the main shop and into the second room her mind was working hard to find a reason why she could not sell them to him after all.

"Oh! Yes, indeed. Yes," he gasped as they entered the room. He darted from one mirror to the next, exclaiming at each one, his grin growing broader by the minute. He chatted away to his own reflections as he browsed. "Oh, a lovely piece. . . . Shame about the silvering on that one. . . . Hmmm, pretty . . . Oh, I know just the home for that one. . . . And you will do very nicely for Marlon's new bistro. . . ."

The more he enthused the more Xanthe loathed the thought of him having the mirrors. She could all too easily imagine him gloating to his clients back in Chelsea, not being able to resist crowing about how he helped her and Flora out by taking a lot of rubbish just to get one or two good pieces because they so badly needed the sale. And word was bound to get back to her father.

After a while Theo stopped rifling through the collection.

"Well, Xanthe dearest, I'll be straight with you, there are some nice ones here, very nice, but most of them . . . well . . ." He waved his arm as if to indicate the majority of the mirrors and gave her a look of distaste.

"So just make me an offer for the ones you like," she suggested.

"Oh no, that's not what we agreed, your mother and me. She explained your . . . predicament, and of course I'm happy to help out an old friend. We people in the trade must stick together. But, oh no, it wouldn't be worth my trekking all the way out here just for one or two pieces."

"But you've just said that most of them are not worth much."

"Well, they're not. Not as a bunch. But I suppose I'll find homes for them eventually, so my trip will be a sound investment. But that's the key word, isn't it? *Eventually*. Seems to me I have time on my side, Xanthe, darling, and you do not."

She did her best not to let her expression show how much she hated what he was attempting to do. There was nothing *friendly* about it. She looked at the many mirrors filling the room. It must have taken Mr. Morris years to amass such a collection. He might not have had a very discerning eye, but she felt, she sensed, that he'd made his selections based on what he loved. On what spoke to him. Theo liked to have everyone believe he adored beautiful things, but he was driven by money, pure and simple, that much was clear to Xanthe. The way he had sneered at the lesser pieces made her squirm. It was not right that he should take them, not if he truly had such a low opinion of them. Not after all Mr. Morris's care. Not when even the lowliest of them must have meant something to someone once.

Xanthe shook her head and folded her arms.

"I'm afraid I can't sell them as a job lot, Theo. You know I'd be throwing money away."

"That's not how Flora felt when she invited me here. Perhaps you should consult her before you start making rash decisions."

"It would be rash to let the whole collection go for a pittance."

"As I understand it, your circumstances are somewhat . . . reduced."

She shrugged, trying to look nonchalant but not entirely succeeding. "Cash flow problems, nothing more."

"I've seen bigger businesses than yours go under for want of ready money, Xanthe. If you so easily underestimate the importance of cash flow, you must be even more naive than I thought," he said, inflicting upon Xanthe the same sneer he had earlier bestowed upon the mirrors. That churlish expression was the final push she needed to make her decision.

"I'm sorry, you've had a wasted journey," she told him.

He gasped, seeing that she meant what she said. "Have you any idea how long it takes to drive all the way out here? I want to speak with Flora. She's the one who asked me to come. She's the one who talked me into even considering this lot," he said dismissively.

"My mother isn't well. She's had a flare-up."

"But surely, a quick word . . . ?"

"She was awake half the night in agony. We've only just got the pain under control. You really want me to wake her up now just so you can tell her that her daughter won't do business with you?"

Theo considered this. At last, knowing he was defeated, he strode past her. On his way out he paused and turned.

"It doesn't do to make enemies in this business, Xanthe," he said. "Remember that."

He slammed the door behind him, leaving the old bell clanking dully. Xanthe wondered if the noise roused Flora. She felt suddenly exhausted and stood staring at the dusty collection of mirrors she had just, on point of principle, defended. Had she been right to do it? Were their circumstances truly so dire that they must abandon all professional integrity? She stepped forward and laid a palm against the cool glass of one of the largest mirrors, a full-length one framed in bird's-eye maple. A tired-looking version of herself gazed back at her.

And then, without warning, the image shimmered and altered, distorting and transforming until the face that looked at her was no longer her own, but that of Margaret Merton.

Xanthe gave a cry and staggered backward. As she did so the whole angular figure of the ghost formed in the looking glass. Formed and then stepped forth.

"No!" Xanthe could not help herself shouting. "Not here, too!" She had convinced herself that the specter inhabited only the blind house, and the realization that she might appear elsewhere, particularly in the house itself, was horrible.

"You abandoned her!" Mistress Merton's voice was shrill with anger. "You left my child, let them put their rough hands upon her and take her away!"

"There was nothing I could do." Xanthe backed away until she reached the stack of mirrors propped against the opposite wall and could go no further. "I did try. I promise you, I did. I was looking for the missing pieces of the chatelaine. I tried to get into the house to search for them, but . . ."

"You came back!" In the sharp glare of the electric light the dead woman was revealed in more unforgiving detail. Xanthe could see now that the scars on the left side of her face were burns and that the dirt on her clothes was mostly scorching or soot. Had she been in a house fire, she wondered. Is that how she had died? She could also see a deep crimson stain that covered most of the bodice of her pinafore and dress. It had not been noticeable in the half-light of the nighttime garden and jail, but now it was unmissable and disturbing, as Xanthe was certain it must be blood. What had the woman been through to end up in such a condition?

"I didn't mean to come home," Xanthe insisted. "I was thinking about Mum. . . . It just happened."

"You must return. Go back to Great Chalfield."

"I can't do that, I'm sorry."

"Finish the task. I tell you there is no other who might do it. Without your help my daughter will hang."

Xanthe gasped. She had known, of course, that Alice could be sentenced to death, but to hear it stated, to hear the words, was still shocking. Even so, she shook her head. "You don't know how dangerous it was. I was nearly found out. I don't belong there, and that's obvious. If the mistress of the house had seen me . . . I'd just end up in prison, too. And that wouldn't help anyone. You have to understand, there is nothing I can do."

"You must prove my daughter's innocence."

"I have people I care about, too. What if something happened to me when I was back in the past? What if I got locked up, or worse? What if I was stopped from coming home? I have to think of my mother first. You must see that. She only has me. She can't manage on her own. She needs me."

The ghost hesitated and fell silent for a moment. At last she said, "Your love for your mother is a match for that which I hold for my daughter. That is plain to see."

"Yes," Xanthe nodded. "Then you must see that I can't leave her."

"I see that you would do anything to protect her. Anything to keep her out of harm's way."

Xanthe felt the hairs at the nape of her neck stir, and when she tried to speak again her mouth was dry. "Does she need protecting?" she asked quietly. "Is she in harm's way?"

There was a long, ice-cold silence. Margaret Merton held Xanthe's gaze as she spoke. "I believe I have made clear the situation, and clearer still my intentions. I will do anything, *anything at all*, in order to save Alice."

"Are you threatening my mother?" Fury was taking the place of Xanthe's earlier fear. "What? What would you do? What *could* you do?"

"You think a spirit has no power of action? I may be unable to travel back to my own time, no matter how much I wish it. I have no influence over events then, which is why I must have your assistance. But be assured, I can effect matters in this day. I may cause things to happen as I wish. When I wish. How I wish."

Xanthe searched her mind for her previous encounter with Mistress Merton, trying to recall anything the ghost had done besides scaring her. Had she actually done anything physical? Had she pushed Xanthe back into the blind house, or merely scared her into toppling backward?

Margaret, watching her, guessed what was in Xanthe's mind. She saw her doubt and knew that she remained to be convinced. To this end, Margaret turned quickly, a blur of tattered garments and insubstantial form, whipping the air about her into a whirlwind such that Xanthe felt the force of it. And that force dislodged the full-length mirror from which only minutes before the phantom had stepped. The mirror lurched forward and before Xanthe could react, before she could even attempt to save it, it crashed to the ground, the frame splintering, the glass smashing, the noise of it shattering the quiet of the morning as Mistress Merton vanished.

The sound of such destruction woke Flora from her medicated slumber.

"Xanthe? Is that you? What's happening down there?"

"It's OK, Mum," she called up to her as cheerfully as she could. "I dropped one of the mirrors, don't worry."

"Mirrors? What are you doing? . . . Oh, is Theo there? Look at the time, for heaven's sake. Why didn't you wake me up?"

Xanthe could hear her mother get out of bed and move to the top of the stairs with the familiar clunk and rattle of her crutches accompanying her uneven steps. Xanthe hurried to pick up the broken frame and what was left of the mirror, repositioning the remnants behind some of the others, not wishing Flora to see that it was one of the best pieces that had been broken beyond repair. Her hands were shaking as her mind struggled to take in the enormity of what the ghost had threatened.

"I'd almost forgotten he was coming," Flora called down. "You shouldn't have let me sleep so long. Have you offered him a cup of tea? I'll get dressed."

Xanthe hurried up the stairs to her mother. "Yes, it was Theo. Yes, I offered him a cup of tea. And don't hurry to get dressed; he's gone."

"What?"

"He just left. Without the mirrors."

"Without them?" Flora ran a hand through her disheveled hair in exasperation. "I know some are a bit ordinary, but I thought there were enough there to tempt him. I don't understand why he didn't want them."

"He did." Xanthe took a breath. "Look, why don't you go back to bed. I'll bring you a cup of tea and tell you what happened."

She looked at her daughter closely. Looked at her and saw that she had something to tell her that was not going to meet with her favor. "I don't want tea. I want an explanation."

"Mum, I couldn't let him have them all. Not like that. We'd be practically giving them away."

"No, we'd be selling them. Which is what we are here to do, in case you'd forgotten."

"I know. It'll be OK, I'll find another way."

"Such as?"

Xanthe cast about for a solution. "Look, how about we put some of the best ones on the internet. On eBay. Fix a reasonable reserve and short selling time. That way we can generate some cash without just throwing out all the others."

Flora said nothing for a moment, and then her shoulders slumped, not in defeat, but relief. "I'm sorry, love. I should have talked to you about Theo. I don't know why I didn't. You would have come up with a better idea. Sometimes I . . . I forget to let you make some of the decisions. Silly of me."

Xanthe put her hand on her mother's arm. "Come on, I'm starving, and I bet you are, too. I'll make us both a fry up. There's still eggs and stuff. We'll work something out."

Flora sighed. "You know, there are times I'm reluctant to part with things, too. Things I'd really like to keep."

Xanthe suddenly saw how frail her mother was, saw anew how vulnerable she was. Instinctively she threw her arms around her and pulled her close, fighting back tears. "I love you, Mum."

"Hey!" Flora laughed, returning the hug as best she could while propping herself up with one crutch. "What's all this about?" When Xanthe pulled back, her mother studied her face. "Are you OK?"

Xanthe nodded. "Just . . . well, you know how Theo can be."

"Oh, don't let that bumptious wally get to you. Come on," she said, turning for the door, "I was promised a decent breakfast."

Xanthe almost preferred it when her mother was cross. Her being so reasonable made her feel worse. And love her more.

Which made her feel yet more terrified at the thought of what the ghost might be prepared to do. There was so much to contend with. Theo had come with money burning a whole in his silk-lined velvet pocket and Xanthe had sent him away, leaving them in as much financial trouble as they had been before. Somehow she was going to have to find a way to make some money as quickly as possible, and at that moment, beyond the uncertain business of selling things on the internet, she had no idea how she was going to do it. Nor could she bring her thoughts to bear on the matter properly, not while the face of Margaret Merton swam before her mind's eye, her threat real and dangerous. The notion of going back to the seventeenth century again scared her, but not as much as the thought of what the ghost might do to Flora if she did not go. Could she, would she really do her mother harm? She had proved herself capable. She was desperate. She had nothing to lose. It was a dangerous combination, and Xanthe doubted, at that moment, that she had an answer for it.

In the kitchen she fetched eggs from the fridge while her mother put a pan on the stove.

"Mum, sit. I'll do it," she told her.

"Don't fuss, I'm not an invalid yet."

"Nobody thinks that, least of all me. It's my turn, that's all. And you had a bad night."

"All right, if you insist, though mind you don't break the yolks. I like mine sunny-side up, not an apology for an omelette. And right after breakfast I want to get on with painting some of those drawers and cupboards. They're going to take a couple of coats. That chalk paint is slow to dry." She prattled on, settling herself at the little table, shoving yet another packing box out of the way, but Xanthe was not listening to her. She was watching the shadowy figure that had just appeared to stand behind her mother's chair. Flora looked up. "Are you going to do something with that spatula or just stand there waving it at me?" she asked.

Xanthe dropped her gaze and tried to attend to the cooking. Was Mistress Merton going to be everywhere now until Xanthe agreed to do what she wanted? It was terrifying, the way she was hovering so close to her mother. Her message was obvious. The threat was real. "Sorry," Xanthe mumbled. "Wasn't concentrating."

"Clearly. Oh, if you go out, can you get some ink for the computer? I want to print out fliers for the opening day. Xanthe?"

She made herself turn around again. The ghost had gone. She could not stop herself letting out a loud sigh of relief.

Flora frowned at her daughter. "Did you get any sleep at all last night? You look dreadful."

"I love you too, Mum."

"Sorry, love, but you need your sleep. Can't have you getting poorly, can we?"

Xanthe set plates and cutlery on the table.

"I'm fine, don't fuss now."

"What's that smell?"

"What?"

They both sniffed the air. Flora eyed the rubbish bin suspiciously. Xanthe took a deeper breath, the smell suddenly growing strong enough to make her gag.

"Gas!" Xanthe shouted, dashing over to the oven. Beneath the frying pan the gas was pouring out, but the flame had been extinguished.

"That's all we need," Flora noted, "a faulty cooker. Are we going to be gassed in our sleep? For heaven's sake, we can't afford a gas engineer or a new cooker."

"It's OK, Mum. The flame just got blown out. Must be a

draft in here," Xanthe assured her, relighting the gas, knowing in her heart that there was no draft. Knowing it as a certainty, as from the corner of her eye she glimpsed the form of Margaret Merton flitting from the room.

Flora sighed. "I do worry that this old house will turn out to be a money pit."

"'Course it won't. Now, if you want these eggs perfect, better let me get on with it, OK?" Xanthe said, trying to sound as if there was nothing in the world bothering her beyond breakfast, while in truth her heart was pounding and her mind was rebelling against the realization that the only way to keep her mother safe might just be for her to step back into the blind house once more, to step back in time, and to help Alice. Only this time would be different. This time she could not return without saving the girl. If she did, her own mother would be the one to pay the price.

10

AFTER BREAKFAST, XANTHE HELPED FLORA INTO HER WORKROOM AND LEFT her to get to work on a small chest of drawers that needed sanding and painting. In the end they had agreed Xanthe would put half a dozen of the best mirrors on eBay, in an attempt to sell them at better prices. She also agreed to go out and purchase the ink. That at least felt like a sensible step. She had to decide what to do about Margaret Merton's threat, and somehow dealing with the smaller problems was giving her head a chance to work through the possible options. They were worryingly few. By the time she came to leave the shop and go out she realized she was seriously contemplating returning to the past, and the thought made her feel ill. Grabbing the books Harley had lent her, she decided to call in at The Feathers first, so that she might have the opportunity to talk to him before the pub got busy.

Outside something of a heatwave had taken hold of the town. It was another market day, and the stalls were set out down the center of the broad street, their striped awnings and baskets of flowers gleaming in the late-summer sunshine. Everywhere people were going about their normal lives, doing normal, everyday things, which seemed so at odds with Xanthe's experiences of the previous night. The contrast between the world's workaday activity, her own problems with money, her mother's poor health, her time traveling, and being haunted by a desperate ghost made her feel dizzy. Made her feel disconnected from the solid, sensible, non–time-traveling folk of Marlborough. Made her feel more than a little bit as if she were losing her mind.

The Feathers was quiet, with only a few tourists partaking of a brunch-time drink or coffee. Annie directed her to the cellar where she found Harley changing barrels. The subterranean room was pleasantly cool, but even so he looked puffed and hot as he shifted the new barrels of beer into place.

"Heavy work?" Xanthe asked, sitting on the bottom stair, the books on her lap.

"Aye. Annie reckons it's cheaper than sending me to the gym," he said, pausing to rub his aching back for a moment. "To be honest with you, I'm hiding down here. My wife's not a woman to cross."

"And you've crossed her?"

"Not me, but I'm the only one she can yell at. It's the singer we had booked for Friday night. The lass has let us down. No way we can find another band at such short notice."

"Oh. That's a shame."

He looked at her, bushy brows raised. "Could you maybe persuade Annie to see it that way? Right now she seems to think it's a catastrophe of major proportions that may see us both destitute and on the street at the very least."

"Will it damage takings that much?"

"For the night it will." He was about to resume his struggle with the beer kegs when a thought struck him. "I seem to remember your mother saying you're something of a singer yourself, hen. Is that right?"

"Oh, I'm a bit rusty," she said.

"I'll take rusty."

"I don't have a set prepared. Or a band." She felt a strange amalgamation of panic and excitement at the thought of performing again. There was a part of her that wanted to, though it might have been motivated more by the need for money than by any sort of creative urge. Whatever it was, Harley spotted the glimmer of a possible yes and turned to face her squarely.

"I'll be straight with you, hen, we're in a fix. Have you some backing tapes, maybe?"

"Yes, but . . ."

"Well there ye are then! Tell you what, I'll pay double, seeing as it's short notice. And if the drinkers like you, I'll give you a regular spot. Say once a month. How about it?"

She thought about how she owed it to her mother to do her bit financially. And if she was being completely honest with herself, she also thought about how it might feel to sing again. Perhaps it was time. Time to move on from Marcus and her own messy past. She looked at the books in her lap. Harley had helped her, and there was a good chance she would need more of his knowledge before she was rid of Margaret Merton. She looked up at him and mustered a smile.

"You haven't even heard me sing," she warned.

"I trust you."

"And I can choose, can sing whatever I like?"

"You can sing the national anthem on a loop if that's what'll get you behind that microphone."

A thought, a tentative glimpse of an idea, was forming in her mind, and at once she knew it could work.

"OK, I'll do it," she told him.

"Bloody marvelous!" he cried.

"On two conditions," she said, handing him back his books.

"Name them."

"Double pay, in cash, on the night, like you promise. And do you by any chance have anything in your stash of historical books about popular seventeenth-century folk songs?"

She spent the rest of the day working in the shop, putting up new shelves, helping Flora with repairs to some of the stock, and in general trying her utmost to prove to her mother that all would be well. She found it impossible to shake off the impression that her every move was being watched. Though she could not see Mistress Merton, she frequently felt her presence, and was forever on her guard in case the tormented creature should give a further demonstration of her dangerous capabilities. She did her best to keep her mother's mood up, and, in truth, what cheered Flora most was the news that she had agreed to sing at the pub. She visibly brightened at the thought of her daughter performing again, saying it was precisely the tonic she needed. She still looked tired, her face strained, but she said the pain was easing, and her movements were less stiff, less labored. Xanthe was eventually able to persuade her she needed a rest and to settle her in front of the computer to design and print out the fliers. She then took a deep breath and told the lie she had concocted to explain why she would be absent for a few days.

"You remember my friend Eva? In Milton Keynes?" she asked.

"The one with the whippet and the unsuitable boyfriend?"

"That's the one. Well, he's left her."

"The whippet or the boyfriend?"

Xanthe made a face. "She's heartbroken, really upset. To be honest, I'm worried about her. She's on antidepressants as it is and really doesn't do well in a crisis."

"Poor girl."

"Thing is, I want to go and support her, spend a couple of days. There's no one else, and I don't think she should be on her own right now." Her stomach churned. Such blatant lying to her mother was completely at odds with the relationship they had. The alternative, however—revealing her need to travel through time to try to prevent a miscarriage of justice and satisfy a frightening ghost—was not an alternative at all.

"It's not ideal timing for us, is it?" Flora pointed out with typical British understatement. It was the most awful timing, and they both knew it.

"It'd only be for a couple of days, tops," Xanthe promised. "I can show you what I've done to sell the mirrors online, so it shouldn't be too time consuming for you to keep an eye on them. The shop decorating is pretty much done, and I'll be back in plenty of time for us to set out all the new stock and finish preparing for the grand opening."

"When would you go?"

"I thought Saturday." She paused, studying her mother's face for a betrayal of panic or genuine worry, but Flora was by nature stoic, and even Xanthe was unable to discern her thoughts when she did not wish to reveal them. "But only if you're OK with it," she added. "I mean, only if you think you'll be OK. After last night . . ."

"Last night was a blip. You know flare-ups like that don't last. I'm fine now."

When Xanthe said nothing more, Flora gave her one of her stern, mother-knows-best looks.

"Xanthe, you've been stuck with me for weeks, what with packing up in London, moving here, getting stuff sorted in the shop. And you're right, we're nearly ready for the big day. You should go. Might do you good. Just because I eat, breathe, and live antiques doesn't mean that you want to." She smiled. "And you're singing tomorrow night. You'll have something to celebrate with Eva. Take her mind off things."

Xanthe gave her a hug and went back downstairs, trying not to let the fact that she had been so understanding make her feel even worse about lying. She moved one of the remaining boxes from the center of the shop and as she did so she spotted a familiar pattern on a piece of china. Digging into the wrapping, she unearthed the Minton sugar bowl from the set Gerri had bought. The fresh green of the Lily of the Valley flowers was beautifully painted along the tiny handles of the bowl. The china was so fine when she held it up to the light, it appeared translucent. She knew it would look even prettier filled with golden sugar crystals. Peering out of the window she could see Gerri bustling about in her tea shop opposite.

"I know where you belong," she said to the sugar bowl, folding the wrapping paper around it once more. Opening the door as quietly as she could so as not to disturb Flora, she stepped outside and crossed the narrow cobbled street. Gerri saw her approaching.

"Hello! Come for a cuppa?" Gerri asked, loading a tray of tea things from the nearest table which was nestled against the ivy that scrabbled over the building. She expertly balanced the tray on one arm, wiping the table with a cloth, her 1940s dress with full skirt swirling as she moved, not a victory roll of hair out of place. Even the hectic pace of work in the tea shop had failed to impact on her perfectly applied bright red lipstick.

"Wish I could stop, but this is a flying visit," Xanthe told her, then held up the package. "I've got something for you."

"Ooh! Come inside."

Xanthe followed Gerri in through the bunting-strewn doorway. The interior of the tearoom was delightful, and it was evident Gerri had an eye for period detail. The theme was authentically 1940s, very British, with gingham curtains and floral china, alongside enamel signs advertising soap and tea and clothes specific to the time. It was only a small area, yet Gerri had successfully placed five tables in it, all with red-and-white tablecloths sporting jam jars full of flowers, with thickly cushioned, white-painted chairs. Most were occupied, with people tucking into slices of sticky lemon drizzle cake or crumbly scones with jam and cream. Xanthe felt hungry just watching them.

"That's Thomas," Gerri nodded in the direction of a small boy sitting at a table by the counter, fully absorbed in a game on his tablet. "And this," she said, setting down the tray of dishes and ruffling the curls of a smiley little blonde girl, "is Ellie. My best helper, aren't you Ells?"

Ellie grinned and wiped chocolate from her mouth with the back of her hand.

"I've been testing the cakes," she told Xanthe with a gappy grin.

"Sounds like the best job in the world," said Xanthe.

"A non-teaching day at school," Gerri explained with a shrug.

"Certainly looks like you've got your hands full," said Xanthe. "Here, I found this." She held out the wrapped bowl, peeling back the paper. As she did so, she happened to glance over Gerri's shoulder. She could see the window of her own shop across the cobbles and a movement caught her eye. Thinking her mother must have left the workshop to look for her, she tried to focus on the figure looking out through the small Georgian panes. But it was not Flora. The haggard features of Margaret Merton as she glared back at her were so unexpected that Xanthe gasped, dropping the sugar bowl.

"Oh dear!" Gerri stooped to gather the pieces. "What a

shame!" she said, seeing what it was as she tried to fit the little chunks together.

"Sorry, Gerri, I'm an idiot." Xanthe took the remnants of the bowl from her. "I never break things. How stupid of me . . ."

"I'm sure it can be fixed," said Gerri, and then, looking more closely at Xanthe, she asked, "Are you all right? You look quite shaken."

"I'm fine. It's . . . nothing."

"You sure? Why don't you sit down with Thomas for five minutes. I'll fetch you some brownies."

"No, I can't stay, sorry." Xanthe began to move toward the door. "I'll get Mum to take a look at this." And with that she left, all too aware that Gerri must have realized that she was, in fact, very far from being all right. Summoning all her courage, she marched across the street. Was the ghost going to haunt her even when she stepped outside the shop? Was she supposed to be scared to return to her own home?

"Right, Mistress Merton," she muttered to herself, "you can just back right off." She flung open the door of the shop, making the bell clang frantically. She scanned the room. Nothing. Not even the slightest sense of a presence.

"Xanthe, love?" her mother called through from the workshop. "You going out?"

"No, Mum. Just letting some fresh air in," she called back. She felt anger lending her strength. She might have no choice but to help Margaret Merton, to help Alice, in order to protect Flora, but she was damned if she was going to become a wreck of nerves doing it. She needed to be strong. She was not going to let a ghost reduce her to such a state that she couldn't function properly. Even so, it took some long minutes before her heart rate steadied to something resembling normal.

The time Xanthe spent working on her own allowed her the

opportunity to think about how she could make her next journey through the blind house. She could not go as she had before, simply stepping back unprepared, leaving her dangerously vulnerable. This time she would be ready, all things as helpfully and safely arranged as possible. And part of that preparation involved leaving things in the best possible order for her mother. With that in mind, she began sorting through the mirrors, picking out the ones destined for eBay. It was while she was photographing them that the shop doorbell rang, causing her to roll her eyes at her own stupidity in not locking it.

"I'm afraid we're not open yet," she called through as she emerged from the mirror room. She found Liam standing in the doorway, holding up a bottle of white wine.

"Excellent!" he said with a grin. "I was hoping you'd be free to help me drink this while it's still good and cold."

"Nice idea, but . . ."

"Don't tell me you're too busy. You know what they say about all work and no play making Jack . . ."

". . . solvent?"

He tilted his head and offered her the bottle. "It's a Chablis. I splashed out. You're surely not going to turn me into a sad, lonely bloke who drinks on his own? How about it?"

It was a tempting offer. It had been a long day. She could feel herself flagging, and there were things she could only do once Flora was asleep, so it would be a long time before she could collapse into her bed.

She put the bolt across the shop door. "Come on," she said, walking past him. "I can see I have to save you from such a terrible fate. Let's go and sit in the garden."

Taking two lead crystal glasses from the cabinet they pushed their way through the muddle of the hallway, which was still filled with antiques waiting to go back into the shop. One of the advantages of selling antiques was that there was never a short-age of something nice to drink out of. Outside the evening was hot and still. They sat on the old stone bench beneath the shade of an unruly butterfly bush. Among its purple blooms flitted red admirals and small tortoiseshells. Some settled on the flowers, spreading their wings to catch the last of the evening sun. Sitting so close to the jailhouse made Xanthe's skin tingle and she glanced about nervously for sight of Margaret Merton. It was beyond unsettling, being pulled in two directions at once; she needed to be at home, with Flora, helping her and setting up the business, but she had to take the ghost's threat seriously. Margaret had said she would do anything to save her child, and she had demonstrated that she was capable of doing Flora harm. Xanthe had to accept that she had no choice but to go back to rescue Alice, though heaven alone knew how.

Liam poured the wine. "Here's to screw-top bottles, summer evenings, and a well-earned break," he said, raising his glass.

The wine was sublime. As she savored it Xanthe realized that she had not eaten for several hours and the alcohol was going to go straight to her head. She closed her eyes for a moment and leaned back against the wall, the bricks warm against her back through her cheesecloth shirt. Dappled sunlight danced upon her eyelids. When at last she opened her eyes again she caught Liam gazing at her. He looked away quickly, but there was no mistaking the intensity of the way he had been studying her. She suddenly felt uncomfortable. She liked Liam but was far from ready for any sort of romantic entanglement, and did not want to give him false hope.

Desperate for something to say that would defuse the moment she blurted out, "I'm going to sing in The Feathers on Friday night."

"Hey, that's great!"

"Harley got let down at the last minute, talked me into it."

"He can be surprisingly persuasive. I'll get there early and bag a front-row seat."

"Don't you dare. You'll put me off. Much easier singing to people I don't know."

He nodded, a fellow performer who understood such a foible. "Well, at least let me buy you a drink afterward to celebrate your return to the stage."

"Thanks, but I've got a lot on the next day."

"On a Saturday? I am seriously worried about the way you antique people work."

"You are going to have to stop calling us that if you don't want Mum to take against you. Actually, it's not work. I'm going away for a couple of days, and there's loads I need to see to before I leave."

"Oh?"

Such a small word, but it was full of so many unasked questions. Such as, why are you going anywhere when you claim to be so busy getting the shop up and running? Xanthe tried to tell herself she was merely being overly sensitive.

"Yeah, a friend of mine, in Milton Keynes, she's had a bit of a crisis, you know, relationship stuff. Got herself in a right state. Needs a shoulder to cry on, that sort of thing." She supposed she should have been glad to find that she was such a poor liar, but it was not helpful. She stared into her wine, twirling the glass in her hands. "It's just for two nights," she added.

"That's quite a drive."

"I'm going by train. Less stressful than tackling all those motorways." Even to her own ears it sounded unconvincing. She had realized it would be difficult to hide her taxi somewhere while she was away, so the train was a better option. She had checked them online and thankfully found that there were a couple running on a Saturday morning from Chippenham. "I love my taxi, but she's a thirsty old girl. Would cost me a fortune in fuel to drive that far. No, train's better for a long trip. I'll get a minicab to the station," she told him.

"Don't be daft. Let me give you a lift."

"No," she said, more sharply than she intended. "No, thanks. I'm fine." She felt bad for snapping at him. Of course he could not know how carefully she must plan her "trip." She had spent most of the day thinking about how she could explain her absence, go somewhere Flora would not check up on her, actually appear to leave, yet double back, slip through the shop, and get to the jailhouse. And then there was the difficulty of returning a couple of days later without being seen emerging from the direction of the garden.

Liam showed his good sense by changing the subject back to something she was evidently less prickly about.

"So, are you excited about singing again?" he asked.

"Excited and nervous. It's been a while. And, well, solo is new for me. I used to sing in a band."

"Are they still playing back in London?"

"We broke up. Actually, we pretty much imploded. Marcus, he was our songwriter, keyboard player, and my boyfriend. When he and I split the band did, too."

"Ah. Not easy, being a rock star, all that adulation, adoring fans. . . ."

Despite herself she laughed. "Hardly that! No, Marcus had a habit. Cocaine. And to fund it he sold the stuff. Just to his so-called friends at first, but then, well, he needed more money so he sold to more people. Until eventually he got caught out. Only his stash was in our flat, and when the police found it, Marcus was nowhere in sight. And as the lease was in my name. . . ." She left the statement unfinished and drained her glass.

"Oh my God, he let you take the blame, didn't he?" Liam poured them both more wine. "Selfish bastard."

"Yes, as it turns out. Let the whole thing go to court without speaking up. The way he put it to me was that as he had a previous conviction, if they prosecuted him, he'd go to prison, no doubt about it. Whereas I was Miss Squeaky Clean. No way I'd get a custodial sentence for a first offense." She took another swig of Chablis. "Or at least, that's what he told me."

"Shit! Sorry, but did you actually get sent to jail? For his gear? And he let that happen? That's taking being a bastard to expert level, sorry to say, but it is."

"I'm not going to argue with you. You can imagine how much my mum loves him."

"What about your father? Didn't he try to . . . persuade him to do the right thing?"

"Let's just say my father had other things to deal with. And he's not the strong-arm type. He did shell out for a good lawyer, though, thank God. I spent twelve weeks in Holloway Women's Prison before he got me out on appeal."

"The whole thing stinks."

"Yup, but there it is. You are currently quaffing very fine wine with a convicted drug dealer. Imagine."

Liam thought for a moment and then said, "I think it's great that you're going to sing again. No one should be able to take that away from you. If you've got a talent, if music is part of your life, you shouldn't give it up, no matter what."

"Have you been talking to my mother?"

He smiled. "I guess she's pretty wary of any new men in your life."

"She's not the only one," she warned him.

"OK. I promise not to give your mother any cause to hate me, and I further promise to hide at the back of the crowd tomorrow night, but clap loudly at the end of each song. What sort of stuff are you going to be singing?"

"Ah, that is a secret only me and Harley know about so far. The rest of you are just going to have to wait and see," she said, finally allowing herself to smile. It had not been her intention to tell him all about her disastrous past, but the wine had loosened her tongue. And now that it had been said, now that she had put the whole sorry fiasco into a few short sentences, it seemed somehow diminished. And for the first time in a very long while she began to think that perhaps she could enjoy singing again. Which was just as well, because the only job she believed she might convincingly undertake back in the seventeenth century was that of a minstrel. In both her own century and the one long passed, she was soon going to have to literally sing for her supper.

11

MUCH OF THE NEXT DAY WAS TAKEN UP WITH GATHERING THE THINGS SHE
required for her journey back to the past, and all her preparations had to be done in snatches of time without attracting her
mother's attention. Mercifully, Flora's arthritis flare-up had, just
as she had predicted, subsided, and she was happy to be back
at work cleaning and repairing stock. Xanthe began the task
of putting things out in the shop, which meant she was able to
search through boxes of old coins. Most of what they had were
job lots bought at auction, so that she had to sift through mud-
dles of coins from different periods. There were plenty of Victorian pennies and Georgian coins of various values, but earlier
ones were more scarce. The handful of seventeenth-century ones
she found were mostly from the later years of the century. The
last thing she needed was to be caught in possession of "impossible" money and accused of forging it! In the end she struck
lucky in a shoe box among Mr. Morris's stock, which yielded
four pennies, three shillings, and a sixpence. Hardly riches,
but then she was supposed to be a traveling minstrel, and it
would arouse suspicion if she had too much money in the little drawstring velvet bag she had found to use as a coin purse.
It occurred to her that she might need something as a bribe.

Something silver, she decided. A further search turned up a silver thimble and a silver pocket knife. The knife gave her pause for thought. Should she take a weapon? On one hand it seemed sensible; after all, she would be a woman alone and a stranger in a familiar and yet strange place. But then, could she actually use it? She had never stabbed anyone or even threatened them with a knife. It seemed more likely she might be overpowered and the thing could be used against her instead. And then, were the 1600s really any more violent than the twenty-first century? Somehow she doubted it. She did not wish to go there with the idea of violence in her head. She chose the thimble for its value and left the knife in the glass-fronted cabinet that she had repositioned in the bay window of the shop.

She had already chosen a tatty leather satchel as her bag. It looked suitably well-traveled and not glaringly modern. Into it she could comfortably fit her valuables; a small, rolled-up picnic rug; and a tiny LED flashlight. She knew this was the one item that she must keep hidden but decided it was small enough to conceal in a pocket if necessary, and it would undoubtedly be useful, for such a time would seem alarmingly dark to her.

After lunch and an afternoon helping Flora add to the shop displays, Xanthe showered and then dug through the clothes in her bedroom in search of something suitable for her journey. She kept the chatelaine unwrapped and on her beside table, so that each time she glanced at it she was reminded of what it was she was trying to do and why. Most of her clothes being vintage, she was well supplied with long bohemian dresses, and selected the warmest, plainest one. It was a linen maxi pinafore in dark blue. She tried it over a cream blouse. It might have been summer in Marlborough in the present, but it had been cold when she had ventured back into the past, and she remembered the leaves were turning on the trees. Unable to find a suitable coat, she layered a vest and T-shirt beneath her dress, as well as thick leggings. The layers were helpful for hiding her gold locket, too. The feel of it next to her skin was a constant reminder that it was her ticket home. Her heavy boots were barely visible and would not be a million miles in appearance from the boots of the day, at least the ones the men were wearing. After something of a tussle she succeeded in pinning her hair up and then tying a small cotton scarf over it. She found another thin woolen scarf to wrap around her shoulders in the manner of a shawl, and tied the whole thing together with a supple Sam Browne wide leather belt. She stood in front of the bedroom mirror. The reflection that peered back at her was worryingly unconvincing. More peculiar than medieval. Would she pass for a minstrel? Would her artistic profession grant her sufficient license to look so odd? This was not a harmless game of fancy dress. This was a mission with a very real objective, and the consequences of failure could be grave indeed. As if it could sense her thoughts, and as if it were reminding her of the urgency of her mission, the chatelaine began to sing to her once again—a high, keening note.

"Is that what you're wearing tonight?"

Flora's voice from the doorway made her jump. "What? Oh, no. I don't think so. Do you?" she said, pretending to be seriously considering the awful outfit. She had been so taken up with what she was planning to do the next day she had almost forgotten she would be singing in public again in a couple of hours.

"To be honest, Xanthe love, it's not my favorite look for you," her mother said gently.

"No? Oh, well, maybe not." She pulled the scarf from her head and let her hair down before rummaging among her clothes again. "Must be something here . . ."

"Don't take too long. You should eat before you go onstage."

"It's just The Feathers, Mum. Not the Royal Albert Hall."

"You know what I mean. And you know how you get before a performance. You need food." She turned and headed for the stairs. "Half an hour," she called back as she went.

Suddenly Xanthe was pulled back to the demands of the present with an unpleasant jolt. As quickly as she could she removed her traveling clothes and slipped on a shorter, red ditsy print tea dress. She teamed it with her faithful boots and a pair of antique garnet stud earrings. Her face had caught the sun so that she looked reasonably healthy, if a little tired. She seldom wore makeup, but decided the event called for a bit of effort and glamor, so she applied some dark-red lipstick as deftly as she could. Next, she grabbed some balm, rubbed it into her hands, and then combed her hair with her fingers to give a smooth gloss to her ringlets. Butterflies had taken up residence in her stomach, not helped by the thought that she had not had nearly enough time to rehearse her new songs. She stood for a moment and took some long, slow breaths, then began to sing, quietly at first, but with growing strength, picking her way through the songs she had selected. She had practiced that morning in the shower and while working in the shop, but only quietly, as much to familiarize herself with the new tunes and words as anything else. This time she let herself sing at full volume, drawing encouraging cheers from the kitchen between songs. As she still had to keep checking the sheet music and Harley's books to remind herself of the words, she decided she would keep them in front of her for the performance to avoid the risk of standing onstage with a blank mind and no memory of what she should sing next.

She was just folding the sheets to put in her pocket when she felt rather than heard Margaret Merton enter the room. The ghost stood in the doorway as if to say she was in charge of where Xanthe went and when.

Xanthe felt her mouth dry at the sight of the specter. She tried to tell herself the woman was acting as a mother, protecting her child at any cost. But this line of thinking only led to the realization that it could be Flora who paid that price. Xanthe dug her nails into her palms, determined not to be cowed, not to let Mistress Merton shake what courage she had summoned for what lay ahead—both singing again and traveling back to Great Chalfield.

"Step aside," Xanthe said, keeping her voice low so that her mother would not hear. "There is something I need to do. Somewhere I need to go."

"There is only one place you should be going," Margaret Merton insisted.

"I can't just leave. If I'm going to have a hope of helping Alice I have to plan carefully."

"There is not time."

"I am leaving tomorrow, OK? Soon enough for you?" She stepped forward, steeling herself to push past the ghost if necessary.

But Mistress Merton was not ready to let her go. With startling speed she slammed the door shut. Xanthe gasped as it swung completely through the phantom, shuddered in its frame, and then clicked as the key turned.

"How do I know you are not trying to run away?" hissed the older woman, leaning forward so that her disfigured features were only inches from Xanthe's face.

Xanthe held her ground, willing herself not to look away.

"I have told you, I'm going back to Great Chalfield tomorrow." She felt her stomach turn over as a ghostly exhalation, lighter than breath, heavier than nothing, seeped around her, twisting up her own nostrils, carrying with it the scent of burned flesh and singed hair.

"Remember this," Mistress Merton whispered. "I will see my daughter freed, and I will do what I must to bring that day about. I do not make hollow threats." So saying she turned her gaze to the gold chain Xanthe was wearing. Slowly, with cold deliberation, she caused it to twist, over and over, shortening it, so that it tightened against Xanthe's throat. It took every ounce of Xanthe's self-control not to snatch at the thing, not to claw at it. She refused to give way to panic. Even as she felt herself beginning to choke she did not struggle.

"Kill me," she whispered, "and you kill Alice's last hope."

Margaret Merton hesitated, letting the chain tighten just a fraction more, then stopped, so that it spun undone, loose and harmless once more, her point made. With a blur of movement, she was gone.

"Xanthe!" Flora called up the stairs. "What are you doing thumping about up there? Supper's ready."

Xanthe waited until her breath had returned to normal, checked in the mirror that the redness around her neck was not too noticeable, hiding it with a dab of makeup, and then went downstairs.

They were having something her mother had named Wiltshire Whimsy, which she insisted was a local recipe.

"Looks suspiciously like an omelette to me," Xanthe said. It seemed so trivial to be discussing food after what had just taken place upstairs, but she badly needed to put the encounter behind her. She had to sing. She had to stay strong.

"Ah yes, but this one has a secret ingredient that makes it special."

"There is something . . . unusual," she agreed, picking at a pink lump with her fork. "Rhubarb, Mum? Seriously?"

She gave a shrug and passed the bottle of brown sauce, which she believed improved the flavor of everything. "Organic and locally grown, got it at the market."

Xanthe chewed on. It was surprisingly tasty, but her appetite was disappearing fast. In truth, she would have had trouble getting anything down, her stomach was so afflicted with nerves. Knowing her daughter well, Flora had put small bottles of beer on the table and Xanthe drank deeply from one, hoping to take the edge of the complicated tension of worrying about both the performance and what she was planning to do the next day. At that moment she was uncertain which was the more terrifying.

It was a beautiful summer's evening. The hanging baskets and window boxes outside the pub were overflowing with warm, fragrant blooms. The sharp yellows and rich purples of the pansies added vibrant color to the softer hues of the building itself. It was nearly eight when Xanthe and her mother arrived. She hoped Harley would not be in a panic, as she was due to start her set in barely ten minutes, but she could not face getting there early and having to wait while her anxiety levels rose higher and higher. Better to just turn up and jump right in.

It was unnerving to find the pub already almost full. There was a good-natured feel to the crowd of early evening drinkers, with some people enjoying meals. She made her way to the bar as confidently as she could. She had learned long ago that there was nothing that put an audience off a singer more quickly than picking up on her nervousness. They had come out to relax, to have a good time, to be entertained. Her job was to give them better than they were expecting, not show them the raw state of her nerves.

"Here she is!" Harley's enthusiastic greeting gave away his relief that he had not been let down. "The lass herself, and looking very decorative, if I might say so. Annie, shall we give the girl a drink before she sings?"

Annie smiled from behind the far end of the bar.

"Would you like something, Xanthe?"

"No, thanks. I'm fine. I'll just take a look at the microphone, then I'll be ready to start."

"Right you are, hen." Harley lifted up the bar flap and the drinkers parted to allow him to lead her to the area at the end of the room where there was a small platform. It was barely a stage, but enough to lift singers up out of the melee and house a couple of speakers. Xanthe glanced back at Flora, who gave an encouraging wave. She saw Liam invite her to join him at a table. True to his word, he'd found seats at the back. Xanthe noticed Gerri there, too. The rest of the room was just a collection of strangers, and she was thankful for that. Harley fussed around, offering her a stool, which she declined, and adjusting the height of the microphone. They checked to make sure the thing worked and that there was no feedback, and suddenly there she stood, clutching her sheet music in her trembling hands, hearing her own name announced with great gusto and drama as Harley introduced his latest discovery, listening to the welcoming applause, about to restart her stalled singing career.

Her mouth was dry, her tongue like sandpaper. She could hear her own shaky breathing as she stepped forward wearing a wobbly smile. The chatter in the room quieted. She raised her chin and began. She had chosen "Scarborough Fair" as arranged by Simon and Garfunkel to start with because she thought many people would recognize it, and a familiar tune could help an audience to engage with a performance. The microphone was an expensive one, carrying her voice easily across the room, but though the quality of the sound was good enough, there was something not right about the artificial edge it gave the song. She was singing without any backing track or instruments, and the song was ideally suited to be carried by the voice alone, but the amplification was at odds with the style of the piece. She knew she was singing well enough. Her voice had once been described as

"Florence Welch meets Kate Bush," which made her blush, but was fairly accurate, on a very good day. She was rusty, and a little hesitant, so was not singing at her best, but still better than most. She could see people nodding in recognition of the song and smiling, but after the first minute or so she noticed many of them drifting back into quiet conversation, or returning their attention to their food. Their reaction was plain enough. It clearly said *nice, but nothing special.* Xanthe glanced over toward the bar. Annie was too busy serving to pay much attention to what was going on, but she could see thinly masked despair on Harley's face. Although she was relieved to find her voice working well, she could tell she was losing the audience. Suddenly, she could see her mistake. She had played safe. By choosing something she thought everyone would know, she had not, in fact, given herself an advantage, she had merely given the audience a pale imitation of something they already had in their heads. And without the sublime guitar backing they would subconsciously have been expecting. This was hopeless. Whoever said compromise was death to art knew the truth of it. She must do the thing properly, commit to it wholeheartedly, or not do it at all. When she finished the song—to a round of gentle and polite applause—she switched off her microphone and signaled to Harley to dim the lights in the room. Being an August evening it was still daylight outside, but the small windows and low ceiling kept the room softly dark. Harley left on a single light, the one shining directly on Xanthe. When the audience heard the microphone click off they turned to watch, probably thinking she had given up and was about to leave. She stayed silent for a moment, letting the tension build, using the curious hush to draw their attention a little more. Then she closed her eyes, offering a silent prayer that she would not forget the words, and began to sing.

This time her voice was free from the distortion of the sound system. It sounded purer, cleaner, and far more suited to the medieval lament that she had selected. It felt right, so that this time she did not hold back. She had chosen "The Willow Song" which was a sixteenth-century ballad of betrayal and heartbreak, the mournful, swooping melody matching the poignant words. Xanthe kept her eyes closed, and instead of a pub full of people she saw the view through the casement window in the paneled room at Great Chalfield. As she pictured it, she recalled the smell of woodsmoke from the enormous fireplace and the slight dampness of the cold, stone flags when she had stood there, a few days and a few hundred years ago, watching Alice running for her life out across the rolling green of the Wiltshire landscape, her figure pinched and stretched by the imperfections of the ancient glass windowpanes. And as she sang she wondered who it was who had betrayed Alice, and whether or not she would be able to get her out of that terrible place and save her from a fate she did not deserve. And she pondered the possible consequences were she to fail. And she let all that emotion pour out through her voice. When she came to the end of the song there was a taut silence in the room before the cheering and applause started. And this time, it was well meant.

"Wow," said Liam after three more songs, when Xanthe finally got to join him and Flora at their table. "That was incredible. You are incredible." He smiled broadly and gave her a spontaneous peck on the cheek. "Really, I mean it. You are amazing."

"I keep telling her that," her mother put in, raising her glass of wine in a toast. "Here's to Xanthe singing again. Oh, but you haven't a drink, poor thing. I'll fetch you one."

"Please, Flora, let me," said Liam quickly.

"Absolutely not," Flora said firmly, getting to her feet and stabbing her crutches down with determination. "She's my daughter, I get to buy her the first celebratory drink."

Liam gave Xanthe a look and mouthed the word *oops*. As Flora battled her way through the crowd, Xanthe tried to reassure him.

"She likes to be as independent as she can. Anything that smacks of pity, or suggests she can't do something, well . . ."

"She's one determined lady. And very proud of you, as she should be."

"Do you think it was OK? Really?"

"Really. Harvey will be like a dog with two tails, about having found you. He'll keep you to a regular spot now."

She smiled, relieved, happy to have been back onstage at last, glad to have finally done something to earn her keep, and more than a little bit delighted that people had liked what she had done. She glanced at the bar. Harley was sorting the wine for Flora, and soon she would be back. Xanthe needed to talk to Liam while she had the chance.

"While I'm away," she said, not sure exactly what it was she wanted to say, "d'you think you could, well, pop in and see Mum? Just to check she's OK. I mean, obviously, she couldn't know that's what you were doing."

"Obviously!" He laughed.

"She doesn't really know anyone round here yet. The problem is that she won't ask for help, even when she really needs it, and I worry about her with all those stairs, and I know she'll try to move stuff that's too heavy for her, and—"

"No problem, I'll drop by, give her my number in case she needs it. I'm sure I can think of some reason for showing up. Probably need to buy my own mother a birthday present. Or something."

"Thanks. I owe you."

"Let me take you out to dinner when you get back."

"Shouldn't I be taking you?"

"Either way works for me," he said with a shrug. And then

Flora returned with her drink, and Gerri came over to say how much she'd enjoyed the music.

"It was so moving, Xanthe," she said. "I can't believe I have such a talented neighbor."

"Steady on," Flora said. "Too much praise'll go to her head. I can't afford to lose my business partner to superstardom."

"You can't have it both ways, Mum. One minute you're nagging me to sing, the next . . ."

"I never nag, Xanthe, love, just encourage."

And Gerri and Liam laughed at that, and Xanthe would have really enjoyed the rest of the evening had it not been for the lingering apprehension about what she was about to embark upon. A fear that did not diminish the more she thought about it, nor become more manageable the nearer the moment came to depart.

Xanthe slept badly and woke wishing she could leave as quickly as possible, while at the same time wanting desperately to put it off. She had never felt so conflicted about what she was planning to do. Before her mother woke up, she packed a small rucksack, carefully putting the things she had chosen to wear underneath her pajamas in case Flora took it into her head to open the bag while she wasn't looking. She turned over and over in her mind how she was going to make her plan work. As far as Flora knew, she was going to stay with Eva from Saturday morning until Monday morning. Forty-eight hours, which would give her several weeks back in the seventeenth century. If she returned sooner, she would just have to stay away somewhere until Monday. Or else come home early and say Eva had made it up with her boyfriend. More lies. There was a hard lump of guilt sitting in the pit of Xanthe's stomach, and she doubted anything could remove it. She was fairly confident she could leave via the old jail without Flora seeing her do it, but she would have less control over getting home again. She would just have to hope her mother was busy in the house, sneak out, change her clothes, and listen at the back door for a good moment to reappear through the shop. Somehow that moment seemed too far off to worry about in any more detail. Far more daunting tasks lay ahead of her before then.

She forced down a breakfast of toast while Flora chatted on about what she would be doing while she was away. She knew she should be chatting too, but every time she spoke she seemed only to utter another lie. She was happier discussing the online sales of the mirrors they had selected, and settled her mother in front of the computer.

"You've put reserves on them, haven't you?" Flora asked, bringing up the site.

"Yes. Reasonable ones. We want them to sell, but we don't want to give them away. Here, see?" Xanthe showed her the pages. "You might want to check in from time to time before the auction ends, see how they're doing. Are you going to get that Facebook page for the shop going?"

She grimaced. "You know how allergic I am to social media. I'll spend a little time on the new website first, I think. Start with something I vaguely understand."

"OK. Well, I'm off now," she said as casually as she could, picking up her bag. "I'll get a cab from the taxi rank on the high street. You'll be OK?"

"Of course," Flora said, barely looking up from the screen as her daughter leaned in to kiss her good-bye. She gave her hand a reassuring pat. "Have a nice time, Xanthe, love. And find a moment to try out some more of those lovely songs! You were such a hit last night."

She left quickly. It would have looked odd, making too much

of going away when she was, after all, only going to Milton Keynes for a short time. Even so, her heart was constricting at the thought of leaving her mother on her own so soon after the move. And at the thought of leaving her under the ever watchful eye of Margaret Merton. And somewhere deeply buried was the terrible fear that she might not be able to get back home. She forced herself to ignore this particular fear, for if she dwelled upon it she might lose the courage to step into the blind house ever again.

Once downstairs she made a point of opening and shutting the front door of the shop, letting the bell clang as loudly and freely as possible. She stood for a moment, breath held, then tip-toed through the passageway to the back door, which she opened with maddeningly slow care so as not to make a sound. She could hear Flora up in the kitchen, chatting to herself and the com-puter in the way she always did when pitting her wits against technology. Xanthe crept out into the garden, thanking her luck that the kitchen window looked out on the other side of the house, and then she ducked behind the blind house to change into her medieval clothes. It was awkward, pulling off her boots and jeans while stooped under one of the butterfly bushes, and it seemed to take forever to get into her many layers. The weather was still warm, so that she was horribly hot by the time she had finished. She paused for a moment to take hold of the locket beneath her T-shirt. It was reassuring to touch it, to know that it was safe, to know that, as long as her theory about it was right, she could use it to come home when her task was done.

Hiding her rucksack among the shrubs, she moved cautiously to the door of the jail. She had left it ajar, partly to air the place, but mostly to give herself the sense that she could go in and out, back and forth, easily and whenever she chose. She hesi-tated, waiting for the presence that she knew must come. And so it did. She felt rather than saw the ghost move inside the little stone building. Mistress Merton was evidently not leaving Xanthe's actions to chance even then. It was as if her attending this moment, this instance of journeying back in time, was to underline the reasons for her doing it, and to remind her of the threat that would hang, like the sword of Damocles, suspended over her mother until Alice was saved.

Xanthe's pulse began to race as she stepped inside. The half-light, the stale air, the confined space, all stirred up unwelcome memories. She reminded herself that this was a reality for Alice. That she had no choice. And no hope without Xanthe. With her leather satchel over her shoulder she stood as calmly as she was able, closed her eyes, and waited. Nothing. Nothing happened. What was wrong? Why wasn't the doorway to the past working? And then it struck her.

"You idiot!" she said to herself, exasperated at her own dim-wittedness. In her haste to leave, and her anxiety about being found out, she had forgotten the chatelaine! It was still sitting on the table beside her bed. Cursing her stupidity, she edged back out of the blind house. She would have to go back in and get it. She considered changing her clothes again, but it would all take so long. Better just to make sure she was not seen. She ran across the garden and gingerly opened the back door again. As she started to climb the stairs she could hear Flora arguing with a search engine. It was Xanthe's good fortune that anything computer-based tended to take up all her mother's concentration. She made painfully slow progress trying to avoid any creaking floorboards. She had just started up the final flight, which led from the kitchen to the bedrooms, when she became aware Flora had stopped clicking and typing.

"Hello?" Flora said. And then again, "Hello?"

Xanthe froze. Had she been heard? How was she going to

explain what she was wearing and what on earth she was doing? Her mind raced, searching for a plausible excuse.

"Hello? Oh, there you are. I wonder if you can help me, I want to place an advertisement in the *Marlborough Gazette* for this coming Thursday. Yes, on the Events page, I think. We are having an opening day for our new antiques shop."

Flora was on the telephone! Xanthe felt giddy with relief. As her mother explained to the salesperson what she wanted in the newspaper, Xanthe dashed up the rest of the stairs and snatched up the chatelaine, clipping it to her belt. If felt hot against her side, even through her clothes, and set up a discordant buzz in her head as she slid back down the stairs. She was certain her footsteps, and even her breathing, were horribly loud, but Flora was busy insisting the advertising rates were ridiculously high, and did not hear her.

Outside, Xanthe ran back across the scruffy lawn and all but flung herself through the door of the jail. She was in such a hurry to avoid being noticed by her mother that she had no time to hesitate, no time to be frightened. She simply stumbled to her knees upon the gritty floor, clutched her leather bag to her side, and pressed her other shaking hand over the pulsating chatelaine, struggling to catch her breath. She heard Margaret Merton bidding her farewell and Godspeed, but before she had time for so much as one last glance back through the door a heavy darkness descended, a lurching movement threw her onto her side, and in that instant, she was falling back through time once again.

12

XANTHE KNEW SHE HAD TRAVELED, KNEW THAT SHE WAS NO LONGER IN THE blind house, but she could not make sense of her surroundings. It was as if she were fighting to wake from a deep, dream-filled sleep. There was darkness, and noise, and a sense of confusion, and through it all she found it hard to draw a proper breath. What if something had gone wrong? Something in the way she had moved back through time? Was she lost in some terrible limbo? She fought against rising panic, struggling to get to her feet. As before, the Victorian parts of the chatelaine had traveled with her and were still in her hand where she had held on to them as she made the jump. Her bag was still over her shoulder. Gradually she became able to discern voices through the muddle of sounds. Shouting, urgent voices. Above everything, unmistakably, came the smell of smoke. She rubbed her eyes and at last was able to see that she was in an old building, much bigger than the jailhouse, though it was hard to tell what it was, exactly, because the space was filled with billowing, choking smoke. Now she could feel the heat. The fire must be dangerously close. She began spluttering and coughing. She must find a way out. She had not made that leap through time only to perish the moment she arrived. The smoke was making her eyes stream, but she could see broad floorboards beneath her feet and concluded she must be on an upper floor somewhere. And there was hay. The hayloft above the stables! In one corner was a bed of pallets and sacking with a rough blanket, but Peter was nowhere to be seen.

From below came shouts, and the sounds of the terrified horses banging against their stalls. Their snorts and whinnies were becoming increasingly frantic. Xanthe could make out Willis's voice as he tried to calm them, and the clatter of ironclad hooves over the cobbles as they scrambled out to safety. She had to get out before the flames took hold of the wooden ladder and she became trapped in the hayloft. Dropping to her knees in an effort to avoid the worst of the smoke, she scuttled across the floor. It should have been easier to breathe lower down, but the smoke was also billowing up through the gaps between the boards. At last she reached the opening and took hold of the top of the ladder. Already the smoke was making her feel dizzy and she could not stop coughing. Swinging her legs over the edge of the gap, she was about to start lowering herself down the ladder when she heard a whimpering. She peered through the gloom and noticed something moving in the corner of the hayloft. It was a dog. A small, spaniel type. It looked petrified, cowering beside some empty feed sacks.

"Come on, boy! Here, come on, come with me!" she urged it, but it was too frightened to leave its hiding place. Cursing silently, she tugged the scarf from her hair and tied it around her face so that it covered her mouth and nose. She took as deep a breath as she was able and crawled along the floorboards. They were hot beneath her hands and knees, and the fire below rumbled in a way that suggested it would quickly consume the whole building. She tried to coax the little dog forward, but it was too terrified to move, so she had to get right into the corner to grab hold of it. There was too much smoke for her to even try to say something soothing to it now, so she was relieved when it did not struggle, but instead pressed itself against her as she tucked it into the shawl tied around her shoulders and waist. She began her painful journey back toward the ladder, but at that moment a burst of flames shot up through the opening, the ladder itself ablaze. An ice-cold fear gripped her. Strangely, she did not feel panic. Did not have the urge to scream or cry. She was immobilized, as the dog had been moments before, her body frozen with dread. Suddenly, there was an almighty crack as one of the main joists supporting the floorboards gave way. In a heartbeat, the floor upon which she had been kneeling dropped, and she and the dog descended with it. There was no time to think about what was happening. She crashed to the ground, her fall broken by the hay and feed sacks that made the drop with her. She landed heavily, the impact knocking from her what choking breath she had. She was briefly aware of more shouts and cries, of blurred figures looming through the smoke, of terrible heat and the redness of the fire. And then, nothing.

When she came to, the first thing she noticed was the smell of singed hair. Was it her own? She blinked and rubbed at her stinging eyes, trying to prop herself up on one elbow.

"She's awake!" said a girl's voice close by.

Firm hands steadied her. She could make out a large woman standing over her, who spoke with a rolling Wiltshire accent and a gruff, no-nonsense tone.

"There now. Do not distress yourself with effort. Lie still. All will be well, the danger is passed."

She tried to speak but this only resulted in a painful bout of coughing, which culminated in her vomiting over the side of whatever bed she had somehow been put into. Embarrassed, she dabbed at her mouth with the back of her hand and tried once more to get her streaming eyes to clear. She was in a high, narrow bed in a small room. The window on the far side was open but still all she could taste was smoke. Slowly the second figure swam into focus and she recognized the well-to-do young woman she had seen on her previous visit. She was holding the spaniel. He had lost quite a bit of fur, but looked otherwise unharmed. Xanthe realized that someone had undressed her, so that she now wore only her underwear, vest, and leggings. They must have found her clothes exceedingly strange. A sudden terrible thought gripped her and her hand flew to her throat, relief flooding through her when she found her locket still in place. As her vision cleared further she could see her clothes on the little window seat and her satchel was there too, still buckled up. The room was sparsely furnished, just the bed, a stool, and a chest for clothes. There was a worn but beautiful rug on the floor. She noticed that the walls had no expensive wood paneling, but were just roughly plastered with a lime wash over them. It felt like a second-best guest room. Not posh enough to mark her out as special, but nor was it a servant's room.

The woman, whom Xanthe thought, now that she could see her better, to be in her fifties, helped her to sit up against the bolsters.

"You'll be right as rain in no time," the woman said. "Though heaven knows, God must have been guiding you, for 'tis a wonder you weren't burned to a crisp," she added with some relish.

The younger woman stepped forward. "Mary, fetch father. He will want to know that Pepito's savior is awake," she said. The maid bobbed a curtsy and went to do as she was asked. "Look, Pepito, here is the one who brought you safe from that terrible fire. You must say your thank-yous like a good little dog." As she spoke, the dog wagged its tail rather feebly. "There, you see?

He's grateful to you. What a clever boy he is!" she enthused. Xanthe could not help thinking that a clever dog would have found his way out of that burning building pretty quickly, but she thought it best not to say as much. The girl was sweet looking, with chestnut hair smoothly arranged beneath a starched white cap. Her gown was simple but expensive, made of a fine green wool, with a square lace collar and cuffs. She appeared healthy and confident, clearly enjoying the benefits of being a beloved daughter in a wealthy household.

"I'm glad your dog is unharmed," Xanthe said, choosing her words with great care. Being a minstrel would only grant her so much leeway. She had no wish to say anything that would make her stand out or arouse suspicion. "Can you tell me what time it is?" she asked, aware that for her there were clocks ticking in two different centuries.

"Time? Oh, you mean the hour. Well, it was three in the afternoon when we went to table; Father likes to dine late in the day. That was when I noticed Pepito was missing. And the very moment I missed him we heard cries from the stables. The fire took hold so swiftly, it is a mercy no one was killed."

"And the horses?"

"All survived, so Willis tells my father."

At that moment the door opened and Master and Mistress Lovewell came into the room, apparently eager to inspect the curious stranger who had emerged, sooty and unconscious, from the flames.

"How fares our mysterious visitor who delivered Pepito from the inferno?" the master of the house inquired. "Ah! You are quite recovered, I trust, Mistress?"

His wife looked less impressed by what she found. "Mistress? Better say vagabond."

They made an odd pair. He was soft and short and round,

his ample belly belted with braid and his clothes showy. Mistress Lovewell evidently preferred to dress plainly, her hair scraped back off her face severely and completely hidden beneath her white cap. She had a hardness about her that started with her angular features and continued through her steely stare.

"Come, come," said Master Lovewell, "we must extend the hand of charity to one whose acts have benefitted us."

"We know nothing of the girl," his wife pointed out, not for a moment taking her gaze off the stranger in the bed.

"Oh, Mother, we know that she saved Pepito," her daughter put in.

"We know that she acted bravely and selflessly," Master Lovewell added.

"We know no such thing. She saved herself, and it may be that she saw the dog as a token for trading when her hiding place was no longer available to her."

"Oh," the master replied, smiling gently at Xanthe, "I doubt anyone would be capable of such clear and mendacious thought while the fire raged about them. I am certain I would not."

His wife gave a dry snort. "There are some more suited to mendacity than others," she said, leaning in to inspect the girl more closely. "Where are you from?" she demanded. "Who is your family?"

Xanthe sat up, doing her best to hit a note that was a blend of humility and honesty. Her voice was unhelpfully husky. "My name is Xanthe Westlake," she said. They repeated it, puzzled, so that she quickly went on, "I am come from the west to perform at the fair. As for family, I have none."

"Perform?" Mistress Lovewell's narrow eyes narrowed further.

"I am a minstrel."

"How jolly!" declared the master of the house.

"But how came you to be in our stables?" his wife wanted to know.

She trotted out her prepared story, praying it sounded more convincing than it felt.

"The band of players I was traveling with have gone their separate ways. I must find a new troupe, or else, perhaps, a private employer. I was weary when I arrived and did not want to present myself at your door without resting first. I confess I stole into your hayloft for a nap. When I awoke, the place was ablaze."

"Oh, Mother! The Willoughbys at Harefield Manor have their own minstrel. It would be such a feather in our cap if we were to have one, too," her daughter insisted.

"There are more important things than expressions of grandeur, Daughter. We have no need of a minstrel."

"Let us not be too hasty, my dear," said her husband. "Clara is right in what she says. It would be a demonstration of our elevated status, to have a singer in our employ. Imagine how such a thing would benefit our entertainments."

"We do not entertain with sufficient frequency to warrant keeping a musician."

Clara was all but jumping up and down, "But, Mother!"

"Your mother is right, Daughter," Master Lovewell told her. "But it happens that we are also in need of a maid." He allowed a little pause for his family to remind themselves of the fact that Alice was no longer available for work, now that she was locked up in the Marlborough jail. Xanthe glanced at the mistress's face but she was giving nothing away. "I have heard," her husband went on cheerily, "of those who employ a minstrel who, when their artistic talents are not required, works otherwise within the house. Tell us"—he turned to Xanthe—"have you experience as a lady's maidservant?"

"Husband, you cannot mean for me to take this . . . unknown person as my own maidservant!"

"Oh, well, if you are uncertain as to her qualifications . . ."

"I am uncertain as to everything about her."

"Then perhaps, work in the kitchens?" He raised his particularly mobile brows, first at his wife and then at Xanthe.

She made sure not to let her disappointment show. She needed to be as close to the mistress of the house as possible if she was to find out what happened to Alice, to find the chatelaine pieces. From what little she knew of the times, kitchen maids were seldom allowed anywhere near the private bedchambers of the family. They were also worked half to death. And yet, it was a chance to remain in the house, and the best offer she was likely to get.

"Oh yes, sir," she answered brightly. "I am a hard worker as well as a good singer. I promise I will not disappoint on either count."

"There, Wife. What do you say about that?"

"I say we are short a maid. Mary can attend me, and you will take up her duties in the kitchens. One month's trial. Make no mistake, girl, if you are not as you profess to be I shall have you thrown out."

"As you wish, Mistress Lovewell," she said demurely. "I thank you for your kindness."

Clara was all for hearing her sing then and there, but her father pointed out that she was still suffering from a surfeit of smoke. It would be unfair to put anyone's voice to the test until fully recovered and on best form. Xanthe was permitted to rest for a further hour, after which Mary would fetch her, show her where she would sleep, and then take her to the kitchen to learn her duties.

She waited until the family had left the room, when their dwindling footsteps and voices told her they were safely out of the way, before climbing out of bed. She winced as she stood up. She had been fortunate not to break any bones when falling through the floor in the stables, but she had certainly acquired some painful bruising, mostly on her back and shoulders. Her left elbow was swollen, the joint unhelpfully stiff, and there was a small but nasty burn on her right calf, which had been dressed with a sticky salve and a piece of muslin while she lay unconscious. She hobbled over to the window, cursing her shortsightedness at not bringing a first aid kit, or at least some painkillers, with her. As she unbuckled her satchel she noticed that her hands were trembling. The combination of leaping back through time and narrowly escaping dying in the barn fire had left her shaken. Not to mention the tension induced by the danger her mother was in. The thought of the fearsome ghost watching and waiting sent a chill rippling down her spine. Her own safety was far from assured. Clara and Master Lovewell seemed easy enough to convince of her good character and harmless intentions, but Mistress Lovewell was shrewd and sharp. Xanthe was going to have to tread carefully around her, which was not going to make helping Alice any easier. It looked as if no one had interfered with her bag or its contents. No doubt with a smoldering stable block and a singed spaniel, they had other things to think about. It was a mercy they had not started digging through her possessions. The chatelaine attachments that had traveled with her were still there. She wrapped them inside her headscarf and put them underneath the picnic rug. Next, she looked at her precious flashlight. What if they had checked her things and found it? How on earth would she have explained it? She had been lucky, this time, but to trust so much to chance was a dangerous tactic. She quickly took out the flashlight and tucked it into her bra. Looking out of the window she could see the family walking across the courtyard to examine the stables. The fire damage was extensive, with the roof almost completely gone and one end of the building collapsed. The Lovewells were going to have to spend a fair amount of money to put it right.

Xanthe felt horribly woozy, and the smoke had left her throat so sore that she could not swallow without difficulty, but however tempting it was to climb back into the featherbed and rest, she knew she must not waste the opportunity to begin her search. Once she was in the kitchens and put to work it would be more difficult to sneak off on her own. And at this moment Mistress Lovewell was out of her bedchamber. That was where the chatelaine pieces had gone missing. That was where she had to begin seeking answers.

After pulling on her blouse, dress, belt, and boots, she crept from the room. She found herself on a long, upstairs corridor. Most of the walls were paneled with smooth, dark, polished wood. The floorboards were bare, which made them unhelpfully noisy beneath her heavy boots. She moved toward the front of the house, reasoning that the main bedrooms would be located there. There were deep casement windows at the end of the hallway allowing enough light for her to see what she was doing. She lifted the latch on the first door, but a quick peek told her this was Clara's room. Even in the seventeenth century, generations before the term had been invented, there were telltale signs of a teenager: brightly colored damask drapes on the four-poster bed and at the windows, piles of ribbons and lace upon the dressing table, more than one mirror, a warm fur throw upon the bed, and a collection of beautifully dressed dolls. Xanthe hurried on to the next room. This one was very grand and had a more grown-up feel to it. At its center was the biggest four-poster bed she had ever seen, intricately carved, with an impressive canopy and drapes. A status symbol, as well as a place of warmth and comfort that must have been rare in the 1600s. The room boasted beautiful rugs on the floor, two heavily padded chairs, as well as a cushioned window seat at the generous window. The glass was of fine quality, allowing in plenty of light, and some of the panes were even of stained glass, which must have cost a fortune. The Lovewells were clearly keen to shout about their wealth and position, however much the mistress of the house might like to pretend otherwise.

On the far side of the room was a small table with two wooden boxes on it. The little stool in front of it and the hand mirror and hairbrush suggested it was Mistress Lovewell's dressing table. Xanthe hurried toward it, wanting to check the boxes.

"What business have you in the mistress's bedchamber?!" came the shout from behind her.

She wheeled around to find Mary standing in the doorway. The statuesque maid who had tended her when she was brought out from the barn looked a picture of fury and suspicion at finding her where she absolutely should not have been.

"Forgive me, I . . . became lost," she stammered. "It is such a big house. I wanted some air but could not find my way out."

"Indeed? And why would a person seeking a way out of a place not walk toward the flight of stairs that would take them downward? It is curious that a stranger should find their way so conveniently to the very room where the mistress of the house might keep her valuables."

"I promise you, I am no thief."

"You will have to do better to convince me than effect a winsome countenance. Your prettiness will not move me, so do not seek to use it."

"Truly, I meant no harm. I really was looking for a way out of the house. You must believe me."

"Must I now? Who is to say so? And who is to say Mistress Lovewell will accept your protestations of innocence? Come. Away with you. We will see what the good lady of the house has to say."

13

AS MARY MARCHED HER FROM THE ROOM, XANTHE'S MIND RACED TO FIND A way to prevent herself from being delivered up to the mistress. She was certain the woman would take snooping in her bedchamber as being all the proof needed that she was untrustworthy. At the very least she would be sent packing. Mistress Lovewell might even have Xanthe dragged away and locked up as Alice had been. She needed to think fast, but her head was still fuzzy, and her breathing had not yet entirely recovered from inhaling so much smoke, so that she was having trouble catching her breath as Mary bundled her down the stairs. The sweeping staircase led down to the broad entrance hall. As they reached the bottom the door opened and the family came in. Xanthe felt Mary straighten up. She opened her mouth to speak, but at that moment Pepito grew tired of being in Clara's arms and jumped to the floor. On seeing his rescuer he came running, wagging his tail and making small squeaks by way of greeting.

"Oh, see?" Clara laughed. "He knows you, and he wishes to show his appreciation. Pepito, you have a new friend." She clapped her hands as the little dog ran in tight circles. Xanthe reached down and patted him, taking care not to touch the patches where he had lost his fur.

"I see you are recovered," Mistress Lovewell observed. She frowned at the faux minstrel's clothes. "Mary, find the girl something to wear more suiting her position in the household. And endeavor to do something with all that hair."

"My lady . . ." Mary started, but she got no further, for her mistress was already striding across the hallway, her hand raised.

"I have not time to spend further on the matter. We are in disarray. This dreadful fire, and all remedies no doubt will cost us dear. Let the girl prove her worth and see that she stays in your sight while she does so."

Mary looked at Xanthe, her face set, arms folded. "That I certainly shall do, my lady," she said. "That I shall do."

She took her to the rear of the house, whisking her along the narrow passageways and through low doors at such speed that Xanthe had little chance of taking it all in. She was endeavoring to get her bearings, to make a note of which door led where, but Great Chalfield was all unexpected twists and stairs and corridors, suggesting the core of the house, with its great hall and important rooms, had been built earlier than much of the rest, with further rooms being added over the years. Xanthe attempted to remember what it had looked like in the modern day when she'd attended the auction, but had only her impression of the exterior on which to make a judgment. It had certainly finished up bigger, with less timber frame and more stone, but that was all she could bring to mind. At last they came to a locked room. Mary had a ring of keys at her belt; nothing so grand as a chatelaine for her, just a loop of metal for her keys. She found the one that opened the door into a small room filled with tall cupboards and nothing else. When she opened the nearest one Xanthe could smell soap and starch and saw that all the shelves were filled with neatly folded linen. The Lovewells might not be nobility, but they were certainly wealthy. All that fine bed linen, table linen, and clothing would have not only cost a great deal to buy, but cost time and money to launder and repair.

"You will have use of these garments for as long as you are a servant in this household and not a day beyond," she announced, selecting things from the linen press and handing them over. "Keep them in good order. The mistress will not tolerate waste nor carelessness with what is given you. You bear responsibility for losses, and woe betide you should you present yourself in an unclean state." With that Mary strode from the room, calling after her. "Do not dawdle, for there is ever work to be done and hours too few in which to do it."

Xanthe scurried after her out of the room. Mary locked the door and took her up a tightly twisting wooden staircase that led two floors up to the rooms in the attic. They passed through one with a single bed in it and eventually came to another at the very end of the house. They were in the roof itself, the ceiling sloping, rafters and beams exposed, with tiny windows set in one side. There were two mattresses, straw-stuffed and lumpy, upon wooden pallets. One was made up, next to the other were folded some basic-looking bed linen and blankets. There was a stool, a low table with a candle stub in a little earthenware holder, and above the beds a sampler reminding all who stood before it to give thanks to the Lord. Xanthe was assailed by a strong feeling of sorrow and thought she could hear sobbing. She whipped around, but there was no one else in the room. She knew then that this had been Alice's bedchamber. Alice's little bed, where she had been living out her little life before everything had gone so disastrously wrong for her.

"For now, you shall share Jayne's bedchamber. She is also a kitchen maid, so your working days will tally. You may keep your own clothes in here. You are given one candle per week—do not squander the mistress's generous allowance. We attend church on Sunday morning and evening, and Wednesday even-song. Sunday afternoon is your own time if there are no guests staying in the house."

Mary stood, waiting, watching her new charge. Xanthe knew she must have already seen her strange undergarments, and probably her locket. What would she make of a lowly min-strel owning such a piece of gold? It struck her that Mary was not the type to give away what she was thinking, unless it was to bark instructions. Xanthe began to unbuckle her belt and Mary turned away, leaving the room with her customary pur-poseful stride.

"See to it that your cap covers that hair," she said as she went. "Come to the kitchens directly and you will be given your du-ties. Be quick." She paused and then added, "This night I shall give you balm for your burn. Mind you tend to it. We've no room here for an ailing maidservant."

It was a relief to be on her own again. She took her clothes off, glad she could keep her own underwear, seeing as she was no longer under Mary's scrutiny, and put her outer garments in what she hoped passed for a neatly folded pile on the little table. Her bag she stuffed beneath the mattress. She had been given a shift of cream cotton which she slipped over her head. Next came a brown kirtle, which was essentially a long-sleeved dress cut in the most unflattering way imaginable, devoid of shape, with a square neckline and nothing by way of embellishment or even nice stitching. She pulled it over her head. The fabric was coarse enough to be itchy, so she was glad of the shift beneath it. It fell to her ankles, not quite covering her heavy boots, which would no doubt gain her some curious glances. Finally, she tied an apron, stiff with starch, around her waist. On the table were a handful of hairpins. She already had a band, but even so it was a struggle to get all her hair into a sufficiently tight bun to force it beneath the starched white cap she had been given. She was glad there was no mirror, as she was certain she looked awful, what with the shapeless dress, the drab colors, and the dangling flaps of the headgear that would, to modern eyes, look completely ludicrous.

She took one more look around the room. What was so striking was just how little of Alice there was to be found. There were some things in the corner that she supposed belonged to the other kitchen maid, Jayne. But what of Alice? Had her own clothes already been thrown out? Or taken to her? Had she no other possessions? No mementos of her family even? Willis had mentioned them only as traitors, so perhaps Alice had been compelled to get rid of anything that connected her to them. It seemed a sorry story that had only grew more sorrowful. Xanthe paused in the doorway, reluctant to leave her own few connections with home, but she was still wearing her locket. She could still return to her own time, when she was ready, when Alice was free, and when Flora would be safe.

She took the back stairs and followed her nose to the kitchen. This was not, in fact, one room but a collection of spaces, all given over to the preparation and storing of food for the household. Xanthe did a quick tally and reckoned that, with Willis and Peter and Mary, the carriage driver, the servants she could see now, probably gardeners as well, and the Lovewells themselves, that meant feeding at least twelve people, presumably two meals a day. Which explained the hectic pace of work that was going on. The main room—the one that most resembled a modern-day kitchen—was huge, with its most noticeable feature being the enormous open fireplace set into the far wall. There was a fire burning in the hearth, with pots set over it, either on stands or hanging from chains. She could see a spit put to one side that would no doubt be used on feast days. To the left of the fire was an oven door, through which a stick-thin man was using a wooden peel to push trays of bread dough for baking. A young girl was emptying pails of water into a barrel, and two young men were carrying in crates of stoneware jugs that Xanthe guessed contained beer of some sort. Mary saw her and put her hands on her hips, clearly not impressed by her attempts to look neat and tidy. Tutting, she tightened the stays of Xanthe's apron and repositioned some of her hair pins, all the while issuing instructions and warnings, none of which she really understood. Even her gruff voice was difficult to hear above the general noise in the kitchen. She pointed out a darting figure scarcely bigger than a child, and stated that this was Jayne. The girl gave a fleeting smile as she hurried past with a basket of eggs. Through one door Xanthe could see a flagged passageway that looked like it led to the dairy in which she had hidden on her previous visit. At the other end of the room the young men were endlessly bringing things in—crates of beer, a churn of milk, baskets of vegetables, armfuls of logs for the fire—or taking things out: buckets of ashes, slops, vegetable trimmings, and general rubbish. The little baker snapped out orders, and she quickly understood that he was in fact the cook and in charge of the kitchen. A maidservant scurried through another door into what appeared to be a storeroom for all of the tableware. Xanthe glimpsed shelves and tables stacked with pewter or silver plates, wooden platters and serving dishes, and silver and glass goblets and beakers. It was all on such a huge scale, just for a family of four people! But then there would be the "entertainments" Master Lovewell had hired her for. And there was the team of staff to be fed, too.

"Mind your backs!" shouted a burly man with a red face as he carted a side of pork through the kitchen and hefted it onto the table at the center. Xanthe stepped out of the way, wondering who among the servants knew Alice best and who she could make a friend of, who might answer some of the dozens of questions she had stored up. The cook looked as if he never had a free moment. Mary was already suspicious of her. Judging by their clothes, the manservants seemed to be mostly from outside the house, possibly employed in the gardens or somewhere else on the estate, and probably only fleetingly seen indoors when muscle was required. Jayne was now scrubbing pots with what looked like a handful of straw and some ash. She could not have been more than thirteen. Xanthe was about to sidle up to her and introduce herself when a bark from Mary summoned her.

"Here," Mary said, shoving a cloth-covered basket into her arms. "Take this out to Willis and the boy. The Lord knows they will be in need after their terrible morning. Inform Willis the mistress has had beds made up for the pair of them in the hoard house. There they will find clothes to replace those they lost. Do not stand and stare like a dumbkin, girl, away and make haste!"

Xanthe hurried out of the kitchen, glad to be free of the noise, the heat, and the smell of the place. She had only been in it a matter of moments, and on a workaday afternoon; what would it be like toiling in there on feast days from dawn till dusk with few chances to rest or eat, she wondered. Outside the day was mild but cool, the leaves on the creeper climbing the west side of the house already turned to autumn reds and golds. The smell of smoke hung about the smoldering stables and grew stronger the nearer she got. For a moment she hesitated, her stomach lurching, the memory of the fire, of the heat and choking smoke, of falling, transporting her back to that very real danger. What if she had been unable to escape? What would have happened to Alice? To Flora? She pressed on, having no time to dwell on what-ifs.

Although badly damaged by the fire, the main structure of the stables remained standing. As she reached the arched doorway that led to where the carriages were kept, Willis emerged carrying armfuls of harness, Peter trotting along behind him.

"I am happy to see you both well," Xanthe said. "Mary sent this for you. You are to have beds in the hoard room, and new clothes."

Peter laughed. "Will be the first time I've been allowed in there!"

She had no idea what a hoard room was, or why Peter would have been kept out of it, but did not wish to show her ignorance. Clearly it was something commonplace, yet not open to young boys. Only later would she learn it was a place for hoarding fruit and vegetables through the winter months.

Willis made no move to take the basket, but stood and stared hard at her, clutching the straps and buckles tight as if she might try and snatch them from him.

"I told you to leave," he said levelly. "How was it you were in the hayloft?"

"I had to come back. I have to find a way to prove Alice isn't a thief."

"You'll find nothing up there." He jerked his head in the direction of the wrecked roof.

"I was waiting . . . for a chance to enter the house unseen."

"Happen a fire would make a good distraction. All the better for you."

"What? You think *I* started it? No! I promise you, I did not."

"'Tis curious the fire began when it did, then."

"I don't know how the fire started, but you will find another explanation. I would never do such a thing."

"She saved Pepito," Peter reminded him. It was only later she would remember how the boy looked when he spoke. He looked . . . ashamed. Guilty, perhaps. At the time it meant nothing, but she would later recall that Peter loved to steal stubs of candles from the house. She knew he hated the dark: it made perfect sense. For a naked flame and an attic full of hay are a dangerous combination, especially when in the hands of a young boy.

"What of it? What better way to win favor with the family?"

She took a step forward, knowing she had to convince him.

"Willis, I could no more start a fire in those stables than you could. I would never risk harming the boy. You must see that."

He considered this. She could tell he was remembering the night she had stayed, the time she had spent with Peter. At last he seemed to satisfy himself that she was not capable of putting a small boy's life in danger, not if she were truly come to help Alice. He nodded at Peter.

"Give him the victuals," he said. "We've not time to stop, mind. Everything's to be moved from here over to the grain barn. Though it'll be the devil's own job to keep the mice from the master's leather." He shook his head in dismay.

"And the horses?" she asked. "All are well?"

"They are. Will likely set them back, that's certain. A scare like that . . ." He left the thought unfinished and moved on. Peter followed, peering under the cloth, hungry for the contents of the basket.

Xanthe waited until they had their backs to her and then slipped behind the barn. She knew she would soon be missed and must return to the kitchen, but she wanted to look once more at the stables. Why had the chatelaine brought her precisely there? The first time she had arrived on the road as Alice passed in the carriage. She had thought that might have been connected to the vision of the dark woods with the birds apparently singing at night, but there weren't many trees by the road, only the ditch and open pasture. The second time she had arrived directly inside the manor house. What was it about the hayloft? She feared she might never find the answer, as the whole thing had collapsed into the building. Nothing up on that level had survived. Even the window in the end wall, surrounded by wattle and daub and timbers rather than stone, had fallen, charred and ruined, to the floor. She turned and stood facing across the sweeping countryside, as if she had been looking out of the window. On the occasion when she had arrived in the house she had been looking southward, so that she had witnessed Alice being taken. Perhaps she was not supposed to notice something *in* the hayloft, but something she could see looking *out* of it. The swath of green swept downward, the direction being the same Alice had taken when she ran to get away from the men taking her to jail. The land was well grazed by sheep, with some impressive trees here and there. In the distance Xanthe could see a track and a stream meandering along the valley. There was a copse—could that be linked to the woodland the chatelaine had shown her? It was possible, but she could see nothing remarkable, nothing that meant anything, nothing obviously significant.

Her thoughts were interrupted by the sound of horses' hoof-beats and men's voices coming from the front of the house. It seemed the Lovewells had visitors. She was unable to see them from where she was and was glad she would not be spotted by people coming out of the front door to greet the new arrivals. She found she could get into the stables and decided to creep through the ravaged building, so that she might make her way back toward the kitchens without being seen. The fewer people she had to encounter the better, unless they could be in some way useful. At this point she needed to be as invisible as possible, until she was more certain of whom she could trust, and who might be able to help her. The inside of the stables still stank of smoke and wet wood where the fire had been doused. It was surprising that the whole building had not been lost. The fact that the main part of the stables were built of stone rather than cheaper wood and lathe and plaster was what had saved it. The interior that remained was in a poor condition, however, with heaps of charred harness and blankets, piles of sodden hay, and everywhere blackened pieces of beams, rafters, and floorboards. At times she had to lift a fallen floorboard to go on. She picked her way through the debris and had nearly reached the doorway on the other side, clambering over the remains of a manger, when a voice startled her so much she almost lost her balance.

"Take not another step!" commanded the man who had just entered the building through the carriage doorway. "Not a single one!"

She stood as still as she could, at the same time trying to turn to see who was shouting orders at her. There came a young man, well dressed, slightly dour-looking. As she turned, the manger shifted under her hand and she stumbled, falling back against an upright beam, which wobbled, causing a shower of filthy ash and wet charcoal to rain down upon her. When it stopped moving she held her breath, waiting to see if more would fall. As the cloud of dust and ash cleared, the stranger came into view, climbing over the wreckage on the floor.

"Here," he said, reaching out to her, "take my hand."

She did as she was told. She expected him to carefully help her out, but instead he hauled her across the debris, pulling her from where she stood with such force and so little care that she could not stop herself from shouting.

"Hey! Steady on!" She protested as she was all but dragged from the corner of the stall, wincing as the burn on her leg brushed against a charred plank of wood.

She would have said more but at that second there was a terrifying rumble and a large section of the stone wall came crashing down, sending up plumes of mortar dust and more ash. When it settled she saw how close she had come to being crushed. If she had not been pulled out when she had been she would have ended up underneath most of what fell.

The stranger was still holding her hand.

"You are unharmed?" he asked.

"Yes," she coughed, then tried again. "Yes, I am. Thank you—"

"Do not waste what breath you have on thanking me, mistress," he interrupted. "I would rather you put your mind to your own safety, so that you might not cause any further devastation."

"What?" She wiped grit from her face, her hand coming away smeared with soot, and she realized she was covered in the dark residue of the fire.

"Your actions not only placed your life in peril, but have brought about further damage to the building. Damage that will not be put right without both cost and effort," he insisted, gesticulating at the gap where the wall used to stand. He let go of her hand and regarded her with a stern stare. She considered he might not have been quite so sure of himself had he been able to see that he too was reduced to looking quite ridiculous, being similarly covered in wet soot and ash. "If you care not for your own neck," he went on, "spare a thought for the work of others and, I pray you, resist adding to their burden if you are able."

"Now wait a minute," she said, snatching the ruined cap from her head and attempting to shake ash from it and from her hair. "You make it sound like I was trying to get myself killed. For heavens' sake, I was just running an errand from the kitchens. I don't know what you're doing in here, but it seems to me that I'm the only one trying to do any work." His clothes, even through their layer of soot, did not have the appearance of those worn by someone who spent his life toiling in the fields or acting as a servant to others. His frown had altered into a look of puzzlement, and only then did she realize that her little outburst was full of modern phrases that must have made him think her decidedly strange.

The sound of laughter came from the doorway and another young man entered. Xanthe recognized him as one of the three she had seen visiting the house the last time she had been there. Now that she looked more closely she remembered the other one, too. He was the reason she had hidden in the dairy. He was the one she had feared might have seen her.

"For truth, brother, what curious creature have you cornered here?" asked the newcomer. There wasn't much of a family resemblance. This second one looked younger, fairer, and had an easy smile. The first had dark looks to match his temper.

"A person endeavoring to bring the remnants of the rafters down upon her head," he said.

His younger brother gave a wide smile. "It seems she near succeeded, judging by the state of her."

Xanthe frowned, jamming the cap back onto her head. This only amused him more, causing him to start laughing again.

His brother shook his head. "Joshua, I have not time for such . . . foolishness."

"Come, Samuel, you are not currently giving the appearance of seriousness yourself," he said, raising his brow a little.

At this, the older brother looked down at his filthy clothes, took out a handkerchief, wiped his face, and gasped in irritation at the soot that came away.

The younger one continued to laugh even as he bowed toward Xanthe with mock formality, pointedly taking off his velvet hat, which he swept low, then replaced firmly on his head, backward.

With a sinking feeling, she reached up to pat her own cap and found that she had indeed put it on back to front. She removed it, stuck her chin in the air, turned on her heel, and strode with what little dignity she could muster out of the disintegrating building, the sound of Joshua's laughter accompanying her and Samuel's glare following her as she crossed the yard back toward the house.

{ 14 }

MARY WOULD NOT ALLOW XANTHE TO SET FOOT INSIDE THE DOOR.

"What manner of calamity has befallen you? Such a state! Get out before you press soot and filth upon the rest of us," she snapped. "Jayne, for the sake of us all, take her to the pump. And do not return until you are in a fit condition!" she added, pushing the young maidservant out toward Xanthe and slamming the door on them both.

Jayne trotted off ahead. "We must be quick," she said as she ran toward the water pump behind the dairy. She grabbed the handle and began pumping water from the spout. "Mary will set about us if we tarry. Here, place your hands beneath the spout. We can do nothing about your clothes until they are cleaned, at least." She spoke as she worked, her tiny body so much stronger than it looked. Xanthe soon learned that Jayne did everything at double speed. She had so many duties, was supposed to be in so many places at once, her only hope of getting everything done was to work at a run. Xanthe tried to imagine a modern teenager doing all that this scrap of a girl had to do. Tried and failed.

The water was so cold it sent painful shocks up Xanthe's arms as she used it to rub the grit from her hands.

"Your face, too," said Jayne. "Heavens, whatever were you doing to get in such a messy state?"

"I tried to walk back through the stables. I . . . didn't want to be seen by the visitors," she explained, reasoning that servants were accustomed to keeping out of sight.

"Oh, you mean the Applebys?" Jayne could not hide her interest and even blushed prettily.

"They are brothers?"

"Master Samuel and Master Joshua Appleby, yes," she said, a wistful note in her voice. "They are here with their father. Engaged by Master Lovewell to undertake improvements to the house. They construct such fine buildings! The most sought after of master builders in the country, some do say."

Somehow Xanthe thought Jayne's interest in the young men had little to do with their profession. "They were looking at the damage done to the stables. Perhaps they will help with rebuilding those, too," she suggested, handing Xanthe her blackened cap.

Xanthe took it between finger and thumb, horrified at the sight of the wretched thing.

"I do hope so, for then they should be right here outside the kitchens for many weeks to come!" Jayne beamed at the thought.

Xanthe tried a smile. "So which of the brothers do you favor?" she asked.

"I?" She turned even pinker. "'Tis not for the likes of me to think of them so!"

"Maybe not, but, well . . . if you had to say?" She leaned in so that the maid could whisper.

Jayne glanced back at the house with a giggle, then blurted out. "Joshua! Oh! He is a fine young man, do you not think so?"

"I haven't known him long enough to form an opinion."

"But you have eyes to see! His are the very bluest, like the sky at midsummer. And he has the brightest smile, did you not notice?"

"I had other things to think about," she told her, indicating her ruined apron.

Jayne took that from her, too. "I will lend you one of mine. And another cap. We can wash these later, so Mary will have no cause for handing out punishments. You don't wish to go without your supper, do you?"

"She would do that? For a bit of soot?"

Jayne gasped and shook her head. "What manner of household do you come from where maidservants might ruin the clothes they have been given and not feel the weight of their actions? Or were you treated differently because you are a minstrel as well as a servant?" She offered her a clean corner of Xanthe's apron for drying her hands and then took her up to the attic room they were to share. She skipped up the two flights of stairs and was barely out of breath when they reached their humble quarters. Xanthe fell to a bout of coughing, trying to get the last of the smoke from her lungs. She could happily have flopped onto the mattress and slept again, but there was no chance of that. Jayne bundled her into a fresh apron, making her promise to return it in good condition so that she would not get into trouble. She struggled to set another cap upon her head.

"I never did see such curls!" she said. "Mistress Clara will be wanting hers tonged and teased to be just so, mark my words. Makes me pity Mary this once, that she will be the one to have to try to please her. She has not Alice's touch with dressing ladies' hair." At the mention of Alice's name Jayne's natural brightness dimmed.

"You must be worried about her," Xanthe said gently. "You shared a bedchamber and worked together. You were friends, I should imagine?"

"Such a kind, sweet girl," she said, her eyes filling with tears.

"You do not believe her to be guilty of stealing?"

"Never! She was good, and honest, and could not do such a thing! It has all been a terrible misunderstanding."

"But the pieces of silver, the chatelaine attachments . . . they are still missing."

"That is precisely what they are: missing. Not stolen! Yet Mistress Lovewell appears determined to see Alice branded a thief and sent away to some dreadful fate."

Xanthe put a steadying hand on the girl's arm. "We must do what we can to help Alice. The house was searched for the missing items, wasn't it?"

"The master had us turn it upside down! But we found nothing. And since nothing else is missed, and only Alice was permitted in our mistress's chamber . . ." Jayne sniffed loudly, wiping the tears from her eyes with the back of her hand. "And now poor Alice sits in the lockup in Marlborough, alone and terrified, with no one to come to her aid! Mary says she will be soon taken to the inquest in Salisbury and judgment passed before we can do so much as take her food!"

Xanthe took Jayne's hands and squeezed them. "This is not justice, Jayne. And Alice is not without friends. Do not give up hope. We will help her, you and I."

They would have talked further, but Mary's stern voice carried up the stairwell, demanding they return to their duties at once.

As the morning went on, Xanthe did her best to fetch, carry, and clean without revealing her lack of experience, trying all the while to fathom what she must do to prove Alice's innocence. She'd come this far—and it was very far!—but what now? She could not take herself off to town and hire a lawyer to defend the girl. No more could she face Mistress Lovewell and remind her she had no proof and insist she withdraw her accusations. And it was fantasy to think she could reach the lockup and somehow release Alice from what she knew to be a strong and secure building. More and more it seemed to her that the answer lay with finding the missing pieces of the chatelaine. And her best chance of knowing where to look was to talk to Alice. If she had not taken them, she might at least have an idea of who else could have, or where they might be. However tense Xanthe's own situation, however bewildering her tasks and exhausting the work, it was so much worse for Alice. Every time she thought of her locked up in the dark—cold, hungry, scared, and trapped—her chest tightened and she felt panic rising inside her, robbing her of breath. It was as if their connection was strengthened by their shared experience of being incarcerated. Of hearing that door slam shut, the lock turn, and knowing that they were alone and confined. And no amount of weeping or shouting or pleading would change that. The idea of such powerlessness, such helplessness was in itself a terrifying thing. On top of which, the closer Alice's fate came to being sealed, the greater the danger for Flora. Xanthe found that every time she let her thoughts turn to her mother she was consumed by a feeling of desperation. She had come here in order to protect Flora, but she felt so far away from her. Mistress Merton had clearly demonstrated what she was capable of. Would Flora be safe in the house with her? How long would the ghost wait for Xanthe to do what she wanted? Might she not lose patience, or hope, and take her frustration out on Flora? Xanthe's mind was jolted back from such thoughts by Jayne's excited voice.

"Look!" Jayne beckoned to her and pointed out of the kitchen window. "The Applebys!"

Sure enough, the brothers were there, taking measurements of the wreckage of the stables. Their father had joined them and seemed to be directing the work. He looked prosperous but not grand. When Master Lovewell appeared, there was a marked contrast between the two older men. Where the architect wore his clothes with understated elegance, Master Lovewell was all show and bluster, trying much too hard to pass himself off as nobility. He might have been the richer man, but he was a strutting bantam cockerel beside the master builder's subtle but powerful hawk. Xanthe wondered how they were viewed by their own society. Which one was more respected? Did money talk louder than intelligence and refinement in the seventeenth century? Probably. Why was it that the things her own time had in common with this slice of the past were mostly the things everyone would be better off without? Were people only capable of passing on the worst of themselves to future generations?

The cook, known only as Randolph—she never knew if this was his first or second name—paused to look at what had taken the girls' interest.

"Only our master would see fit to employ the most expensive builders twixt here and London to build a house for the horses!" he snorted.

Jayne smiled. "I believe it to be one of the master's better decisions!"

"Ha!" Randolph was clearly enjoying the chance to have a good moan about his boss. Something else that hadn't changed over centuries! "Master Lovewell sees only another opportunity to flaunt his riches. It would not surprise me were he to have marble pillars fitted in the stalls."

"I shouldn't mind if he did," said Jayne, "so long as 'tis the Appleby brothers who must put them there."

The cook shook his head. "They are too grand to heft stone, even if it were marble. No, they will set some lowly mason to the heavy work and return to enlarging the master's house."

At this Jayne sighed. "As if there are not rooms enough for us to be tending."

"Hush now! Jayne, remove your nose from the master's business and return to your own!" Mary had entered the kitchen without being noticed and clapped her hands, sending most of the servants scuttling. "Shame on all of you for your mean words. The master deserves our respect, and he shall have it from you, girl, have I to beat it out of you."

Randolph frowned at her. "Master Lovewell acts only to feather his own nest, to please himself, to raise his own family up. He cares not who he stands upon to get that elevated view. Why you see fit to defend him I cannot fathom. You owe him nothing."

"I owe him my living. The roof above my head. The food in my belly. A place of safety in a time of turbulence. And we'd all do best to remember that," she said pointedly.

Later Xanthe thought about what Mary had said. In the early seventeenth century the laws to protect property were stricter than those protecting a lowly person against misuse, and the penalties harsh. Members of a household, whether lowly kitchen maids or more important staff, they all depended on the good nature and integrity of their masters. To lose your job meant being turned out of your home, too, often with nothing and nowhere else to go. If you had the good fortune to work for someone who treated you well, you could not afford to be choosy about how they wished to spend their money, or whether or not you actually liked them. Was that why no one had felt able to speak up for Alice? They all seemed to respect her, to think well of her, or to be fond of her, but none of them had done anything to keep her from jail. To do so would be to risk too much. They had too little. They knew they stood scant chance of making a difference. It seemed to Xanthe that Alice was not the only one who was trapped. There might not be stone walls and iron bars surrounding Jayne and Randolph and Mary, but they too were imprisoned, in a different way, each held in their place with precious little chance of ever escaping. And entirely at the mercy of those for whom they worked.

Xanthe learned that the main meal was usually eaten in the middle of the day, with a lighter supper taken in the evening. So it came as something of a surprise to see the amount of food they were to take up to the family. There were three "courses," which were actually served at the same time, this not being a formal occasion. The first was a side of salmon with whole pike beside it, then a venison stew served up with an enormous cob of fresh bread, followed by a truckle of hard cheese and a dish of preserved strawberries and quinces. Nobody drank water if they could possibly avoid it, so instead jugs of weak beer were fetched, together with a carafe of watered-down red wine that smelled terrible.

By now Xanthe herself had a terrible thirst, and when she asked Jayne if she could have some water the maid shrieked with laughter. She had to quickly explain it was to keep her singing voice sweet. At that Jayne took her a bit more seriously and offered her a ladle of frothy milk. Her stomach clenched at the warm, pungent drink, but she was able to keep it down. She needed something and could not imagine only drinking alcohol. She would also have to choose what she ate with care, as much of the food was unfamiliar to her. She had already had to use the "necessary house" at the far end of the kitchen garden and had no desire to be making frequent dashes there because of an upset stomach.

Even though they were not entertaining guests, the Lovewells still took their meals, light or otherwise, in the Great Hall. Xanthe followed Randolph up the steps from the kitchen, along the passageway, negotiating several heavy doors, all the while carrying a weighty tray of food. She was only entrusted with the bread, she noticed, with Randolph taking the meat, Mary the fish, and a boy she did not know hurrying behind with the drinks. Jayne and Mary had already set out the table, so this was the first time Xanthe had been in the main room of the house. It was double height, the ceiling vaulted into the rafters of the house, and had a minstrel's gallery at one end. There was an enormous fireplace set in one wall, big enough to get half a tree in at a time, with a mighty stone lintel above it. Everything about the room was solid, sturdy, on a grand scale, giving the impression not just of wealth but of permanence.

The Lovewells might be newly raised up in status but they were here to stay. They would make their family important, respected, influential, and a permanent fixture in society. On one side of the great hearth a floor-to-ceiling window was set in a generous bay, complete with beautiful glass that was of the quality that did not distort anything seen through it. Each pane was encased in finely worked lead, with the family crest set at the center of the window. Two of the other walls, the one opposite the fire and the one at the top end, were hung with richly colored tapestries, chosen for warmth and decoration, no doubt, but also for the symbolism in the scenes they depicted. Xanthe was too busy trying not to trip or drop anything to get a proper look at the one to her right as she marched past, but she could see a religious theme, merged with scenes of nature and abundance. Across the far wall the main table was placed, slightly raised, lifting the family quite literally above everyone else.

"Ah!" exclaimed Master Lovewell when he saw Xanthe. "Here is our songbird. Fully restored to good health, I trust?"

Jayne gave her a shove forward so that she was standing in front of the top table, opposite the master of the house.

"Yes, thank you, sir," she said, trying to sound appropriately humble and taking care to lower her eyes when she spoke to her employer, as she had seen the other servants do.

"Excellent."

"Oh, Father," said Clara, struggling to restrain the wriggling spaniel on her lap, "let us hear her sing!"

Mistress Lovewell gave a disapproving look. "There is surely no cause for celebration and merrymaking, Clara. Our stables are in ruins, we shall have to find a deal of money to repair them, and we were spared loss of life only by God's grace."

However pious Mistress Lovewell tried to sound Xanthe could not help noticing that she mentioned the financial cost of the fire before worrying about anyone being hurt. Perhaps she would have taken a different view had the house itself been ablaze.

"But, Mother, do you not wish to assure yourself of the quality of her voice? We should not risk embarrassment, after all. Let us be certain of her talent before setting her before any guests." Xanthe was astonished to see Clara give her a sneaky wink. It seemed the young lady was smarter than Xanthe had first thought, and more than capable of manipulating both her parents.

Her father saw the sense in what she said and, first taking a deep swig of his wine from a silver goblet, smiled warmly. "Well, child, are you recovered sufficiently to bestow the gift of your voice upon us?"

This was an important moment. Xanthe felt her mouth dry at the thought of what was at stake. If her singing failed to please them it was doubtful they would permit her to stay. She took a steadying breath or two, squared her shoulders, readied herself to give a performance that would secure her position in the household, and opened her mouth to sing.

It was then that she saw it.

The tapestry behind the top table, the one now directly in

her line of vision just beyond the family who were looking at her so expectantly, was a colorful scene of biblical characters, probably taken from one of the famous parables. It was not the main picture that caught her eye, though, but the broad, intricately decorated border that made her gasp. The border was worked with a tangle of woodland plants, weaving and twining together. There was a profusion of brambles with cruel thorns and glossy-leaved vines, and among the dense foliage and choking tendrils were tiny birds. Birds that looked to be singing, even though it was dark as night. Xanthe knew with absolute certainty that this was what the chatelaine had shown her. The very first glimpse she had had of Alice's story was not, in fact, of a nearby patch of woodland; it was right here, inside the Great Hall of the big house. It was that very tapestry.

"Well?" Mistress Lovewell said, her stern tone jolting Xanthe from her thoughts. "Have you voice or not?"

She quickly pulled herself together. Though her heart was racing at this new discovery, and her mind frantically trying to figure out how it might be of help, she forced herself to think only of her singing, and found it helped to imagine she was singing for her mother. To recall how Flora's face lit up when she listened to her daughter. She chose "The Willow Song," reasoning that it was very popular, and had nothing bawdy about it that might offend her new employers.

> The fresh streams ran by her, and murmur'd her moans
> Sing willow, willow, willow
> Her salt tears fell from her and soft'ned the stones.
>
> Let nobody blame him, his scorn I approve
> Sing willow, willow, willow
> He was born to be fair, I to die for his love. . . .

She had begun a little hesitantly but slowly grew in confidence, encouraged by the looks on the faces of her small but important audience. When she had finished Clara let go of Pepito to clap enthusiastically.

"Oh, that was a delight! You must sing for me on my birthday, don't you think so, Mother?"

And so it was agreed. Xanthe had passed the test. She would be required to sing for Clara's guests when they came to celebrate her birthday in three days' time. Xanthe left the Great Hall feeling both relieved and confused. Her place at Great Chalfield was secure, at least for the moment, but she would soon have to prove herself all over again by singing in front of a much larger audience. More importantly, another piece of Alice's mystery had revealed itself to her. After three more hours of hard work Xanthe was at last allowed to go to her bed, where she turned over and over in her mind what the true significance of the tapestry might be.

15

HOWEVER TIRED SHE WAS, XANTHE COULD NOT AFFORD TO LET HERSELF fall asleep. Her bruises were aching less, but the burn on her leg still smarted, which in any case did a fair job of preventing her from sleeping properly. She dozed fitfully, listening to Jayne's soft snoring, waiting until the house was quiet and she was as sure as she could be that everyone else was sleeping soundly. Wearing her borrowed nightdress, she took her flashlight from its hiding place and crept out of the little garret room, holding her breath as she tiptoed past Mary in the next room, and padded down the stairs. The house itself felt like it was sleeping. It was in total darkness, with the cloudy night merely a suggestion of a lighter black through those windows that had no shutters. There was a gusty October wind blowing outside, and the house creaked and groaned as it was buffeted, like a galleon tossed on a stormy sea. As Xanthe descended to the ground floor, the faint smell of dampness and of lavender unsuccessfully masking that of chamber pots was replaced by the scent of woodsmoke and extinguished candles. The smooth floorboards felt warm beneath her feet, but the stone flags of the Great Hall were cold enough to make her gasp. Every door wanted to scrape the floor as she opened it, and every hinge seemed determined to make a noise. She crept into the cavernous space of the hall, which seemed even larger in the dark, its ceiling invisible in the blackness above. From the tapestries, faces of the saints and the saved peered down at her as they were picked out by the narrow beam of her flashlight. With the fire no more than ash, the temperature in the room had dropped sharply, making her wish she had paused to put something on top of her shabby linen nightdress.

She stopped at the point in front of the top table where she had sung earlier and directed the flashlight upward and forward. Spotlighted by its harsh beam, the songbirds seemed almost luminous against the dark background of the forest where they had been placed. Xanthe searched for a meaning, a significance beyond the symbolism of purity and innocence and nature they might have been originally used for. What had they to do with Alice? What had they to do with the chatelaine? What had they to do with Xanthe? Nothing suggested an obvious connection. She walked around the table, slipping behind the heavy wooden chairs so that she might touch the tapestry. Running her hands over its densely stitched and woven surface she could trace the outlines of the birds with her fingers. They had been exquisitely worked, the tiny stitches carefully re-creating the appearance of feathers.

"What is it?" she whispered. "What secret are you hiding?"

Somewhere in the passageway a door slammed, startling her so much that she dropped her flashlight. She fell to her knees and just managed to take hold of it as it started to roll between the chair legs and under the table. She remained crouched, her heartbeat thudding in her ears, waiting, listening. No one came. It was only the wind keeping her company. She stood up again and went back to studying the wall hanging. Following the border, she reached the corner, which was briefly disturbed by a forceful draft coming from the window. Carefully, she turned up the heavy edge, wondering if there might be a name or a signature of some sort on the back. Nothing. Just as she was beginning to think the whole thing was a dead end, she noticed some loose stitches. It seemed odd, such carelessness in a work of such precision and fine craftsmanship. Looking closer she found that there was a wayward thread coming from the turned-up hem of the hanging. It struck her then that it had not worn loose, nor come free just through wear and tear, nor from being moved, perhaps. No, the way the long thread was out of its keeping stitches, the way the whole hem appeared poorly secured and in danger of dropping, all seemed to point to it having been deliberately undone. With another quick glance toward the door to make certain she was not about to be discovered, Xanthe took hold of the flashlight between her teeth so that she had both hands free. She unfurled the rolled hem as gently as she could, knowing that she would have to tuck it back up again and secure it without the help of a needle. At first she thought she was going to draw another blank, but then her fingers touched something hard, something almost sharp, hidden in the folds of fabric. She probed cautiously and took hold of what was inside. Her heart sank as she realized that it was not the missing needle case and scissors. The shape and texture of what she could feel was all wrong for that. She pulled out the hidden item and snatched her flashlight from her mouth, shining it on the object in her palm.

Beads. Silver chain.

A crucifix.

It was a rosary! The beads gleamed dark red and were quite possibly semiprecious stones, probably garnets. Similar stones were set into the little silver cross at the end of the chain, too. No doubt about it, it was a rosary used for counting prayers. Catholic prayers. In a steadfastly Protestant household. At a time when following the wrong religion could get you into all manner of trouble. She racked her brains for remnants of history lessons, attempting to recall what the penalties for practicing Catholicism were in the reign of King James I. Most of her knowledge of the past came from the antiques she had grown up surrounded by, along with the ones she had studied, bought, and sold over the years. She was unclear as to the details, but the Stuarts had been Protestants, and as far as she could remember, Catholics did not have a good time of it when James was on the throne. Was the possession of a rosary enough to get you hanged? It seemed possible. She recalled what Willis had told her about Alice's family all being executed as traitors. Was this thing Xanthe now held in her hand all it took to get a person tried for treason? Had it been Alice's? Perhaps a final legacy from her mother, one that she could not bear to part with, but that just might get her hanged? Xanthe tucked it back into the hem of the tapestry. It was a good hiding place, and there was nothing to be gained by moving it. The consequences of it being found among her own possessions did not bear thinking about.

As silently as she was able, she hurried back out of the Great Hall, up the stairs, past the large, slumbering shape of Mary, and back into her own chilly bed. She huddled beneath the rough blankets, shivering, rubbing her arms in an attempt to warm them. So, it seemed Alice was a Catholic after all, and she had continued to hold to the faith, knowing the risks. Now Xanthe understood why she might have taken the needles and scissors. Not to sell, but to use. To stitch and unstitch her precious heirloom, the one connection she had left to her family and her faith, into that clever little hiding place. She thought about the loose thread. Had Alice been disturbed one day putting the thing back? That could explain the undone stitches. It might also explain why she had not had the chance to return the silver pieces to her mistress's bedchamber. Which meant she had to have hidden them somewhere else.

But where?

The next morning, as a gray dawn struggled to lift the gloom of their bedchamber, Jayne shook Xanthe awake.

"Make haste, sleepyhead," she said.

Xanthe rubbed her eyes. "Surely it's still nighttime?"

Jayne laughed. "'Tis near six o'clock! Mary will be fit to spit if she must call for us."

Xanthe dragged herself out of bed. The shock of the cold air in the room was effective at waking her up. She did not like to think about how freezing it might be in the winter. As quickly as she could she wriggled into her unfamiliar clothes.

Jayne picked up her roommate's boots, staring at them in horror.

"I never did see what a minstrel wore on her feet before. Such ugly things. I imagined players to have fancy clothes, finery sometimes, to be all color and shimmer and show. I could not have conjured in my mind . . . these!"

Xanthe took them from her. "We do a lot of walking," she said flatly. "Getting from place to place."

"When the master and mistress were entertaining here in the summer there were minstrels of all sorts," Jayne said. "Players of lutes and pipes and drums, singers, and dancers with bells and ribbons. The master let all the servants come up to the Great Hall to watch the dancing. Oh, how I should love to have danced with Joshua Appleby! So light on his feet, and yet such strong arms. Which were, alas, for the most part about the waist of Mistress Clara," she added with a look of exasperation. "She is not the maid for him. That's plain for a fool to see."

"Oh? You know someone better?" Xanthe teased.

Jayne blushed again and then looked a little sad. "Master Joshua cannot be seen giving his attention to a servant."

Xanthe studied her face. The girl's choice of words suggested that it would be fine for a well-to-do young gentleman to flirt with a girl of thirteen, servant or not, so long as it was done in secret. "Have you ever . . . talked with Master Joshua?" Xanthe asked.

"Me? Oh no! Though he did once smile at me."

"Really?"

"Yes! I had to fetch his cape from the parlor where it had been cleaned for him. They arrived one day in such weather as you never did see, all mud-splattered, horses and men, and we set to cleaning their outer garments while they went about their work, and later, when I took him his cape all clean and dry, he thanked me so politely, like I was a proper lady, and he did smile at me!" She clasped her hands to her chest at the memory of it.

"Must be quite something, that smile of his." Xanthe thought how hard it must have been to live and work as a servant, never mind the added angst of impossible teenage crushes. It was a good thing the Applebys seemed to be respectable men. She wondered how often servant girls were taken advantage of and then cast aside. Jayne was sufficiently infatuated, naive, and pretty to be at risk. At least she had a dragon in the shape of Mary to protect her virtue. Xanthe let her help force her hair under the starched white cap, a garment that struck her as the manner of headgear that would make anyone, however pretty, instantly unattractive. Perhaps that was the reason behind their design!

"Jayne, how well did you know Alice?" she asked as casually as she could.

"'Tis as I told you, we worked together, we shared a room. She is a good person."

Xanthe hesitated only a moment before uttering the words she knew would shock the girl. "And a Catholic?"

Jayne's expression was that of a person who had just received a slap.

"What makes you ask such a thing?"

"I want to help her. I'm trying to understand—"

"No good comes of scratching at old wounds," she interrupted, no longer meeting Xanthe's eye. All the easy chat was gone in an instant and replaced with something else. Fear. "Come," she said, holding open the door. "We shall be missed and begin the day flinching from the sharp edge of Mary's tongue."

Clearly the conversation was at an end. Xanthe followed the girl out of the room and Jayne did not say another word all the way to the kitchen. As they went about their work that morning two things went round and round in her mind. The first was that she absolutely had to find a way to talk to Alice. She had no idea how, but she would have to make it happen somehow. The second thing that kept nagging at her was something that simply did not fit. If Alice was a Catholic and continued to practice her faith, she was putting anyone connected with her in danger, too. If her whole family were executed as traitors, she would already be under constant suspicion herself. Why then, would the Lovewells have taken her in? They were Protestant, and they were clearly a family determined to claw their way up the social order, to establish themselves as important, which had to mean gaining the king's favor. To do that they needed to be of spotless reputation, so why on earth would they give house space to the daughter of convicted traitors and known Catholics? It did not make sense.

As if the kitchens were not already a place of constant activity and hurrying to keep up, the approach of Clara's birthday celebrations increased the pressure on the staff noticeably. More and more food was brought in, all of it carried by wet and be-draggled servants, as the weather outside had worsened to heavy rain as well as strong winds. Randolph went into a frenzy of cooking pies and puddings, all the silver and pewter had to be cleaned, and the workload seemed to double. On top of all this, there were workmen rebuilding the stables who had to be fed, and the Applebys in the house, having resumed their work on the improvements and extensions, who also needed to be given meals.

It was nearly noon when Mary called Xanthe over and handed her a tray of beer, bread, and cold meats.

"Take this up to the Great Hall," she said. "Master Appleby and his sons are doing their work in there this day, so Mistress Lovewell has chosen to take her food in her sitting room with Clara. 'Tis a sensible woman who leaves the men to their business. Now, you have not to serve them, simply place the tray where they may take what they wish. Wait and ask if there is anything more they require, then return here without delay." She stressed the last two words to make the point she had not yet forgiven or forgotten Xanthe's trip to the stables the day before. Xanthe wondered why she did not choose someone else for the task, and as if reading her mind, Mary added, "I would send one of the boys, but they have all been called upon to assist with the stables. And as for Jayne . . ." She tutted at the sight of the girl. Not much got past Mary, it seemed, and she wasn't about to give the youngster the chance to make a fool of herself. "Hasten!" she said, clapping her hands.

The tray was so wide Xanthe had to turn sideways to get through the doors, and so heavy she doubted she would be able to go all the way to the Great Hall without setting it down at least briefly. But there was nowhere suitable, so she struggled on, clumsily maneuvering herself through the last heavy door backward, to arrive, puffing, in front of Samuel Appleby. She had expected to find him with his brother and father, as well as Master Lovewell, so she was surprised to discover him alone. He was dressed in dark clothes to match his own looks, with his black hair loose to his shoulders. His long jacket was deepest plum velvet and the doublet over it—a sleeveless jacket—was black with black and silver braid stitched onto it and looked very different from the starched white collar and cuffs that many wore. It was as if he wanted to be absorbed into the shadows rather than be seen. He wore long black leather boots which came over his knees, and black hose. He was bent over some plans which were spread out on the high table, his attention entirely taken up with whatever they showed. Xanthe looked around for somewhere to set down the tray, but he was taking up the whole table. She could hardly put the thing on the floor, but her shoulders and arms were burning from the weight of the thing, and she was in danger of dropping it if she did not do something quickly.

She tried noisily clearing her throat, but the man was oblivious to her existence.

"Excuse me, sir," she said at last, "might I be permitted to put this down, somewhere?"

He answered with a grunt, something that could have been a nod, and a wave of a hand, without for one second taking his eyes off his precious plans.

She tried again. "Your refreshments, sir, where would you like them?"

He turned to look at her then, his expression somewhere between distracted and annoyed. It strangely suited him. Xanthe blamed her fortune for getting the awkward brother to deal with.

"Where shall I put it?" she asked again, this time a little desperately.

"I care not. Where you will."

Her arms had begun to shake with the effort, and she was fast losing patience. "The table?" she suggested, nodding in the direction of the plans.

"There is no room here," he replied, as if she had failed to notice, and as if he could not possibly do anything about it.

Fine, she thought, two could play at that game. On the point of dropping the tray, she took a step forward and plonked it down on the table, on top of a section of the drawings.

Samuel gave a shout of horror, leaping over to snatch up the tray again.

"Does Master Lovewell now invite imbeciles into his house?" he demanded, turning circles to find somewhere else to put the tray.

Xanthe fought her natural response to defend herself. *Keep meek, think humble*, she told herself, *you are a servant.*

"Begging your pardon, sir, but I feared I might drop—"

"Do you not know your duties?" He strode off to a high sideboard on the far side of the hall and slammed the tray down with such force that every plate jumped and rattled and beer slopped from the jug, spilling all over the bread.

Xanthe was about to apologize when she saw what it was he had been poring over. The plans were drawings of an intricately carved screen, beautifully drawn, meticulous measurements and specifications marked with infinite care. They were a work of art in themselves, a perfect example of expert draftsmanship, showing hours of loving work, and the object they described was breathtaking. She recognized it at once. She had seen the real thing, rendered in gleaming mahogany, ten feet tall and broad enough to bisect another great hall, set in place in one of the grandest houses in the north of England. Drillington Hall was famous for the number of craftsmen employed over decades to work on its interior, and there was no mistaking this highly decorative screen.

"Oh, this is exactly how it looks! Are these the original drawings?" The words were out of her mouth before she could stop them. She held her breath, terrified she had just given herself away. She frantically tried to remember when the screen at Drillington had been installed. If it was later than 1605 then she had just admitted to knowing about something that did not yet exist.

Now she had Samuel Appleby's full attention.

"You know the Drillington screen?"

"Well, I . . ."

"You have seen it?" He marched back to stand close to her. "Truly, you have seen it for yourself?" In his face she saw real passion for the thing. This was a man who understood matchless craftsmanship, who loved and appreciated the beauty of an object such as this one.

Xanthe reasoned that if he was asking about it, it must at least exist. Relieved, she nodded. "Yes. I have."

"But your words, your demeanor, are not of the north. How came you to be in the Earl of Yorkshire's home?"

"I am a minstrel," she explained. "As musicians, we travel a great deal, visit many great houses." She was not lying about having been to the place, but by the time she had got there it was in the care of the National Trust, you had to buy a ticket to get in, and the screen he was talking about was more than three hundred and fifty years old.

"And you recognized it from these drawings?" He brushed past her and smoothed the plans carefully, running his hands over the area where she had put the tray, almost reverently brushing away the tiniest specs of dust. Xanthe noticed that he smelled of bergamot and sawdust and ink.

"I did. They are so well done," she said, turning to study them again. She remembered then that she had once watched a BBC documentary on the history of the Earl of Yorkshire's house. The screen had been featured in that, an iconic and important piece. This was hardly something she could share with Samuel, though! She glanced up at him and saw how absorbed he instantly was in his project. "Did you draft them?" she asked.

"I did, and I fear they are but a shadow of those for the original screen." He waved a hand at them, shaking his head. "I have endeavored to re-create what is at Drillington, but my information comes from the reports of others, and from rough sketches only. Having not seen the screen myself—"

"You haven't visited the Hall? Surely, if you want to make something similar—"

"Not similar, the same!" He gave a dry laugh. "Master Lovewell is a man of borrowed taste, but it is nonetheless good taste for that. He wishes to have an exact copy in his own home. I will do my utmost, but I fear I cannot reproduce the detail, the finesse of the one at Drillington, my information being so scant."

"Can you not take a few days, I mean, some time?" She tried not to sound ignorant of how long the journey would take, but really she had not a clue, never having ridden from Wiltshire to Yorkshire. "Surely, it would be worth the time?"

He nodded at this. "Indeed it would. Alas, a person such as Master Lovewell is determined to make his ascent through the ranks of society without being seen to try. Commissioning the screen is one thing, openly owning to having your craftsman copy it is quite another."

"Ah," she said.

He looked at her then, more closely. "Ah, indeed." He seemed to regard her differently, as if before she had been merely some

flibbertigibbet maidservant, given to blundering around in un-
safe buildings or narrowly avoiding damaging his work, but now,
now that he knew that she knew something important, something that mattered to him, well, perhaps she was a proper person after all. "Would you look again," he asked, "as closely as
you are able, and tell me if any irregularities strike you?"

"Irregularities?"

"Deviations from the original. Departures from what you recall of the Earl's screen."

She leaned over the table and scrutinized the plans. They
were incredibly detailed. He must have had such patience, such
skill to produce them, particularly if he'd never actually seen
the thing. She tried to translate the lines and measurements
into the solid object of her memory. It had been tall, set in a
double-height room just as the one they were standing in, used
as a sort of partition at one end, beneath the minstrels' gallery.
It was intricately carved with leaves and scrolls, and the amount
of wood cut away must have been almost impossibly difficult to
carve without rendering the whole thing unstable. As far as she
could see, the plans would produce something similar, but there
were differences.

"The drawings are wonderful, but . . ."

"But? You detect imperfections?"

"Well, not imperfections, as such, just small things that aren't
exactly the same."

"Where? Show me. In what way does my design differ?"

She pointed to the doorway set into the screen. "Here, for
example. This was definitely narrower."

"You are certain?"

She remembered stepping through the door of the screen and
having to wait while a queue of people went in front of her, one
by one. It would not have been possible for them to have passed

through it side by side. "Yes," she told him simply. "I'm certain. A shoulders' width, no more."

He snatched up a quill and a sheet of paper, grabbed a pot of ink and led her to the window. "Come, see here," he instructed, setting the page down on the windowsill so that the sharp autumn light fell upon it. "You say narrower, so the arch above it must have been steeper, like so?" He sketched quickly. "Or like so?" He did another sketch.

"Well . . ."

"Have a care," he warned. "You must be certain."

"I am as certain as I can be, doing it all from memory," she reminded him, beginning to feel a little hectored. He looked at her, holding her slightly grumpy gaze, his face so full of hope, his dark eyes shining with the joy of creating something, with the love of his work. It was a hard face to say no to. "It is like the second one," she pointed at his sketch. "Exactly like that."

"I see. Yes, that would be more pleasing to the eye, though harder to construct, stability already being a matter of difficulty. . . . In what other ways are my drawings inaccurate? What else can you detect that does not fit?"

"Well—"

At that moment the door opened and Master Lovewell came in, all smiles and good humor.

"Good morning to you, Master Samuel, I trust you are being well cared for. Have you all that you need? We must not have our genius going hungry. Surely no person ever heard the whisper of his muse above the growl of their own empty belly, don't you think?"

"Thank you, I am well supplied."

"But you have not eaten! This will not do. Come, let us dine together. Girl . . . your name again?"

"Xanthe, Master Lovewell."

"Ah yes, very curious. You may go now. Tell Mary to send up some of her venison pie. We must have meat to fuel our endeavors, must we not, Master Samuel?"

She turned to go, but as she did so Samuel put his hand on her arm. It was a fleeting gesture, a reaction to the thought of such a valuable resource leaving him, no doubt. Still the contact was startling, his touch firm, and the look he gave her suggested it surprised him, too.

She left the room and went in search of Mary to relay the master's request for pie. She found her at the door of the kitchen talking to Willis. They did not notice her at first, and she was able to overhear their conversation.

"I am to go to Marlborough this afternoon," Willis said. "I must visit the tannery and see the costermonger. The fire has left us short a number of pieces of harness that will have to be repaired or replaced."

"Come to me before you leave," Mary told him. "I will have a basket ready for you to take to Alice."

"She may be there a while yet. Best send all provisions you can."

"All I can without the mistress noticing."

"'Tis a shame the girl is come to this. I will not believe her to be a thief."

"It is not for us to judge. But we may at least provide her with sustenance. She should not suffer hunger on top of all else."

"Mistress Lovewell must know her to be innocent. Surely she will retract her accusations."

Mary gave a shrug. "On the matter of Alice, the mistress is conflicted, Willis, we both know this."

At last Xanthe saw a chance to talk to Alice! A move closer to securing Flora's safety and being able to return home. Xanthe stepped forward, making Mary start and Willis frown.

"Please, might I be allowed to accompany Mr. Willis? I would very much like to take the food to Alice."

"The habit of eavesdropping is a dangerous one, maid," Mary warned. "Do you not know that?"

"Forgive me, but I couldn't help overhearing. Please let me accompany Mr. Willis. He will not have time to sit with her, but I could. It would surely be a kindness for Alice to have someone to talk to while he goes about his errands. At least for that short time, she would not have to be alone."

Willis shook his head. "I doubt they will let you inside the jail. You would have to content yourself with speaking through the grille."

"It would be better than nothing."

Mary put her hands on her hips and drew herself up. She was a strong, tall woman, her body toned from years of hard work and fortunate good health. "You have duties of your own. Who will do your share of work if you are gone half the day? We are already in disarray with the preparations for Mistress Clara's birthday celebrations."

"I will make it up to you, I promise. I'll work late. Whatever you want. Only let me go, let me see her."

"Why do you care so much?" Mary asked. "What is she to you?"

What answer could Xanthe give to that? She was not a relative or someone Alice was even known to have met. What answer, save the truth?

"She is, I believe, a young girl wrongly accused, shut away from the sun, alone and afraid, awaiting an uncertain fate. She needs the hand of friendship extended. Are we not all of us, at some time or another, dependent on the kindness of others? Would we not wish someone to act selflessly for our sake?"

Mary pursed her lips and then gave an impatient sigh. "Very

well, you may accompany Willis. But see to it your tasks are finished this night. There will be no rest for you with things left undone."

"Of course. I promise."

"Come," she said, walking toward the pantry. "We will find what will not be missed."

"Oh," Xanthe said, suddenly remembering her instructions, "Master Lovewell has asked for venison pie."

"Has he indeed?" Mary picked up the plump pastry case, but instead of setting it on a platter for her master she wrapped it in cloth, tied it tightly, and slipped it into a deep wicker basket. "'Tis a shame, then, that there is none left," she said, shoving the basket into Xanthe's arms and fetching apples and cheese and bread to go with it. When the basket was brimming she looked at her sternly. "Tell no one else what you have been given or for whom it is meant. And for pity's sake take off that apron before you leave! Care you nothing for the reputation of this household?"

16

BY THE TIME XANTHE CLIMBED ABOARD THE CART, TAKING HER PLACE NEXT to Willis on the front seat, the rain had stopped. There was still a cold wind blowing, and she was thankful for the thick woolen cape Jayne had loaned her. One look at Xanthe, with her own picnic rug wrapped around her shoulders, had reduced the kitchen maid to helpless laughter. Jayne had been certain Mary would change her mind about letting Xanthe go if she was to be seen looking such a sight, so she offered her own cloak. In her pocket Xanthe had some of the coins she had brought with her from Mr. Morris's collection. At least Alice might be able to use them to pay for more food or bribe someone to help her, if only in a small way. In the back of the cart, beneath some burlap flour sacks, were the charred remnants of a ruined harness and tack. Even days later and in the open air it was still possible to smell the fire on them. No one had yet found the cause of the blaze, but this did not seem to worry them greatly. Perhaps such fires were commonplace, and people were only relieved they had not lost any of the horses, or servants. Or perhaps Willis had his own suspicions about Peter's fear of the dark and carelessness with candles and chose to keep them to himself.

There was a single brown mare pulling the cart. No fancy

carriage for this journey, but Xanthe did not care. Here at last was the chance she had been hoping for. She would be able to reassure Alice that she was not alone, and to ask her where she had hidden the chatelaine pieces. She could return them to Mistress Lovewell's room, and the charges against Alice would have to be dropped. Her main challenge was going to be getting the poor girl to trust this odd-looking stranger who had suddenly popped into her life. Would she have seen her in a dream, she wondered, in the same way Xanthe had seen her? Had the chatelaine worked its magic for both of them? It would make her task easier if the girl recognized her, though it might terrify her. This was an age of superstition and belief in witchcraft—she might be horrified to see someone from one of her own visions standing in front of her.

The countryside on the way to Marlborough was remarkably similar to how it was in the modern day. Much of the county was given over to arable farming rather than livestock, so that it remained largely unfenced or enclosed in any way in the twenty-first century. Crops did not need walls and hedges to keep them in, after all. The main difference was the road. The persistent rain had turned the muddy track into a rutted mess of soupy soil and sharp stones, so that the horse had to move at a frustratingly slow, plodding trot, and the cart lurched and bounced, demonstrating with every turn of its wheels that suspension was not fitted on such lowly conveyances.

The journey took a full, tortuous hour, making Xanthe think wistfully of the way her beloved black cab had beetled along the same road. Had it only been a matter of days since she bought the chatelaine at the auction? It felt as if she had done so in another life. The wind was still doing its best to dislodge her hair from its cap and pins, as the cart finally crested the hill that led down into the town. The sight of the town took her breath away.

She had not felt the distance between the date she was at and her own time as keenly as she did at that moment. The town was so small! Most of the buildings she knew were not yet there. It was little more than a village, by modern standards. There was a church at either end of the broad high street, and she recognized the grand merchant's house, the town hall, and the pub. Her heart lurched at the familiar sight of the low-beamed inn. Its sign declared it to be The Three Quills, not The Feathers. One day she would be sure to tell Harley about that. The main street was almost as muddy as the road, and the bad weather seemed to be keeping most people indoors.

Suddenly, without her being in any way prepared for it, there was the jail. It looked even smaller than she remembered, set as it was partially into a high wall that ran along the north of the town. What struck her most, though, was what was *not* there. No shop. No home. Flora's precious antique shop did not yet exist. She felt her heart constrict at the thought. Somehow she must have held the idea of her mother being just down the road all the time she was at Great Chalfield. Now she had to face the fact that they were separated not by a few miles of rough track and rolling barley fields but by yawning centuries. She had to fight the urge to take hold of her gold locket. She longed to feel connected to her mother again, but she dared not risk slipping back to her own time. She was so close to Alice now. So close, she hoped, to finding a way to save her. She could not take the risk of disappearing, for even if she found her way back again, how would she ever explain that to Willis? She would never be allowed to set foot anywhere near the Lovewell household and would surely be branded a witch.

They drew to a halt beside the swath of green that led across to the jail. Despite being set in the wall, it looked so isolated, so lonely, as if the point was being made that whoever was in it was no longer part of the community. Their actions had put them beyond reach. There was no sense of innocent until proven guilty, and she doubted many people who were sent to the jail escaped a conviction of some sort. Willis nodded toward it.

"Get yourself over there. I'll inform the constable you've brought provisions for the maid."

Xanthe climbed down, her boots sinking into the wet mud of the street. She clutched the basket to her and leaned against the wind, making unsteady progress across the rough grass to the jail. It was strange seeing it in its original state. The circular building was built as part of the long wall that ran off toward the older houses, forming a protective boundary for the little town. The stone tiles of the roof were new and free from moss. The walls looked horribly solid, and the only openings were the tiny air vent at the top of the stonework and the door itself, which was wooden and studded with iron bolt heads and hinges. Set into this was an opening too small to really be called a window. It was about twelve inches square, near the top of the door, without glass, but with thick metal bars.

Xanthe was about to call through the grille when something made her stop. She had the sensation of being watched. More than that, of being scrutinized. She turned and saw, standing on the far side of the green, a tall figure, his wide-brimmed hat pulled low, long blond hair caught up by the wet wind. She shuddered, uncertain as to why this stranger should so unsettle her. She was accustomed by now to feeling out of place and being on her guard, yet something about this man frightened her. She turned her attention back to the blind house. Back to Alice. She leaned against the door, calling through the bars at the tiny opening.

"Alice? Alice, can you hear me?" Her voice was whipped away by the wind. "Alice?"

"Who is it? Who's there?" came the faint reply.

"My name is Xanthe Westlake. I have been sent from Great Chalfield."

"I do not know you. Who was it sent you?"

"Mary. I have food for you. Willis brought me."

She heard a movement inside the jail. It occurred to her then that maybe those tiny structures were called blind houses not because they had no windows—or eyes—for people to see out, but because the interiors must have been so dark the people inside might have thought they had gone blind.

She felt the door shudder slightly as Alice stumbled against it. At least, she assumed it was Alice. For the first time she contemplated the thought that the girl might not be alone in there. Which would be worse, she wondered, to be shut up on your own, or with some drunk or possibly violent criminal?

"Alice, are you . . . unharmed?" Xanthe asked.

"I am quite well," she said with admirable grit. "But a little hungry."

Xanthe looked at the narrow gaps between the bars. It would be almost impossible to pass the food through. "Willis has gone to tell the constable I am here," she explained. "As soon as he comes I will give you the basket. There is fresh bread and cheese, and even venison pie."

She heard a weak laugh. "Master Lovewell would not willingly give up such a favorite, I think."

"Well, Mary didn't think it necessary to bother him with the details of your basket," she said.

"She must not take risks on my account. No one should."

"You have friends, Alice. Do not give up hope. You are not forgotten." Xanthe glanced over her shoulder, in the direction of the buildings in the high street. She could see Willis's cart outside the costermongers, the horse dozing at the rail, its ears turned against the wet weather, but there was no sign yet of any constable. The wind whined around the jail, and at that moment it seemed a heartbreakingly bleak and cruel place to keep a person. "Alice, I want to help you. I don't believe you are a thief. Let me prove to Mistress Lovewell that you are not," she said.

"Who are you that you would wish to help me?"

"I am a minstrel, only recently come to the area. I heard of your plight," she told her, choosing her words with painful care, trying to make them sound less modern and at the same time sincere, while not actually being able to tell her the truth. "I . . . I know what it is to suffer an injustice. I will do all I can to help you gain your freedom."

"You think I did not take the silver pieces from the chatelaine?" she asked.

Xanthe took a deep breath. There wasn't time to tiptoe around the matter. The constable could appear at any minute, and this might be the only opportunity she got to talk to Alice alone.

"I think that you did take them, Alice."

She didn't respond to this, though Xanthe thought she heard her gasp.

"I think you took them for an innocent reason; to use them, but not to steal them and sell them. You planned to return them before they were missed, but something prevented you from doing that. And when the mistress discovered they were gone the household fell into uproar, and it was too late."

There was a moment's tense silence and then Alice asked, "For what purpose would I have taken them?"

"You needed them to sew up the hem of the tapestry, Alice. I found the rosary."

This caused her to cry out. "Leave me be! You cannot help me."

"I can. All I have to do is put the silver pieces back. No one need ever know why you took them. I have told no one about the rosary, I promise you."

"I don't know who you are! I know of no such rosary!" she insisted, her voice growing hoarse with fear.

"I know it's hard for you to trust a stranger, Alice, but believe me, I can help you."

"I know of no rosary, I tell you!"

"You must realize how serious your situation is."

"You think I do not?"

"Those pieces, the needle case and scissors, they were very valuable. The law regarding such thefts is harsh, cruel even. The very best you can hope for if you are convicted of stealing them is transportation. You could hang, Alice. I'm sorry, but that's the truth of it."

"It is a truth that haunts my every moment, waking or sleeping, here in this place of darkness and despair! It is a fate I am resigned to."

"But you don't have to be!" Xanthe grabbed hold of the iron bars of the grille, pulling herself up, trying to peer in, to see Alice, to let her see that Xanthe was just a girl, like her, that she could be trusted. That she *had* to trust her. "Just tell me where you hid the pieces. I will put them back in Mistress Lovewell's bedchamber. She may never know where they have been or why, but she will have to drop the charges against you. You will be freed, Alice."

"I tell you I know of no rosary! Do you wish to see me condemned as a traitor? Do you wish me to suffer a traitor's end?"

Xanthe thought then about what Willis had said about her family. All of them executed as traitors. Only Alice spared. The family name tainted forever. This was her greatest terror then, not transportation, or even being hanged, but to be confirmed as a Catholic, a follower of the old religion, a traitor to the crown.

"Alice, I—"

Suddenly, the girl jumped at the door, grabbing hold of the grille and pulling herself up so that her face was close to Xanthe's. In the bleak autumn light she saw the deep shadows beneath Alice's eyes, the pallor of her skin, the fear in her expression. She looked, more than anything, like a caged animal.

"I escaped the fate of my family by the narrowest scrap of fortune. My punishment was to be left orphan, alone and entirely without support in this dread world. But that was not enough for those who would stamp their preferences upon us all and allow no other. I was made to suffer a greater torment, for they forced me to watch my loved ones go to their deaths. My mother and grandmother they burned before me. My grandmother was weak and mercifully not aware of what was being done to her, her frailty robbing the spectators and accusers alike of their cruel sport. My dear mother held my gaze as long as she was able until the smoke obscured us from one another. With his last gold, my father had bribed the executioner to step up and slit her throat, so she at least was spared the greater torments of the flames. He had no riches left for his own defense, however. He was dragged through the streets, humiliated and pelted with rotten vegetables and sharp stones. He was strung up by his neck until he was half choked to death. Then he was taken down and opened with a scythe, his innards pulled from him and burned on the fire so that he and I both could smell them as they cooked. Only then did they take an axe and remove his sweet head. His body was divided and scattered about the city. His head was put to decay upon a spike outside the tower." She paused then, the fury and the fight seeming to go out of her. More softly she asked, "Who will find gold to pay for mercy for me? Tell me that." She let go the bars and slipped back into the darkness.

"Alice." Xanthe scrabbled to reach her with her fingers, as if she might pull her back and make her understand. "I promise you, I have told no one of the rosary, nor will I ever. Only tell me where you hid the pieces and you will be safe. You have my word on it."

From the direction of the high street came the sound of rattling and heavy footfalls. She turned to find the constable almost upon them, a large ring of keys in his hand.

"Alice, we must be quick!" she hissed through the opening. "Tell me where I should look."

But there came no reply. She was too terrified of what the consequences might be if she trusted a stranger.

"Stand aside there, missy," said the jailer. He cast an eye over the basket, lifting the cloth that covered it. He pawed the contents. "Got to check there's nothing here as should not be." He whistled at the sight of the pie. "Fine food for a felon," he declared, and Xanthe wondered how many times he had used that line hoping for a little of what he found.

She pulled the basket away from him. "All sent by Master Lovewell, who will hear of it should something fail to reach its destination," she told him.

He gave a snort and turned his attention to finding the right key for the lock. All the while, Xanthe was trying to think of a way of getting Alice to tell her what she needed to know, but time was running out, and the presence of the constable was only likely to make the poor girl more reluctant to speak. The key turned in the lock and the door was dragged open, heavy on its hinges, as if reluctant to let air or light in, or to allow anyone out. The constable made to take the basket, but Xanthe held it tight.

"I shall deliver it myself," she told him with as much author-ity as she could summon. Reluctantly, he let her pass. She had prepared herself for how strongly standing inside the blind house would affect her. The instant she stepped across the threshold she felt dizzy, short of breath, assailed by panic and the sense that all the suffering in the place was embedded in the rough, cold stone of its walls. What was more, she felt the heavy presence of Margaret Merton, no doubt lingering, a helpless ob-server, come to see that her daughter's release was secured. In the darkness Xanthe could only just make out Alice's pale form.

"Here," Xanthe said gently. "You must stay strong. I implore you to trust me!" she whispered urgently. She feared that the chance of saving her mother was slipping through her fingers. Might she fail? What if she could not find the wretched silver, and Alice was condemned? The thought that her mother's life hung in the balance, and that she was the only one who could save her, felt suddenly too great a weight to bear. "Alice, *please!*"

But, still, the girl would not talk to her.

"Come on, missy," the constable chivvied. "I've better things to do with my day than stand out here in this sharp wind. Give the girl what she don't deserve and come away now."

She pushed the basket into Alice's arms and briefly took hold of her hand. She turned her palm up and pressed into it the coins she had brought with her.

"I will return," she told her. "I'll come back so you can tell me. Do not lose hope."

"Oi!" The constable had lost patience. "You wish to find yourself keeping the wench company all night?"

She stepped out of the jail, the lost souls who had once inhabited it whispering mournfully in her ear as she went, and above them all the sound of Mistress Merton calling her daugh-ter's name.

✳ ✳ ✳

Back at Great Chalfield Xanthe was given little time to think about what she was going to do next. The preparations for Clara's birthday feast seemed ridiculously elaborate and labor intensive. It seemed this wasn't just a jolly party for a young girl and her family and friends, but a chance for the Lovewells to wine and dine influential people, and generally show off. Nothing was too fancy, too expensive, too rich, too flashy. Xanthe sensed that Mistress Lovewell fought against some of this excess, displays of wealth not sitting comfortably with her more puritanical way of dressing and presenting her family, but her husband was unstoppable. He wanted the world, or at least the part of it he cared about, to see how successful and grand he was, and he wasn't going to stint on this opportunity to impress as many people as possible. In his daughter he found an eager supporter. Clara delighted in every bolt of silk brought in to decorate the hall, every crate of fruit arrived from London, every armful of flowers and herbs fetched from the gardens to scent the house. She flitted about, Pepito either in her arms or trotting at her heels, exclaiming and commenting on every item that passed under her nose. While her mother might not have shared her enthusiasm for all the trimmings and show, she was determined that everything should be done well. With Mary as her sergeant major she saw to it that every servant in the house was kept busy for the remainder of that day and well into the night.

Despite being completely exhausted, Xanthe slept badly. Her dreams were filled with pale faces looming at her from the darkness, and she woke from a nightmare where she had been locked up in the blind house herself, knowing no one was going to come to her rescue. And all the while, coloring everything was the knowledge of the danger her mother faced. It took her an age to get back to sleep, all the memories of her time in jail having resurfaced in a way that dreams so successfully provoke. In the daytime she could guard against the feelings those memories brought, could steel herself, distract herself, reason and make sense of things. At night she was assailed without any such barriers, and left feeling the wounds raw and new.

The next day continued at an even more hectic pace. As she went about her increasingly exhausting duties Flora was constantly in her mind. Her hope was that Alice would think about what she had said. Think about her, and decide that she had no choice but to trust the one person who was going to offer her help. Xanthe's fear was that time would run out. The authorities would not keep Alice in the lockup for long. Soon she would be moved to a city where her trial would be held. And the further away she went the harder it would be for Xanthe to reach her, to talk to her, to gain the vital information needed to clear her name.

Clara's birthday was one of those rare, bright days when the wind takes a break, the dirty October clouds go somewhere else, and there is just enough frost to touch everything with a crisp sparkle. It was as if the weather were bestowing a little gift of its own upon the birthday girl. The gardens looked enchanting, and the honey-colored stone of the house gleamed beneath the flattering autumn sunshine. Nevertheless, Mistress Lovewell fretted that the wreckage of the stables was an eyesore, that the weather was set to turn again to further ruin the road, and that the colder weather would mean more fires needed to stop guests taking a chill. Between her carping, Mary's barking instructions at the servants all day long, the impossible workload, the biting cold, and Xanthe not knowing what she was supposed to be doing or how she was supposed to be doing it half the time, she barely had time to draw breath, let alone think of what she was going to do next for Alice. At one point, rushing through the kitchen with a tray of bread, Xanthe slipped and fell, dropping the entire batch.

"Doltish girl!" Mary shouted. "Not content with being the most useless of kitchen maids, now you are set upon wasting good food! Get up, girl. Get up and get on!"

Jayne came scurrying from the pantry and knelt beside Xanthe to help pick up the bread.

"Pay her no mind." She grinned. "She's had the mistress on her back since yesterday, and she passes it on to us."

A nursery rhyme came into Xanthe's head. "'Big fleas have little fleas upon their backs to bite 'em, and little fleas have lesser fleas, and so *ad infinitum*.'"

Jayne let out a squawk of laughter, which drew withering stares from both Mary and Randolph. Together they rescued the best of the bread, putting the pick of the dirtied rolls into the servants' basket, and the worst into the pig bucket. Xanthe was certain at that moment that a maidservant in Great Chalfield was definitely one of the smallest of fleas.

The feast was to be held at six o'clock. Guests would be greeted at the door by the master and mistress of the house and Clara, on this occasion, and shown into the Great Hall. A feast would be served that would last, she was told, for hours. There would be music and dancing, and Xanthe would be required to sing whenever Master Lovewell deemed the moment appropriate. By five thirty, the hall was at last ready, the food mostly prepared, the house scrubbed and polished, and all of those who might possibly be seen by the guests sent to change into clean aprons, cuffs, collars, and caps. From her attic bedroom she heard the first of the carriages arrive. It was obvious that guests came in families. Unmarried girls certainly couldn't attend unaccompanied, and in any case, Xanthe imagined the care with which the guest list had been drawn up. Master Lovewell would have been making certain that anyone who counted, anyone who might be of use to him, or who might improve his standing just by visiting his house, would have had an invitation. It passed through her mind that there might well be a judge attending. A judge who might one day hold Alice's fate in his hands. Would she be able to find him and speak with him? To put in a plea for her, just in case she failed to find the chatelaine pieces? It was unlikely Jayne would know who most of the guests were, and anyway she was too humble in the order of servants to be allowed to wait at table. Xanthe decided she would have to risk asking Mary.

The carriages came in many shapes and sizes but all suggested a level of wealth. In her mind she translated the picture to her own era and saw top-of-the-line Audis, BMWs, Mercedes, and even Rolls-Royces scrunching over the gravel.

One of the smaller conveyances—a modest covered carriage with a single driver, no liveried footmen or flunkies, two black horses, and elegant but understated paintwork of burgundy and gold—stopped a little further from the house than the others, as if aware of its own lack of glamor. As the occupants climbed out she recognized them at once. Master Appleby alighted first, wearing a long cape with fur collar, followed by Joshua, all swagger and open smiles in an emerald-green jacket, and then Samuel, who was dressed in his preferred black, a little gold embroidery on his long jacket his only concession to the occasion. Samuel appeared to hang back from the others as if reluctant to join in. He didn't strike her as a man who would enjoy a party, unlike his brother, who was already making elaborate bows and kisses over the hands of a red-haired girl and her mother. Even from the distance of her garret window Xanthe could see that Samuel wore an expression that said he would rather be anywhere else. At that moment he raised his head and looked straight at her. It was as if he had felt her watching him. She stepped back into the shadows of the room, telling herself the idea was nonsense. Even so, it truly did feel as if he had seen her—properly seen her—and she felt exposed under such scrutiny.

Jayne burst through the door. "Xanthe, cease your dreaming! Mary is fit to bust waiting for us all. Make haste, now."

She followed Jayne downstairs. She had been loaned yet more dun-colored clothes, but at least the freshly starched white cuffs and collar lifted the look a bit. It made her think about how the modern notion of vintage clothing never included such humdrum everyday stuff. She had taken care to make sure her locket stayed out of sight, to avoid being questioned about owning something so valuable. Mary must have seen it when she undressed her after the fire, which was no doubt one of the reasons she didn't entirely trust her. Jayne had helped Xanthe pin her hair beneath the grim cap but had persuaded her she could leave a few curls loose, given that she was as much singer as servant just for this one evening at least. A glance in the long hall mirror as she passed on her way to the kitchen confirmed that Xanthe did look a little less severe. Not that it really mattered. Why should she care about how she looked? The important thing was to go as unnoticed as possible, not to draw attention to herself. Even so, however much she liked to think she was no more vain than anyone else, it was surprisingly hard to go about knowing that she looked drab. More than that, she did not look like herself. Another modern-day idea, it seemed: the importance placed on the individual. A servant was barely a person in the eyes of their superiors, more a commodity. And that low regard appeared to give those same servants little self-worth, as if they understood they were easily expendable, speedily replaced, living largely invisible lives that left no trace.

The heat in the kitchen should have been welcome after the

chill of the bedchambers, but it was overwhelming. The intense fire in the hearth seemed to be sucking all the air from the room. The spit had been set in place and on it turned a hog, basted and rotated by Peter, who had been taken from his beloved horses specifically for the task. He worked on with a grim face, resigned to his work, already flagging from the blast of the fire, splattered with spots of fat as the roasting pig spat angrily at him. Randolph looked almost as hot as the hog! He had stripped down to his hose and a thin linen jerkin, and still the sweat made his clothes cling to him in damp, pungent patches. Everyone performed their duties at a breathless run, and it was a wonder no one ran into anyone else. What air remained in the kitchens was heavy with the stink of cooking meat, burned sugar, boiled vegetables, and the acrid tang of sweat that only unwashed bodies could produce. Xanthe was grateful when she was at last instructed to take food up to the Great Hall, if only so that she could gulp fresher air.

The clamor of the kitchen was nothing when compared to the noise of the party itself. Although still early in the evening, there was a hearty buzz of excitement and good humor. It was not sufficient merely to be having a good time, everyone had to see—and certainly hear—that you were having a good time. The hall had been set out with the high table accommodating the family and what Xanthe took to be the most important guests. These included, on Clara's right, a man with a particularly wide white ruff that somehow made him look as if his head were being presented on a platter. He was middle-aged, and not attractive, and could not take his eyes off of Clara. It did not take a genius to surmise that this was her father's intended suitor for her. Poor thing. In certain matters she had even less freedom than the servants. Xanthe noticed that the girl's own gaze repeatedly fell on one of the other tables that lined the room, and one guest in particular: Joshua Appleby. Even from halfway across the room he was managing to flirt with her. Samuel was seated between two women who were trying to engage him in conversation without much success. The room itself did look wonderful. There were flowers everywhere, from pink and white posies on the tables, to swags of ivy and tiny white flowers over the fireplace, to Clara's requested rose bower above where she sat. Pale green silk had been unfurled on the walls, covering the dark tapestries, giving the illusion of grass or perhaps leaves, so that the whole place felt like a flower-filled garden in summer, rather than an imposing stone house in October. It smelled a great deal sweeter than the kitchens too, with herbs strewn over the floor, releasing their uplifting scents as they were crushed underfoot.

Trays of food were set down upon the tables, following Mary's instructions, and the servants scuttled back to fetch more. On and on it went, more and more food, more and more drink. There might have been forty people in the room, but Xanthe could not believe even that number could eat everything that was set in front of them. There was a clear beef soup, whole steamed salmon, pies of all shapes and sizes, a centerpiece of four different birds stuffed one inside the other, the roast pork, the whitest of white bread, glazed fruits, flummeries and syllabubs and even jellies. All achieved without a single gadget, let alone a fridge. Following the custom of never drinking water, and given that beer or ale would have seemed a little lowly for such an occasion, everyone was supplied with red wine in their silver goblets or pewter tankards, so it wasn't long before most of the guests were moving beyond merry into downright tipsy, and fast approaching drunk. After an hour of ferrying food up the stairs, clearing away discarded bones and half-eaten plate-fuls, and pouring yet more wine, Xanthe noticed Clara whisper something in her father's ear and he rose, a little unsteadily, to his feet, clanging his bone-handled knife against his silver goblet to gain everyone's attention.

"My Lords, ladies, honored guests, dear friends," he addressed the room, beaming, the proudest of proud parents, happy to have his daughter, and his home, the focus of attention by so many people, if only for one evening. "It is a delight of the highest order to have you here tonight, to welcome you to our home, in order that we may give thanks to God for his bounty, and celebrate the anniversary of the day my sweet daughter was born."

Here he paused to allow clapping and cheers. Clara smiled prettily. She was wearing a dress of the palest pink silk, with tiny green leaves embroidered on the tight-fitting bodice. The style of the time dictated that an unmarried woman could wear a low-cut gown, but she might preserve her modesty with a little lace or gauze tucked into the neckline. Clara had found what looked like fine chiffon, which was so sheer it actually hid nothing at all. It must surely have been the most daring thing she had ever been allowed to wear, and she knew precisely how beautiful she looked.

Her father went on. "They say a man lives on through his sons, and that may be so. Alas, the Lord has not seen fit to bless us with sons, but instead we have the gift of the sweetest, the most charming and dutiful daughter any parents could hope for. And, my friends, my greatest wish is to please her. Why would it not be?" He laughed, encouraging the guests to agree with him. "And my darling daughter tells me it is time for music!"

At this there was an uproar—stamping of feet, shouts and cries, and more thunderous clapping. If Xanthe had been expecting some genteel affair with everyone behaving formally and primly she was having her eyes opened to what feasts were like in the seventeenth century. This was no staid dinner party.

There might be important people present, nobles, people of rank and power, but they were here to enjoy themselves, and given the amount of wine they had already guzzled, they were going to enjoy themselves noisily and rowdily.

To her horror Xanthe saw that Clara was on her feet and was beckoning her to step closer to the top table. She had known she would be asked to sing, of course, but had put it to the back of her mind.

"Soon we will have the musicians play and there will be dancing," Clara said to the room. "But first, something to lift your souls, one and all. See?" She indicated Xanthe with a sweep of her hand. "We have our very own minstrel!"

There was an appreciating bit of oohing and aahing.

"She is newly arrived in Wiltshire, never heard before in this region. I promise you a rare treat indeed!"

Again there was a deal of foot-stamping and cheering.

Xanthe's stomach clenched. This was not the crowd she had been expecting. She had a horrible feeling "The Willow Song" was not going to find favor with all these half-drunk revelers. How would they have the patience to sit through something so gentle and quiet? And why would they want a sad song to spoil their upbeat mood? The other servants were sent from the room, and a terrifying hush began to fall. After much shushing and admonishments the hall was at last silent. With Xanthe standing at the center of it, without so much as a glass of water, sweat sticking her hair to her neck, her face horribly shiny, she cleared her throat as best she could. This was no time to give a feeble performance. She must not allow nerves to get the better of her. If she let Master Lovewell down in front of all those people he would have no desire to retain her to remind him of the humiliation. She took two deep breaths. She had to forget that she was a servant, had to forget that she was hundreds of years from home. She had to forget everything except the song and the music and her own voice.

"Come, come, girl," the master chivvied. "Do not keep our guests waiting. What song have you for us?"

"By your leave, Master Lovewell, sir, I shall sing 'The Willow Song' to start," she told him. He gave a little nod of approval, which encouraged her sufficiently to pitch in. As she sang, a respectful air of listening came from the guests, which surprised her. Although the song was gentle and melancholy, they seemed to like her voice and were content to listen to it, at least to begin with. As she went through the verses, however, some began to fidget. She reached the end, but only just, sensing the mood in the room was changing. She had to regain their interest. She forced herself to change her stance to reflect the manner of song she was about to deliver. She was a performer, not a servant, though heaven knew it wasn't easy feeling like one, dressed the way she was. More out of desperation than anything else, she snatched the cap from her head and tossed it over her shoulder. As luck would have it, it was Joshua who caught it, with a whoop of glee, making everyone laugh. Xanthe pulled the pins from her hair and shook it so that her ringlets tumbled down around her shoulders. While everyone was still a little stunned—she heard Mistress Lovewell gasp and dared not meet her eye—she firmly placed her hands on her hips and proceeded to walk as saucily as she knew how up and down the space in the center of the hall. "And now," she told them, "I shall sing something altogether different. Perhaps you know it? It's called 'The Counterfeit Bridegroom'! At this there were squeals of delight and peals of laughter. She strode about, trying to glance at everyone and no one in particular, doing her best to avoid the mistress, but noticing Clara cheerfully clapping her hands as she began to sing the bawdy song that was more commonly heard in taverns than grand houses. Xanthe sang with verve and gusto, holding nothing back.

> *Come all ye young frolicsome jilts of the town*
> *Whose trade like yourselves is uncertain*
> *Since whoring and other professions goes down,*
> *I'll show you a new way to good fortune!*

And it felt good. Just for those few moments, when her voice worked its magic, when the music took her, when the audience were completely caught up in the song and the fun of it all, it was good to be singing again. She knew that her mother would have been proud. When she came to the end of the song Joshua leaped to his feet.

"Again! I say, again!" he cried, and the rest of the guests shouted their agreement.

So she sang it again. Twice. Each time with a little more confidence. If the mistress disapproved she did not show it, for her guests were loving every minute of it. They were entertained, and they would remember the evening for it. Master Lovewell even joined in the chorus. Finally, Xanthe shook her head and said she would make way for the musicians and the dancing. She knew she had done well, and she almost managed to slip away with her reputation and position secured. Almost. When she went over to Joshua to ask for her cap back, he smiled and shook his head.

"I don't think our songbird should vanish back into her disguise as a servant," he said, loudly enough for everyone to hear.

"I beg your pardon, sir," she said, "but I have duties to attend to." She held out her hand, but he merely frowned at the wretched cap.

"Such an ugly thing should not hide such pretty hair. Nor

should we be deprived of such talent." He jumped to his feet. "I say our songbird should be allowed to stay and join in the dancing!"

All around him people shouted their agreement. She tried not to look as panic-stricken as she felt. She could never manage one of their complicated dances, having no idea of the steps, a fact which would quickly become obvious to everyone. How would she explain that? She was supposed to be a singer, part of a troupe of players, of course she should know how to dance.

"If you please, sir . . ." she tried again, but Joshua was unstoppable.

"What say you, Master Lovewell?" he called across the room. "Shall she be permitted to stay and dance, or will you return our little songbird to her cage of servitude?" There were raucous jeers and boos at this idea.

The master hauled himself to his feet again and announced with mock formality, "She shall stay!"

There were further cheers and some laughter, and Clara clapped her hands and the musicians up in the gallery began to play, and Joshua was in the process of bowing at her to ask for the dance when Samuel darted out from behind the table and snatched up her hand.

"The first dance is mine, I believe," Samuel said, and led Xanthe toward the quickly gathering throng of dancers.

17

IN THE GALLERY THE CONSORT OF MUSICIANS STRUCK UP WHAT WAS, BY seventeenth-century standards, a lively tune. Around Xanthe, women curtsied to their partners. Her mouth went dry. She froze. This was it. Surely this was the moment she was to be found out. Shown to be a fraud. Samuel still had hold of her hand, which was by now trembling.

"Mistress?" he said softly, his voice questioning her sudden apparent inability to move.

"I can't," she murmured.

"What's that you say?" He stepped closer to try and catch her frantically whispered words.

"Forgive me," she said, "but I cannot dance."

"You cannot?"

"Not . . . dressed like this," she told him, indicating her servant's clothes. "It would not be appropriate. I should be ridiculed. Laughed at." When he looked as if he might protest at this she hurried on, "Mistress Lovewell would be displeased, and I fear she would send me from the house the minute the party is over."

This seemed to strike him as a real possibility. Quickly, he pulled her hand through his arm and led her off the dance floor and back to the table. He signaled for an extra chair to be brought, and one of the serving boys swiftly set a place for her beside him. She sat down, relieved but her heart thumping, and glanced anxiously in the direction of the top table.

"Fear not," Samuel reassured her, "I wish to talk with you, for I would question you further on your knowledge of the Drillington screen. Your mistress will not object. I shall speak up for you, should the necessity arise."

"Thank you," she said, and meant it, painfully aware of how close she had come to being exposed as a fraud. As Samuel took a carafe of wine and poured some into a silver goblet for her, she experienced a flashback to drinking wine with Liam in the garden. How different the occasions. How different the men. Where Liam was as open and sunny as the Wiltshire country-side, Samuel was an enigma, and a dark one at that. *What on earth would he make of the real Xanthe Westlake*, she wondered. Could a man at the beginning of the seventeenth century ever really see a woman as an equal?

And so they talked of the screen. While all about them the revelry grew more and more boisterous, the dancing more and more exuberant, he quizzed her upon the carvings, the steepness of the arches, the finish of the wood, the thickness of the uprights, every tiny detail, all of which she struggled to recall as the wine found its way to her tired brain. After twenty minutes she noticed Mistress Lovewell staring at her with fierce disapproval. Samuel's wishes might only count for so much, and she could not risk setting her employer against her. She rose to her feet.

"I thank you, sir, for the wine, and for the opportunity to rest a while, but I must return to my duties."

He stood up. It was a small gesture but one that suggested he no longer saw her as a servant. She noticed Joshua watching, his expression one of amusement. His attention was quickly claimed by Clara, however, who had threaded her way through the crowd to insist he dance with her.

Samuel bowed a farewell and then a thought struck him.

"Tell me," he asked, "are you able to draw?"

"Draw?"

"If I furnished you with pen and ink and paper, might you be able to draw what you recall of the screen?"

"Well, I can render a passable likeness," she said, thinking of her sketchbook back home. Her drawings were quite good, but to pull so much detail out of memory—she wasn't certain she could do it. She went on, "But I'm not used to using ink, and I've already told you all I can remember."

"Please, say at least you will consider it."

He put his hand on her arm again and gave her such a beseeching look she did not have it in her heart to say no. And in any case, she had to consider how he might, in some way, be able to help *her*. She had not been successful in tracking down a judge among the guests, and still she did not know where the chatelaine pieces were hidden. It would not harm her cause to have someone of influence owing her a favor. She would just have to think hard about what she had seen on her visit to Drillington and to dredge up from her mind images from the documentary she had watched.

"If my mistress does not object . . ." she said.

He smiled then. It was a fleeting thing, but in that brief moment his features were transformed, lightened, warmed. "I will speak with her at the first opportunity," he said, finally, slowly, removing his hand from her arm.

The day after the party involved hours of clearing up, which was every bit as exhausting as the preparations had been. The

Lovewells were nowhere to be seen, presumably recovering from a very late night, enormous amounts of food, energetic dancing, and no doubt nursing sizeable hangovers. The guests who had stayed over emerged in dribs and drabs throughout the day, summoning their carriages and drivers, to be borne away as gently as the rutted roads and gusty winds would allow. There was no sign of the Applebys, and Jayne told Xanthe with a sigh in her voice that the master had halted work on the house and stables for a day or two so that the family could rest without the annoyance of builders and their noisy ways. Xanthe was surprised to find herself a little disappointed that she would not be doing the drawings for Samuel. She quickly convinced herself that this was only because she had hoped to build up his trust so that he might help her free Alice. At least with the family shut in their bedchambers and the house quiet, she was able to do a little snooping and searching. Alice had chosen such a clever hiding place for her rosary, but how would Xanthe ever find the silver pieces? She took the attachments she still had out of her satchel and sat with them, hoping for perhaps a glimpse of something or somewhere that might lead her to the needle case and scissors. But nothing came. No vision. No voices. Nothing.

She took every possible chance to search in bedchambers, passageways, storerooms, and outhouses, but she was searching for some very small things in a very large house. That night she lay awake trying to invent a better approach. If Alice had not had the time to return the chatelaine pieces to her mistress's room, she must have been in danger of being caught with the things on her. Did that mean she still had them when the constable and the sheriff turned up to take her away? Xanthe cast her mind back to her first proper visit to Alice's time, when she had seen them trying to put her in the carriage. She had broken free for a moment and run off. They had taken a while to get her back.

Where had she run to? She might well have put the pieces some-where then, knowing that she would be searched. But Xanthe had been in the stables and had not been able to see exactly where Alice had gone. At least it set her thinking that she must have put them somewhere outside the house. Which made her realize, with a sinking heart, that she had been looking in the wrong place all along! She silently cursed herself for being so dim-witted. The worst thing was, if the house was an enormous place to search, outside was impossibly vast. She had seen Alice break free of the men and run, but where? How far did she get? Xanthe stood and looked out of the window of the first-floor landing, where she was supposed to be cleaning. The Great Chalfield land swept away as far as the eye could see. If Alice had made it past the stables, the gardens, and the barns—which she might not have done—there were acres of rolling greenery, a small stretch of woodland, the road, ditches, and a valley with a stream in it. It would take weeks, months to search it all. And with all the rain that had lately fallen, such tiny items could easily have sunk deep into the mud.

Xanthe's best hope was still that Alice would have had time to think about her offer of help and be ready to trust her. She had to go and see her again. She thought about the cold weather and how Alice must be suffering in the damp stone building and decided to plead with Mary to be allowed to take her some more warm clothes and bedding. She knew she would beg if need be. She wondered again how Flora was coping without her, too. She kept telling herself it was only a short time, a matter of hours that barely formed days, and that her mother's flare-ups occurred rarely. In her heart, however, she knew it was the threatening pres-ence of Margaret Merton that made her stomach turn. If she had had any choice in the matter she would never have left Flora under the watchful eye of such a dangerous companion.

Mary's response to her request was not at all what Xanthe had expected. Instead of pursed lips and a rant concerning work to be done and not enough hours in the day to do it, she looked saddened. She looked at Xanthe carefully, still trying to explain to herself her interest in Alice, and then said levelly, "You cannot go to her in Marlborough, because she is no longer there."

"What?"

"She has been moved to the jail beneath the courthouse in Salisbury."

Xanthe swore under her breath. "When?"

"This morning, so Willis tells me. He heard it from the saddler who delivered some of the repaired harness. The magistrate's wagon came through, doing the rounds of the blind houses. They scoop up the prisoners as if they were picking stones from a plowed field, throw them in the back of the thing, caged and heaped together, innocent and guilty alike, and haul them off to await trial at the court."

"But Salisbury is miles away. When will the trial be?"

Mary tutted, losing patience. "Now why would anyone bother to tell me that? Alice is beyond your reach now, girl. There is nothing any of us can do for her save pray." Mary turned on her heel and went about her work, all brisk efficiency, but Xanthe could see by the set of her shoulders, by her rapidly blinking eyes as she passed, that even Mary, made of iron, was close to tears. She had given up hope.

"You think she's doomed, don't you?" Xanthe snapped, unable to stop herself, angry at how quickly the woman was defeated. "Well I'm not giving up on her so easily!" She stomped down the stairs and strode out of the door at the back of the house. She could hear Mary calling her name, but if she did not get out, did not put some distance between herself and such contagious despair, she might not be able to stop herself from saying unforgivable things. Things that would see her sacked. She needed some air and marched through the kitchen garden, ignoring the surprised stares of the gardeners. The weather was horrible, gusty winds rattling the few remaining brittle, brown leaves on the apple trees in the orchard, heavy clouds blotting out any autumn sun there might have been. She allowed the elements to blast her, let the cold air and the uneven ground and the lowering sky thrash her anger from her. She felt, at that moment, useless. Helpless. Hopeless.

At last she came to a huge oak tree. She leaned back against its rough bark, staring up into the crooked branches. Most of the leaves had gone and lay in rusty heaps at her feet. How could she begin to search even one tree, one heap of leaves? As she stood there she noticed a horse and rider approaching. They came galloping up the driveway, swift and sure-footed, and she could see it was a fine horse, fast and sleek, though its rider was dressed soberly. Not one of Master Lovewell's noble friends, then. Soon she was able to recognize the visitor: Samuel Appleby. The drive described a curve from where it left the road and turned up to the house, so he did not see her standing close against the oak tree, disguised in her muted servant's clothing. He must have known there was to be no work on the stables or house that day. And he was coming alone. Was he there simply to see her? For the sole purpose of asking her to draw the screen for him? It seemed likely. It also seemed likely that she needed a friend now more than ever, if she was not to fail in her mission. She experienced a shudder at the thought of what that failure might mean. If Samuel cared so much about his work, he might just be prepared to strike a bargain with her. Her help in return for his. At that moment, it did not feel like her best option, it felt like her only option.

She leaned into what was fast becoming a gale and strode back to the house. The wind whipped the door from her hand as she opened it and blew through the passageway, disturbing the rug and rattling the pewter jugs and tankards on the tallboy. Mary stuck her head out of the kitchen.

"There! I was to send Peter running for you. What were you thinking? Disappearing like some will-o'-the-wisp! And the state of you! Here, straighten that cap and brush those leaves from your skirts. The Lord knows, but people will think you sleep in a hedge." Before Xanthe had time to make apologies, Mary continued, "Master Samuel is asking for you. You are to go up to the library. He's there with the master. Well don't stand gawking and gaping, girl, go! Make haste!"

She did as she was told, hoping that Mary would not notice the mud she was shedding from her boots as she ran up the stairs.

The library was a lovely room in the oldest part of the house, walls lined with shelves and bookcases crammed with leather-bound volumes, two tapestry sofas, and full-length windows overlooking the herb garden. It had a huge stone fireplace, in which a fire had been hastily lit. Master Lovewell had his night-gown under a silk house robe and wore an embroidered cap on his head. Clearly he had not been expecting the visitor. When she entered the room Samuel, who had been standing by the window, walked toward her. He was still wearing his narrow-brimmed black hat and short cape. Not for the first time Xanthe was struck by his restlessness. It was as if good manners kept him in check, otherwise he would be allowing himself to hurry everywhere, to rush at things almost recklessly, to speak out on things about which he was required to be silent. She imagined how he might be in the twenty-first century. It crossed her mind that he had been born into the wrong time. He would have been much better suited to her world, where he could say what he liked and be whoever he wanted to be. At least he was free to express himself through his work, which was clearly hugely important to him.

"Ah!" exclaimed Master Lovewell. "It seems the girl is found. Come in, my dear. Shut the door, let us not invite the weather to join us."

She closed the door and bobbed what she hoped was a polite and correct curtsy.

"Forgive me, sirs, I had just stepped outside."

"No matter," the master waved his hand, eager to get to the point, no doubt so he could get back to his bed. "Master Samuel requires your assistance in the matter of the new screen for the Great Hall. He tells me you are familiar with the one at Drillington? Excellent. Then I am happy for you to be of use to him."

"It would aid me greatly," said Samuel, addressing not Xanthe but her master, "if you might spare your maidservant, Master Lovewell. A matter of hours only, I am sure of it. However, I would need to take her to my own home."

"Your home? Can she not talk with you here? Have we not ink and paper for sketches and such in this house?"

"Indeed I could want for nothing here," he assured him, "it is only that in my studio I have sections of the screen already prepared. I wish to have the girl look at them, at the carvings, at the style. I am hopeful she will confirm the accuracy of my design, as well as be able to supply me with drawings of what she recalls. The weather is too wild, the road too rough, to risk transporting the pieces. Better for her to see them at my place of work."

So the conditions were too awful for his bits of wood, but she could be dragged through the countryside no problem at all! Yet again Xanthe was reminded of the low value put on servants.

"I see," said Master Lovewell, considering the idea while keeping his rear end as close to the warmth of the fire as was safe. "And you suppose her knowledge of the original will be . . . accurate?" He looked at her as if he couldn't imagine anything of quality being stored in her mop-capped head.

"I do," Samuel told him.

"Well, I have sent Willis about his errands, and my driver is gone for the day. There is the cart, but—"

"Please, do not put yourself or your household to trouble on my account," Samuel said. "My horse is strong and well mannered. The maid may ride with me."

"Oh? Then I see no further obstacle," said the master with a happy grin, sensing he could wave them off with no further interruption to his day of leisure.

He might not have seen a problem with the idea, but then he was not to know that Xanthe could not ride. Her entire experience of horse riding was an hour-long pony trek in the Lake District as a child, but it was impossible for her to admit to the lack of this vital skill. The majority of people in the seventeenth century knew how to sit on a horse. In any case, it did not appear that Xanthe had any choice in the matter.

She was given a moment to dash upstairs and fetch her borrowed cape and then meet Samuel outside the front of the house. On her way she encountered Mary, who would not let her leave the house in her laughable boots a second time, fearing for the reputation of the household. She had Jayne fetch a pair of shoes that she insisted were more suitable. They felt horribly flimsy and girly, and Xanthe would far rather have worn her own Dr. Martens, but this was not a moment for argument.

She found Samuel waiting for her outside, standing next to his black horse, holding its bridle as if it were the tamest, quietest thing in the world. To her it looked dauntingly tall and lively.

She must have let some of her fear show on her face because Samuel patted the horse's neck.

"Raven is a gentle creature," he insisted. "He will convey us swiftly and safely."

"I'm sure any horse of yours would not dare misbehave," she said, trying to sound confident and relaxed but unable to keep a frightened squeak out of her voice.

As he helped her up into the saddle she was certain she caught a look of amusement on his usually inscrutable face. Her nerves made her irritable, but she resisted snapping at him. She needed this man to help her; she had to hold that thought. He'd sat her sideways, but she knew she would fall off if she tried to ride like that, so she quickly hitched up her unhelpful skirt and shifted so that she was sitting astride. Samuel opened his mouth to comment on this but evidently thought better of it. He swung himself up behind her with practiced ease, wrapping one arm around her waist while holding the reins in his free hand. He uttered a word to Raven, and the horse plunged forward. Before Xanthe had time to think further about it they were cantering down the driveway, the wind whipping past her ears, threatening to snatch the cap from her head. She clung to Raven's long mane, too nervous to do anything but sit tight and trust Samuel to know what he was doing. She thought longingly of her taxi and how much she would rather be traveling in it at that moment. The thought of what Samuel would make of a London black cab made her give a yap of laughter. Unfortunately, Samuel interpreted this as a sign that she was enjoying herself, so he urged his horse to go faster. When Raven jumped through a deep puddle, lurching slightly as he did so, Xanthe felt herself slip to one side. Samuel quickly tightened his arm around her, pulling her close to him, without for one second slowing their speed. She forced herself to stop worrying. In fact, she did feel safe. Safe and yet daring at the same time. After all, she was not required to do anything but sit and hold on, and Samuel was clearly an expert horseman. She had ridden pinion on a big motorbike once, and remembered the buzz of excitement that had given her, but it was nowhere near as thrilling as charging through the stormy countryside on such a powerful horse with a strong man holding her tight.

Without warning it began to rain heavily. What started out as a sharp, cold shower quickly developed into a serious downpour. Her cap was soaked in a minute, and she could feel water forcing its way through the wool of her cape. Raven's mane became saturated and difficult to hold. Samuel let the horse pick his own way over the uneven, stony road that was fast becoming waterlogged. Mud splashed up at them as they cantered on. By the time Marlborough came into sight, Xanthe was wet through and aching. It seemed all sorts of muscles she did not usually call upon were required to work just to stay upright in the saddle. They slowed to a trot once they reached the town, clattering up the high street, past the inn and the town hall, up beyond the church at the far end. The street opened onto a green with houses on three sides. Raven needed no urging to find his way home and without being asked turned beneath an archway that led to a barn. An ostler ran out into the rain and helped her down. Her legs were weak when she tried to stand. Samuel issued orders for the horse to be rubbed down, thatched with hay, and rugged up before being given water to drink. Only then should he be offered a feed of warm bran mash. All this was shouted above the noise of what was by then a full-blown storm.

"Come!" Samuel took her arm and steered her across a courtyard, under another brick archway, and through an iron gateway. She glimpsed a garden before they reached the rear door of the house and he bundled her inside. Once through the door he removed his hat, dropping it onto a nearby chair, and called out, "Philpott! Where are you, man?"

There came the sound of scurrying footsteps and a thin, balding man appeared. He had pale eyes and an expression that seemed to say he was constantly disappointed by life but rarely surprised.

"And there you are, drenched through and through!" He took Samuel's cape from his shoulders, shaking rainwater from it and muttering darkly about October chills bringing Christmas grief.

"Enough of your doom-mongering, Philpott," said Samuel. "Take the mistress's cape. Is the fire lit? Good. Bring us toddies. And oatcakes. And paper and ink. No, wait. We will go to the studio a little later."

Philpott gingerly took what was in fact Jayne's cape between finger and thumb and gave Xanthe a glance that took in everything in a well-schooled second: her strangeness, her youth, her servant's clothes, and, she felt, in particular, the fact that she was a woman. For this was a man's house, that much was obvious even in the dimly lit hallway where they stood. There were no flowers, no herbs to perfume the rooms, the paneling was unadorned, not a picture or a wall hanging or so much as a bolster on a window seat. She followed Samuel through to what she guessed was the main reception room. It had two tall windows at one end, giving onto the green and the town beyond. The furniture and furnishings were of excellent quality—the antique dealer in her could not help put a price on the elegant table against the wall between the windows and the wrought-iron sconces on either side of the mantlepiece—but things had clearly been chosen for function rather than frivolity. Even the dark red rug, the one concession to color and comfort, had a masculine feel to it.

"Here." Samuel pulled a wooden chair closer to the hearth.

"Sit you down. The fire will soon drive the rain from your clothes."

She was happy to do as she was told. The cold had got to her, adding to her tiredness from hard work and not enough sleep, on top of the unfamiliar effort of horse riding, so that she was shivering. Her teeth began to chatter. Samuel looked alarmed.

"No, this will not do," he said, taking her hands and pulling her to her feet again. "Forgive me, but this must go." He took off the sodden headgear and dropped it onto the fireguard where it set up a hissing. The few pins she had in her hair were not equal to the weight of it when wet, so that it fell down in waterlogged ringlets. She shook her head, much like a dog trying to rid itself of water, causing the fire to spit and set up more hissing.

Samuel laughed. "I have not seen such a sorry sight since last I joined the hunt with Lord Avebury! The hounds looked just so."

Xanthe raised her eyebrows at him. "Perhaps you should take a look in the mirror," she said, forgetting her place.

He turned to check his reflection in the large looking glass that hung over the fireplace. They both looked ridiculously soggy and bedraggled. He turned back to her a little sheepishly.

"You make a fair point, mistress. We are neither of us at our best, nor fit for company."

"Unless it is a spaniel," she suggested, thinking of Pepito and his own floppy ears and glossy ringlets.

Philpott came bumbling into the room carrying a tray with steaming cups and plates of oatcakes. He set the things down on the low table in front of the nearest sofa. There was a pot of honey with a drizzler next to the freshly baked biscuits. Samuel handed her a chunky ceramic cup. She sniffed its contents warily.

"Milk," he promised. "With just a pipkin of rum. Philpott

swears by it as a cure for all ills, do you not?" he asked his man-servant.

"Better safe than sorry, sir," he said, putting more logs on the fire, taking a poker to the embers, and generally fussing around. "A west wind brings sickness, and there's no better answer to that than good food and a little rum. And dry clothes," he added, pointedly looking at them both.

"We shall fare well enough by the fire. Thank you, Philpott," Samuel told him.

Dismissed, the doleful man gave a nod and left them.

"Please, eat as you will," Samuel said, nodding at the tray.

She had not realized how much she missed eating something sweet. The Lovewells liked their sugar, but it was a rich man's treat, and none of it found its way to the servants. The sight of the golden honey almost had her drooling. She took a small pewter plate and piled on warm oatcakes, holding the drizzler high to allow plenty of honey to swirl over them. She considered sitting on the sofa to be nearer the food, but she needed to dry her clothes and hair. Taking her feast back to the hearth, she indicated the rug.

"Would you mind?" she asked. "It's the only way I'll get my hair to dry."

Samuel looked puzzled, as if the idea of a woman sitting on the floor was completely baffling. Before he could protest she plonked herself down, folding her legs beneath her, turning her back to the heat of the burning logs, and tucking into the crumbly oatcakes. After so long without chocolate or cake she thought then that she had never tasted anything so delicious. For a moment she was reminded of Gerri's wonderful baking and felt a pang of homesickness, wondering whether Flora would have been over to the tea shop while she was away. She looked up to find Samuel watching her in astonishment. She stopped, mid chew, horribly aware that there was honey running down her chin. She tried to wipe it off with a finger as casually as she was able. "These are very good," she said, being careful not to spit crumbs.

To her surprise, Samuel helped himself to a plateful and came to sit on the floor opposite her. He gave a brief smile and then began devouring his food. For a few minutes they both ate hungrily and gulped their hot toddies while the fire crackled and spat and their hair and clothes steamed gently. There was something incredibly companionable, almost intimate, about that shared silence, that shared moment. Xanthe felt bad about using it, but knew that she must.

"Master Samuel," she started cautiously, choosing her words with care, "I am happy that I can help you in some small way with your work. I will do my very best to draw what I remember of the screen, and to recall as many details as possible."

This time it was Samuel who struggled to stop honey dropping from his biscuits into his lap. He quickly licked his fingers. In the firelight he looked less stern, somehow. Younger. More relaxed. It occurred to Xanthe that he was always the shadow to his brother's sunshine. He was quite different when he was not with Joshua.

"Your knowledge will be of great use, I am certain of it. It is my immense good fortune that you arrived at Great Chalfield when you did."

"As a matter of fact, it is the misfortune of another that keeps me here," Xanthe said. "There is someone else who has need of my help, but I fear I will not be able to do enough."

"Someone else?"

"A girl. A maidservant at Great Chalfield. Her name is Alice, and she was taken in by the Lovewells when she . . . lost her family. She has been the victim of a terrible misunderstanding, accused of a theft she did not commit. You may have heard her name mentioned while you were at the manor house?"

"I believe so," he said, giving nothing away in his voice.

"You will certainly have heard of the jail in this town," she went on.

"You are referring to the lockup?"

"Yes. It is there that Alice was first taken when she was arrested, there that I was able to speak to her. A dreadful place. Constructed not just to hold people but to torment them, having no light, precious little air, only cold darkness and rough stone. It is beyond my understanding why such a place would be built, why a young girl should be locked away from everything and everyone when she is convicted of nothing, not yet even given a chance to be heard."

At this, Samuel stopped eating. He placed his platter on the floor, and his face once again looked closed and distant, the tension returned to his body. He raised his eyes to hers and held her gaze. "I know the place of which you speak," he said. "How could I not? For it was I who built it."

18

SUDDENLY XANTHE FOUND THAT SHE COULD SCARCELY SWALLOW HER FOOD. Samuel could not have known the impact this revelation would have upon her. How could he? He could tell by what she had said that she hated the place, that she considered it cruel, which might have struck him as strange, as such lockups were commonplace at the time. What he could not have realized was how personal this one was to her. How it connected her to home, to her real life. How it linked the future to the past. How the suffering that lingered in it entered her soul every time she went near the place. And this was the man—this clever, talented, complicated, and she believed, kind man—who had created the thing. Did that make the link between the two of them stronger? Or was it a point that would always stand between them? That he could build such a place, and that she was someone who knew a little of what it must be like to be thrown into one and locked away?

"We are a young company of architects, mistress, only recently recognized as such."

"Please, you don't need to explain."

"I feel that I do. That is, I wish to." He turned to stare into the fire as he spoke, flickering shadows playing across his face.

"My father was a master builder, and he himself the son of a master builder. The family built their reputations in the stone of their creations over many years. The work was hard, steady, respectable, and provided a good living, but the times in which my forefathers lived were more dangerous even than these. Allegiances shifted with the tides. To declare one's friendships or one's relationship to God was to risk everything, for what was in the morning acceptable could by the morrow be deemed traitorous. Many of my father's friends were unable to keep their footing on such treacherous ground. Many were . . . lost. My father prevailed due to a combination of wits and skill. With so many newly ennobled, the demand for grand houses, or improvements to ones no longer considered sufficiently grand, brought about a need for men like him. As years went on, men like us. My brother and I followed our father's craft, though now it is at last considered a profession. In truth, Joshua's talent does not lie in the conception of buildings, nor in draftsmanship, but he is adept at business and is content to see himself as the merchant of the family. We did not, you will understand, achieve our position of stability, of safety, without climbing many steep steps. We chose our commissions with care, and those that were of a civic nature saw us rooted in the order of the day. We could not risk giving offense by turning down the task of providing the community with a means to maintain a peaceful society. To do so would be seen as disagreeing with the ruler who made the very laws that govern the country. It fell to me to design and oversee the construction of the lockup."

In the silence that followed his speech even the fire seemed to quieten. It was clear Samuel had been conflicted about building the jail, but in the end he had done what he had to. How could she judge him? She had not lived through an era where a monarch could send people to the executioner for holding beliefs other than his or her own. Or for refusing to uphold the rule of law. Or even for not declaring oneself fully as a supporter of the crown in every way.

Xanthe wanted to say something to make him see that she understood.

"Samuel . . ." she began, and he started, surprised at her using his name. She got no further, however, as there came sounds of someone entering the house, the front door banging open and then shut, wind rattling anything that wasn't tied down in the hallway, shouted greetings, Philpott's trotting feet, and then the door of the sitting room being thrown wide. Joshua, clothes wet, hatless hair disheveled, eyes bright, strode in.

"Hell's teeth, what a tempest rages without, Samuel . . . Oh!" He stopped, taking in the curious sight of his brother sitting on the floor with a woman, both of them rain-damp and sticky with honey and crumbs. "What's this? A new fashion of entertaining, brother?" He laughed, tugging off his gloves and dropping them carelessly on a chair. "I know you, do I not? Why yes, it is our little songbird. What strong wings you must have, to have flown against this stormy blast."

Samuel scrambled to his feet, plainly cross at being teased by his younger brother.

"Your mouth opens and nonsense falls out of it, whatever the weather, Joshua," he snapped, pushing his hair off his face and dusting down his velvet jacket. He was taller than his brother and slightly broader at the shoulders. There were small similarities about their features, but otherwise there was nothing to suggest they were related at all. Xanthe noticed that the instant he was in Joshua's company the other, more inhibited, more unreachable version of Samuel reappeared. "Mistress Westlake is here to help me with the drawings for the screen. She has seen the one at Drillington Hall. Now, if you'll excuse us." He held out his hand and helped Xanthe to her feet. She let him lead her past his smirking brother and out of the room.

They walked along a narrow hallway and through two more doors. She had the impression that the home of the Applebys was a fine example of a townhouse of the day, but a long way from the grandeur and space of the Lovewell's manor house. The studio was at the back of the building and formed one side of a small courtyard, one other side being the rear of the house itself, and the two others high brick walls, one with the gateway that led through to the stables and barn. There was a small herb garden, cobbles set in careful geometric patterns, an espaliered fruit tree, and some rose bushes beside a seat. Somehow she doubted the men spent much time drifting about among the flowers. The studio was one large, airy space, the room without a ceiling and open to the rafters. Priority had been given to light rather than warmth, with as much in the way of windows as could be fitted in. There were desks and cupboards on one end, with drawing boards and tables at the center, while the far end, more than half the building, was taken up with carpenter's tools, samples of wood and marble, bits of slate, tiling, stone-work, and just about anything that might one day form part of a building. Samuel and his father might not actually heft the stones themselves anymore, but they clearly liked to work their designs closely with the materials, using this type of stone or that type of wood to inspire and inform their work. She could smell sawdust and plaster and the wood itself.

Samuel seemed not to notice the cold, but it made Xanthe start rubbing her arms. It did not help that her clothes were still damp. He had been in such a hurry to escape his brother he'd forgotten all about Philpott's dire warnings of lethal chills. Xanthe decided she would wait a while to bring up the subject of Alice again. She needed to get him on her side before asking for his help, and she was not even clear in her mind what that help would look like. How much power and influence did the Applebys have?

"Here," he said, unfurling drawings on the central table. "These are the altered plans I have worked on since we spoke. See, I have adjusted the angle on the arch above the doorway. And to balance it, the uprights are more slender . . . here and here. Is it as you recall?"

"Wow. I mean, yes, much more like it. It's going to be a nightmare to actually make, isn't it? All that cutaway wood . . . Really fragile for something so big."

"It is a challenge, certainly. And the wood the carpenter must work in is unhelpfully prone to splitting." He went to a corner where pieces of dark wood were leaning against the wall. He selected a section that had already been planed but not carved and brought it over for her to look at.

"But it is beautiful," she said, running her hand over the burnished surface. The rich brown glowed with flashes of deepest red. She smiled at him. "It will reward the effort, don't you think?"

He looked up from the wood sample and did not answer straight away. His expression of surprise and interest made her realize it was probably the first time he had ever seen her smile. Her time at Great Chalfield, her time in *his* time, had been so fraught, so full of anxiety, with the possibility of being caught out in a lie always with her, as well as the likelihood that she could fail Alice and that Flora would pay the price for it, not least because she might accidentally step back to her own century, all these things meant she must have looked constantly tense, worried, even frightened. But then, with Samuel, in his home, sharing a love of beautiful things and exquisite craftsmanship, just for a moment, all of that had slipped her mind.

It was just him and her, in his place of work, in his life, sharing his hopes and dreams, glimpsing what it meant to be him in his world that was so strange to her, and yet in some details strangely familiar, too.

"You have an eye for such things," Samuel said at last. "It is not something given to all."

And so they turned all their attention to the work at hand. She was given fresh paper and pen and ink, which she began with messily and clumsily. Samuel was patient, letting her find her way with the drawing pen made of wood and swan's feather, until slowly her drawings started to make sense. He made his own sketches from her descriptions too, and they talked about how best to achieve the look of the original piece. The storm buffeted the building, making the roof creak and the branches of the fruit trees strain against their ties to scrape at the walls and windows. The relentless rain continued all afternoon. There was a small stove in the studio, but it gave out a feeble heat which was hopeless in such an open, drafty space. Xanthe found that she did not care. She quickly forgot about the cold, and an hour passed, and then another, as together they worked on, totally absorbed in what they were doing, removed from the world and all its worries.

The heavy skies and gathering gloom had already forced Samuel to light lamps when Philpott entered the room apologetically.

"Forgive me, Master Samuel, but your father is returned. He brings news of the road north—it has flooded two miles out of Marlborough, and he informs me there is no possibility of either horse or carriage successfully making the journey back to Great Chalfield today."

Samuel and Xanthe exchanged glances. She had almost forgotten she would have to return to the Lovewells that same day.

Now, it seemed, she would not have to, after all. She felt a little flutter of happiness at the news, quickly followed by a nervousness when she realized it was staying in Samuel's company that made her feel that way.

Philpott asked, "Shall I have Amelia prepare the guest bedchamber, sir?"

"What? Oh, yes. We will convey Mistress Westlake home in the morning. No doubt the storm and floods both will have abated by then."

"No doubt, sir. Also, Master Appleby requested that supper be served as soon as possible, and asks that you and your . . . guest join him in the dining hall at your earliest convenience."

"We will come this minute," said Samuel, putting things away as he spoke. "The light is too poor to work further as it is."

"How early it gets dark in October," Xanthe murmured, seeing her own face reflected in the black glass of the window.

Samuel gave a light laugh. "I have surely kept you here too long," he said. "Do you not know this day is the first of November?"

"Already? The time is passing so quickly," she said, fighting a jolt of panic at the thought that for herself, and for Flora, the clock was ticking.

They trooped back into the house and went to the sitting room. Joshua was nowhere to be seen, but Master Appleby was standing by the fire, warming his hands over the flames.

"Ah, Samuel, there you are. Good. I must dine soon lest I faint for want of food. All day at the home of Lord Avebury, discussing plans for the east wing and not offered so much as a crust of bread." He stopped, noticing Xanthe, taking in her unpinned hair and shabby maid's clothes. He did not ask why she was there, so she guessed that he already knew why Samuel had brought her to the house. He frowned, turning to his son.

"Your guest looks every bit as in need of food and rest as I. You have been a poor host, I fear."

"Father, Mistress Westlake has been of tremendous assistance to me with my work on the screen for Great Chalfield. I confess I had not noticed how time had passed."

Master Appleby took a step toward her. He seemed to be studying her closely, and she sensed he was less than pleased about having his son spend so much time alone with a maid-servant. She expected to be sent to the kitchen for her food and dismissed for the evening. Instead, he took her hand, bowed briefly over it, and then smiled, the same face-transforming smile that his son had inherited.

"I hope you will forgive Samuel's social ineptitude, mistress. Allow me to right his wrongs. You are most welcome in our home. The inclement weather prevents us from returning you to the care of the Lovewells this night, but I trust you will be content to remain here a little longer. Let us go to table. Samuel, fetch your brother, if you please. And instruct Philpott to send for Amelia's grandmother, so that she may stop the night here."

"Amelia's grandmother?" Samuel asked.

"Yes, for pity's sake, would you so recklessly risk Mistress Westlake's reputation? She cannot spend a night alone in a house peopled entirely by men. Amelia, as is her habit, will return to her parents' house after dark. Show some concern, Samuel, some interest in the good lady's well-being. In truth, mistress, at times I despair of my son's ability to conduct himself in company. Now, will you join me?" He offered his arm, which she took, and he escorted her to the dining room.

If any space in the Appleby's house could be said to en-capsulate the difference between their home and that of the Lovewell's it was this one. No Great Hall for them. This was not a room for showing off, nor for entertaining on a grand scale or demonstrating wealth and status. This was a room for intimate dining, for the sharing of food with family and friends, for quiet meals and close conversation. It was large enough to accommodate a long, oak table at its center, around which were ten chairs, plain ones at the sides and more elaborate carvers with arms at either end. The walls of the room were paneled not with the dark, somber wood used at the manor house, but with soft, light oak, waxed and burnished to allow its natural color and richness to glow. At the far end of the room was a deep fireplace with a stone mantelpiece above it. Set into one side were two mullioned windows that overlooked the green and the other handsome town houses outside. On the other long wall were oil paintings, portraits of slightly austere ladies in plain but elegant clothes and similar men. Ancestors, Xanthe decided. The room was lit mostly with candles in pewter sticks on the table, or iron sconces on the walls. The feel of the room was warm, relaxed, and friendly. The table was laid with good quality pewter, with simple wooden or plain silver spoons. People would have their own knives. The only concession to luxury was the glass goblets, which were palest blue and had small red stones set into the stems. The floorboards were bare, so that their footsteps rattled as they entered the room. She was given a seat halfway down the table. Joshua arrived and amid good-natured jostling everyone took their places, Master Appleby at the head of the table, Samuel to his right, next to his guest, and Joshua to his left. Philpott and the maidservant, Amelia, brought watered wine in a carafe; warm bread; a thick, beefy broth in wooden bowls; a dish of mashed vegetables; a large grilled trout dressed in an herb sauce; and two roasted birds that looked too small to be chickens. Xanthe guessed at guinea fowl. There was also a bowl of apples and a truckle of cheese with a shiny yellow rind. It was good, wholesome food, carefully prepared, the level of meat showing this was an affluent household but one that did not believe in excess or waste.

Philpott addressed the master of the house. "Grandmother Garvy has arrived, sir. She will sup with us downstairs before Amelia leaves for home and will sleep in the attic bedroom. Will there be anything more, sir?"

"Nothing, Philpott. Get you to your supper, man. We will not be up late tonight, I think."

Joshua gave a light laugh at this. "So say you, father. Samuel mayhap has plans to keep our guest awake until dawn breaks so as to further bother her with details of his beloved screen."

Samuel refused to take the bait. "Some of us keep work in the forefront of our minds, brother."

"Oh? Are you accusing me of shirking my duties?" he asked with a grin, tearing off a chunk of bread and dunking it in his broth bowl.

"Unlike you, Joshua, I take little interest in the business of others."

"Ha!" Master Appleby put down his wine goblet. "You will not persuade your brother of the good sense of that, Samuel." Xanthe wondered what he meant by this, but he did not elaborate. Instead he turned to her and said, "You see we are a home without the improving presence of a woman, Mistress Westlake. My dear wife was taken into the Lord's loving arms four years since, and I fear we are rough company without her. My sons are all but feral at times."

The idea of such well-mannered men being described as wild made her laugh out loud. She felt all eyes watching her then. It was hard to keep thinking, every minute, of how a seventeenth-century girl would react, would behave. Would someone in her position, someone from the servant classes, who had nothing and nobody, would she think these people unrefined? Would she allow herself to laugh in their company? There was a very good chance she would give herself away with everything she did and said. She had to hope her being a minstrel, and therefore someone already outside normal society, would excuse most of her strangeness.

"Please do not concern yourself on my account," she told Master Appleby. "I have been shown every consideration." The language felt strange to her, overly formal, and not, in fact, what she had been using with Samuel. Had he noticed? They had been so busy working, perhaps he had not been paying attention to the way she spoke. She saw, in that moment, that she had the attention of the whole family. She could not let the opportunity pass. "I wonder, Master Appleby," she went on carefully, "have you heard of the young woman from Great Chalfield who stands accused of theft? Her name is Alice, and I believe, indeed I *know* her to be innocent."

"Master Lovewell did mention something of the matter, though I'm afraid he does not hold your opinion of the girl. Seems she will not speak up for herself, beyond insisting on her lack of guilt, and the mistress of the house is adamant no one other could have taken the pieces of her chatelaine. They were of some value. . . ." He let the statement hang, shaking his head as if to say this was enough to explain everything that had happened. And everything that would happen to Alice as a consequence.

Samuel surprised Xanthe by saying, "I have agreed to look into the matter, Father. Mistress Westlake is distressed that the maidservant is being treated unjustly."

"Why, Samuel," Joshua poured himself more wine, "do you see yourself as a gallant knight, galloping to the defense of a damsel? Or two damsels perhaps." He paused to look Xanthe over in a way that was all too familiar and not in any way limited to the 1600s. "The evidence before me suggests it is our guest you wish to help. An understandable wish, if I might be permitted to say so."

Samuel narrowed his eyes at his brother. "The day has not yet come when you require permission to say whatever fevered thoughts come into your mind."

"Brother, have I hit the nub?"

"Joshua," Master Appleby flapped his napkin at his son, "mind your manners. Samuel, I shall make inquiries regarding the case, though you know as well as I, there will be little I can do if no evidence is brought forward to support Mistress Westlake's belief in the girl's innocence."

Xanthe put on her best smile. "I would be so very grateful, Master Appleby, if you could try."

She felt all three men staring at her then and became suddenly painfully conscience of her loose hair. She knew enough of the customs of dress of the time to know that it was quite shocking to be at dinner with men, unchaperoned, in such a casual and unladylike state. Somehow adding a bright smile only made it worse, made her seem as if she were flirting. Why had she not taken time to read up on seventeenth-century etiquette before landing herself among people who noticed such tiny details and read enormous amounts of importance into them? It did not help that everything she was given to drink seemed to contain alcohol. Useful for steadying the nerves but potentially hazardous when it came to playing a part she knew so little about. She did her best to look a little more serious and tried not to meet anyone's eye.

"I wish only to help someone who has no one else to stand for her," she said quietly. "It surely cannot be her fault that she has lost her entire family and finds herself alone. Who better to take up her cause than me, a young woman who must also find her way in the world without the support of wealth or kin? After all, are we not measured by the way in which we treat the most vulnerable members of our society?"

At this, Xanthe felt a subtle shift in the way she was being regarded.

"Quite so," said Master Appleby, sufficiently reassured of her good character to continue with his meal.

"Mistress Westlake." Joshua was still looking at her more hungrily than his father was regarding his food, but his tone was altered somewhat—there was less joshing, more respect, she thought. "I stand rebuked and deservedly so."

It was Samuel's turn to laugh. "My little brother brought to heel!"

Joshua laughed off the jibe. "I have ever known my place with women, Samuel. I also know life does not have to be all grim endurance each and every day. Something you might remind yourself, from time to time."

"You do not know me as well as you suppose you do, brother. I am not incapable of merriment, it is only that I, for the most part, concern myself with matters that demand my serious attention. Matters that concern us all. Or should do."

Master Appleby and Joshua exchanged glances, and Xanthe sensed an ongoing conversation she had not heard the beginning of.

"Have a care, Samuel," his father said.

"I believe we may speak freely before Mistress Westlake. I am of the opinion she would share my views on matters of social justice, of liberty, of the right of the people to determine their own fate."

"Samuel . . ." His father sounded another note of caution, but his son would not be so easily silenced.

"Can we not speak freely in our own home? If not, then we have, in faith, allowed ourselves to become mute subjects, our tongues imprisoned behind the bars of our teeth, our thoughts no more at liberty than that poor girl who found herself in what is, after all, a lockup that bears the Appleby name."

"It is not *our* lockup, Samuel," said Joshua. "No more than the extension to Lord Avebury's house is ours, beyond our having built it."

"Only two days ago," Samuel went on, "I was in conversation with Francis Tresham. He sees as I do that our individual freedoms, our rights to the very thoughts in our own heads, for pity's sake, they are being taken from us one by one, as the pebbles can be taken from a beach. In this way the loss at first goes unnoticed, until it is too late, and all that remains is the shifting sand beneath what once was."

Joshua shook his head. "Francis Tresham is a dangerous man, as are many of your acquaintances."

"Enough!" Master Appleby brought his sons to order. "Let us choose a subject more suitable for the company we are fortunate enough to have."

After that exchange the conversation was kept to less-contentious subjects and soon, oiled by the wine, the mood relaxed. After the rigid hierarchy and grandeur of Great Chalfield, Xanthe enjoyed being in the presence of intelligent, liberal-minded people. Slowly she was able to let down her own guard. She detected an amount of social conscience within the family, even though they expressly avoided talking politics again. These were people who knew what it was to be poor. They had made a success of their profession at a time when it was new for this to mark a family out as acceptable or even noteworthy. Their work as architects was valued, and modest wealth had followed. They had not forgotten their more humble origins, though, that much was clear. She also saw that beneath Samuel's quiet seriousness lay something of a firebrand who took the fate of the common man to heart. Although he kept his feelings guarded, Xanthe still felt the bond they had established while they worked together. She liked being in his company. She liked sharing his passion for his work. She liked sitting there, with his family, watching him gradually relax a little more. She liked him.

It was after midnight when they eventually went to their rooms. Philpott had reappeared to clear the table, the candles were extinguished behind them as they went up, and she was given a small lamp and shown to her own bedchamber at the rear of the house. She had forgotten how tired she was until she sat on the edge of the high bed and pulled off her shoes. It had been a long day, with an early start, an exhilarating but exhausting ride into town, taking a soaking, working in Samuel's studio, and then a lengthy, entertaining but slightly charged evening. At least she felt she had won over some allies to Alice's cause. She had no way of knowing if any of the Applebys had sufficient influence to intervene, to fight in her corner and make a difference, but she was as certain as she could be that they would try. And it felt a relief not to have everything resting upon her own shoulders. With each passing day she was reminded in one way or another just how powerless she herself was. *Alice needs more than me if she is not to end up hanged,* Xanthe thought. It could be that her knowledge of the Drillington screen and her meeting Samuel would be the things that tipped the balance in Alice's favor. At last Xanthe felt there was hope. Real hope.

Wearily, she took off her dress, shift, and petticoat. A nightdress had thoughtfully been found for her and was laid out on the bed. It was simple, white cotton, with long sleeves, loosely gathered at the neck, with just a little lace at the front. She wondered, fleetingly, if it had belonged to Mistress Appleby once. How differently she was treated in this house. The Lovewells, for all that they liked her singing, saw her as a servant. A breed beneath them and somebody not to be given a second thought, except when she might be of use. The Applebys seemed to accept her, if not quite as an equal then at least as someone worthy of respect and consideration. She slipped the nightdress over her head and shivered as the cool cotton touched her body. Outside, the storm was still blowing with fearsome force, and the temperature in the room was low even for autumn. The bed looked wonderfully inviting, with its deep feather mattress, over-stuffed pillows and bolsters, thick blankets and bedspread of crewel work in blues and reds. She was just pulling back the covers, eager to climb in, when she heard a light tapping at the door. She snatched up her shawl and threw it around her shoulders, crossing it over at the waist.

"Who's there?" she asked.

"Mistress Westlake?" The reply was so softly spoken and muffled by the door she could not be certain who it was.

Xanthe stepped forward and lifted the latch, opening the door just a few inches. Joshua was standing on the landing, his jacket undone, his shirt untucked. He smiled, his eyes in shadow, but still able to twinkle somehow. Like most good-looking men, he knew the effect he could have on a woman. Some used it like a weapon, some did not. Joshua was most definitely of the kind that did.

"Such a turbulent night," he said. He kept his voice low and moved closer to the door. "I was concerned that you might not be able to rest. That you might be afraid."

"Of the wind?" she asked, hoping her own voice told him just how ridiculous he sounded.

"It played on my mind, mistress, that you are, after all, in a strange house, unaccompanied, a woman alone. . . ."

"You forget, Master Joshua, I am accustomed to traveling, for it is a necessity of my work. And I am often alone. Also, I believe I have a very able chaperone in the room above mine in the shape of Amelia's grandmother."

"A good woman indeed," he said, nodding. "Alas quite deaf. Has been so for many years." As he shared this gem of information, he placed his hand on the door and gently but firmly pushed at it.

Xanthe pushed back, jamming her foot behind it, wishing she still had her good heavy boots with her.

She opened her mouth to protest, biting back the instinct to tell him exactly what she thought of him in very twenty-first century terms, when a door further down the hallway opened.

"Joshua!" Samuel's fury at finding his brother at her door was unmistakable. In three strides Samuel was upon him, grabbing Joshua by the collar and dragging him backward. "For shame, brother!" he hissed at him.

Joshua laughed. "Samuel, what ill temper! Could it be you are driven to such rage only because I was quicker to the sweet mistress's door than you?"

At this Samuel slammed his brother up against the wall. Through gritted teeth he snarled at him. "Do not seek to dress me in the same colors you would choose for yourself! It was my knowledge of the workings of your mind and your incontinent desires that brought me from my bedchamber!" He gave Joshua a shove in the direction of his own room. "Get thee hence, and do not speak to me on the morrow, for I may be less willing to rein in my anger when I am rested."

Joshua gave a shrug and a smile, holding up his hands as if to say the prize was worth a try but of little consequence. Samuel watched until his sibling had shut himself in his room and then turned to Xanthe.

"I beg pardon for my brother, mistress. You do not deserve such treatment. Father would view such behavior toward a guest with horror, as do I."

"No damage done. Please don't let it sour things between you and your brother. He was just . . . being himself."

He regarded her closely for a moment, though she wondered if he could read her expression at all in the gloom of the hall-way. Had she made too little of the incident? Did he think she wanted Joshua to come to her room? She hated that idea, that he might think that of her. And she realized then that it was not because of her precious reputation that she cared, it was because she did not wish him to think she would have chosen Joshua over him. Because, in fact, the opposite was true.

Samuel bid her a rather formal goodnight and left her then. She closed the door, leaning against it for a full minute before the chill of the room drove her from her thoughts and into the high bed with its warm, heavy bedclothes.

19

SAMUEL AND XANTHE WERE BOTH UP AND BREAKFASTED BEFORE JOSHUA was awake. Master Appleby had agreed to try to talk to the magistrate on Alice's behalf, and as she knew this was her best hope, Xanthe felt less frantic, and more able to give herself over to helping Samuel. Neither of them mentioned the incident of the night before, and any awkwardness quickly vanished once they were back in the studio working together. She had a sharp pang of homesickness when he showed her a piece of stonework that he had commissioned for the planned extension to the manor house. It was a gargoyle, beautifully detailed and carved, and Flora had always had a soft spot for the gruesome little creatures, snapping them up if she ever found any at auctions or salvage yards. It was strange to meet a brand-new one, the stone still smooth, not yet pitted by weather or adorned with mosses and lichens.

"It will look very fine on the new wing of the house," she told Samuel. "You enjoy your work, don't you?"

"I do, though there are aspects of it that test me," he said.

She laughed. "The patrons? I can't imagine the Lovewells are easy to please."

"They are paying the piper; they must call the tune. Even so,

I am often conflicted when they request something that I consider unsuited to the building, or a poor fit. And yet I know I am blessed to be creating buildings that will last for generations, buildings that will stand as examples of how what can be imagined can be brought into being. I confess to sinful pride at the thought of our work surviving through the decades. Mayhap centuries."

"Centuries," she agreed.

"You believe so?"

"I'm certain of it." She thought of Great Chalfield in her own time, its exquisite seventeenth-century additions still there, still doing exactly what Samuel hoped they would do; withstanding wars and fickle fashions and weather and fires, so that hundreds of years of history continued within their walls. She wished she could tell him. Wished she could let him know that he'd succeeded, he created wonderful things that would live on. And that thought led her to the next unavoidable one: Samuel's work would survive into her own century, but of course Samuel would not. A shiver wriggled down her spine. She was talking to a ghost. She was standing so close to him, breathing in his warm scent of sandalwood and beeswax and woodsmoke. Close enough to see his broad chest rise and fall. To feel the life in him. To see the faint blue pulse in his throat. And yet, he was already long gone, in her own reality. Nothing left in his grave but dust and bones. Xanthe's head hurt with the madness of it all.

Samuel, knowing nothing of the chaos he was causing in her mind, continued to speak about the Lovewells. "I am fortunate that the times have produced such families, in truth. Their desire to show themselves as elevated in society has resulted in a great deal of work for master builders and architects alike. It is because of them that I am able to do what I do. It does a man no good to set himself above others, for that way I would not see one stone set in place. Master Lovewell has the ambition and the riches to build a great house. I merely provide the expertise."

"Oh, I think it's more than that. It's not just about knowing how to build something," she insisted. "It's about vision and passion. Nothing lasting and beautiful was ever made or built without them."

"Or without the ebb and flow of political change in the land. New nobles, families newly in favor, these come about only after alterations concerning those in power. And a new king is the clearest example of this."

"And the Lovewells are clear examples of new money."

"Ha! New money! I like this expression. You have a curious way of putting things, Mistress Westlake."

"Please, do you think you could stop calling me that? I realize it is . . . unusual, but I'd much prefer it if you called me Xanthe, at least while no one else is around."

He hesitated, then softly said, "Xanthe," trying the name out. "Xanthe," he repeated, and she felt goose bumps prickle her arms. "A curious choice, but maybe not so for a child of minstrels and troubadours."

"We are an unusual bunch of people," she agreed, hoping that would make him feel more comfortable with such informality.

"Very well. But you, then, must call me Samuel."

"I will. Samuel," she said, and then found that they were both standing there, staring at each other. She tutted and looked away, affecting interest in a piece of marble in the corner of the room, babbling on about Italy and shipping heavy stone and the cost of the thing. But all the while she was simply trying to shake off the way she had felt when he had said her name.

"Did you know," he said suddenly, "that it was Mistress

Lovewell who chose to take Alice in? It was she who knew the girl's family."

"I didn't know that. I always assumed it was her husband; I don't know why. He just seemed, well, kinder. As if it was the sort of thing he might do, particularly if Clara talked him into it. Something Willis told me made me feel Mistress Lovewell was against having the girl in her home."

"Alice's mother and Mistress Lovewell grew up together." He paused and then looked at her closely, as if watching for her reaction, when he said, "They were both of them raised in the Catholic faith."

"Mistress Lovewell is a Catholic?" Xanthe was amazed. Why would Alice have had to go to such lengths to hide her rosary, to keep her own beliefs secret, if her mistress was also Catholic?

"No longer," said Samuel. "She renounced her faith when she married. She has made a point of being a visibly devout Protestant ever since that day."

"But she still felt some allegiance to her childhood friend? She must have, to have taken a known Catholic and daughter of executed traitors into her home, even as a servant."

Samuel said carefully, "The thought entered my mind that it might suit Mistress Lovewell to be rid of the girl. It may be that the threat of being tainted by her past proved harder to endure than the mistress had anticipated. And, she may have come to fear for Clara's safety, to doubt the wisdom of what may have been an impulsive act of charity. She would, ultimately, be happier without the girl, I believe."

"And if Alice were convicted of a crime then the mistress couldn't be blamed for severing all contact with her, could she?"

"It is a . . . possibility."

A cold heaviness settled in the pit of her stomach. "Which

means she's not going to be ready to believe in Alice's innocence, however much proof is put in front of her."

Samuel nodded. "If you are able to find such proof it would be prudent to ensure it is revealed as publicly as possible. Better not to put in Mistress Lovewell's way the temptation to . . . obscure the truth."

She looked up at Samuel. "Thank you," she said. "For caring about Alice. You cannot know what it means to me."

"Life is full of hidden perils," he said. "If we cannot help one another when we are able to do so, then I fear for all our futures."

She thought of the distant future. Of her future, where there was no Samuel, and she found it was painful to imagine. She made herself bring her attention back to where she was, to his reality.

"Joshua said last night, at dinner, that one of your friends is dangerous? Why would that be so?"

He hesitated before saying "There are men far braver than I who put themselves at risk for the greater good. Joshua would rather we protect our own. He considers it enough that we do what we must for our family, no more." He paused and then added, "I find myself, at times, unable to remain merely a bystander to the world's events. In particular those about which I have the opportunity to be of use. To do something to save lives, perchance."

"You are not afraid? For yourself and your family?"

"Can we allow ourselves to be ruled by fear?"

Xanthe thought about how fear of what Margaret Merton might do to her mother had been the galvanizing force behind her own actions. However much she told herself she was helping Alice, it was exactly fear, more than anything, that drove Xanthe now. Fear for someone she loved. "It is easier to be brave for oneself," she said quietly, "than for someone we care about, don't you think?"

Samuel nodded. He seemed to consider something for a moment, studying Xanthe closely, and then made his decision. He offered her his hand.

"Come with me," he said. When she hesitated he said, "Please. There is something I wish you to see. Something . . . important. I can trust to your silence, can I not?"

"Of course." She took his hand. She needed his help. She had to prove she could be trusted.

Samuel led her to the rear of the workshop and opened a narrow door that gave way to a flight of steps leading down. He took up a lamp and descended the flight ahead of her. The steps twisted along a rough stone wall and into a low-ceilinged cellar. Samuel hung the lamp on a hook. As Xanthe's eyes adjusted to the gloom she could see there were barrels and crates and piles of sacks.

"There is a cellar beneath the main house where we keep our wine and beer and most of the stores for the kitchen: tallow, lamp oil, candles, flour, and so on. The two cellars are connected by that door there." He pointed to a plain wooden door just visible in the gloom of the basement. "In here we keep further stores, winter vegetables and salted meats, as well as items for our work that we need only infrequently."

Xanthe wandered the space, running her fingers over the worn barrels, peering into crates. She identified carrots put into sand to preserve them, apples set carefully apart from one another on a cool stone shelf, another taken up with scallions and turnips. There were crates covered in burlap and labeled GYPSUM or LIME or other items that might be used for the finer aspects of building. The air in the space was dry at least, with no hint of damp, but the height of the ceiling and the darkness all began to work

on Xanthe's deep-rooted fearful memories. While she wanted
to gain Samuel's trust, she hoped she would not have to linger
in the dark cellar.

"It is all so . . . orderly," she said. "And useful." She came
to stand in front of him, looking at him levelly. "But I don't
think you brought me down here to impress me with your
housekeeping, did you?"

Samuel shook his head. He turned to a pile of flour sacks
and set to shifting them, one by one, until the floor was revealed.
The flagstones beneath were large and smooth and had the appearance of having been laid many years before. Samuel scuffed
the small amount of spilled flour and sawdust laid down against
any rising dampness. Only now Xanthe could see that there were
three small holes in the nearest flag. Samuel took an iron bar
from a nearby hook and inserted its hooked end into one of the
holes. With some effort he heaved at the flat stone. It scraped
against the gritty earth and onto the flag beside it, revealing a
cavity beneath. Samuel fetched the lamp and held it so that its
faltering light fell at their feet. Xanthe leaned forward and saw
that there was a small space cut into the floor, lined with wood.

"What's it for?" she asked.

"What do you suppose?"

"Valuables, maybe? To keep money?"

"It is indeed for something precious, for it may be all that
protects our greatest freedom; that which allows us to follow our
hearts and preserve our souls."

Xanthe frowned, and then, at last, she understood. She recalled visiting a grand house in the north of England, when she
was only a child, and being shown just such a place by a tour
guide. A hiding place. She shivered as she recalled the purpose
for these constructions and the fate of people who might have
been desperate enough to use them.

"It's a priest hole!" she said, dropping to her knees to inspect it more closely. The cavity was barely six feet long and three feet wide. Just big enough for a man to lie down in. It was cut deep into the ground, so that he would also have been able to crouch or sit. The boards that lined it were of hardwood, free from mold or moisture, but affording no comfort. She imagined what it might have been like for a priest to flee for his life to this place, to scramble down into the hole to avoid discovery and evade searching soldiers, no doubt with a jar of ale and a piece of bread thrown in after him, and to have the horribly heavy stones dragged into place above his head. There would have been no light other than that which could enter through the three tiny holes, which might anyway have been covered by sawdust and sacks. It must have been distressingly cramped and claustrophobic.

"But, there would be no air," she said, shaking her head. "Samuel, how would anyone breathe in such a place?"

"That is something I thought very carefully about when I built this," he told her.

"You made this?"

Samuel was too busy explaining the finer points of the ventilation system he had constructed to answer such an obvious question. *Of course he had built it,* Xanthe realized. This must be what the family had argued about the night before. The Applebys were Catholics, though not openly so, and they welcomed a priest into their home to observe mass. A hanging offense, for the priest and for the family. A priest hole was the last resort. If the authorities came knocking at the wrong moment, or indeed anyone who might betray them, their best hope was to be able to hide the priest. Xanthe recalled now that many houses had had priest holes built into them, behind false walls, under floorboards, between rooms. She had been impressed by the ingenuity involved in hiding them so well, and repelled by the idea of being shut away in such a tiny space, but she had never before really considered that someone had to design and build them. And that someone, in this case, was Samuel. As he told her of the vital conduit for air that he had modeled into the structure, with tiny tunnels and grilles that allowed the flow of outside air in two directions, she wondered how many other priest holes he had secretly installed in the houses of his patrons. Was there even one at Great Chalfield?

"You have made others too, haven't you?"

He sighed and turned to her. "How could I refuse?"

Xanthe reached out and put her hand over his. "You are a brave man, Samuel."

"Not as brave as the poor wretches who must take to these pitiful hiding places. When the authorities are at the door, or the soldiers are sent to search a house, the priest must stay silent and still in his bolt-hole, not coughing, nor sneezing, nor giving way to panic, else he will be discovered. The hardest part of his incarceration is that he cannot know how long he must abide. And he cannot free himself, for such places, of necessity to make them well hidden, cannot be opened from the inside. We must, as you see, pile all manner of objects upon them, to make their hiding so complete. If, as sometimes happens, the family of the house are taken away, often the servants too, for questioning, the priest may remain here for days. Weeks." Samuel ran his hand through his hair. "I confess when I first agreed to make them I told myself I was making a place of safety. The sad truth is at times they prove to be nothing more than tombs."

As if deciding he had said too much, Samuel clapped his hands, rubbing them together against the cold. "Enough of this. Such maudlin thoughts. It was wrong of me to bring you here, to show you." He began hauling the flagstone back into place.

"No," Xanthe said quickly. "I'm glad you did. I understand so much more now."

At last, when she had helped Samuel replace the flour sacks, she said, "Thank you, for trusting me."

"Knowing what you do, you might choose to distance yourself from us now."

She shook her head. "Your secret is safe with me, I promise. We will help each other."

He smiled then and ushered her back up the steep stone steps and into the workshop.

"And now, to work. See?" He pointed through one of the long windows. "The storm is easing. Soon the flood will have receded and I shall have to take you back to Great Chalfield. Let us complete as much of the detail of the screen as we are able."

Again, they worked well together, absorbed in what they were doing, content to forget the wider world and its dangers and difficulties, more than happy to be in each other's company. They talked as they worked but only of things related to what they were doing. Of the great houses which they both knew and the treasures within them. Of craftsmanship and skill and the execution of ideas. Of the beauty of an object, of its lasting qualities, of their own likes and dislikes. It was a surreal experience, discussing things that were, for her, antiques but were, for Samuel, examples of modern creativity. When he talked about new techniques and innovations, she had to pick her words cautiously when responding, and it was hard to hold back. She wanted to tell him about styles of art, about methods of architecture, about houses and glorious paintings or movements in silver work or jewelry that had not yet been invented. When she thought about things he would love, of ideas and developments that would fascinate him, it seemed almost mean to keep them from him. But she could not tell him any of it. Ever.

They continued to work for most of the day. Samuel had Philpott bring them some simple food for lunch. Xanthe had already conquered her embarrassment the night before and asked Amelia's grandmother where the necessary house was, so she was able to excuse herself when she needed to and make the stormy journey across the courtyard. The little building that served as the toilets for the house was dark and the roof and door rattled in the wind, but it looked clean enough, and private. She had washed that morning in cold water with fragrant lavender soap. Somehow she always imagined life years ago being for the most part uncomfortable and grimy, but she could see now that this was not the truth of it. Not if a person were lucky enough to be somewhere near the top of the social order, at least. The Appleby household was not full of servants and luxury, but it felt safe, friendly, and comfortable.

At around four o'clock the light of the shortened autumn day began to render detailed drawings impossible to make, so the pair admitted defeat and went inside. The truth was, they had all but finished work on the plans for the screen. There was nothing more she could usefully offer in the way of information on the thing. Which meant there was really no reason for her to stay any longer. As soon as the road was useable again, she would be returned to Great Chalfield.

Inside, they found Master Appleby sitting by the fire.

"Ah, I was beginning to wonder if Samuel would ever permit you to emerge from the studio, Mistress Westlake. Such diligence is laudable, Samuel, but you must guard against becoming a hard taskmaster." He stood as she entered the room and invited her to take the chair opposite.

Samuel went to the table to pour them both wine. "The plans for the screen are much improved, Father. I could not have produced anything so accurate without Xanthe's help."

His father looked surprised at the use of her first name but said nothing about it.

"I am pleased to hear it. As no doubt Master Lovewell will be, both for the sake of the improvements to the Great Hall and for the return of his minstrel. I am told the flood water has receded and the stage was able to pass along the north road earlier today. We shall be able to deliver Mistress Westlake back to her home before dark."

Samuel opened his mouth to reply to this but changed his mind. What could he say? What possible reason could there be for not returning her? Other than that he didn't want her to go. Because she could see that he did not. She took a deep swig of wine and then said, "Master Appleby, you have made me so very welcome in your home. And I know you have taken up the cause of Alice on my behalf. Will you not allow me to repay your kindness? Perhaps I might sing for you after supper? Of course it would mean my staying here one more night. . . ."

Samuel jumped in. "That would be most welcome. Would it not, Father?"

The older man looked hard at his son. He cannot have been pleased to think of his eldest and finest falling for a maidservant, but he must have seen it was becoming a real possibility.

Master Appleby sighed. "It is already late, so perhaps it would be best not to attempt the journey until the morning. And yes, indeed, it would be most diverting to hear you sing again, Mistress Westlake."

Samuel and Xanthe exchanged the briefest of glances.

"On the matter of Alice," Master Appleby continued, "I do not, I'm afraid, have encouraging news. I have spoken to the magistrate himself, my business having taken me close to Salisbury this morning. He told me the girl is still refusing to defend herself beyond saying she is no thief. Without anyone to speak for her, and without the missing items being discovered, there is little hope she will be found anything other than guilty. I am sorry for it, but I can do very little to help her."

Xanthe felt suddenly swamped with guilt. How could she have been so easily and completely distracted from what she had come here to do? All the time she had been enjoying herself working with Samuel, getting to know him, her mother had been in no less danger than the moment she had arrived. She had been much too quick to hand over responsibility for her fate to someone else. What had she been thinking? Flora's safety, her life, rested in her hands, no one else's. And now she was deeply ashamed of letting herself lose sight of that.

She was about to question Master Appleby more on what the magistrate had said when the sound of the front door being opened followed by animated voices in the hallway interrupted their conversation.

"Joshua is home," Samuel noted.

The door was thrown open and his brother came in, his face aglow, his whole being lit up with something. At first she thought it was good humor, then she smelled alcohol on his breath, and detected a note of anger in his voice, however polite his words.

"Father, Samuel, ah, the lovely Mistress Westlake, still with us, I am happy to note," he said as he all but bounded across the room.

At that moment there was a hammering on the door and seconds later Philpott arrived with a letter for Samuel. He took it from him, breaking the wax seal and unfolding the message to read its contents. His face darkened as he did so.

"Further word from Salisbury," he told Xanthe, pausing to look up at her. "The date of Alice's trial has been set. She is to go before the magistrate on Wednesday morning."

"The day after tomorrow?" She shook her head. "But, that is so soon. We haven't time. . . ."

Samuel put a steadying hand on her arm. "All is not lost," he told her.

"What time is the trial?"

"The court sits at ten. Hers will be among the first cases of the day to be heard."

"Will she be given a lawyer?" she asked. "I mean, someone to speak for her. Will they call witnesses?"

It was Joshua who spoke up then, his voice for once somber.

"Mistress Westlake, it pains me to tell you this," he said. "Without support in her defense in the way of proof, there is little a lawyer could do. The trial is merely a formality. It is a process for announcing rather than determining guilt. And," he hesitated and then went on, "it is the moment in which what is deemed an appropriate sentence will be passed."

20

LATER, WHEN SHE HAD TIME TO THINK ABOUT IT, XANTHE WOULD BE ashamed she had not been more grateful for the care the Applebys had shown her, but at the time she was too consumed with worry to properly appreciate it. As soon as Joshua explained to her how serious, almost inevitable, Alice's fate was, she had allowed herself to become angry. How could this be justice? Why would no one see how unfair, how unreasonable such treatment was? Was someone's life really of no more value than a few silver trinkets? Samuel had tried to calm her and reassure her: they would go to the trial and speak up for her. Master Appleby had sent a letter to a man of the law who might be able to think of a defense for Alice, and Appleby had trusted no one but Philpott to deliver it. Joshua had poured wine for everyone and called for sweetmeats from the kitchen.

After two hours of exploring every possibility and finding nothing helpful, Xanthe realized that there was something she could do, but she had to do it without Samuel. She made her excuses, claiming fatigue, which men of the day appeared to almost expect women to suffer from on a daily basis, and went to her room. She sat on the bed, waiting until she heard all three men climb the stairs and go to their own rooms. Only then did she step over to the window, ignore the frantic racing of her heart, open her gold locket, gaze at her mother's gentle face, and wish herself home.

The journey was startlingly swift. There was the falling sensation and the dizziness, with sounds of distant voices and a rushing of air pressing against her, and then she was once again on the gritty floor of the blind house. She stayed crouched, panting for a moment. When she felt steady enough to get to her feet the first thing that struck her was how cold she was. It might have been summer in her own time, but the thick stone walls of the blind house kept out the heat. The second thing that surprised her then was that she was still fully clothed. She had been in such a hurry to make the leap through the centuries she hadn't stopped to think that she might arrive naked. Mercifully, her seventeenth-century garments had traveled with her. Running her hands over the skirt, she could detect a roughness she hadn't noticed before, as if the fibers had worn or been somehow weakened by their journey through the centuries, but the clothes were still there, still intact. There was so much to process and no time in which to do it. She tried to take stock, then tensed, detecting at once the heavy presence of Margaret Merton. Something shifted in the darkness, though still remained invisible.

"I know you're here," Xanthe spoke into the gloom of the little building. "There's something I need to do. To help Alice. I will go back as soon as I've done it, I promise. You are going to have to trust me on this."

She waited, fearing the ghost would appear and slow her down, or worse, prevent her from leaving, sending her back again, perhaps. The air seemed to thicken, the vibrations subtly alter, but nothing more. How much Mistress Merton could see of what was going on in the past Xanthe could not be certain. She pushed the door open a little further and used the incoming light from the streetlamp on the other side of the garden wall to find the chatelaine. There were just the seventeenth-century parts, of course. The Victorian pieces were still in her room in Great Chalfield. She found the silver chains and clasp lying on the dirt. They were her only way back to Alice and Samuel. She placed them carefully on the right-hand side of the door so she would know where to find them when she needed to return. Then, hitching up her skirts, she pushed the door open and peered out. The garden was mercifully dark, and all was quiet. Xanthe thought about going to get her own phone, retrieving it from where she had left it beside her bed, but the risk of waking her mother was too real. And what if it was out of charge? No, she would stick to her plan and make her way to Liam. There wasn't time to change into the clothes that she had hidden in the garden. She would just have to hope she wasn't spotted by anyone she knew, and she was fairly sure that the way she was dressed was not going to be the most difficult thing to explain to Liam.

She retrieved her house keys from her hidden bag and moved quickly and quietly across the lawn. The key sounded loud in the lock of the back door. Inside, the smell of beeswax furniture polish, paint, wood glue, and the dust of ages made her feel instantly at home. It was hard not to nip upstairs to her mother's room. Just to see her. Just to reassure herself that Flora was well. But she could not risk waking her. She opened the front door of the shop as carefully as she could, given that it needed quite a tug to get the old wood to free itself from the doorjamb. In her haste she had forgotten the bell, which clanged loud enough to wake the whole street. She grabbed hold of it. She waited, heart pounding, listening for sounds of Flora stirring. Nothing. Had she had to take extra painkillers or sleeping pills because her arthritis had flared up again? She felt the now familiar wrench at leaving her as she slipped out of the shop and down the cobbled street. The town was asleep, blurred beneath the dull glow of the streetlights. Everything was so unchanged, so normal, and yet she could never look at it in the same way again. The space at the end of the street was where the original blind house had once stood. Above The Feathers, a sign had once swung proclaiming it to be THE THREE QUILLS. At the top of the hill, hidden by another church now, was the little green surrounded by old brick town houses, one of them once the home of the Applebys. She squared her shoulders and quickened her pace. She could not let herself become disturbed by the enormity of her newfound ability to journey through time; there was something she had to do. She had brought her attention to bear on that, to the exclusion of everything else. She hurried down the narrow street, relieved to find Liam had left the gates to his yard open. The flat was in complete darkness, and his front door lacked a doorbell. She thought of hammering in the door but dismissed the idea. She didn't want light—sleeping neighbors waking up and seeing a frantic woman, apparently in fancy dress, desperate to wake up a young single man in the middle of the night. She couldn't risk someone recognizing her, or mentioning to her mother that she had been seen. The possible complications were too difficult and too time consuming to risk. Instead, she searched around for some small stones— not as easy to find in a street as one might think—and threw them up against Liam's window. She was on her second handful when Liam appeared, bleary eyed. He opened the window and frowned down at her.

"Xanthe?" was all he managed.

"Sorry," she began, the first of many times she was to say that to him over the next hour. "Can you let me in?"

She must have looked more than a little deranged, dressed as she was and babbling at him. Liam, dressed in tracksuit trousers and pulling on a T-shirt, refused to do anything until they had some tea. The idea of pausing for refreshment when she wished only to make progress with her urgent mission made her become even more incoherent, which only made Liam insist. She could see he was not prepared to agree to anything otherwise. Fighting her own growing sense of panic at time passing, she let him lead her up the narrow stairs into his little flat. Once they were sitting at his kitchen table sipping strong, sweet Assam and eating shortbread biscuits, he tried to make sense of what little information she had given him.

"So, putting aside for the moment the fact that you're dressed for some sort of Civil War reenactment . . ."

"It's complicated. It would take too long to explain," she said, noticing then that the colors of her dress were strangely faded. It was only now, in the cheerfully lit kitchen, that she was able to see that the hues had definitely become more faint. Had it happened straight away, she wondered, or was it an ongoing process? Liam's voice shook her from her confused thoughts.

"Let's just deal with the fact that you're back from Milton Keynes, except that you never really went there, because the friend who lives there didn't really need you in the first place, but someone else does, only you can't tell me who. And your mother mustn't know you're here, and you can't tell me why. OK, that's all brilliantly clear so far."

"Sorry," she said again, and meant it. She knew she was going to be asking a lot of Liam, and there was no reason he should just help her without question. "Really," she said, "I know it all sounds ridiculously mysterious."

"Your words, not mine."

"But, well, there is stuff I can't tell you. It's too complicated."

"For my basic little brain?"

"I didn't mean that. It's just . . . let's say the secrets are not mine to tell. But someone is in deep trouble, and I may be the only hope she has."

He munched a biscuit and shrugged. "So what is it exactly, in simple words that I will be able to understand, that you want me to do?"

"Nothing. That is, I just need to use your computer. I need the internet."

"Not working in Milton Keynes? Oh, wait, you haven't been there!"

"Liam, please?"

He shrugged and held up his hands in surrender. "OK. Internet. Why not?" He fetched his laptop and set it up on the table for her. "Am I allowed to ask what it is you're looking for?"

"That," Xanthe said, punching out broad searches on the worn keyboard, "is something I'm curious about myself." She frowned, biting her bottom lip as she deleted one search and typed in another. Not for the first time she cursed the vastness of the web, the swathes of useless information that had to be plowed through before anything useful, or even relevant, could be found. It was difficult to know where to start. Searches about laws in the seventeenth century were far too vague. Questions about loopholes in the law regarding theft in the 1600s were too specific and sent two different search engines fizzing off at unhelpful tangents. Xanthe could feel low-level panic coloring everything she was doing. She couldn't leave until she had found something that could work as a defense for Alice. But what?

After half an hour of tense silence, save for the clicking of keys and the occasional exasperated sigh, Liam collected the mugs from the table.

286 :: PAULA BRACKSTON

"More tea," he said, and set about making it. "I'd be happy to help," he called over his shoulder, "if I knew what it was I was helping with."

"If I thought there was any way you *could* help, but it's . . ."

"Complicated. I think you mentioned that."

"I'm not being deliberately cryptic." Xanthe turned and caught the unconvinced expression on his face. "OK, I need to find out if there's some way a person about to be tried and convicted for theft can be got off, I don't know, on some sort of technicality. A loophole."

Liam looked serious for a moment. "Has your old boyfriend been in touch again?"

"What? Oh, no. Nothing like that. This is . . . a friend is in trouble. She's relying on me."

"Does she have a lawyer?"

"Not as such."

"Good place to start, I'd have thought. Did this friend actually steal anything?"

"Well, yes, but . . ."

"Hmm, tricky. Might be best to fess up and appeal to the judge's better nature. Say sorry, promise not to do it again, that sort of thing."

"She certainly won't get to do it again if they hang her." As soon as the words were out of her mouth Xanthe regretted them.

Liam plonked the freshly filled mugs of tea down on the table and stared at her hard.

"What worries me most about that statement," he said, "is that you don't look like you're joking."

"I'm sorry." Xanthe began to rub her temples, closing her eyes against a burgeoning headache. "I know it doesn't make any sense. I'm talking about the law as it was in the early sixteen hundreds."

"Of course you are." He sat down opposite her.

Xanthe opened her eyes and met his stare. "I don't have time to convince you. Just humor me." When he gave another why-not shrug, she went on. "There must be something we can argue in her favor."

"Mitigating circumstances, sort of thing?"

"Maybe." She scrolled through more pages of repetitive information.

"Did someone else make her do it, d'you think? Would coercion be grounds for . . . something?"

Xanthe shook her head. "There was no one else involved. Damn it, I'm getting further away from what I want. So much rubbish."

Liam chomped another biscuit thoughtfully for a moment and then suggested, "Try another angle. You know, come at the thing differently."

"Differently how?"

"Well, when I'm struggling to diagnose a problem with a car, I stop looking at what I think the problem is and start thinking about what I think a solution might look like."

Xanthe looked up from the screen, about to say something dismissive, but then she stopped to consider what he had said. Perhaps looking at how to defend someone vulnerable and guilty was all wrong. There could be another way. She tried to think about how a powerful person would get out of a similar situation. "You might have a point," she said, thinking aloud. "If a person with good connections needed a way out. Or someone with money, or influence . . . a high position in society, say, well, they'd have ways of getting away with things."

"Friends in high places and lots of money, yup, I reckon they'd find that loophole."

"OK"—Xanthe resumed her typing—"so who are those people. Or rather, who were they?"

"Way back then? Aristocrats? Landowners? Who else had power?"

"The church," Xanthe said at once, thinking of how it was the particular manner of Alice's faith that had got her and her family into so much danger. "The clergy." She deleted her last search and tried again:

How would a member of the clergy benefit from his position if charged with a crime?

Possible answers pinged up on the screen.

"Well?" asked Liam.

"Bingo!"

"Really?"

"Listen to this: 'When standing trial, a priest could claim Benefit of Clergy. This entitled him to be tried by a bishop, rather than a magistrate, who was empowered to choose his own sentence. As the Church protected their own, this was guaranteed to be far more lenient than anything the accused could expect from the secular law. In fact, where a first offense had been proven and the accused was likely to hang, the clerical church would usually impose a term of one year's imprisonment instead.'"

"Is your friend a vicar?"

"No, but wait, it goes on: 'Over time this law was extended so that people outside the Church could also use it, the test being that they be able to read a passage from the Bible.' Alice can read!"

"So it worked for women, too?"

Xanthe scanned the document in front of her. "Well, there's a record of it having been used by nuns, and it doesn't say anywhere here that ordinary women aren't allowed to claim it."

"If it's that easy I should have thought everyone would be using it."

"Everyone who could read, maybe. Which was, believe me, a really small percentage of the population." Xanthe thought about the Lovewells' household, running through their names and faces in her mind. Most, she knew, would have been illiterate. But not Alice. Alice was born of a wealthy family. A family who knew their Bible. Even if it was, politically, the wrong one. "There is a risk," she said, more to herself than Liam.

"Yeah?"

"Well, this whole mess came about because of . . . let's say because of what my friend's family believed in. She has had to keep her faith secret. To use religion as her defense, well, it's playing with fire."

"You reenactors take this stuff very seriously, don't you?"

Xanthe looked up from the computer and studied Liam's face. She saw there that he didn't really believe she was engaged in some sort of Civil War role-playing, but that he was prepared to go with it, to let it be, not to press her further, if it was easier for her. It was a measure of his character, of his ability to put someone else first. She liked him for that. She was truly grateful.

"We do," she said, turning her attention back to her search. "Have you got a piece of paper and a pen? No, hang on, make that a pencil? I need to write some of this down."

As soon as she had made her notes Xanthe got up to leave. As she did so she noticed tiny fibers falling from her clothes, and that the colors had faded even more. It seemed anything she brought back with her was at best unstable. How long before the garments disintegrated altogether, she wondered. She folded the paper and tucked it into her deepest pocket.

"You're going?" Liam asked. "Can I drive you somewhere?"

"No, I'll be fine." Xanthe found herself wishing she could

confide in him. She stepped forward and gave him a peck on the cheek. "I would have been stuck without you, Liam. Thank you."

He looked at her thoughtfully. "Will you tell me what this is really all about, one day when you're not in such a tearing hurry?"

She nodded. "One day," she promised, not knowing if she would ever be able to keep her word.

After convincing Liam she didn't need him to go with her anywhere, Xanthe hurried back through the deserted streets of Marlborough and crept back through her house. All was still quiet and dark, and she reached the blind house without bumping into anyone. On the threshold she hesitated, looking longingly up at the little bedroom windows. It was hard to leave without seeing her mother, without checking on her. In that moment of hesitation she felt the heavy presence of Margaret Merton growing stronger. There was no time to dwell on anything, no time to waiver, no time to be afraid.

"I'm going, OK?" she said to the deeper shadow in the blackness within the blind house. "I'm keeping my side of the bargain. Just make sure you keep yours and stay away from my mother."

{ 21 }

XANTHE HAD NOT DARED THINK ABOUT WHERE SHE WOULD APPEAR WHEN she arrived in the seventeenth century again. As far as she could work out, each time she had traveled, she ended up near something significant, or at least looking at something that mattered to Alice, something that was connected to the story of the chatelaine. She could think of no way to control where she emerged, and it was too scary to stop and consider the consequences of turning up somewhere dangerous. On this occasion, to her immense relief, she found herself in Samuel's workshop. She knelt on the dusty floor, allowing her breath to return to normal and the giddiness to fade. The space was unlit but not in darkness, and mercifully empty, so that there was no one to see her materialize. She got to her feet, brushing down her skirts and moving to the window. As the light fell upon her clothes she realized that they had regained their original colors, and that there were no more fibers falling from them. It was as if, by returning to their own time, they had been restored.

Xanthe peered through the thick glass into the small courtyard. The weather was still wet and unsettled, with a brisk breeze rustling the few remaining brittle leaves of the ornamental trees that sheltered the herb beds. It was difficult to know what time it was. She tried to do the math that would tell her how many hours had passed while she was away. She calculated that she had spent little more than an hour in her own time, which should mean something like a day in the 1600s. She had left in the early evening. It was too cloudy to see where the sun sat in the sky, but the day did feel as if it were drawing in somehow. As she stepped outside she heard very few birds, confirming that this was not the pale light of dawn but the softness of twilight. She felt chilled rather than cold, as if her hasty dash to her own time and back again had disturbed her equilibrium, leaving her slightly weakened, almost feverish. She needed to marshal her thoughts. She would have to explain her sudden disappearance.

"Mistress Westlake!" Samuel's voice made her start. She turned to find him emerging from the door of the house. She tried to read his expression as he strode toward her. "We have been concerned, mistress. You left without word, without explanation." She felt the sting of him addressing her so formally. She could not afford to lose his trust, not now.

"Forgive me, Samuel, there was something I needed to do. I . . . sought the help of a friend. Someone who might be able to help Alice."

"A friend? But, you are not from Marlborough. I understood you knew no one in this area save the Lovewells."

"No one who lives here permanently," she answered quickly, hating herself once again for the lies that she was forced to tell. "My friend is a fellow player with the troupe I once worked with, a musician in fact. I knew him to be visiting the town again briefly."

"Him?" An unmistakable flash of jealousy passed across Samuel's face.

"An elderly man, a grandfatherly figure to us all. Someone I have known for many years and whose advice I have sought before."

"And you did not think to inform me that you were to be absent? I had no way of knowing where you were, what you intended . . . whether or not you would return."

"I feared he would leave before I could speak with him. There was not time."

"And this musician is also an expert in matters of law?"

Xanthe could see he was far from convinced.

"Samuel, I—"

She got no further, as at that moment Philpott came from the house. He gave a stiff bow in her direction and then addressed Samuel.

"Master Appleby sent me to inform you, sir, the guests have arrived. He requests that you join him at once."

Samuel frowned, evidently torn between doing his father's bidding and pressing Xanthe further on the matter of her curious friend. She could see that he was hurt by what he might see as a slight, or perhaps a lack of trust. What had he imagined, she wondered, when he discovered her gone? Had he really thought he would never see her again? And did it matter to him? It seemed it did.

"Samuel!" Joshua came bounding from the direction of the stables, the wind ruffling his already unruly hair. He smiled at the sight of Xanthe. "Ah! The songbird has returned to us. We shall have entertainment this night after all. Excellent! Come, let us join father, for he frets if left to play host to men of business by himself, you know that, brother. Mistress Westlake . . ." He made an elaborate bow to let her go before him.

Xanthe had no choice but to be shepherded indoors. She remembered with a sinking heart that she had promised to sing for the Applebys. It was the last thing she felt like doing, and besides, she needed to speak with Samuel. Needed to explain her plan, to sound him out about it, to convince herself that it wasn't a mad and dangerous idea. As she drew level with him she took the folded piece of paper from her pocket, wishing she had written her notes more clearly, and pressed it into his hand.

"Read this," she said. "Please."

Wordlessly he took it from her and tucked it into the breast pocket of his black velvet jacket.

In the dining hall, Master Appleby was doing his best to make his guests feel welcome. There were three well-dressed men, prosperous, Xanthe judged, but not nobility. The reason for the gathering was evidently to strengthen connections, one man being an importer of marble, another a wine merchant, and the third a master mason. The introductions made, they went to the table, where a fine spread was provided, with an abundance of meat and fish. Joshua was in his element with their guests, full of witty remarks and easy laughter. Samuel became even quieter in such lively company. When they had dined, Xanthe sang for them, doing her best to put her heart into it. She was a performer. She had to ignore her own tiredness, her own anxiety and tension, and focus on the song. She closed her eyes as she sang a gentle ballad, letting the notes soothe her and calm her. After that she treated the guests to something a little more daring and upbeat, which was very well received.

The evening wore on, and even when all the food was eaten and what Xanthe considered to be unhelpful amounts of wine drunk, still the visitors showed no sign of leaving. Master Appleby looked tired, but Xanthe could see he would never be so rude as to suggest the visit should come to an end. It dawned on her then that they were waiting for her to go to bed. That there was probably another phase to the evening that could not begin with a woman present. A woman they were no doubt wishing would see sense and leave them to their men's ribald talk. Exasperated, she saw that there was going to be no chance of her talking to Samuel, no possibility of waiting for a quiet moment when everyone had gone home.

She got to her feet, her chair scraping against the flagstones.

"If you will excuse me, gentlemen, I have an early start in the morning," she said, bobbing a polite curtsy. She left the room to murmured thanks and slightly slurred farewells. Samuel caught her at the door.

"We will talk further in the morning," he told her, lightly placing his hand on her arm. It seemed he had forgiven her for her earlier disappearing act. "Courage," he said. "All is not yet lost."

Weary from the long, confusing, and demanding day, Xanthe was annoyed to find she still could not sleep. She was too restless, too anxious. At last she climbed out of bed, wrapping herself in the crewel bedcover, and took up vigil by the window. She dozed fitfully, half worrying and half dreaming about the day to come. By the time the sky outside began to lighten slightly she had snatched no more than two hours' sleep. She heard the clock in the hallway strike six and then sounds of the household stirring. Hours of sitting on a hard wooden chair in the chilly room had left her aching. She got up stiffly, rubbing her neck and shoulders, thinking of her mother and wondering how she was and praying she had not been suffering another flare-up while Xanthe was not there to help her. She jumped when someone knocked on the door.

"Who is it?"

"Samuel. Forgive the hour, but we must leave before seven. I have something for you," he said.

She opened the door and saw he had some clothes draped over his arm. He held them out for her.

"I believe we will fare better if you are not seen first as a maidservant," he said. "I had Grandmother Garvy fetch a gown and cape for you. And a headdress. I hope I have not offended you."

"Of course not. Thank you, Samuel. It was very thoughtful of you," she said, taking the clothes from him. "My note, about the Benefit of Clergy . . ."

"Yes, I have read it, of course."

"And?"

"And I would not give you false hope, Xanthe; our mission is a difficult one with little chance of success."

"But it could work, don't you think?"

A shout from downstairs snagged Samuel's attention.

"Forgive me, I must answer my brother. We will discuss the matter on our journey, but, I have to tell you, there is no certainty in anything you suggest."

She nodded. "I know. But I have to try."

She refused his offer of Amelia to help her dress but happily accepted the suggestion that Amelia bring her up a tray of breakfast. They arranged to meet at the stables in an hour and he left her to get ready. She laid the clothes out on the bed. There was a fine cotton underdress, a cream petticoat, a stomacher, a long kirtle, a laced velvet bodice, and a snood with a decorative band for her hair. It was something of a struggle getting everything on by herself, and she was glad of Amelia when she arrived with eggs and hot milk. She helped her tie the stomacher in place, laughing at her clumsiness, and then battled bravely with her hair. It took a fair amount of pins to get it fixed firmly, but once the headdress was tied and pinned on top it felt secure. She drew Xanthe over to the looking glass and she was surprised at the results. Instead of a lowly maid, scruffy and shapeless in drab colors, she was transformed into a well-to-do young woman of the day. The combination of layers was quite flattering, with part of the petticoat and the underdress showing through the cut of the dark green kirtle. The bodice was a lighter shade of green with a lovely shimmer due to the nap of the velvet. There was a tiny bit of embroidered braid at the square neckline, matching the piece at the front of the snood, which was far more flattering than the horrid cap she had been compelled to wear before. Amelia had done a good job with her hair, smoothing it into a neat coil beneath the headdress, which was set back on her head so that at least it was not all hidden, giving a much less severe look.

As Xanthe reached the top of the stairs she heard voices. The tone of them caused her to hesitate. That and the fact that she heard her own name mentioned. Samuel seemed to be taking her part.

"I gave my word I would not see Mistress Westlake stand alone in this matter."

"Noble of you brother," said Joshua, the growl in his voice suggesting this might, for him, be a very late night rather than an early morning. She wondered if he had left the house after they had all gone upstairs. Reveling seemed to be Joshua's way of shaking off a bad mood, by all accounts. "To take up the cause of a young woman of such scant acquaintance."

"She has no one other to assist her. Nor, it seems, has Alice while she stands accused of theft."

"Theft from the Lovewells, or had you forgotten that?"

"I had not."

"They are our most important clients to date, Samuel. It would ill serve us to displease them."

"You consider me unaware of our position?"

"I believe you may have put it out of your mind, while your attention is taken by such a striking and intriguing maidservant."

"Is that your true objection, Joshua? That she is a servant?"

"You know that I would not brook such an objection!" Joshua's voice was raised now. "You know where my true allegiances lie, brother, but still I must keep the interests of the family, of our business, to the fore. Even if you will not. I may not have your talent, but it is I who watches over our finances when you and father consider such things beneath your artistic natures. And I tell you now, pit yourself against the Lovewells and we will be the poorer for it. Not merely for the loss of their own business and patronage, either. For if they choose to spurn us because you have caused them embarrassment, others will follow."

"I care not for the Lovewell's pride!" It was Samuel's turn to sound truly angry. "I will not have my actions dictated by such people."

"Such people? Do not set yourself above them, Samuel. You forget how much our families have in common."

Xanthe stepped on a creaking stair tread and the conversation stopped. She appeared as casually as she could, trying hard to give the impression she had not heard what they had been saying. Joshua bid her good morning and then took himself off. Samuel stood and stared at her, taking in the transformation.

"You look . . . exceedingly well," he said at last.

She was unable to hide a small smile. Part of her wanted to laugh at his feeble attempt at a compliment, part of her was pleased he had noticed. But this was not a day for thinking about herself, and any happiness was a fleeting thing. Under everything was the knowledge that Alice was a step closer to her possible doom, which meant disaster for Flora, and still there seemed to be precious little any of them could do about it.

Samuel offered her his arm and together they went out of the front door. It was a surreal experience, stepping into the waiting carriage, settling onto the small, padded bench seat while Samuel sat opposite her, the driver flicking the reins and urging the two, sleek, black horses into a brisk trot around the green and onto the high street.

Xanthe leaned forward in her seat.

"Please tell me, Samuel, what do you think about using the law of Benefit of Clergy? Do you think it might work?"

"It has certainly been used for centuries, but usually in defense of men."

"But there is nothing written to say women can't use it, too."

"Your friend told you this?"

She nodded, adding, "The test seems to be that she must read a passage from the Bible."

"The neck psalm."

"Sorry?"

"The Fifty-first Psalm is known as such because it is the one required to be read, and, if annunciated correctly, can save a fellow from the gallows. *Miserere mei, Deus, secundum misericordiam tuam*—'O God, have mercy upon me, according to thine heartfelt mercifulness.' It is not unheard of for the accused to learn the passage by heart so that he may appear to be able to read and deliver the words that will save him."

"You do know about this rule, then?"

"I've heard of it, but there are risks, Xanthe. You have to understand that."

"But Alice was brought up in a well-to-do family, she must be able to read."

"Let us hope so. The courts have become wise to such tricks as memorizing the psalm so they will now more commonly choose a verse at random. An unschooled villain would certainly be caught out by pages of Latin."

"Latin?"

"A Bible in any other language is rare indeed."

"But, prayers, readings in church, what language would they have been in? I mean, what language are they in?"

He raised his eyes at her not knowing this. "Why English, of course." Out of habit he lowered his voice a little before adding, "Unless a person follows the Catholic faith."

"Yes! Of course. Everything would be in Latin." She sat back in her seat, shaking her head and allowing herself a small, hopeful smile. "For once Alice's beliefs might actually help her. She should be able to read any passage they throw at her."

"And therein lies a part of the risk," Samuel reminded her. "For the daughter of a traitor, the orphan of a condemned family, for her to use the very thing that saw them executed as her defense . . . it is a dangerous path to tread, Xanthe."

"I know. I know. But what else can we do?"

"Let us try all other avenues open to us first. I will speak for her. I will attest to her good character, to the lack of evidence. Only if these entreaties fail, in that case, I will claim Benefit of Clergy on her behalf."

They fell silent then, and both sat watching the landscape of Wiltshire as they rattled through it along the stony road.

There were moments when Xanthe could almost forget that she did not belong there, in that time, with those people, that it was all an incredible, impossible, magical journey. And then there were moments when she felt as though she had stepped through one of Mr. Morris's mirrors into another reality. It could not be real, and yet it was. She was in a carriage speeding along the rough, wet road south from Marlborough. She was sitting opposite a disturbingly attractive and enigmatic man. She was the only hope Alice had of not going to the gallows. And her own mother's safety, possibly even her life, depended upon her succeeding. This was her reality for the time she was in it. It was not a dream. Every lurch of the carriage that jolted her body told her that. Every pinch of fear she felt when she thought she could be exposed as a liar and a fraud. Every knot in her stomach reminded her she might fail Flora and watch Alice hang. Every time her blood stirred when Samuel's eyes met hers. It could all go so terribly wrong. She could be hurt. She could cause hurt. There would be consequences to her actions. And what then? What if she did keep Alice alive? Would that somehow change the future? She was meddling in something much bigger than she had a hope of understanding. What if by doing some small good thing she altered the course of history and made something terrible happen? She felt as if she were in deep, fast-flowing water and might go under at any moment. What had ever made her think she was up to the task she had been given? She blinked away tears, staring determinedly out of the window, aware that Samuel was watching her closely.

"Do not distress yourself," he said gently. "The weather has eased, the roads are clear, we will make good time to Salisbury." When she only nodded in reply he went on, leaning forward in his seat. "All is not lost, Xanthe, I promise you." He watched her for a moment longer. "I know how your fear for your friend troubles you, and yet I sense there is more. Something of which you do not, or cannot, speak."

"Samuel, I—"

He held up a hand. "I would not cajole you into telling me that which you would rather hold to yourself. I say only that I sense a secret, a thing that is burdensome for you to carry. I would share that burden. I hope the day comes soon when you will trust me sufficiently to let me help you carry it."

He sat back in his seat and turned again to watch the countryside as they hurried through it. Xanthe had the impression he was no more able to focus on the prettiness of the scenery than she was. He was doing his best not to press her for answers when he evidently had plenty of questions he longed to ask. He could not have known how grateful she was for his thoughtfulness. Could not have known that she would have had to answer any questions about herself with nothing but lies. And that she did not want to lie to him. She truly did not.

At last the rain stopped completely. The broad skies of Wiltshire emerged blue and clear after days hiding behind a layer of gray that had effectively blocked out all the worthwhile sunlight. As the final, most stubborn clouds disappeared, everything was revealed as bright and richly colored, the landscape changed from dull browns and somber, muddy hues to clear golds and fresh, sharp greens. It was unsettling to have changed not only century but season. She had left home at the height of an English summer and stepped not only into the distant past, but into late autumn. It was strange to discover just how much that small alteration affected her. Even a city girl, it seemed, traveled through the seasons of the year at some deeper level than merely registering the temperature or changing her wardrobe. When she had left Marlborough there had been leaves on the trees, roses blooming, and blackberries ripening in the bramble-filled garden. Now the branches of the oaks and ashes were almost bare, and there was a sense of the darkness of winter approaching.

Perhaps she had already taken on some of the concerns and fears of a seventeenth-century woman. Would the winter be harsh? Would the harvest be enough to last to summer? Would fever and flood visit the household? Would there be enough tallow and candles to light their way through the long, bleak nights? How would she cope, she wondered, if she found herself unable to return home and had to live out her life there, in those conditions, in those far-off, brutal days? She thought of how her mother would have suffered had she been born then, without modern drugs to combat her arthritis. Thought about the wisdom teeth Xanthe had had extracted when she was eighteen. Thought about the time she had broken her wrist falling from a tree when she was nine. Thought about the croup she had suffered as a toddler. Would she even have survived to adulthood?

She looked at Samuel again. He could not have been more than twenty-five, but he had an older soul. It was as if his life, the very fragile nature of existence in his time, made each of those years heavier. A young man of the same age in Xanthe's day might not long have left university, might be in his first proper job, just setting out on his career, building a long, prosperous, privileged future. What did the future hold for Samuel in such unsettled times, with only the most basic of medicine to keep him and his loved ones alive? A cold shudder passed through her, and with it a glimpse of deep, fast-flowing water, and a terrible sense of pressure upon her chest. She gasped, trying to shake off the vision, wondering what on earth it was meant to show her.

"Xanthe? Are you well?" Samuel asked.

"Yes, sorry. Just a little . . ."—she searched for a harmless, coverall word—"fatigued."

He nodded at this, as if it were a common condition for a woman.

She was glad he did not talk further, because her heart was pounding. The glimpse of a possible future—for who, herself? Samuel?—had been so powerful, it took her some time to steady her breathing and feel calm once again.

At last the countryside began to change. The road grew both wider and busier. There were carts and carriages of all shapes and sizes, and people walking toward the city. The farmland gave way to businesses and small dwellings: a cooper, a tannery, a smithy. Then a coaching inn. Streets, some cobbled or paved in one manner or another, some just mud, or so it seemed to Xanthe. This was not a little market town like Marlborough, but a thriving city. The buildings were a mix of timber—mostly painted white with black beams, steep gables, and mullioned windows—or more expensive red brick. The older timber houses were showing their age, with sway-backed roofs and leaning walls. The smarter, younger brick ones stood straight and tall, often two stories clear of their older cousins, with longer windows, showing off the wealth of their owners in the cost of the glass alone. Even on such a cold day and with their own windows closed, the smell of the city was something that could not be ignored. It was so sour that it turned Xanthe's stomach, so putrid that it made her think of aging roadkill or a long-forgotten rubbish bag, with memories of overflowing rock festival toilets. A glance at the street explained where most of it was coming from. A ditch to one side was nothing more than an open sewer, with chamber pots and kitchen slops being emptied into it. There were rotting vegetables from stalls and thrown from inns, and a quick count showed two dead cats, a decomposing dog, and several flattened corpses that were probably rats, no doubt casually dispatched by local people as part of their everyday tasks.

Samuel checked his pocket watch. "It is near ten. We must be at the courthouse in a matter of minutes." He banged on the ceiling of the carriage and shouted up to the driver, "With all haste, Mannering, if you please!" The horses duly lunged forward at a reckless pace, sending pedestrians and slower conveyances scattering and drawing more than a few bursts of swearing and fist waving. Xanthe saw two men abandon their handcarts to throw punches at each other, and another get shoved into a stall of apples.

"Road rage seventeenth-century style," she muttered to herself.

They passed along increasingly crowded streets, one skirting the market square. Here occupied stocks and a grim-looking whipping post served as reminders of the very real fates of people who passed through the justice system. She looked around for a gibbet and was relieved not to find any. The courthouse it-self was a nondescript building, squat and square and solid, with wide steps leading up to heavy front doors. The driver brought the blowing horses to a halt right outside it, and Samuel helped Xanthe from the carriage. She took his arm and they hurried inside.

The trials were already underway and they had to force their way through the crowds in the public gallery, paying a couple at the front for their seats. Xanthe parried flashbacks to her own court appearance; she could not allow herself to revisit her or-deal now. She must keep her mind focused on Alice. The room was large with a high ceiling but felt somehow cramped and sti-fling; there were so many people crammed into it. The smells of the city faded here to be replaced by the reek of sweat and unwashed bodies. There was a low-level murmuring that kept up the whole time, with occasional hushes to listen to a grisly detail of a murder or hear the testimony of an interesting wit-ness, whose words were often greeted with jibes and ridicule until the court usher restored order. Below the upper gallery where Xanthe and Samuel were sitting, the business area of the court was laid out, leaving no one in any doubt as to where the power lay. The judge, complete with wig and robes, sat on a raised platform behind a high desk, his enormous chair ornately carved and the clerks on either side of him all wearing the same dour expressions. The floor of the room housed something like box pews for the lawyers and court administrators. There was a witness box, and at the back, looking more like an animal pen than anything else, was a wooden partition with bars at the sides where the accused were kept. There must have been thirty of them squashed in together. As their names were read out, they shuffled through to the front for their own case to be heard.

"There she is," Xanthe whispered to Samuel, tugging at his sleeve and pointing. Alice was in the middle of the bunch, pressed up against the filthy and the desperate, most of them men, some looking heartbreakingly young, others decayed from old age, hardship, drink, or a combination of all three. Alice herself looked thinner, older, world weary, as if she no longer cared what happened to her, so long as it all came to an end. As Xanthe watched her Alice looked up and caught sight of her and Samuel. Xanthe smiled at her, raising her hand, trying to signal that she should not give up. That they were there to support her. But Alice recoiled at the sight of her, shaking her head and backing away, trying to hide among the crush of bodies in the dock. She was frightened of her. But why? She did not know her, but she knew that Xanthe wanted to help her. Xanthe had hoped she would have believed her when she told her that, would have had time to think about what she said and decided to trust her. It seemed the opposite was true.

"Oh, poor Alice," she said. "She is so frightened. She thinks I will make things worse for her." She recalled what Alice had told her about being condemned as a traitor instead of a thief, and of what punishment that would mean. No wonder she was terrified. What if she had reason to be? What if Xanthe did make things worse? "We must be careful, Samuel." She looked up at him. "Are we sure this is going to work?"

Samuel did not answer, but reached down and took her hand in his. He squeezed it, and their fingers interlaced. It was not a passing gesture of reassurance, it was a declaration; they were in this together. Alice had Xanthe, and she had Samuel, and they would do what they could.

"ALICE MERTON? STAND FORWARD, ALICE MERTON!" THE COURT OFFICIAL called her into view in the dock and announced her trial. "Let the accused make herself known!" When she appeared from the ragged group he gave the details. "Alice Merton, you do stand accused of the theft of two items of silver, being a scissors and needle case from the chatelaine of Mistress Lovewell of Great Chalfield, in the district of north Wiltshire. How do you plead?"

The gathering in the court room quietened, waiting for her response. When none came that quiet grew first restless, then charged.

The court official tried again.

"Your plea girl, let us have it, do you admit your guilt or claim to be innocent of the charge made?"

Samuel whispered at Xanthe. "She must enter a plea!"

"But, can't she stay silent? I mean, she's damned whatever she pleas, perhaps she's right to say nothing," she suggested.

"No." Samuel glanced down at her. "If she refuses to speak she risks *peine forte et dure*. Did not your scholarly friend tell you of this? A person might choose silence to protect others connected to them from also being charged, but they pay a terrible price."

She did remember then reading of this punishment while searching the internet, and the memory of even the brief description of the punishment made her catch her breath. The convicted person was made to lie down facing upward with a large board placed on them. Stones were then put on top of the board, more and more of them, the person underneath being crushed slowly to death. To make the punishment even more cruel, a sharp, pointed stone was positioned underneath the wretched convict's spine. Why would Alice risk such a horrendous death? Who was she trying to protect? It was no wonder the crowd was getting agitated.

The judge leaned forward, his hands clasped in front of him. He looked very old, his face puffy and fat, his eyes cloudy. He did not have the appearance of a well man. He looked as if he had grown heavy and breathless from a life of overindulgence, but perhaps the task of sending people to such awful fates had also taken its toll. Perhaps he was a just person, struggling with an unjust system. Would he see fairness done for Alice? Xanthe held tight to this small bright hope.

"Mistress Merton," he said slowly, his voice also showing signs of age and frailty, "you are required to enter a plea. The charge of theft is a serious one. I understand the items were valued at some—" He paused, consulting with an aide to his left, and then went on. "—a considerable sum, running to several pounds. In which case the charge is one of grand larceny. Do not make a bad situation worse for yourself, child. You must surely be aware of the possible consequences of your refusal to speak."

In the hush that followed, Xanthe was amazed to hear Samuel's voice.

"Be not afraid, Mistress Merton," he called out to her. "Let the truth be your protection."

She looked at him then, and Xanthe could tell in that instant that they knew one another. Was it Samuel she was trying to protect with her silence? He and his family had been cautious in admitting they knew her, but Samuel had confessed to Xanthe that they were Catholics themselves. Alice knew only too well what fate might await them if she gave them away somehow. The poor girl seemed lost for a moment and then at last she coughed lightly, struggling to find her hoarse, faint voice. She stood as straight as she was able, holding on to the top of the partition in front of her, and said, "Guilty, my lord. I plead guilty."

"No!" Xanthe whispered urgently to Samuel. "She can't do that."

"If it please you, my lord," the prosecutor went on, "the accused offered no defense before the trial and has now spoken only to confirm her guilt. In as much, she has confessed to the theft of valuable and personal silver items from Mistress Lovewell and has offered neither a reason for this act, nor has she returned the stolen pieces."

The judged puffed and frowned. "And has money been found on the girl or among her possessions?"

"It has not, my lord. We assume she has secreted the stolen objects in a place from which she later intended recovering them for the purpose of selling them on."

The judge gave a noise somewhere between a groan and a growl. "We cannot have assumption, Master Howard, can we now? Let us concern ourselves solely with the facts."

"Indeed, my lord, and they are these: that Alice Merton did feloniously and deceitfully rob her mistress of her property for her own personal gain and enrichment, and this despite the Lovewell family having shown the girl every kindness after she found herself in reduced, and not to say scandalous, circumstances."

"Is that so?" The judge turned again to his aide, who whispered in his ear, presumably filling him in on the way that Alice had lost her family. He gave another grunt and then peered over his glasses at her.

"Why'd you do it, girl?" he asked her baldly. "You were not, by all accounts, poorly treated, so had no need to go elsewhere. Why would you bite the very hand that so generously fed you?"

The prosecutor detected a softening on the judge's part and was having none of it. "If I may, my lord . . . There was some talk of an elopement."

Alice looked appalled at this piece of nonsense but still did not speak out.

The prosecutor went on. "The girl sought to buy her way out of servitude and take off with a man—we do not have a name—so throwing away what remained of her reputation, her family name already having been ruined."

"He's lying," Xanthe insisted under her breath.

The judge nodded slowly. He looked at Alice, and Xanthe believed she saw sadness in his expression then, for what could he do but condemn her? "Mistress Merton, you have owned your guilt, the crime of which you are guilty carries a grave penalty, and though it gives me no joy to pass such judgment upon a young woman, I cannot allow sentiment to blunt the sword of justice. The law is clear on the matter."

Samuel squeezed Xanthe's hand before letting it go and jumping to his feet. The moment to put their plan into action had come.

"My lord, on behalf of the accused, I claim Benefit of Clergy!" he announced.

This statement brought first incredulous gasps and then ribald laughter from everyone in the gallery and even many of the court officials. The prosecutor raised and dropped his arms in a gesture of disbelief. Alice turned to look at Samuel, astonished by his words.

The judge banged his gavel on his desk, demanding silence. "Benefit of Clergy?" he repeated, frowning. "Sir, are you intent on making a mockery of this court?"

"No, my lord, on the contrary, I wish only to avail Mistress Merton of the law, and there is a law that states should a person be able to read a passage from the Bible they may be tried not by the crown, but by the church. None other than the bishop can pass judgment and sentence upon them. Is that not the case?"

The judge was not pleased at having his own authority brought into question. "You know full well that it is, Master . . . ?"

"Appleby, my lord. Samuel Appleby of Marlborough."

"Well, Master Appleby, it may have escaped your scrutiny, but the law which you cite applies to men alone. Some exceptions were made for nuns, it is true, but the practice was stopped many years ago. As women are not permitted to be members of the clergy they do not fall, under such circumstances as these, beneath the auspices of the church nor the jurisdiction of the bishop."

"With respect, my lord, I believe the law is open to interpretation as regards the sex of the offender. Might we not take 'man' in this instance to refer to 'mankind'?"

There was a murmur of confusion in the public gallery. The prosecutor was shaking his head. The judge sat back in his chair, his aides hastening to look things up in their hefty law books. It was a long shot, both Samuel and Xanthe knew it, but they had no alternative to try. The punishment a bishop would be compelled to pass down was not execution; it was more likely a year's imprisonment and possibly a branding of the left hand. It was cruel, but at least her life would be spared. And therefore Flora's, too.

The prosecutor was on his feet again. "My lord, is this . . . person," he asked, waving his hand dismissively at Samuel, "to be permitted to ridicule his majesty's court and its processes? The law is quite clear; only a man may be a member of the clergy—a clergy*man*. To suggest that a woman may benefit from this law is to show disrespect to monarch and church both."

Xanthe got to her feet, taking Samuel's arm. "Tell them she can read," she reminded him.

Samuel kept his voice level, refusing to be riled by the prosecutor. "Mistress Merton can read the Bible, my lord. That is what is required. Please, let her do so. It may be the passage of your own choosing."

The judge raised his eyebrows. "Oh? I am to be permitted choice in the matter? How very generous of you." He sighed. "I shall allow the accused to read. Have a Bible passed to her," he instructed the court usher.

Xanthe watched as the worn leather-bound book was handed to Alice. Alice looked up at her with such fear in her eyes that for a moment Xanthe feared that she might not, in fact, be able to read. But no, she was originally from a wealthy family. She *must* have received sufficient schooling to read a passage.

The judge nodded at Alice. "The book of Genesis will do well enough, mistress," he told her.

The room was the quietest it had been all morning. Alice turned the pages until she found the right place and then, slowly, haltingly, but with growing confidence, she began to read. Everyone listened, some no doubt hoping she would fail, but she did not. She read on, clearly, calmly. At last the judge held up his hand.

"That will suffice, thank you."

The usher took the Bible from her, and all waited. The judge did not confer further with his aides but sat deep in thought for a moment. Again Xanthe was taken back to her own trial, to that moment before a verdict is passed and then a sentence given, where one's life is in the hands of others, to crush in a moment if they see fit. She thought of her mother then and of how she must have felt watching her precious daughter have her fate decided in just such a way.

Finally, the judge squared his shoulders and gave his judgment.

"The passage was read well enough. There is no doubt in my mind that we have before us a godly and learned woman. She has indeed fulfilled the requirement of the law as it pertains to claiming Benefit of Clergy." There were mutterings around the room. Samuel took hold of Xanthe's hand again. "However," he went on, "there is no precedent for applying this law to a woman in our time if she be not resident in a nunnery, and I am not convinced there is reason enough to set one here. In which case, the accused having confessed her guilt, I cannot do other than pass sentence upon her. Theft from an employer is a matter not to be taken lightly. When that employer is a family of note—supporters of the crown, upholders of the laws of the land, and providers of work—a crime against them is, de facto, a crime against the order of things in this land. To break that trust, to steal property, is a serious offense. The law asks for capital punishment for the crime of grand larceny, death by hanging, but I am minded toward leniency, taking into account the established pious nature of the accused, and the sincerity of those who have spoken for her. I therefore commute the sentence; she shall not hang, but shall be placed upon the next available vessel for transportation to the new penal colonies in his majesty's settlements in America. There she shall remain to serve a term of fifteen years." He rapped his gavel twice more and called for the next case.

As Xanthe watched, helpless and stunned, Alice was jostled by the others in the dock, turning her tear-stained face toward her and Samuel as she was led away.

{ 23 }

THEY HAD GONE TO SALISBURY TO RESCUE ALICE, AND THEY HAD FAILED.
Nothing Samuel said could make Xanthe feel any less guilty,
any less frantic about what Margaret Merton might do to her
mother. She let him lead her out of the courthouse and to the
waiting carriage. She sat heavily, staring at him as he took his
place opposite her. The driver sang out to the horses and they
lurched forward into the melee of the town traffic.

"I should have done something more," she said. "Something,
anything, to stop them dragging her away like that. Back to some
awful cell."

"You did what you could, Xanthe. If there is another way of
securing her freedom I do not know of it." He sat regarding her
closely as the carriage rattled and rocked, the driver having been
told to get them home as quickly as he could. There was no real
hurry, but she knew Samuel wanted her away from the courthouse. She was struggling to hide how desperate she felt, and he
might well fear that she would do something reckless.

"You don't understand," she told him. "I can't just leave her.
Fifteen years in a penal colony? She'd never live through it. Have
you any idea how terrible those places are? Most people struggle
to survive the sea voyage, they are transported in such appall-

ing conditions. By the time they reach America they are already weakened and often ill. They live there in filthy conditions on near-starvation rations and are put to hard labor. There's precious little medical care . . . just hard work and dangerous places to exist and outbreaks of disease. They are just used until they drop. It will kill her, don't you see that? Transportation is every bit as much a death sentence as hanging!"

"You are very well informed on the matter," he said.

She was too angry to care how he thought she knew what she did. "Yes, well, I know what I know," she snapped. "And I know we can't just leave her there. We should have tried harder to get to speak to her."

"I requested time with her, you saw me do it."

"And we were turned away flat."

"There are rules."

"To hell with the bloody rules!" she shouted. Samuel looked shocked to hear her curse, but she was too upset to moderate her language another minute. "I don't give a damn about what we should or shouldn't do! To send someone to their certain death for taking a couple of silver trinkets . . . It's ridiculous. It's unjust. It's barbaric."

"It is the law."

"And the law is wrong!" She could not do it. Could not simply leave. To do so was to condemn Alice to a slow death and so risk Margaret Merton's fury. Risk that she would carry out her threat to harm Flora. *No,* Xanthe told herself, *I am not giving up. I can't!* "Stop the carriage!" she shouted.

"There is nothing to be gained by returning. . . ." Samuel began, but Xanthe was not listening.

"Stop!" She banged on the ceiling of the carriage to try to get her point across to the driver. He seemed oblivious to her cries, but a stagecoach crossed their path at that moment so that he was forced to check the horses. Xanthe leaped from her seat, threw the door open, and jumped out.

"Xanthe, wait!"

She ignored Samuel. She had to go back, had to do something more. If he was not prepared to try then she would go alone. The first obstacle was the mud. What passed for the main street had been transformed by the rain into a rutted track pocked with horse manure, studded with dislodged stones and clods of earth, along with general rubbish and filth. If only she still had her boots. The lady's shoes Jayne had found for her were ridiculously flimsy and unsuited to the conditions, making the going ten times more difficult than it would have been in her own robust footwear, her feet squelching into the puddling clay, the water and mud quickly seeping through the shoes as well was over them. Her clothes hampered her, too. She was compelled to hitch up the long skirts of her dress, which otherwise dragged in the muck, quickly becoming sodden and unhelpfully heavy.

"Make way!" a voice shouted.

She turned just in time to see a rider cantering toward her. Stepping to one side she narrowly avoided being knocked down by a fast-moving gig. There seemed to be no highway code, not even a semblance of who should go where. It was a wild muddle of horses and carriages and wagons and barrows and people, with Xanthe floundering at the center of it. She could hear Samuel calling her name, but she pressed on. She decided that if she reached the side of the street she could make her way back toward the courthouse more quickly and safely. Crossing the street was not a simple matter, though. She was jostled and cursed at and shoved all the way. She glimpsed the Appleby carriage stopping further up the street and Samuel jumping out. Turning away, she ran on. She knew Samuel meant well, meant to protect her, but there was no time to stand and argue about what she was doing. She had to go back and find someone, *any-one*, to talk to, to plead for more time to find the evidence that would prove Alice's innocence. If Samuel caught up with her, he would only slow her down or possibly drag her away. She dove down a side street, planning to take another back to the main road further along. There were fewer vehicles rattling along the narrower lane, but as there was less space it was hazardous merely trying to make any headway at speed. She kept stumbling, bumping against people, or having to spring out of the way of the faster-moving carriages. She was almost at the next corner, about to switch back along a quieter cobbled street, when she failed to notice how little room there was for the carriage and four thundering up the road behind her. Too late, she tried to step out of the way. She felt the horses whistle past, and then a painful blow as the side of the carriage caught her as it sped by. She was thrown to the ground. For all its layer of mire, the landing was harsh enough to knock the wind from her body. She pushed herself up to her knees, refusing to give way to panic, waiting for her lungs to remember how to function properly.

"Mistress?" An unfamiliar voice spoke softly. "Have a care, do not hasten to rise, lest you faint away," the stranger advised. He took hold of her arm and encouraged her to lean on him as she struggled unsteadily to her feet. Xanthe was too breathless to reply but grateful that someone at least, in this pitiless place, was prepared to lend a helping hand to a person in difficulty. "There," he said, yet holding her arm. "Are you all alone, mistress?" She tried to focus on him, her vision a little blurry from a lack of breath. He was middle-aged, with wary eyes and stubble shadowing his chin. Even to her faulty eyes, he did not look like a typical Good Samaritan.

"Xanthe!" Samuel's voice cut through the fog in her brain as air at last started to work its way in and out of her lungs.

She opened her mouth to thank the stranger, who had turned to see that she was not in fact on her own. In an instant he altered. His hold on her arm shifted from supportive to bruising. She squealed in protest as he shoved her backward, her back slamming against the rough wall of a house. Before she could react he raised his free hand and snatched the locket from her throat.

"No!" she screamed, her voice forced into action by horror at what he was doing. She threw herself at him, scrabbling to grasp the gold chain that now swung from his hand. Muttering oaths, he pushed her away with such strength that she fell to the ground again. Before she could get to her feet he was off and running, weaving his way nimbly through the throng. In a moment he would be lost in the crowd, and her locket gone forever. Her only way of ever returning home vanished in an instant!

"No!" she yelled again. "Stop him! Thief!" She cried out in desperation, pointing at the quickly diminishing figure.

"Are you hurt?" Samuel was at her side, helping her to her feet. "Did he hurt you?"

"Forget about me, he has my locket!" She dragged herself from his grasp and lunged after the running man.

"Your locket? But we will not catch him now. Wait. . . ."

"We have to! You don't understand." She tore away as fast as she could, her breath still ragged, her back sore where the carriage had struck it.

Seeing she was not to be stopped, Samuel too gave chase. He dashed past her, telling her to stay where she was, and charged after the thief, shouting for others to stop him or else *for God's sake get out of the way*. Xanthe struggled to keep up, and even though Samuel ran swiftly, the gap between him and the stranger was widening. Terror gripped her, real and overwhelming. Without the locket she would have to stay in the past forever. She could never go home. Would never see her mother again. Never live in her own time. What had she done? How had she been so stupid as to risk everything? And for nothing, because she had failed Alice, too. At that moment she felt defeated, beaten, broken. She wanted to give in to despair, slump down into the mud and howl. She could see Samuel battling to get past a vegetable barrow and a gaggle of bemused shoppers. The thief was almost out of sight. Almost gone. And then, just as it felt like everything was beyond her, out of her control, and hopeless, she felt such a surge of rage course through her that she let out a roar of frustration and anger. She would not give up! She would not let someone snatch away her life like that. Her home. Her mother. She started to run again, and as she did so she saw the thief dash to the left down a narrow alleyway. It appeared to run parallel to the nearest street, on her left. Both routes led back to the high street. It was a shortcut.

Xanthe charged down the rubbish-strewn road, screaming at people to step aside and let her pass, ignoring shouts of protest as she pushed and shoved and swore her way onward. It seemed an impossibly long way to the main road, but at last she emerged onto the frantic route that ran east-west through the town. She did not hesitate, but turned and ran on. Just as she drew level with the exit from the alleyway the thief came barreling out of it. She liked to think she tackled him and brought him down, but everything happened so fast and the truth was he blundered straight into her. They crashed to the stony road together. She was a woman possessed, her only thought to get the locket, as she grabbed and clawed at him. The thief swung a punch and missed, then another that connected with her chest. She gasped, doubling over with the pain and force of the blow, but still held on to his shirt with one hand, digging her nails in so that he could not shake her off.

"Give it back," she gasped. "My locket, give it to me!"

"Get off me, wench!" He took hold of her wrist and wrenched her hand from his shirt. He was horribly strong, but she was easily as tall as him. She hurled herself forward, flinging herself over him so that he could not get to his feet. As she grappled with him she saw the glint of sunlight on the gold he still clutched in his hand. She tried to make him open his hand but he would not. Without a second thought, she leaned forward and bit his knuckles. She could never have imagined actually biting another human being, but even as she felt her teeth break his skin and tasted his blood she did not stop. Nothing was going to stop her from getting back her passport home.

"Argh! Cursed woman. Vile bitch!" he yelled, raining blows on her head with his other hand.

But he could not keep hold of the locket. She forced him to let go, so that he could snatch his hand away from her teeth. She grabbed the locket and rolled on top of it, curling into a ball to avoid the kicking he was now giving her. For a moment she thought of opening the locket. Considered shutting out everything else—turning away from the brutality of her attacker, from the weight of failing Alice—and letting herself be taken home again. What good was she doing, after all? What use had she been? But she knew she could not simply admit defeat. Too many people depended upon her carrying on.

Suddenly the kicking stopped. Hearing a cry she looked up to see Samuel hauling the man off her before landing a punch that put him down. He took a firm hold of the ruffian's collar as he looked at Xanthe.

"Are you wounded?" Samuel asked, breathless from running, his eyes full of both fury and fear. Fear for her safety, her well-being, she realized.

She shook her head and climbed unsteadily to her feet, hastily dropping the locket into her pocket, shutting her mind to the pull it was exerting upon her. "I'll live," she told him.

He dragged the struggling thief to his feet. "You, sir," he hissed at him, "will take a short walk with me to the constable, and a shorter one still on your own to the gibbet!"

Xanthe shook her head again. "No, Samuel." She waved a hand at the man. "Let him go."

"What? What do you say?"

"Let him go."

"But, you cannot..."

"You think I want more of what passes for justice around here?" she shouted at him. "The same sort of justice that Alice got? A system so cruel, so harsh, so completely without fairness? Do you think I want to be the one to put someone through that, to be responsible for their death?" Her shoulders slumped as pain and exhaustion took hold. "I have my locket back," she told him quietly. "Let him go." She did not wait to argue further but started making her painful way back to the carriage.

The journey home was terrible. With every mile she felt she was getting further from any possibility of protecting her mother. The roughness of the road and the resulting lurch of the carriage were constant reminders of the beating she had just taken. Samuel had fussed at first, wanting to take her to an apothecary. It had taken her some time to make him accept that she had sustained no serious injuries. They journeyed out of Salisbury in silence after that. Frustration at her own uselessness got the better of her, so that she had to bite her lip against threatening tears and turn to stare out of the window. She felt so helpless. Ignoring the look on Samuel's face, she pulled at her ruined shoes and kicked them off before curling her feet up beneath her. Gingerly, she took the locket from her pocket and set it on her lap, examining the chain as best she could while not wishing to handle it. The clasp was broken. Defeated again, she leaned against the padded back of the seat, closing her eyes. It was then that she felt Samuel move from his seat to sit beside her.

"Let me," he said. He took the locket from her and used his pocket knife to work the broken clasp back to a functioning shape. He held it up, and Xanthe leaned forward so that he could fix it around her neck once more. Then, wordlessly, he slipped his arm around her shoulders and pulled her against him. Grateful and weary, she leaned upon him, resting her head on his shoulder. After another jolting mile, with the shadows lengthening outside, fatigue overcame her and she fell at last into a deep, dream-filled sleep.

When they reached Marlborough the driver dropped them at the front door of the Appleby house. Samuel told her there was no question of her going back to Great Chalfield and her duties there that evening, but that he would see that she returned there in the morning.

Inside, Philpott fussed about taking their capes and hats.

"Where is my father?" Samuel asked.

"Gone up to London on business, sir. Not expected back until Friday."

"And Joshua?"

"Not at home," was all the explanation the manservant could give.

"We will take supper—"

"Not for me," Xanthe interrupted. "Thank you, but I have no appetite."

"After such a day, you must keep up your strength," Samuel said.

"I'm not hungry," she said, feeling that all she wanted to do was go to her room.

"At least allow me to have Amelia fix you a tray of something. And send up a draft for the pain, and some balm for your bruises."

She nodded. "Thank you, Samuel." She made herself look at him. *It was not his fault*, she kept telling herself. He had done what he could. "Really, I mean it," she said. "Thank you for helping me. For trying to help Alice."

"I only wish we could have had greater success," he said.

She could think of nothing else to say. He was looking at her with such genuine concern, such sympathy, she knew she was in danger of weeping. She doubted her ability to remain composed if he were to be nice to her again. She turned and trudged up the stairs. With each step it got harder not to whip round and run back to him. But how could she explain how desperate she felt? How could he answer the question that now screamed inside her head: Would Margaret Merton consider her daughter saved, or would she punish Xanthe's failure by taking her revenge on Flora?

Philpott had lit a fire in her room, but it remained chilly. The storms of the previous days had gone, to be replaced by a severe drop in temperature. She rubbed her hands by the fire for a moment, bracing herself for the business of getting out of her cumbersome clothes. She marveled at the thought that women had to go about their daily lives, all day every day, laced and tied into so many heavy layers. No wonder noblewomen were treated as semi-invalids half the time. The higher up the social scale you were, it seemed, the more restrictive and elaborate your clothing, the less you were able to actually move. For a while she knelt in front of the hearth, removing the many pins that secured her headdress until at last she could let her hair down. She ran her fingers through it, relieved to release the tension such a tight hairstyle provoked in her head. It felt to her as if everything a woman had to wear was designed to remind her just how much freedom, how much control over her own life, she did not have. Eventually she forced herself to get up and undress. Amazingly, she had not suffered anything more than bruising, from either being knocked down by the carriage or from being thumped and kicked by the would-be thief. Even so, she felt sore and fragile. She winced as she pulled the bodice back off her shoulders and thought longingly of a deep, hot bath. She had removed all of her clothes except the underdress when there was a knock at the door. Expecting Amelia with her food she opened it, only to find Samuel standing there. Seeing her in a state of undress he struggled not to look flustered.

"I have brought your supper. And some wine," he mumbled, holding up the tray.

"Oh, I thought Amelia . . . Um, thanks. Thank you," she said, stepping aside so he could bring it in and put it on the table by the fire. She followed him, so that when he abruptly turned around they were standing face to face, very close. The light in the room was all shadows, jittery flashes from the fire, steadier glows from the candles, nothing but fading twilight through the window. He seemed about to say something, but instead he reached out and touched her hair, taking a ringlet between his fingers, feeling the soft springiness of the curl. He looked at her so intensely, so searchingly. She felt her pulse quicken. She scarcely knew him and yet she was strongly drawn to him. It was more than just his dark good looks, his lean, muscular body, and the sensitivity and kindness he had shown her. She felt a connection. Something on a different level altogether. As if he had been a part of her traveling back in time that she did not yet fully understand. Part of the reason, though whether for her sake or his, she was unsure. Either way, she knew she had no wish for him to leave her. She wished him to stay. To step closer. To touch her again. To hold her.

"Xanthe," he murmured. "You are as if come from a foreign land, a distant shore, across seas not yet charted. A person apart from all others. Unknowable. And yet I would know you. Unclaimable, and yet I would with all my heart claim you."

He lifted his hand and went to stroke her cheek but hesitated, holding back. She took a small step, just a tiny movement toward him, not taking her eyes from his, all the time watching him as he watched her. It was all the encouragement he needed. He slipped one arm around her waist, pressing the thin cotton shift against her skin. His other hand he slid beneath her hair, cradling her head, titling it up toward him. As he kissed her she felt any sensible restraint, any common-sense resistance, melt away. She was tired of being sensible, of being strong. She was worn out from thinking. She did not want to try to make sense of everything anymore, she only wanted to give in to the powerful desire she had for this man. She wanted to feel his mouth upon hers. She wanted his strong arms holding her. She wanted to feel the press of his warm, firm body against her own. She longed to forget all the impossible things she was trying to do and to only feel instead.

He stopped kissing her and pulled away a little, his arm still holding her, but with caution now. He studied her face again, his own expression serious.

"I would not see you harmed or ill used for all the riches in this world," he told her, his voice low. "But, Xanthe, you stir such passion in me, such desire, such a need for you. . . . If you wish me gone, if you would save your honor and my heart, then send me away now."

Now it was her turn to hesitate. Whereas Samuel was trying

to check himself to safeguard her reputation, thinking about the morals and social etiquette of the day, she had other, stranger, more confusing matters to consider. Such as the fact that a shared love between them was doomed, for soon she must leave and they would be separated by centuries. And that if she gave in, if she allowed herself to make love with him the way she found she badly wanted to, then her feelings for him would be deeper, her connection with him more intimate, more meaning-ful. This was not a matter of simple lust, and they both knew it. There was something more emotional taking place. And at the same time, something that could cause them both a great deal of pain. They would be parted, forever, and she would never be able to explain to him why that was. But then, at that moment, she thought of how dangerous and fragile life was, especially for him, especially in his world. She thought about how moments of beauty and love were fleeting and rare. Was it really better to turn away from them when they were offered? Was it really right to pass up on the chance of happiness, however brief? Samuel's life, like everyone's at that time, could be snuffed out in a matter of days by sickness, or an accident, something simple and curable and fixable in her own day but that would see him dead and gone for want of antiseptic or antibiotics or anesthetic. How often, in the modern world, were people told to be mindful, to live in the moment, and to be fully present in the experience and wonder of that moment? What sense was there in running away from this moment with Samuel? It would have been so easy to talk herself into doing what, deep down, she knew was something she would later regret. Just as she knew, after what she had been through the past few days, she was in no state to make sound judgments, to act rationally.

Samuel, sensing her confusion, stepped back, letting her go.

"Forgive me," he said. "It was wrong of me to even consider . . . and you have suffered today. . . . I was being, at best, insensitive."

"No, you weren't. . . ."

"I shall leave you in peace."

"Wait," Xanthe put her hand on his arm. "I don't want to be alone. And I don't want you to go. Could you just stay with me? Could we just . . ." She struggled to find the words.

With a sigh Samuel slipped his arms around her, lifted her with ease, and carried her to the bed. Taking care not to cause her to wince from her bruises, he laid her down and pulled the covers over her. Wordlessly, he removed his boots and climbed on top of the heavy, embroidered bedspread. Instinctively, gratefully, Xanthe snuggled up to him, reveling in the warmth and closeness and reassured that nothing more was expected of her.

"I know not where you come from," Samuel said, "but I thank God that he sent you into my life. With such a wandering existence as yours must be, we might never have met, our paths coming close yet not converging. I see now how empty my life was before you stepped into it."

Xanthe breathed in the warmth of him, tracing the pulse in his throat with her finger, watching his life force and at the same time knowing he did not exist in her own world. It was enough to make anyone lose their mind. It was too much to properly take in.

"It does seem as if we were meant to find each other," she told him.

"I believe that to be true," he agreed. "I know there are things in your life of which you cannot speak. Secrets. That is not uncommon in these dangerous days. We all must guard our very thoughts. You saw that Alice recognized me, at the trial? The truth is my own mother counted the girl's family among her friends. She was appalled by what happened to them. To witness her distress was hard for my father, for us all. Our hearts were softened by her suffering, but hardened by the knowledge that we could do nothing to help the family. And that if we tried, we were putting our own in peril."

"Can it really be so bad? I mean, just by speaking up for people in trouble, could you have ended up prosecuted, maybe executed, too? Your father is well regarded, he has friends at the king's court because of his work. Why wouldn't they protect him?"

"Alas, friendships are fickle things when the shadow of the executioner's axe falls upon them. No person, however well regarded, can rely upon the support of others if his own past includes adhering to a faith that is now seen as traitorous."

"Your family were openly Catholics once, too?"

"My mother was raised as such, though she, like many others, renounced her beliefs when she married my father and raised us as Protestants. Public Protestants but secret Catholics."

"Just like Mistress Lovewell."

"A common practice. A necessary adjustment to the shifting rules of law that determine all our futures."

"And of course Alice knew about this. That's why she looked so fearful when she saw you at the trial, isn't it? She was afraid if you spoke out, your own background would come to light."

"Which would have served both of us badly." He nodded and gazed down at her, his expression earnest. "Do not return to Great Chalfield. Stay here with me. You are no servant, that much is plain as a pikestaff. And when you sing, your voice is something precious. Let singing be your sole occupation."

She smiled up at him. "Why, Master Samuel, are you suggesting I live here as a kept woman, singing for my supper on a nightly basis?"

He looked confused for a moment, about to protest that he had her best interests at heart, worried that he might have offended her by suggesting something improper.

She laughed. "I'm teasing, Samuel. No need to panic."

"The truth of it is I do not wish you to step one pace from my side."

She ran her hand over his strong shoulder. "I have to go back to Great Chalfield," she told him carefully. "The missing pieces of the chatelaine are there somewhere. Alice hid them outside the house before she was taken. They are the only things that can save her now. I have to go back and find them."

He thought about this for a moment. If he believed there was, in fact, no hope, he resisted saying so. "Then I will come with you," he promised. "We will search together." He frowned. "But I am a selfish fool. I have not so much as let you take the draft that Philpott prepared for you against your pain, nor applied the balm for your bruises. Tell me, where is it that you feel pain?"

She smiled at him. "You have a way of taking my mind off the bits that hurt," she said.

While looking at her throat and neck he found her locket and paused, taking hold of it, running his fingers over the smooth gold. She wondered, fleetingly, if he might trigger it. And what then? Could he travel back with her? Even after all the craziness that she had come to see as normal, that was too big an idea to comprehend.

"This holds great importance for you. Does it contain the picture of a lost lover, perhaps?" he asked, only half joking.

"Open it," she told him. She would have done it for him, but dared not.

Carefully he did as she suggested. When he saw the photo of Flora inside he gasped, sitting up to take the candle from the bedside table and hold it closer so he could see more clearly.

"Such fine draftsmanship!" He said. "I have never seen a miniature executed with such precision, such finesse. Who was the artist?"

"Mr. Kodak," she said, enjoying her own little joke. "That's my mother. It's . . . all I have of her." Which did not go halfway to explaining anything, but it was the best she could offer.

Samuel nodded. "It is a hard thing, to lose a parent." He must have felt her tense slightly because he refrained from asking all the questions he must have badly wished to ask. Instead he put the candle back and gently snapped shut the locket. "I can see why it is precious," he said. "I'm happy we did not let that wretch take it from you."

"We?" She laughed, and the moment of awkwardness and guardedness was gone. "I seem to remember I was the one who got it back."

"And was it not I who rescued you from the resulting attack?"

"I didn't need rescuing. I was managing perfectly well on my own, thank you very much."

He looked at her then, his expression more serious.

"In truth, my love, you are the one who has rescued me." He planted the lightest of kisses upon her brow. "Now, sleep. The morning will come soon enough and you must rest. Tomorrow we will search for the chatelaine pieces. All will be well."

Xanthe closed her eyes but knew that she must not allow herself to fall asleep. Even as she had been telling Samuel that she had to return to Great Chalfield to search for the missing silver, a thought had occurred to her. A thought about how she could most effectively search, about what would give her the best chance of success. In that moment she saw a way, something that could work. It seemed at once both wonderfully simple and almost impossible. Impossible in the sixteenth century, but not in the twenty-first. Once the solution had come to her, she knew she had to try it, despite the risks.

She waited, feeling the rise and fall of Samuel's chest beneath her head. When his breathing was steady and deep she opened her eyes and watched him for a while, marveling at how beautiful he was. At how close they had grown, and how easy it would be to fall for him. But that would be to fall for a ghost; that was the long and the short of it. She softly kissed his brow and then carefully climbed out of bed. Whatever she had said to him, she knew that trying to find those small pieces of silver in such a big area would be an impossible task, and yet they were crucial. If Alice was to be saved, and Flora's safety assured, she must find them. She knew what she had to do. She knew where she had to go. And Samuel could not go with her.

The floorboards were cold beneath her bare feet as she moved away from the bed. Leaving Samuel, without explanation, without any word of how she felt, was a hard thing to do. She stood by the window and took hold of the locket at her throat. The gold felt warm in her fingers, warmed from her own flushed skin. She opened the locket, took a deep breath, and focused her attention on home. She made herself look at the fuzzy photo of her mother. The sight of her gave Xanthe a little courage. Courage she badly needed.

And then, as she felt herself begin to grow weak and dizzy, as the shadows of the room seemed to reach out to claim her and she had the sensation she was falling backward, the last thing that she saw before she stepped through time was Samuel's eyes as they opened and his expression of confusion and fear as he watched her disappear.

XANTHE ARRIVED IN THE BLIND HOUSE DIZZY, BREATHLESS, AND FURIOUS with herself for being so careless. How could she have let Samuel see her vanish like that? What could possibly be going through his mind now? He would think her some sort of witch. She got to her feet, a little shaken but determined not to give in to the, by now, familiar feelings that followed stepping through time. She had work to do, and little time in which to do it. She shivered, rubbing her arms against the shock of the cold night air on her bare skin, her flimsy underdress offering little warmth. She was about to walk out into the garden when the heavy door slammed shut in her face, and Margaret Merton appeared before her.

"Your task is not yet complete!" the ghost said, her thin voice cutting through the air as if it were an icy wind.

Xanthe took a step backward. "Alice will not hang," she said. "She is safe for now."

"She will perish if her sentence of transportation is carried out! You said as much yourself."

Xanthe began to shiver, partly from the cold, and partly from the thought of her every move in the past being watched over by this vengeful spirit.

"There is something I must do," Xanthe explained. "Here, in my time."

"How can I trust what you say?"

The ghost moved closer, its shadowy form seeming almost to drape itself around Xanthe. The sensation was deeply disturbing.

"I have said I will do what you ask," said Xanthe. "You have to let me do it my way."

"Do you need reminding what will happen if you fail?"

Xanthe resisted the urge to scream at the ghoul. She must remain calm. Stay resolute.

"Every minute I spend here is an hour in Alice's time. We don't know when her ship is to sail. Do you want to keep me talking, listening to your threats, when all the while she is in greater and greater danger, or are you going to let me do what I have to do?"

There was silence for a moment as Mistress Merton considered this. At last she hissed, twisting into a vortex of shifting air and dust before disappearing. Xanthe waited until she could no longer hear the thud of her own, frightened heartbeat against her eardrum, and then pushed open the door of the jail.

She peered out. Dawn, she decided. Birds were singing, and the day felt as if it were beginning rather than ending. Trusting to hope that her mother would still be asleep, and crossing her fingers that any overlooking neighbors would also be in their beds and not at their windows, she dashed out and retrieved her hidden bag, clothes, and keys from behind the butterfly bush. Back inside the jail, shivering, she pulled on her jeans, sandals, and black T-shirt. Only then did she have a chance to properly register what had just happened. Moments before she had been in Samuel's arms. Moments or centuries, depending on which way you looked at it. She could still smell him on her skin. Her body still held the memory of his body. Was he horrified? Disgusted? Terrified? Did he now think she was some sort of ghost or witch? Was he ever going to even want to speak to her again, let alone give her a chance to explain? And just how was she going to explain?

She picked up the few pieces of the chatelaine that had not traveled with her and dug a little hole in the dry dust of the floor in case Flora chose this day to come poking around inside the blind house. As she handled the chatelaine it began vibrating in her hands and she was terrified it would transport her back again. She dared not hold on to it for a second longer than she had to. Once she was satisfied it was safely hidden she crept outside. It was a relief to be free of the oppressive interior of the cramped building, and to step away from the call of the chatelaine and the company of the ghost. She was assailed by dizziness from traveling through time, and her stomach rumbled and cramped unhelpfully. She ignored it as best she could. She had to be quick. For one thing, she needed to get away from home without being seen. For another, a few hours in the twenty-first century could mean a day back in Alice's time. The girl could be bundled aboard a ship at any moment. One way or another, time was against her.

Xanthe ran across the lawn and made her way through the house as quietly as she could. She could hear sounds of the ancient plumbing working. Flora was running a bath. It was worrying that she was up so early, as it could mean she was suffering a flare-up of her condition, and she might be anywhere in the building when Xanthe had to try to get back through it. On the other hand, at that moment it allowed Xanthe to get in through the back door and out through the shop without being heard.

Along the length of the high street shuttered windows showed the shops were not yet open for business. A solitary milk truck made its slow progress from doorstep to doorstep, the whistling milkman hopping out to leave bottles for essential early morning tea. When she reached Liam's workshop it was no surprise to see the curtains of his flat still closed. She hammered on the door for what felt like forever, risking waking the neighbors but reasoning that she was less likely to arouse suspicion in daylight, rather than in the middle of the night when she had turned up on his doorstep last time. At last she heard stumbling footsteps on the stairs inside.

Liam opened the door, half dressed and half awake.

"Xanthe. Another surprise visit. I'm honored."

"I need you to drive me out to Great Chalfield."

"Where we met? How romantic." He stood to one side. "You know the routine by now: tea first, madcap schemes after that."

She hurried past him, running up the stairs. "We'll have to go as soon as possible. That way I'm less likely to be spotted. When we get there I need you to help me find something. Oh, and on the way I need to buy a metal detector."

"A what?" he asked, not unreasonably, following her into the kitchen and putting on the kettle.

"A metal detector. A good one. You know, the type that can look for specific metals. In this case silver. Otherwise we'll be there forever turning up bits of nails and rubbish. I need to get back really quickly."

"Back to the place that isn't Milton Keynes?"

Xanthe nodded. "Do you think we can buy one somewhere between here and Great Chalfield?" she asked. "We might have to make a bit of a detour. I don't know, Chippenham? Salisbury?"

"That's some detour!"

Liam put tea bags in mugs and spooned sugar into both. He glanced at Xanthe. "In jeans today, I see. I quite liked the medieval maid kit."

336 ☙ PAULA BRACKSTON

"Seventeenth century is not medieval."

"Course not, how stupid of me."

"Oh, and please can you lend me the money to buy the metal detector?"

"This gets better and better."

"I promise I'll pay you back as soon as I . . . come back again. Here. In a day or two. Only I haven't got any cash with me and nothing in my bank."

"Whoa." He held up his hands. "First off, I'd be happy to lend you the money, but it won't do you any good."

"Why not?"

"Because today is Sunday. Shops'll be closed."

"Sunday? Shit!"

"Should I be worried you don't know what day it is?"

"Bristol!" she nearly shouted. "There's a big shopping center there that's bound to be open on a Sunday."

"Lucky for us that won't be necessary. As it happens, I know a man who has just what you're looking for."

"You do? That's great. Will he let us borrow it? Can you phone him and ask? Where do we have to go?" She paced up and down even as Liam pressed a mug of tea into her hand, impatience beginning to get the better of her.

Liam sipped his hot drink and then said, "You can ask him yourself. And we only have to go there." He pointed out of the window at the back of the kitchen toward the building behind. Toward the pub.

"Harley?" she asked. "Harley has a metal detector?"

"Used to be quite the enthusiast. Are you going to sit down or what?"

Xanthe forced herself to perch on one of the kitchen chairs and did her best to gulp the scalding tea. "Sorry to do this to you," she said. "Again."

"What are friends for? Just to be clear, your mum still thinks you're in Milton Keynes, right?"

Xanthe nodded. "Have you seen her lately?"

"Spotted her buying chutney at a stall in the Saturday market yesterday."

"How did she seem?"

"I could hear her haggling, trying to beat down the price of the pickle."

Xanthe smiled, relieved. "That sounds like Mum." She drank her tea, avoiding Liam's gaze, hoping to avoid difficult questions. He clearly picked up on her restlessness and eagerness to get on with what she had to do, as he got up and pulled a leather jacket on over his T-shirt before pushing his feet into sneakers.

"Come on," he said, picking up his car keys. "We'll go and wake up Harley, you can use your very best smile on him, and I promise we'll have you up at the manor house before sensible people are out of their beds." He nodded in the direction of the kitchen clock that plainly said the time was a quarter to six.

They decided there was more likelihood of getting Harley to hear them if they tried the rear of the pub. Liam helped her climb over the locked wooden gate that led into the small yard where barrels of beer were delivered. They walked around a store shed and on to the kitchen entrance, where they both set about knocking and calling. After what felt like an interminable wait there came sounds of heavy footsteps and muttered Scottish curses. Locks were turned, bolts pulled back, and the door finally hauled open.

Harley appeared, a shirtless vision, his upper body a wealth of tattoos mapping his youth, his beer-grown belly just a little too much for his jeans to contain, his bare feet strangely vulnerable. He opened his mouth, no doubt to let loose a stream of bad language to vent his fury at having been dragged out of bed at such a painful time on a Sunday morning. When he saw them standing there the surprise of it took the wind from his sails. He looked from Liam to Xanthe and back again and then gave a low growl.

"This had better be good," he said.

It took a maddening ten minutes to make him understand what they wanted, and to convince him they were not planning some manner of robbery. He clearly hated not being given all the facts, his natural curiosity as an amateur historian demanding answers. At last he saw that Liam could not give him any, and that Xanthe would not. Reluctantly, he led them up to the attic, where they dug through endless boxes, piles of books, a large vinyl record collection, and several leather biker jackets before Harley spotted what was wanted.

"There she is, the little beauty!" he cried, removing the long-stemmed gadget from its dusty box. The thing resembled nothing so much as a bagless vacuum cleaner. He flicked a few switches. "Haven't had her out in years. Aye, but we had some hunts, out in the misty mornings, looking for coins and so forth. Annie wasn't so keen on me wandering off looking for treasure when we'd a pub to run, though. I kind of got out of the way of it, you know. Now, has the old girl got any charge left in her?"

They waited while he twiddled knobs. Small lights came on. He waved the machine over a nearby random bicycle wheel. It made no sound, not a single beep. Xanthe began to feel desperate. They were wasting valuable minutes, if the thing wasn't going to work they would have to drive miles to find another one. Just then there was a jittering bleep and then an earsplitting screech from the machine. Liam and Xanthe flinched, throwing their hands over their ears, but Harley laughed, delighted.

"There she blows! Will you look at that. Years of ignoring the poor wee thing and she's still ready for action. Here." He handed the detector to Liam, no doubt thinking a mechanic would know how to use it. "Take good care of her, laddie. I might just find time to start using her again, now that you've stirred the idea of hunting treasure in me."

They thanked him, made all sorts of promises regarding both the metal detector and future explanations, and left as quickly as they could. Back at his workshop, Liam took Xanthe into the main bay of the garage.

"Time to give my latest project a run out," he said. "I've been doing some fine tuning. Was looking for a moment to put her to the test." With a flourish, he pulled back a dust sheet to reveal a gleaming red, soft-top classic sports car. She vaguely recognized it as the one Liam had been driving when he'd pinched her parking space at the auction. It had the top down to show off its cream leather seats, walnut dashboard, and leather steering wheel. He was obviously waiting for a reaction.

"Very nice," was all she could manage.

"Nice? This is only a mint condition MG V8 Roadster. Nice, indeed!"

"Does it go?"

He clutched at his heart. "I am wounded! Just get in. You'll see."

He put the metal detector on the tiny space behind the seats and opened the door for her, before jumping into the driver's seat. They left Marlborough, and the pretty summer countryside flashed by as the MG purred along. She was relieved Liam did not question her further. She realized then that his apparent flippancy was his way of letting her off the hook. If he admitted he could see how serious the whole thing was to her, he would have to know more about it. This way he could help her without pressing her for more answers. Impossible answers to impossible questions. There was no traffic to slow them down.

Even the tractors seemed to have taken a day off. With each passing mile she worried more and more that she would not find what she was looking for. It was a huge area to search, even with a metal detector. At last they came to the village that had sprung up around the estate, and wound their way along the lanes to the house itself. She asked Liam to stop at the top of the long driveway. For a moment she felt completely disorientated. Great Chalfield had been extended and enlarged over the years but was still recognizably the same house, and just for a few seconds she was unsure not *where* she was but *when*. She could have been sitting in the back of an open carriage rather than an open-topped car. She could have been about to call on the Lovewells, or meet Samuel in the Great Hall. With a pang she thought of his beloved screen and how she had loved working on it with him. Was it there, she wondered. Had he succeeded? Had his creative vision been translated through craftsmanship into something that had lasted centuries? Because the auction had been held in the old barn she had not been inside the house itself. She wished she could do so then, so that when she next saw Samuel she could make him believe that all his hard work and skill would bear fruit.

"Where d'you want to start?" Liam asked, jolting her from her thoughts.

She glanced around. "Can we park the car here somewhere? I don't want to get too close to the house or we might be seen. I need to look in the area to the south of the stables. It reaches down across the fields to a small stream."

Liam turned the car off the drive onto a farm track and found a place for it behind some trees. The track only led to more fields, and they decided to trust to it not being used so early on a Sunday morning. Taking the detector, they made their way as far along the drive as they dared before dropping down across the sloping pasture. Xanthe heard a dog bark somewhere, but no one seemed to be up. The day was already beginning to heat up, the cloudless sky hosting a warm sun, despite the early hour. She had grown accustomed to the autumn weather and found herself squinting at the brightness of the morning.

"When do you want to use this?" Liam asked, holding up the detector.

"Not here. Not yet. Alice . . . the person who hid the pieces, she ran from the house, past the stables, down across the parkland. There were no hedges or fences here then. . . ."

"Then?"

She did not respond to his query. "I don't think she could have found a hiding place out here in the open." She stopped, hands on hips, looking around. The landscape had changed little, but there were changes, and they weren't helpful ones. Had that small bunch of trees been there in 1605? Or that run of hazel hedge? Or that pond? They walked on. Further down the slope the stream came more clearly into view. It had quite steep-banked sides. Alice might have been able to reach it, and then those muddy banks would have provided a place where she could have squashed the scissors and needle case in. It would have been the work of a moment. Liam followed Xanthe as she started to walk along the water's edge.

"Here," she said, pointing. "Can you search the bank on this side?"

He switched the gadget on. There was a nerve-racking moment when the flickering charging light seemed to indicate loss of power, but then it steadied and set up a quiet, rhythmic beeping. To cover as much ground as possible they had to move horribly slow. They had made sure to set the detector to silver, so there were no time-wasting finds along the way. Just the *beep-beep-beep* of nothing to see here, nothing found. They trudged on.

With a heavy heart she realized that anything pushed into such soft, wet mud, washed over by the river year after year, could easily have been dislodged. In fact, it was more than likely that the banks would have eroded, so that something so small and light could easily have been swept along and carried downstream to who knew where. She was on the point of despair when they reached the little stone bridge. She stopped so abruptly that Liam almost tripped over her.

"Seen something?" he asked.

"I'm not sure. Actually, yes, in a way, I have seen something." She could not tell him she had seen it in a vision the first time, and then the second time when she had stood at the fire-damaged stables and looked down toward the stream. She had noticed the bridge then, but not thought of its possible significance. Only at this point did she work out that, when she had traveled back that time and arrived in the middle of the fire, if the building had not been burning, if the hayloft had not been filled with smoke, and if she had looked out of the loft window, it was this very bridge that she would have seen. That was what she was supposed to see. That was why she had been sent back to that exact place.

Suddenly, she felt hopeful. "It's here somewhere!" she told Liam. "Here in the bridge, I'm sure of it. If Alice ran quickly she could have reached here before they caught her. And if she hid the chatelaine pieces among the stones, not in the mud, they could still be here."

Liam did not question her thinking but raised the detector and swept it slowly from side to side over the start of the bridge. They paced across it. Nothing. They searched in the low stone walls on either side. Still nothing. Not a twitch from the machine. Not a glimpse of anything out of the ordinary. Just stone and stone and more stone.

"Not a glimmer," Liam said, shaking his head.

"It has to be here. It has to be." She walked back to the house side of the stream and stared at the bridge. If she had been Alice, running, breathless, terrified, knowing she had seconds maybe before she was caught, where would Xanthe have hidden those things that might get her hanged? What would she have done? And then it struck her. "Underneath!" she cried, scrambling down the bank beside the bridge. "It makes sense. They wouldn't be able to see what she was doing as they caught her up."

Liam followed her as she waded into the stream, the cool water making her gasp. It was no deeper than her knees and the flow gentle, but the weeds grabbed at her ankles, and the chalky river bed was unstable beneath her sandals so that she nearly fell in. Liam splashed through the water behind her, holding the detector high.

"Try it there," she told him. "Right under the arch of the bridge."

He did as she asked and almost at once the device started to squeal. It gave a high-pitched whine that rose and dipped depending on where it was pointed. Liam followed its lead, moving in the direction that appeared to set the thing off most. The sound grew louder, stronger. Xanthe searched where it seemed most definite, pulling at the moss that had grown to cover the gaps and crannies between the stones. There was mud. There were smaller stones. There were snails. She searched on. At last the detector settled on its highest note, insistent and shrieking. She clawed at the loose mud, mortar, and moss.

"Anything?" Liam asked.

"No. No ... wait ... there is something here. Jammed between these two stones. Look, here!" She scraped away a layer of lichen and yet more moss and then could clearly see something smooth and metallic and dully gleaming in the shadows. It was the handle of the scissors. Carefully, she wiped the mud from it with her T-shirt. She was then able to grasp the tiny handle between her fingers. At first it felt stuck solid, but as she wriggled it she felt it give. A tiny amount of movement became more, and then more, and at last she was able to pull the scissors free. She stared at the tarnished, muddy silverwork in her palm. Such a small thing, and yet of such significance to Alice. And to Flora. She probed inside the tiny gap again and easily found the needle case, which came free with less persuasion. She turned to show Liam their treasure.

"Cool," he said. "I'm not going to ask how you knew they were there, or why they are so important, but they look like they might have been something special once."

"They were. They still are," she said, smiling.

"That's better," he said, smiling back.

At that moment they both heard the barking of dogs. Dogs getting nearer.

"Someone's up," he said, "and it sort of sounds like they've seen us. We should go."

"Wait, I have to put these back," she told him.

"Put them *back*?"

"Yes. Otherwise they won't be there when I go to look for them. And they can't travel back with me because they are already there." She hastily jammed the pieces back into their hiding place.

"Run that by me again?" Liam could not keep the bafflement out of his voice.

"There isn't time. I can't explain." She pushed moss over the gap, sealing it with more mud.

The dogs were close now, and a man was with them.

"Who's there?" he called out. "This is private property." He was less than pleased to find two strangers on his land before breakfast.

Liam scrambled up the bank and gave a cheery wave. "Good morning! Hoped we wouldn't disturb you, getting out here so early," he said.

"There is no footpath on this part of the estate," the man informed them, peering past Liam to try and see what Xanthe was up to.

She joined Liam on the riverbank.

"Sorry," she said, mustering another smile. "We were treasure hunting and following this lovely stream. Got a bit off the path, I suppose."

"Yes, you did," said the landowner. His expression suggested he was a long way from being convinced. His dogs, two black Labradors, turned out to be laughably friendly. Not the fearsome guard dogs Xanthe had anticipated, they panted and wagged around Liam and Xanthe and did nothing more than jump up with muddy paws.

"Sorry," she said again. "We'll go straight away, of course. Could you point us in the best direction?"

The man refused to soften, however polite she was. "Go straight up to the drive and follow your nose. Away from the house." He gave another hard stare and then turned on his Wellington-booted heel and marched away. His dogs bounded after him, oblivious to any tension.

"Right," said Liam, shouldering the metal detector, "I think we've earned a decent breakfast."

She tried her best to dissuade him. All she wanted to do was return to Marlborough, return to the blind house, and return to the seventeenth century. But Liam argued that it would not take long, and that she looked in need of a proper meal. She realized that this was his way of not letting her simply disappear again. However hard he was trying not to quiz her, he must have wanted to know more about what on earth was going on. How was he to know that minutes with him could mean hours or even days for Alice, either in the stinking prison in Salisbury, or already embarking on her fatal journey to the colony? In the end Xanthe decided it was quicker to agree with him and do what he wanted than it would be to argue. Twenty minutes later they were parked in a clearing off a busy road that led to the motorway, ordering bacon-and-egg sandwiches from a mobile stall that regularly served there.

"Best bacon butties for miles," Liam assured her as they leaned against the boot of his car, tucking into their calorie-laden breakfasts, ketchup dripping onto their laps. "Lorry drivers stop here to refuel before the M4. Don't worry. It's a faster road back to Marlborough from here. I'll have you back in no time. Although, I have a hunch you will be off somewhere else the minute we arrive. Am I right?"

She nodded. "Yes. And, no, I can't tell you where. I'm sorry. You've been such a help. I would have been stuck without you."

"Oh somehow I think you'd have found a way, even on your own. I don't think there's much Xanthe Westlake can't do if she sets her mind to it. Just don't ask me to try to make sense of it all. You turn up at silly o'clock on a Sunday morning, desperate to find something, which you then leave where you found it?"

"I had to know if it was there."

"Right."

"And now I do."

"So you can . . . send someone else to get it?" He was trying his utmost to keep up.

"Something like that. The important thing is that it is there, and I know it is there." As Liam chewed his bacon sandwich she went on. "One more thing," she said, wiping ketchup from her lip. "Please, don't tell Mum you've seen me."

"OK. Any idea how long I'll have to keep it a secret? Or don't you know when you're coming back?"

"Mum's expecting me on Monday afternoon. God, that's tomorrow. How can it all be so soon and yet..." She left the sentence unfinished. She would have to deal with the confusion and bewilderment of the time differences between the centuries on her own. "Have you seen her, apart from at the market yesterday?" she asked. "Since I went away. Would you say she is coping?"

"Called round the afternoon you went wherever it is you didn't go. She was in her workshop, removing old paint off a chair like a woman possessed. Very focused on the shop opening. Seemed more than fine to me."

"Thanks. For calling in." She looked at him closely then. He was still undeniably good-looking, and kind, and funny. And she knew that he was interested in her. That he was beginning to care. She was aware she was comparing him to Samuel. Liam looked up and caught her studying him, making her blush. "I'm sorry," she said for the umpteenth time. "For dragging you into all... this."

He gave a shrug. "What are friends for," he said again.

Once they were back in the car, speeding toward town, she allowed herself to let go of some of the unbearable tension she had been holding inside her. She now knew where the pieces were. She would go back, fetch them, return them to Mistress Lovewell in a way that suggested they were never stolen in the first place, and then Alice would be released. And she would see Samuel again, provided he wanted to see her. What could she say to him? How could he take her into his home again, having watched her dissolve in front of him? What could he tell his family about her now?

"You OK?" Liam asked, glancing at her.

"I will be. Once I've figured it all out."

There was a short pause and then he said, "You can trust me, you know. If you need to tell me . . . stuff." He reached over and put his hand on hers.

She gave him a small smile. "I know. And maybe I will be able to tell you. One day."

"One day," he repeated, slowly removing his hand and returning his attention to the twisting road home.

By the time they reached Marlborough it was nearly nine, and the town was awake but moving at Sunday speed. Liam drove straight into his yard and parked up in the workshop.

"Do you need a lift to a train station, or somewhere?" he asked.

"Actually I need to get something from home. Or rather, from the garden behind our shop. I'll . . . go on from there."

"There's a door in the wall at the back of your house? I didn't realize."

"It's sort of hidden," she told him, uncomfortable with having to tell yet more half-truths.

"And you're sure you don't want your mum to know you've been around?" When she nodded he shook his head. "OK, you're the boss. Come on." He started for the street, and when she hesitated he called over his shoulder, "You'll need a decoy, don't you think?"

When they arrived they found the shop door propped open. From inside came sounds of the radio and someone sweeping. By the look of the shop itself Flora had been busy putting an extra bit of elbow grease into making the place look good for the opening. It tugged at Xanthe's heartstrings to think of it all going on without her. She had to tell herself she would be home in a few short hours, just one more day. Liam gave her a reassuring wink and a smile and then walked into the shop ahead of her. She slipped in and hid under the sturdy Victorian desk that they had kept as our counter.

"Mrs. Westlake?" Liam called out. "Flora, are you at home?" He continued through to the back of the shop.

From her hiding place Xanthe heard her mother emerge from the workshop, surprised and pleased at the sight of her visitor. She was impressed, and even a little appalled at how charming Liam was, and how quickly he persuaded Flora that it was a Sunday, and too lovely a morning to be stuck inside working, and he insisted she join him for a glass of something cold at the little cafe down by the river behind his workshop. However dedicated her mother was to the shop she allowed herself to be persuaded. Xanthe waited, heart thudding, as they walked past her, Flora on her sticks, chatting all the while, locking the front door as she left. Only when she was convinced they were not going to return for some reason did Xanthe unfold herself from under the desk. She dashed upstairs and grabbed her peasant skirt, quickly wriggling out of her jeans and stepping into it. She added her cheesecloth shirt and tied a scarf around her hair. She would have to rely on her artistic profession to excuse her bizarre appearance again.

Outside the garden was full of sunshine and birds, their cheerfulness at odds with the weight Xanthe felt in her heart. It seemed so wrong to be lying to people she loved. Whatever her reservations, though, as soon as she stood inside the blind house again she felt the powerful pull of the past and heard the chatelaine begin to sing once again. Quickly, she dug in the dust and uncovered the chatelaine. She brushed the dirt from the grooves of the silver, closed her hands around the gritty metal. She was at the point of shutting her eyes when Mistress Merton appeared before her.

"I can see her still, still feel her despair. She languishes in another place of squalor and filth!"

"They will not hold her long in Salisbury." Xanthe faced the ghost calmly. She knew what she had to do and there was no time to argue about it. No time to waste being scared. "I am going back now," she said. "And I have to know you won't harm my mother while I am gone. Promise me."

"When my daughter is safe, so will your mother be," the ghost insisted.

There was nothing more to be said. Xanthe rubbed the chatelaine with her thumb, closed her eyes, and allowed herself to be transported back through the centuries once again.

{ 25 }

AS SHE TRAVELED BACK THE THING THAT WORRIED HER MOST WAS WHERE, exactly, she would emerge. She never felt she had any control over it, but this time she focused as strongly as she was able on the missing chatelaine pieces, holding a picture of the bridge in her mind, willing herself to arrive near them. She offered up a hasty prayer that she would be set down at least in sight of where they were. She tried to push to the back of her mind the fear that Alice, in such desperate circumstances, might somehow call her directly to her. What use would Xanthe be alongside her in a prison cell? Or, worse, aboard a transportation ship somewhere in the Atlantic? Surely she could not have been sent away so soon? She could not know. All she could do was hope.

Which was why she almost whooped with relief when she opened her eyes to find she was lying in the grass only a few strides from the little stone bridge. To know that she could in fact, exert some influence over where she ended up was huge. Her head felt groggy, her vision slightly blurred, but she didn't care. She was so close to putting things right. This was not the time to give in to fatigue or trivial complaints. It was daytime, the air crisp with a frost just thawing. She hauled herself to her feet and hurried to the water's edge, stepping carefully down the muddy river bank. She ran her hands over the damp stones of the underside of the bridge, trying to locate the exact spot, looking for the familiar padding of mosses. Somewhere nearby, crows cawed as if disturbed by someone. She could not afford to be found. Not now. Not while she was so close to succeeding. She scrabbled at the stones and at last felt the hard, smooth nub of the scissors handle. It took a deal more scratching and tugging before she was able to shift the tiny stones and mud around them and pull the silver pieces free. She quickly dunked them in the stream, rubbing off the grit and grime until they shone as good as new. Her gypsy skirt had an ornamental pocket that was helpfully deep. She tucked her treasures deep into it, scrambled up the bank, and ran toward the house. As she ran she had to face the fact that she had no proper plan beyond returning the chatelaine attachments to Mistress Lovewell's bedchamber and placing them in such a way that they could have been lost, rather than stolen. To do this she must enter the house unseen. If any of the Lovewells or Mary saw her, she would no doubt be shouted at for going missing and then either sent packing or put to work. She had time for neither. She made for the stables. There were ladders up against the damaged walls now, and piles of wood and stone, as rebuilding work had already begun. Thankfully there was nobody there at that moment, though she could hear voices and hammering coming from inside. She made her way around the side of the stricken building, taking care to keep out of sight of the windows of the house itself. She was just about to make the dash across to the low-roofed dairy when footsteps behind her made her wheel around.

"Oh, Peter!"

"Where have you been?" the boy asked, excited at finding a runaway. He cast a surprised glance over her outlandish clothes but said nothing about them. "Everyone has been searching for you. They said you'd probably stolen something that would later come to light, but I said no, you were no thief. I said you were a wandering minstrel and it was only to be expected you would go roaming again. Mister Willis agreed with me. I was right, wasn't I?"

She smiled at him. "You were. I'm not a thief. And, yes, I will need to move on, very soon."

"But I wanted to hear you sing again," he said, his face falling as he kicked at a small stone.

"I'm sorry," she said. "But my stay here could never be permanent. I must find a troupe of players, and that means traveling to a city."

"If that is so, what is it that brings you back to Great Chalfield?"

"Well, I left my things here. My bag. My boots." She wriggled her toes in her sandals to make her point.

Peter laughed at the sight of such peculiar footwear. "Why, yes, I can see you cannot walk far in those!" he agreed.

"I must take my things without being seen," she explained. "Will you help me, Peter?"

He nodded without hesitation.

"I don't want to get you into trouble," she said.

"Fear not on my account, for I come and go into and out of the house without being seen as I please. I am very good at it."

Xanthe recalled him finding her in the paneled reception room the first time she had come to the house. He certainly had had no more business being there than she. She remembered too what he had said about knowing where to find stubs of candles. Not something he should have been doing, and yet he had never been caught.

"Very well. Will you go ahead of me, check that there is no one I will meet on my way?"

He nodded again and then scampered across the yard, darting behind the dairy. She followed, struggling to keep up with his nimble little legs. He led her through the herb garden, past the water pump—after first checking there was no one using it—and to a door at the rear of the house that was seldom used. It was unlocked, and he waved her in. As they went up a back staircase she whispered, "Where are the master and mistress?"

"Taking their breakfast in the Great Hall. They had guests staying, Lord and Lady Pemberton. Nothing is too much trouble for them," he said, not pausing as he scurried up the slippery, twisting wooden stairs.

She could see that he was taking her straight to the attic, but she needed to stop at the mistress's bedchamber. She put a hand on his arm.

"Wait. Please, wait here. There is something I must . . . see to. But you must not speak of it. Can you do that, Peter? Can you keep a secret? Someone's very life may depend upon it."

"I am not a child," he insisted. "I know how to keep a secret."

She nodded, smiling at the thought that it was precisely because he was a child that he would be able to do so. He waited at the end of the long landing while she went to the front of the house on the first floor. As she passed the top of the main staircase she could hear sounds of conversation and laughter. The hosts were still busy entertaining their guests. A fleeting glimpse of Mary carrying fresh linen into another bedroom made Xanthe jump, but she was not seen. She all but ran into the mistress's room. She had thought about what she was going to do, so she went straight to the dressing table. Jayne had told her this was where the mistress sat every night before bed. This was the exact place where she would remove her chatelaine. It was different from a modern dressing table, having no fixed mirror, and drawers instead of a knee hole. Xanthe took the scissors and needle case from her skirt pocket and reached down behind the cupboard. The gap between the wooden back of the furniture and the wall was, as she had hoped, only just wide enough for the pieces to fit. By giving the dressing table a hard shove she was able to jam the chatelaine attachments in place, hidden, yet secure, and very difficult to see. A whistle from Peter alerted her to someone coming. She ran from the room, charging along the landing, and was on the point of crossing the top of the main stairs when she heard the unmistakable voice of Mistress Lovewell.

"Girl! What are you about? How came you back into this house, and without word or explanation? Master Lovewell, husband, come quick!" she called. Within moments the master, Clara, and the guests all appeared at the bottom of the stairs, staring up at her.

Master Lovewell was keen to make light of the situation. Anything to save face in front of his noble friends. "Ah-ha! Our missing songbird has flown back to us. And dressed as if for some performance, I believe. I am happy to see her once again. You were present at Clara's birthday celebrations, Lord Pemberton. You will recall the beauty of our minstrel's voice, no doubt?"

The guests nodded, but Mistress Lovewell would not be so easily put off dealing with the errant servant.

"She is a feckless maidservant, no more no less, and one who has yet to earn our trust. I would remind you she claims to be a friend of a proven thief."

"Come, come, my dear," Master Lovewell said, putting a hand on his wife's arm. "One bad apple need not spoil the whole barrel, not since the apple has been removed. The maid was doubtless returning to her duties."

"She has no business being near our private rooms. What

were you intent upon, girl? Speak up now, or it will go badly for you."

If Xanthe had wanted witnesses to the finding of the pieces, the Pembertons would serve very well indeed. She took a deep breath and said as clearly as she could, "I went to find the silver scissors and needle case. I know where they are."

There were gasps from the Lovewells and murmured questions from their guests.

"It is as I thought!" the mistress declared.

"I know where they are because I have spoken again to Alice." Another lie. When did she become so adept at duplicity? It was terrifying. "She is certain she knows what befell the missing pieces, and she has directed me to look where I might find them."

"Ha!" Mistress Lovewell shook her head. "The word of one thief to another."

"We are both honest people, mistress. I promise you. Let me show you now where you may find your silver."

The mistress opened her mouth to protest but her husband saw an opportunity to display his fair-mindedness, to show himself in a good and kindly light in front of his guests. "Come," he said, taking the mistress's arm and beckoning to the others, "let us go up and have this matter happily settled once and for all."

They trooped into the bedchamber, by now accompanied by Mary, who had heard the commotion and come running. Clara edged her way ahead to peer more closely at her clothes. Xanthe heard Lady Pemberton mutter "shocking" under her breath as she passed.

"Well?" The mistress of the house indicated the room with a sweep of her arm.

"Better you discover them for yourself, mistress. Alice believes that during a moment's inattention on her own part they slipped down between the dressing table and the wall. Would you care to look?"

"I would not!"

"Oh, Mother." Clara stepped forward, pushing Pepito into her father's arms. "Let me." She leaned over and reached her hand and slender arm down into the barely existent gap. "I can detect nothing. . . . Oh, wait . . . what is this?" And with that she pulled out the silver pieces and held them up for all to see.

"Well done, Daughter!" Her father dropped the dog in order to applaud, and the Pembertons joined in.

Clara returned the attachments to her mother.

"As ever they were, Mother," she told her.

Mistress Lovewell turned them over in her hand. She looked up at Xanthe and her face plainly said that she knew she had been tricked, but that she lacked any evidence to prove it.

"And now at last," Master Lovewell was herding everyone back toward the door, "life may resume normality."

"I beg your pardon, sir," Xanthe said, stepping in front of him, "but for Alice, that depends on you now. Will you send word to Salisbury of her innocence?"

"Well, I . . ."

"She has been convicted," Mistress Lovewell insisted. "She is beyond our reach."

"But she has committed no crime," Xanthe insisted. "Master Lovewell, are you not a man of influence? The court would listen to you, would they not?"

He glanced at Lord Pemberton, torn between his desire to appease his wife and his wish to look good in front of his influential and powerful friends.

"It is possible, if I were to write a letter. . . ."

"Husband, do not concern yourself. The matter is out of our hands. And besides, with the stables in disarray, the horses moved, some unfit for use, who would undertake such a task? There is no one."

"I will take the letter," came a voice from the doorway.

Xanthe's heart lurched, and she turned to see Samuel standing there. "Samuel," she murmured.

Lord Pemberton thought it beneath such a sought-after architect to run errands. "Surely a manservant can be found."

Samuel insisted. "A messenger will not suffice. The case for Alice's immediate release must be presented along with Master Lovewell's letter. Please allow me to see this thing done," he said, addressing Master Lovewell.

After that, everything happened quickly and amid a deal of flapping and bustling about, so that there was not a hope Xanthe could speak to Samuel. He was bundled out of the room by Master Lovewell, keen, no doubt, to have him back working on the house as soon as possible. Lord Pemberton volunteered to add his own signature in support, and Clara offered to show his wife the grounds while they waited. Mary took the first opportunity to scold Xanthe for not returning when she was expected and so landing the other servants with her share of the work. Through it all the mistress watched her closely, still holding the chatelaine pieces, still attempting to unravel the puzzle of how she had been duped, by whom, and exactly why. Mary was all for sending Xanthe back to work but Mistress Lovewell would not hear of it.

"A moment, Mary. Step forward, girl," she said to Xanthe, glancing at the door to make certain she was not overheard. "I know not the reasons behind your actions, nor do I care to know them. I am certain, in any case, that they are not borne of affection or duty for this household. I will not keep a servant under this roof if I cannot trust them. In short, I will not keep you. My husband has a soft heart, my daughter has a young maid's fancies for entertainments. Neither is here to plead your case now. I would have you gone this day, this very hour. Collect your things and go."

There was no point in attempting to argue with her. Such a dismissal was unfair, it was unnecessary, and had Xanthe really been what she claimed to be it might have meant hardship for her, but she was only ever there because of her desire to protect her own mother, and now it was time to return to her.

"I am sorry that you think so of me, mistress," Xanthe replied, bobbing a curtsy and walking quickly out of the room. Mistress Lovewell might have been surprised that she did not fight for her position, might have wanted to question her further, and Xanthe was not going to give her that opportunity.

Upstairs she had changed her sandals for her boots and nearly finished pulling her own faux medieval clothes on over her cotton skirt when Jayne ran breathlessly into the room.

"Oh, it is true then! You are to leave, and only this minute returned! I had hoped so very much you would stay," she said, tears brimming.

"I'm sorry, Jayne, but don't worry about me. I'm used to moving on often. I like it," she insisted. "New places to see, new adventures."

"But . . . I shall miss you," she said in a tiny voice, her lip trembling.

Xanthe gave her a hug and then took three silver coins from her bag: a penny and two shillings. More money than the maid would see in months. "I want you to have these. Buy yourself a new dress for fayre days, and keep the rest safe. That way, if anyone ever treats you ill, you will be able to leave and take up another post."

This brought more tears, and it was a while before Xanthe could leave her and go downstairs. If she had expected any sort of farewells from the family she was to be disappointed. As she made her way down the stairs she saw them all walking in the rose garden, the whole matter no doubt already put behind them. Such was the lack of importance servants held in their lives. Looking up she saw Samuel galloping Raven out through the gates at the far end of the drive. Would that be the last she ever saw of him? She continued down the stairs and was about to go out the arched front door when something made her pause. She turned instead and entered the Great Hall. Samuel's drawings of the screen were in place on the high table, all their alterations and additions included, reminding her of what it had been like to stand beside him and work with him, making Xanthe long to be that close to him again. She forced herself to focus on what she had to do. Glancing quickly over her shoulder she slipped behind the ornately carved chairs so that she could reach the wall hanging. The stitching on the hem of the tapestry was still loose from when she had undone it. She gave the thread a tug and it unrolled easily. Alice's rosary felt cool in her hand, the smooth garnets gleaming even in the low light of the hall. She tucked it deep into her bag and was just adjusting the strap over her shoulder when Mistress Lovewell appeared in the doorway.

They stood looking at one another. There was so much in that silence, so much that passed between them. She had seen what Xanthe had taken from the tapestry. At that moment, the mistress understood what Alice had done. Of course she had known all along about the girl's beliefs, and now she realized that Xanthe knew so much more than she had admitted to. Was this the instant where Mistress Lovewell would denounce her, too? Was Xanthe to be arrested as a secret follower of an illegal faith? Would the mistress of the house go that far, even though she herself was once a Catholic?

"Would it have been so hard to just let Alice be?" Xanthe asked. "You could have turned a blind eye."

"And risk my own family?" She shook her head slowly. "If you think my husband could protect us from prosecution you know little of how this world works. You see a man puffing himself up, surrounding himself with grandeur, playing the fool for minor nobles to ingratiate himself. Do not be quick to judge. I see a man who will do what he must to secure his family's safety and their future. What manner of wife would I be were I to allow my past, my personal history, to undo all his efforts? What manner of mother would I be not to put my own daughter's security above all else?"

She was right, of course. Xanthe was in no position to criticize her. It was no good using her twenty-first-century view of life to judge what the mistress did, what she had to do, in order to survive in a very different time. There was no more to be said. Xanthe hoisted her bag over her shoulder and walked out of the room, passing close enough to Mistress Lovewell to smell the lavender in the scent bottle that hung from her chatelaine, but she did not try to stop her.

Outside the day was all crisp autumn freshness, with clear skies. The muddy road had dried out, now that the rain had stopped, and been hardened by frosts. Xanthe marched away from Great Chalfield sorry not to have been able to thank those who had helped her and say good-bye to them. She attempted to estimate how far Samuel would have traveled. When would he reach Salisbury? Raven was a swift horse, sure-footed and fit, but it was many miles to gallop. And would Alice still be there? Would Samuel get there in time? As she walked on it occurred to her that she did not know where she was going or what to do next. True, she had put right the injustice Alice had been accused of and cleared her name, but had all her efforts been too late to save her? She could not leave until she was certain Alice was free. Certain that she had rid her mother of Margaret Merton's threat.

As she was wondering how long it would take to walk all the way to Marlborough she heard the sound of a cart approaching. Turning, she found Willis driving the old wagon and the chestnut mare. He caught up to her and reined the horse to a halt.

"Seems I have business in town this morning," he said, holding out his hand to help her up onto the driver's seat beside him.

"My good fortune," she said, smiling up at him as she took his hand.

The journey was slow but definitely faster and less exhausting than walking would have been. Willis was a man of few words, and not given to taking them out for an airing often, but they passed the miles companionably enough. She felt he knew more than he would ever admit to and was being careful not to talk about anything difficult. Before he dropped her in the high street she handed him her flashlight, wrapped in a strip torn off her hem. She had a brief moment of panic at leaving something modern behind, but it was such a small thing, surely it would not matter.

"For Peter," she told Willis. "Tell him . . . tell him it is a minstrel's lamp, so that he need not light a candle in the new hayloft to light his way. It is a secret, not to be shared, and it is a fleeting thing so he must use it sparingly. When it no longer shines he should bury it out of sight."

Willis nodded, taking the parcel without examining it, though she suspected the minute she was gone he would be unwrapping it.

"Fare thee well, mistress," he said, touching his cap.

"I shan't forget your kindness," she told him.

"Nor I yours. Alice's fortunes would not have changed without it."

She watched him drive the cart on toward the smithy's, and then headed up toward the green. By the time she reached the front door of the Applebys' house she was stupidly nervous. She knew Samuel would not have had time to get to Salisbury and back. She only hoped she would be allowed to wait for him.

Philpott answered the door. He looked aghast at her muddle of clothing but let her in and asked her to wait in the hallway. She could hear voices, and then Master Appleby emerged from the sitting room.

"Mistress Westlake, a pleasure to see you again."

She ducked an awkward curtsy. "You have heard? Of Samuel's mission?" she asked. When he said he had not, she began to explain but he stopped her, summoning Philpott, instructing him to send mead, and offering Xanthe his arm to escort her to a seat by the fire in the sitting room. Only when Philpott had poured them both small glasses of the honeyed and herbed wine did Master Appleby let her tell him everything that had happened that morning at Great Chalfield. At last he sat back in his seat, nodding thoughtfully.

"I have received no word of the girl having been moved. God grant Samuel is in time, which I believe he will be. In which case, with the letter bearing two such signatures, along with Samuel's own testimony, I am certain Alice will be freed within the day."

"I can hardly believe it. At last," she said, sipping her mead, feeling suddenly weary.

"It is through your efforts, my dear. The girl has you to thank for her freedom. For her life."

She looked at him, trying to see in his face what he truly made of her. "It was what I came here to do."

"And now that it is done . . . you will depart?"

"I have no choice."

"Samuel will miss you."

She looked away then, not trusting herself to speak about how much it would cost her to leave Samuel. Seeing that she was struggling to hide her emotions, Master Appleby put on a more cheerful voice.

"As will we all. Indeed, I for one will lament the loss of your sweet voice. A gift. And I sincerely hope you will return soon to bestow it upon us once more some day not too distant."

She did her best to smile. "I would like that," she said.

As there was nothing left to do but wait for Samuel they fell to talking about great houses that they knew, and the wonderful furniture and craftsmanship within them. Philpott brought them food at one point, but she was still too keyed up to eat anything much and happy for the distraction of engaging conversation.

It was nearly four o'clock when they heard hooves clatter under the archway beside the house, signaling Raven returning to the stables. Xanthe stood up, anxious beyond endurance to find out if Samuel had been in time and Alice had been released. She suddenly was horribly conscious of how drab she looked, her hair a mess, her clothes a hodgepodge of her own garments that looked even less authentic to her than when she had first put them together. She had not slept for hours and was suffering from something resembling jet lag, with all the flitting from one time to another. No matter the century, she was still vain enough and insecure enough to wish she looked better for Samuel.

And then, there he was. Standing in front of her. His hat was dusty from the long ride. When he removed it his hair was wild and fell into his eyes. Eyes that he did not for one second take off her. She knew he said her name, but she scarcely heard it. This was the man who had held her in his arms and then watched her vanish. This was the man to whom she was close to losing her heart. It was Samuel's father who cut through the moment to ask the burning question.

"Did you succeed in your task, Samuel? Is the girl freed?"

Samuel took a breath and then said levelly, "She is."

"The Lord be praised!" Master Appleby cried, calling for Philpott and the best claret in the house.

"Oh, Samuel," Xanthe said. "I am so relieved. So pleased!" She did her best to say the right thing, but all she could think of was how at last her mother was safe. Margaret Merton would not harm Flora now. The danger was over. She took a steadying breath and stepped closer to Samuel. Whatever he thought about her now, she would always be grateful to him for what he had done. "I can't thank you enough for going to Salisbury," she said. "Did you see Alice yourself?"

"I did."

"How is she?"

"Frail. In a state of confusion. I believe she thought her fate set and was almost unable to accept such a change in her fortunes."

"Where is she now?"

"I found her lodgings in the town. She was in no condition to travel. She will bide there until she is recovered from her ordeal."

"And then?" she asked.

"She cannot return to Marlborough, that much is plain," said Master Appleby. "Her position with the Lovewells is no longer tenable."

"But," Xanthe protested, "her name has been cleared."

"Father is right," Samuel said. "She would not be welcome there, nor would she wish to return."

"Then, what is to become of her? Have we secured her freedom only to send her into a life of begging? We can't let that happen."

Master Appleby shook his head. "Once the girl has regained her health and strength, a new position can be found for her. I myself will write a letter of recommendation. And I will see to it that she has one from the Lovewells also."

"Mistress Lovewell will never agree to it."

"Perhaps not, but her husband is of a more . . . pliable nature."

Samuel said, "It would be better for Alice to begin life anew, somewhere her past is not known."

Philpott arrived with the wine and Master Appleby made a show of pouring it, passing round the elegant Italian glasses, declaring it a moment for celebration. As he chatted on, giving Philpott instructions for the supper, Samuel and Xanthe stood looking at each other. She tried so hard to read his expression. What did he feel for her now? Did he regard her as some sort of ghost? Did he feel lied to, cheated, tricked? More than anything she wanted to be alone with him, to try to explain the inexplicable. They went into the dining room for supper, where Master Appleby, fueled by the wine, talked so much that all she and Samuel had to do was agree with him occasionally. By the look on his face, Samuel was finding the whole evening as difficult as she was. As the meal was being cleared away, his father said he would send for Grandmother Garvy again, as their guest would be staying the night in the house.

"There is no need, sir," she told him. "I thank you for your thoughtfulness, but the time has come for me to leave."

"What? Now? As night falls?"

"There is a late stagecoach leaving from The Quills this evening," she said, hoping he was not familiar with stage timetables.

"Samuel, talk to Mistress Westlake, make her see how much better it would be for her to leave in the morning."

Samuel shook his head. "The mistress knows her own mind and is in charge of her own destiny, Father," he said, getting to his feet. "I shall, of course, escort her to the stagecoach."

Minutes later, after saying a warm farewell to Master Appleby, she found herself walking through Marlborough on Samuel's arm. To anyone who cared to notice them, they must have appeared a normal couple, or good friends, taking the crisp autumn air, strolling through the little town like any other couple might. Except that they were neither normal nor natural. They were two people caught up in somebody else's story. Alice's story. And now that her world had been set right again, Xanthe no longer belonged in it. She had her own home in her own time, and she must return to it. When they reached the inn Samuel turned to her.

"I do not believe you will be taking the stage, even if there is one at this hour. Where is it you wish to go, Xanthe?" he asked, his eyes still guarding his feelings, his expression still unreadable.

"There is only one place. Will you walk me to the blind house, Samuel?"

"The jail? But . . ."

"That place, that cruel little building, it is what connects us, you and me. I don't expect you to understand, but that's the way it is."

Suddenly, abruptly, he let go her arm and stepped back, cutting the air with his hand in a gesture of desperation and barely concealed anger.

"So this is how it is to be? You are to vanish from my life a second time?"

He kept his voice low, and there were few people close enough to hear their conversation. Even so, she glanced about, worried they would attract unwanted eavesdroppers.

"Samuel, I—"

"Without explanation? Without words that at least could go some way to stilling the teeming thoughts in my mind? Have I taken a witch into my home? Am I cursed to chase a phantom for the rest of my days? Will I only ever see your face again as you haunt my dreams?" He paced about, all the time keeping up a barrage of unanswerable questions and declarations of confusion and hurt. "You have appeared as if out of no place that ever existed, with your strange ways, your curious manner, your absence of family or past or present, it seems to me. All these things I dismissed, I excused, I refused to give weight to. Because I wanted you. I was drawn to you as a moth to a candle flame, knowing even as I stepped closer that I would be burned, perhaps even unto death, by that very strangeness, that brightness that lured me in. And now you are to melt into the night a second time, and I am certain it is not in my power to stop you." He marched back to her then and took her in his arms, holding her so tight it took her breath away. "But stop you I would, if there were a way. I would pay the price, make a pact with the very devil to keep you, my golden, shining, love. Tell me what it is I must do to have you stay. Only tell me."

"I'm sorry," she murmured. "I'm sorry, but you have to let me go." She made herself slip from his arms and take his hand. "Please, take me to the jail."

For a moment he did not speak. She wished she had answers for him. To leave him wondering about so many things was a terrible thing to do, but how could she explain? Where would she begin? After that, he did not question her further and they walked the short distance to the other side of the high street. As they went across the empty patch of ground where the antique shop would be built a full two centuries later, she felt a shiver, as if they were walking over her own grave. At last they came to the blind house.

"It is unoccupied at present," Samuel said, indicating the door standing open.

As they moved closer to it she felt that same oppression begin to weigh her down. Even standing outside it she could hear the whispered pleas and curses of those who had passed through it. She knew she could travel home from another point, if the locket still worked, but this seemed right, somehow. And it was, as she had told him, the strongest link with Samuel that she had. He had built the blind house, and now it was part of her home in her own century. They would always be connected through it.

He took hold of her hand. "Alice was grateful," he said. "She asked me to tell you that you will be ever in her prayers. She considered you heaven sent."

She smiled. "No, not from heaven. Somewhere a little nearer home." She reached inside her bag and took out the silver thimble she had brought as a possible bribe but never got to use, the rest of the coins, and Alice's rosary. "Will you see that she gets these?" she asked him.

He took them, pausing to run the rosary through his fingers. "She was fortunate to have such a champion as you," he said.

"Is that how you see me, Samuel? A champion? After what you saw, the way I vanished . . . Please, don't despise me."

"Despise you?"

"I didn't want to deceive you. I promise you, if I could I would tell you everything, but . . ." She shook her head. "I am not some . . . ghost."

"Xanthe, my sweet." He pulled her toward him one last time, wrapping his arms around her and looking down at her with such tenderness. "I do not understand. I do not know what I saw or what any of it means. I know one thing only: the woman I held in my arms, she is no phantom." He kissed her then, gently. A slow, lingering kiss, full of unspoken promises and unfulfilled longing.

When he stopped she made herself pull away a little.

She tried a smile. "Do you remember once, you told me you thought I came from a distant land, unmapped territory? Keep that thought. It's about as close to the truth as we can get."

She slipped out of his grasp, taking her hand from his, and moved toward the open door of the jail. At the entrance she turned to look at him one last time.

Samuel held out a folded piece of paper.

"Please," he said, his voice a whisper. "Take this. Read it when . . . when you have made your journey."

She ran her finger over the red wax seal on the letter. "You knew. You knew that I would have to leave, didn't you?" She held tight to the note, worrying that it might not successfully travel with her, but knowing there was nothing more she could do but cling to it.

"I doubted the certainty of anything after what I witnessed. How could I even be sure I would see you again? I could not. But I hoped that I would. Even though I believed it would be but a fleeting encounter. It was in that spirit of hope, allowing at the same time that we must part again, that I penned some words, inadequate words." He gestured at the letter.

"Thank you," Xanthe said. Fighting back tears, she turned toward the jail once more.

"Tell me one thing and one thing only, Xanthe, my love. Will you come back to me?" he asked, the break in his voice the saddest thing she had ever heard. Sadder still for knowing that she herself was the cause of it.

She put her hand on the door to steady herself. She looked at him one last time, and acknowledged that in her heart she hoped it wasn't over. That she would see him again, one day, somehow.

"If I can, Samuel, if there is a way," she told him.

And then quickly, before she lost the will to do it, she stepped into the blind house, took hold of the gold locket, opened it, and closed her eyes.

{ 26 }

THAT JOURNEY BACK THROUGH TIME WAS A DRAINING EXPERIENCE. INSTEAD of falling into a dizzying blackness through which she usually passed quickly, she was plunged into a nightmarish world of glimpsed faces, flashes of light, and a discordant chorus of voices. And one voice louder than the others, unfamiliar to her, yet seeming to address her directly as if he knew her. A brief sight of a man's face, with pale, pale eyes.

"Who are you?" his voice rasped. "Where do you go?"

And then he was gone and there was only the jumble of terrible cries and moans that grew steadily louder. She felt as if she were being thrown and jostled and struck on all sides. Why was this time so different? Was it because the chatelaine had done its work and was no longer guiding her? Or was it her own deep resistance to leaving the past, to leaving Samuel? Whatever the cause, it was a brutal passage through the centuries and one that, for a terrible moment, she feared she might not survive. What if she was to be trapped in this chaotic nothingness? Lost in a manner of limbo, neither in one time nor the other? The lurching and twirling began to make her feel as if she were losing her mind, no longer knowing which way was up, or back, or how to right herself, or turn around, or go forward.

And then it stopped.

She came to a jarring halt, crashing onto the floor of the blind house, at the same time hitting her head hard against the wall. She lay where she fell, battered, bruised, and bewildered. The sense of the suffering of hundreds of people was with her even then, the cries of the lost growing fainter at last. She found she could not properly come to her senses. Could not open her eyes and focus through the dimness of the jail, could not hold on properly to consciousness. The fight went out of her, and she let herself be claimed by a deep but restless sleep.

When next she woke, the voices had stopped chattering, the shouts and cries fallen silent. She hardly dared try to move, her body felt so stiff and sore. She felt the letter still in her palm, and her heart lurched at the thought of Samuel, of leaving him, of what he might have written. She tucked the precious note into her waistband. Blinking, she saw daylight falling through the open door of the blind house. She could hear birds singing. The sound of a telephone ringing. A lawnmower. She was home. Properly home this time. She tensed, listening for the reed-thin voice of Mistress Merton, waiting for the arrival of that dreadful presence. But it did not come. She could feel nothing of her.

"She's gone," she whispered to herself, hardly daring to believe it to be true and yet knowing that it was. Alice was safe, Margaret could rest now, her duty to her daughter complete after so many lonely, anguish-filled years.

Xanthe got up, surprised to find that aside from a tender spot on her forehead, she had no other injuries. It was as if all the pain she had experienced had been just illusions, however real they had felt at the time. She was wobbly but otherwise unharmed. She needed to think. She still had to get back in the house without Flora seeing her emerge from the garden. Xanthe retrieved the chatelaine from the dusty floor and put it into her leather satchel. As she handled it, this time, she felt and heard nothing. Its silence was a shock to her after having had such a powerful connection with it. She took off her outer clothes so that she was once again in her gypsy skirt and cheesecloth shirt, and bundled up her mismatched disguise. She peered around the door. The garden was empty, the back door open. As she crept out and retrieved her bag from the butterfly bush she could hear the radio playing up in the kitchen. It sounded as if the day was properly underway and her mother was up. After stuffing all the things she had brought back with her into her backpack she did the only thing she could do: hope to luck and stride out across the lawn. Once again she felt the curious disconnect of going from late autumn to summer so quickly. Gingerly, she stepped through the back door. The door to Flora's workshop was closed, so she hurried past it. She had her foot on the first stair when she saw her. Flora appeared from the kitchen to peer down the stairs at her daughter.

"Xanthe? You're home early! What a lovely surprise."

"Mum!" It was all she could do not to give way to sobbing at the sight of her mother. She sprinted up the stairs and threw her arms around her.

"Well!" Flora laughed, hugging her back. "I missed you, too."

All the fear for her mother that Xanthe had carried every step of her far, far journey threatened to undo her, now that she could at last release it. "You're OK?" she asked, hoping Flora would not notice the tremor in her voice. She pulled back to study her mother's face. "Really, are you well? How have you been while I've been away?"

"Perfectly fine. No more flare-ups." She smiled, and then said, "I didn't hear the doorbell."

"No? Doesn't always work. It's pretty ropy. I think it needs a new clapper," she told her. "We'll have to get it fixed before opening day."

"You look done in. Difficult time?" she asked.

"Sort of." She nodded, squirming at the lies but trying hard to remember what she was supposed to have been doing. "All worked out in the end, though."

"Did he decide he couldn't live without her after all?"

"What?"

"Eva's unsuitable boyfriend. Did he come back?"

"Oh, yes. He did."

Flora tutted loudly. "Men! What a fuss. Come on, I was just about to fix lunch. I found some soup!" she said, using her crutches to turn herself around and head back into the kitchen.

Xanthe followed her as far as the doorway and then paused.

"Actually, Mum, I think I'll have a shower first. Feel a bit grimy from traveling, you know."

"OK, love. You go ahead. I'll save you some of this," she said, waving a packet of instant vegetable soup in the air.

As soon as Xanthe was locked in the bathroom she took out Samuel's letter. She slipped her thumb beneath the wax seal to break it and unfolded the thick parchment. She noticed that already the edges of the paper were beginning to crumble. Samuel's bold handwriting filled the page.

My dearest love,

How do I find words to speak to one who is not of my own world? How do I find thoughts to still my own seething mind when I try to fathom what it was I witnessed last night? You were there and then you were not. As if you had melted away with the night, the dawn light extinguishing your own. In truth, I cannot capture here how altered I am by having known you. All I know is that the greater part of that alteration is not brought about by your magical disappearance but by your more magical presence. Which I hope with all my heart to feel again, and in that hope I pen these inadequate lines, that you may know

you have my heart,
always,
Samuel

"Oh, Samuel," she murmured sadly. "I'm so sorry."

She had never appreciated a shower so much in her life. She stood motionless, letting the water cascade over her head and course down her body. She had not thought about how she would miss being clean. It was bliss to wash away the grit and filth of days traveling on muddy roads, wearing rough, cumbersome clothes, and sleeping inside the blind house. At the same time, she experienced a pang of sadness at the thought that she was also washing away the scent of Samuel from her skin, from where he had held her hand, put his arms around her, kissed her. As if she were performing a final act of separating herself from him. She must have been in the shower an unusually long time because Flora was calling her.

She joined her at the kitchen table and reached across and took hold of her hand.

"How are you, Mum, really?"

"Good. Really. Arthritis has been holding itself down to a dull roar. Sleeping OK. Busy, busy, busy."

"I missed you," she said.

Flora must have noticed the weariness in her voice. She took hold of her daughter's hand and gave it an encouraging squeeze.

"And I missed you. Who else is going to appreciate all my hard work on that walnut desk, or my repairs on that silver candelabra I found under the pile of rugs? Now, eat up."

They shared stale bread and slightly lumpy soup.

"This is truly awful, Mum."

"Nonsense. Perfectly good vegetables in there somewhere."

"Have you been shopping since I went away? Have you had anything decent to eat?"

"Don't fuss. I can survive a few days without your cooking. Anyway, I've been much too busy to eat. Did you see how lovely the shop looks as you came in? I'm really pleased with the way it's all come together. But there is still heaps to do. Opening day on Thursday!"

"I thought it was going to be Saturday?" she said, gulping water to push down the bread and promising herself she would go shopping before the next meal. Suddenly life was all about mundanities: looking after her mother, getting the business up and running, household stuff. How could she even think about things like that when all the time her heart was aching? And nobody knew, not even Flora. And she could never tell her. Her mother was chatting on about having brought the date of the grand opening forward because it was market day and busier and would not be competing with the local county agricultural show on Saturday. Xanthe tried to take it all in but was in a daze of tiredness, relief, and confusion over her feelings for Samuel. After lunch they went downstairs and she helped put out more antiques in the shop and price things up and work on displays and generally immersed herself in what had to be done. And so the afternoon passed, followed by takeout, and then, despite her best intentions, she collapsed into bed, where she finally allowed herself to sleep.

The next two days passed in a flurry of activity. Xanthe welcomed it. The busier she was, the less time she had to brood. As she helped her mother prepare the shop for the opening, she tried to replay in her mind all that had happened, from when she first arrived in the stables at Great Chalfield, to when she tore herself from Samuel and stepped back home through the blind house. It all seemed so long ago now, as if it had happened to her in another life. And she worried about her actions. She spent ages, as she polished an eighty-four-piece silver cutlery set, thinking of what the possible consequences of what she had done might be. Alice was saved, that much she knew, but what if she had never found the chatelaine? What if she had never journeyed back and saved her? Had she somehow crucially altered her own present by changing Alice's future? The thought that she might have started some terrible chain of events that she could not possibly have foreseen, nor know about, worried her more and more. It was only in the small hours of Wednesday night that an answer came to her that seemed to make sense. The present that she knew, the way things were in her time, could only have come about if she *had* traveled back to the past. Her finding the chatelaine, her answering Alice's call for help, those things were necessary to shape the past and bring about the future as it was. She had to believe this. It did work. She was a part of how things had turned out, not an alternative version, but the one she was meant to live in. If she *hadn't* gone back, hadn't taken the decision to help Alice, well, that would have resulted in a different future from the one she knew. From what she knew to be "normal." At first this thought comforted her. She had not brought about some far-flung catastrophe by doing what she had done. All was well. She had done the right thing. But then, as she thought about it some more, the weight of the responsibility of this hit her like an avalanche. What if she had not gone back? What if she had not found the chatelaine? Or had not bought it? Or had messed up when she was at Great Chalfield and seen Alice hang? How different might things have been?

By the time the day of the opening arrived Xanthe and Flora were both exhausted. Still, Flora was buoyed up with excitement, whereas Xanthe had never felt less like partying. The thought of being upbeat and dealing with people the whole day made her weary. But this was her mother's big day, the proper start to the new life she had dreamed of and planned for. For her sake, she did her best to pull herself together, find one of her better sixties boho dresses, and put on a bright smile. At eight o'clock that morning they were both in the shop, running a cloth over the display cabinets, stringing up a line of vintage bunting, and generally making tiny final adjustments. At last Flora stood, hands on hips, and surveyed their handiwork.

"Well, Xanthe, love, I think we've done all right."

"Better than all right, Mum," she said. "It looks wonderful, really it does."

And it did. The freshly painted walls gave the main room of the shop a light, clean background against which to set all the wonderful treasures they had found. Flora's restored and rejuvenated small tables, cupboards, and chairs stood prettily around the room, with carefully chosen pieces placed on them: vintage blankets and quilts, silk tasseled cushions, a dressing table set, silver candlesticks, pewter lanterns, two writing boxes with exquisite marquetry inlay, a gleaming top hat, and an assortment of vases. One piece was particularly successful: a charming little bookcase, with delicate carving that extended over part of the glass doors, nicely showing off the shelf of antique leather-bound books Xanthe had rescued from the original stock.

On the walls they'd hung three of the nicest mirrors from Mr. Morris's collection, a Victorian oil painting of a farm scene, and three 1930s enamel signs advertising Pears Soap. At the back of the room stood the writing desk, wrapping paper and ledger at the ready, the cash tin in the top drawer. Maybe one day they would be forced to buy a proper till, but Xanthe was actually quite glad they hadn't been able to afford one yet.

There were two display cabinets. The first was tall and showed off the finest pieces of china, which included some Wedgwood, three elaborately decorated Spode dishes, and a Minton tea set. The other case, placed in the window to get the best light and so that it could be seen from both inside and outside the shop, housed jewelry and prized silver items. Pride of place, right at the center, lustrous and shining, sat the chatelaine. Her mother had been surprised that she was ready to part with it so soon, but Xanthe knew it had served its purpose. It no longer sang to her. Of course, it still had two pieces missing. Perhaps Mistress Lovewell had not wanted to wear a daily reminder of the whole incident with Alice and so had chosen not to put them back on their chains. Or perhaps they had become separated again, some-where in the intervening years, as many attachments did, par-ticularly ones that could be useful. Either way, the chatelaine itself went on. It had become what it always should have been; a beautiful example of early silverwork that was both ornamen-tal and useful. It had been passed down through generations, altered, added to, sold on, no doubt cherished for centuries. Xanthe was happy to be able to hold it without feeling it vibrate or hearing it hum or picking up whispers or snatches of visions, because she knew that meant Alice was safe. On the other hand, it also meant that it had lost its power. She could no longer use the chatelaine to transport herself back in time, back to Samuel. In truth, she would be happy if someone bought it, as now it was a painful reminder of what could never be.

They were just moving an umbrella stand full of walking sticks and canes into position when the door opened, the bell ringing loudly. Liam stood holding a large, square, flat parcel.

"I met a delivery man looking a bit lost at the top of your street. Think he was panicking about bringing his van down here, so I signed for this for you," he said cheerfully.

"Oh!" Flora clapped her hands together. "I know what that is. I was hoping it would turn up in time. Set it down on the desk, would you please, Liam?"

He and Xanthe exchanged smiles as he passed her. Since she had arrived home she had been avoiding seeing him. They had spoken on the phone once or twice and he'd been sensitive enough to pick up on the fact that she was not yet ready to tell him any more about where she had been. She was thankful he had not pressed her, as she had no idea what she was going to tell him. There were moments when she thought it would be a huge relief to share it all with someone, but then the reality of trying to explain, to make them believe, it was too much to face. Too big a mountain to climb when she was still struggling to put one foot in front of the other on level ground.

"Pass me the scissors, Xanthe." Flora held out her hand. They watched as she snipped the string and tape and peeled off the wrapping around the box. At last the contents were revealed. It was a new shop sign. It had a scumbled white background, with the grain of the wood showing through it. On top of this, in beautiful black cursive lettering, was written THE LITTLE SHOP OF FOUND THINGS. Here and there loops and swirls were picked out with a tiny bit of gold leaf.

"It's gorgeous, Mum. Perfect."

Flora beamed. "I sold two of those mirrors you put up for auction online. Thought I'd invest the money wisely."

"I'll hang it up for you," Liam offered. "Where's your ladder?"

It was good to have his help and his easy presence. The closer they got to the advertised opening time the more jittery Flora became and the less Xanthe wished to be there. Liam's cheerfulness kept them both in check. There was just time to smarten themselves up, which meant lipstick for Flora and some balm dragged through Xanthe's hair. At ten minutes to ten Gerri came across the street with trays of chocolate brownies and shortbread and a tea urn to keep everyone supplied with Darjeeling through the day. Finally, the moment had arrived.

"Ready?" Flora asked.

"As I'll ever be. You?"

She nodded, and turned the sign on the door to OPEN.

Within minutes, people started to drift in. Some were locals, come to see what the newcomers had been up to. Others were market-day shoppers happy to browse. There were tourists with plenty of time to linger and ask questions about the stock. Gerri did a brilliant job of keeping everyone fed and watered, and Liam made himself useful fetching and carrying. By twelve o'clock there was a real crush. Flora's discount fliers had proved popular, with customers eager to claim their 10 percent off whatever they bought. The smaller items were good sellers, as Flora had known they would be. Then a collector swooped on the Minton, and someone else bought the largest mirror. Two of the painted chairs went, and a lovely pink-and-blue quilt. They were so busy it took Xanthe a while to notice an elderly gentleman taking an interest in the chatelaine. She stepped over to answer his questions.

"It's not entirely Victorian, is it?" he asked.

"It's not. The clasp itself, and three of the chains, and the scent bottle, they are much older," she told him.

"Early eighteenth century?"

"Actually, early seventeenth."

"Good gracious. What sort of provenance do you have for it?"

It was a reasonable question. The value, in fact the desirability, of an antique was as much dependent on its history, and the verifiable authenticity of that history, as it was on how it looked and felt.

"Well, those silver pieces aren't hallmarked," Xanthe said, "which fits with the era, as does the thickness of the silver. The later design echoes the pattern, but it can't match its simplicity. And, well . . . let's say I met a relative of someone who inherited it."

"A descendent?"

"In a manner of speaking, yes."

The old man studied her face, trying to decide, no doubt, if she was spinning a story for the sake of a sale, or if her claim was genuine. He gestured at the cabinet. "Could you take it out? I should like to hold the piece and examine it more closely, if I may."

She fetched the key. Lifting the chatelaine from its bed of velvet for just an instant she fancied she felt something. But, no, it was just the anticipation of what it used to do, not what it did anymore. She passed it to the customer, who studied it carefully.

"It is very fine. And very pretty. My wife and I are celebrating our silver wedding anniversary next month and I was looking for something special to give her."

"It is special," Xanthe said quietly. "Very special."

He read the price on the label. She had added only a thirty percent markup, as they needed to get some cash flowing into rather than out of the coffers. The customer looked up at her then. "I say, you have a charming shop, and a very good eye. I'll take the chatelaine. Rest assured, it will be greatly valued."

Flora watched Xanthe take it to the counter and find tissue paper and a box for it.

"Are you OK with that, Xanthe?"

"Completely fine, Mum, honestly."

At that moment the door was flung wide open and Harley arrived, carrying a case of prosecco, Annie following with glasses.

"Good morrow, lassies," Harley said. "A little something here to launch your new venture." He gave Gerri's teacups a horrified glare. "You canna set a ship sailing without a drop of bubbly, for pity's sake. Annie, where are ye with those glasses?"

Soon everyone in the shop was sipping the sparkling wine. The level of chatter increased, and there were one or two impulse purchases prompted by the booze. Xanthe sidled up to Harley.

"This is really good of you. Thanks," she said.

He winked conspiratorially and whispered, "Wine loosens purse strings as well as tongues, ye ken? Mind you, looks as if it's all going well enough already. You've the makings of a solid little business here, lass."

"I hope so. Mum's worked so hard."

"Aye, you can see she's passionate about it. And you? When will you get back to what stirs your heart?" he asked.

For a moment she thought, madly, that he was talking about Samuel, but of course he wasn't. He had not asked for any more explanation about why she'd needed the metal detector so badly, though she wondered if he had questioned Liam. Of course, he was referring to her singing.

"Are you short a singer again, Harley?" she asked, smiling.

"Oh, we're fine. Thanks for asking. But we'll always make room for you, hen. Just say the word, and the spot is yours. You've the voice of an angel and it'd be a sin not to use it. In fact, you should be singing whenever the opportunity arises. And this, if you don't mind my saying, is just such an occasion."

"What?"

"Oh, aye. You've got to bless your mother's new business with a song, lassie. Nothing less will do. Now then!" He put down his glass and tapped the heavy ring on his finger against it to get everyone's attention.

"Harley, no, please . . ." She tried to get him to listen, but he was unstoppable. She saw Liam look toward them and smile. Were they in this together? Had they planned it all along?

"Ladies and gentlemen!" Harley's voice boomed around the small space. "I am delighted to inform you that, in honor of the opening of this new and frankly bloody marvelous wee shop, Miss Xanthe Westlake will now sing for us! Come along, lassie!" He pulled her forward into the center of the room amid much clapping and cheering from everyone else present.

For a moment she froze. She was not prepared, she had not had time to build herself up or warm her voice. She had not practiced or even thought about singing in public again so soon. She caught her mother's eye and it was hard to ignore the pride she saw there, the joy and the love. Flora so wanted her to sing. How could she disappoint her? This was her day, she had earned it, and Xanthe would not be the one to let her down. Besides, Harley was right, it did seem fitting: Flora's passion celebrated with her own. A show of what they could do together. Her vision of a new life for them both, and Xanthe's determination to embrace that life, completely, which meant being there with her, it meant being open to new friendships, it meant being ready to love again, however painful that might be. It meant, for her, singing.

"OK," she said at last, clearing her throat and downing another mouthful of prosecco. "Just the one song today. This is something that means a lot to me. It's a very old song, more than four hundred years old, in fact. And it brings back memories for me of a very special place." She did not add that Marlborough was that place, and not the Marlborough they knew. The song, with its medieval tune and ancient words, would take her back, just for a moment, to long ago, when the town was half the size, and there were no cars or electric wires or lights, no phones or internet. When the world was much smaller and quieter, but no less colorful or challenging. When Samuel lived and breathed and loved. She opened her mouth and began to sing. And as she sang she closed her eyes and into her own, secret vision came Samuel's face, clear and strong and wonderful, and she knew then, as she sang on, that one day, somehow, through another found treasure that would speak to her, she would find a way to return to him.

For I loved my love but I left my love,
Though it broke my heart to go.
And he'll yearn for me, and he'll wait for me,
Though the winter chill his bones.
For I loved my love, but I left my love,
Else the gallows they would claim me.
And he'll sigh for me, and he'll wait for me,
For my love has a heart that is true.

ACKNOWLEDGMENTS

My grateful thanks to Patsy and Robert Floyd, the current owners of Great Chalfield Manor. They were excellent hosts and shared a wealth of knowledge about the gorgeous house, its history, and the local area. I hope the liberties I have taken with the building and its history do not make them wince too much, and that they feel I have caught the essence of the place in this book.

Many thanks to Helen McCook for telling me about chatelaines.

A special mention must go to Melanie Williams for helping me explore Wiltshire. Some say mini-break, I say research trip.

Thanks as always to the team at St. Martin's, particularly my tireless editor at Thomas Dunne, Peter Wolverton, and his assistant, Jennifer Donovan. Starting a new series raised all sorts of challenges for us, and I'm grateful for their insight and perseverance. And for meeting each new idea with equal parts willingness and enthusiasm.

Heartfelt thanks to the design team, for the lovely cover, and the all-around general gorgeousness of the finished book.

I'd send tea and shortbread if I could to all those behind-the-scenes people who each play their vital part in bringing the book into being, getting it out there, and getting it noticed. Thank you.

READ ON TO SEE HOW XANTHE'S STORY CONTINUES
IN THIS EXCERPT FROM PAULA BRACKSTON'S

SECRETS OF THE CHOCOLATE HOUSE

By the time Xanthe arrived back at the shop the day had fallen into twilight and the little town of Marlborough was enveloped in a heavy fog. She shivered as she put the closed sign on the shop door and called out to Flora.

"Mum? I'm home. I'm going to lock up. Where are you?"

The sound of crutches on the tiled floor of the hallway to the workshop gave her mother away. Her arthritis might have made them a necessary part of her mobility, but that didn't mean she moved slowly.

"I was just putting the finishing touches to another mirror frame," she said as she hurried back into the shop. Her fine, fluffy hair was kept off her face by what Xanthe suspected was a polishing rag, rather than a scarf, but still Flora looked appealing, her English rose skin and deep-set eyes maturing kindly. Being in her fifties suited her.

"Leaving the stock at the mercy of shoplifters?" Xanthe smiled as she spoke, but there was a seriousness to her words.

They had been warned about a spate of light-fingered browsers in the town recently.

Flora shook her head. "No one gets through the shop door without that old bell letting me know."

Xanthe thought guiltily about how many times she had done just that, sneaking in and out of the house so that her mother wouldn't know she had been there. Covering her tracks. Protecting lies. Keeping secrets. "I expect that's why Mr. Morris never got rid of it," she said.

"Well, if he used to restore things like I do he'd have needed it. I can't be in two places at once, love, and when you decide to go off on one of your walks..."

"Sorry, Mum. Just needed a bit of air. Clear my head."

"I'm teasing. Doesn't take two of us to man this place, not all the time. What does need your attention, on the other hand, is the stock. Or rather the lack of it."

"I know."

"Christmas may seem ages off, but we can't afford to miss the trade. People start shopping for gifts earlier and earlier these days. And if the things we find need some work doing..."

"OK, you're right. I should be out scouting for more stuff."

"If we don't have it we can't sell it." She paused, her face more serious for a moment. "We need these few weeks to be a success. Your father is still dragging his heels when it comes to agreeing to the divorce settlement."

"Still no news?"

Flora shook her head. "Why would he be in a hurry? He's got the family home and the income from an established business."

"Not to mention whatever his new woman brings to the party."

Flora tutted. "No use relying on any progress this side of the

New Year. We just have to focus on finding treasures and making sales. And we have to prepare for our first Christmas in our new home! Nearly December and not so much as a pudding stirred."

The moment of tension passed as Flora gave way to her irrepressible love of the festive season. Xanthe made a mental note to make sure this would be a happy one, for both of them.

"Oh, and I want to get working on that lovely pine dresser we found in Devizes last week. We need to find a van from somewhere so we can collect it."

"No way that was going to fit in my taxi."

"Why don't you ask Liam if he knows where we can get one from?"

As always the idea of seeing Liam brought with it a tangle of feelings. He had already proved himself to be a good friend, had helped her when she had needed him. And it wasn't as if he was being pushy. But still it was clear his interest in her went beyond friendship. What he didn't know, what he couldn't know, was that Xanthe's heart was still bruised after having to leave Samuel.

She realized her mother was looking at her, waiting for an answer.

"Sure, Mum. I'll call him."

"Oh, look." Flora waved one of her crutches at the window. "No need. You can ask him now."

Liam was standing outside. He was wearing his favorite old, soft, leather jacket and had his hands deep in his pockets against the cold. His stubble, Xanthe noticed, had passed just beyond what was fashionable into something a little more rugged, yet still he was dangerously good-looking. He gave a rueful smile, his light blue eyes crinkling at the corners. Xanthe opened the door.

"I was passing. . . ." He grinned.

"Down a cul de sac?"

"I like to take in the sights...."

"In this fog?"

"For heaven's sake, Xanthe, let the poor boy in and shut the door. It's chilly enough in here as it is. We were just talking about you, Liam."

"Oh?" He looked at Xanthe, who hurried to explain, the expression of hope on his face unnerving her.

"We need a van. To pick up a dresser."

"A lovely piece," said Flora. "We found it at an auction in Devizes."

"Mum wants to work her magic on it with paint."

"Do you have a van?" Flora asked Liam.

"No, but I know a man who does," he said.

"Excellent." Flora turned and stick-stepped her way toward the hall. "I was just about to muster up an early supper. Why don't you join us and we can make plans?"

"Oh, well..." Liam hesitated for form's sake, but Xanthe could see how keen he was to accept the invitation. "That'd be great," he said at last.

"Brave man," she muttered to him as they trooped upstairs to the little kitchen on the first floor. Her mother's singular approach to cooking was not for the fainthearted, and Liam had already chewed through one of her lunches, so he knew what he was letting himself in for.

In the few busy months since buying the property, Xanthe and Flora had transformed the dusty, cluttered shop into a wonderful, light-filled space, stocked with gorgeous things. The living quarters, however, had not received the same attention. There were still packing cases in every room and the sitting room was mostly given over to being an office, apart from the green velvet sofa on which they flopped when time allowed. Nothing had been repainted, and the floors remained covered in nasty carpet or cracked linoleum. In the kitchen, plates and general paraphernalia sat about in stacks and heaps waiting to be found homes.

"Find yourself a seat," said Flora, opening the fridge. She had given up apologizing for the mess. Xanthe suspected she no longer noticed it. It was only when visitors called that she herself saw their home with fresh eyes and felt a little embarrassed.

"We are going to redecorate up here," she said. "Eventually."

"Really? Can't think why," said Liam, moving a stack of *Antique Trader* magazines off a ladder-backed, pale pine chair. Xanthe recalled his own flat and realized that interior design, or the lack of it, was hardly a priority for him. He'd far more likely spend his time and money on his beloved classic cars. Just as she and her mother would rather be restoring a Georgian table, or reframing a set of Victorian prints, or repairing a crucial chip in a piece of powder blue Wedgwood china. She cleared some space on the old kitchen table and fetched bottled beers from the fridge.

"The dresser's a big one," she told Liam, handing him a bottle opener. "The base is over eight foot, three cupboards, and the top half has glass doors. Though we may have to abandon those."

"Nonsense," said Flora. "I've got the perfect set of hinges we can use."

"My mate's van will handle it, no problem." Liam paused to take a swig of his beer. "I'll text him. See when we can have it."

"You don't need to abandon the workshop; I can drive it," said Xanthe, taking a packet of spicy noodles from her mother and putting them back in the cupboard, selecting rice instead.

"Course you can," Liam agreed, "but you are going to need help lifting the dresser in and out of it, aren't you?" He had about him such an easy charm it was impossible not to feel a little better for simply being in his company.

Xanthe smiled at him and nodded. She admired his patience. Some men would have given up on her by now. Would have realized she wasn't looking for a relationship, taken the many hints she had dropped, and looked elsewhere. But not Liam. He was prepared to wait, and while he waited, to be a good friend. She couldn't help liking him for that. And their shared love of music and performing gave them a safe common ground too. He was a good lead guitarist. Better than good, in fact. She remembered the first time she had heard his band play at The Feathers, and the first time she herself had sung there. It was good to have a friend who understood what it felt like to stand up in front of a crowd, to make yourself so vulnerable, to give of yourself in that particular way.

Liam was an undemanding guest, and soon they were all seated at the table, a stub of a candle found for an orphan silver candlestick, more beers, and bowls of rice with chopped-up frankfurters, spring onions, tomatoes, and a handful of sultanas Flora had flung in while Xanthe's back was turned.

"Xanthe's singing in The Feathers again the week after next," she told Liam. "You will come along and support her, won't you?"

"Mum . . ."

"Try and stop me. Looking forward to it. Harley says takings go up every time you sing there, Xanthe. He's always telling people about how brilliantly you sing. What's the word he uses?"

"Stop, you're making me blush."

"*Stupendous*, that's it. He tells everyone you're stupendous!"

"He's a good publican. He's good at selling his events," Xanthe said with a shrug. In truth, she was, at last, enjoying her singing again, welcoming the chance to perform, and to earn some money of her own. She had intended to make herself choose new songs.

Singing the ones that were of that distant time—Samuel's time—only made her melancholy. What was the point in wallowing? And yet, she still felt drawn to the melodies and sentiments of that era. Perhaps singing those ballads and love songs that Samuel would have known, just for a little longer, would help her ease away from him. Perhaps it was a way to prove to herself that she had accepted that she was never going back. The adventure was over. To return to him made no sense. It was too dangerous, and there was, ironically, no future in it for them. She had to focus on home, on work, on her singing. It was the right thing to do.

Liam interrupted her thoughts, checking a text on his phone. "Right, we can have the van on Thursday. That suit you?"

Flora answered for her, adding a liberal amount of brown sauce to her supper as she spoke. "Perfect. We've got a house clearance to do at Laybrook first thing tomorrow. I want to be back here by eleven at the latest so we don't have to leave the shop shut too long."

Xanthe nodded. "I took that booking. A lady who lived in the village all her life. The nephew is dealing with her estate. He said there's nothing large, as the family have taken the major pieces of furniture. Mostly paintings, china, rugs, some glassware."

Liam frowned. "Don't you find it creepy, sifting through a whole lot of stuff that belonged to someone who just died? Sort of ghoulish?"

"No," Xanthe said. "It's fascinating. We get a unique glimpse into someone's life through the things they chose to keep close to them. It's very revealing. And it's a privilege."

"Not to mention a treasure hunt," said Flora. "And Xanthe is always on the lookout for something that sings to her, aren't you, love?"

Liam leaned forward, gesticulating with his fork. "Your daughter

396 ❖ PAULA BRACKSTON

has been very cagey about her special talent, Mrs. Westlake. Plays it down every time I try to ask her about it."

Xanthe helped herself to another beer. It wasn't a secret, the fact that some of the antiques they found spoke to her, giving her glimpses of their past, but it wasn't easy to talk about it without her feeling she must come across as a little bit bonkers. "Yes, well, I might find something special, I might not. Can't know until I get there. More rice, anyone?"

She let the subject drop, but privately she could not help being excited at the prospect of this kind of house clearance. By all accounts the old lady's house was something special in itself, and the village had a reputation for being one of the prettiest and best preserved in Wiltshire. They were almost certain to find some interesting and beautiful things for the shop, and that was what mattered. She told herself firmly that it might even be for the best if nothing in particular sang to her. No more mysteries. No more traveling back through time. She had to root herself in the here and now.

Arriving in Laybrook the next day, however, it was all too easy to believe she and her mother and even her black cab had journeyed to a bygone age. The little village was picture-postcard perfect, shown off to its best advantage beneath the flattering winter sunshine. The last of the russet leaves held fast to oak and ash, with evergreen climbers glossy over low stone walls. Road signs and markings had been kept to a minimum. Cottages, shops, pubs, and houses had all been painstakingly preserved, with not a modern window or clumsy extension anywhere to be seen. The National Trust had bought the village some years earlier and now managed it with meticulous care, but this was not a museum. Laybrook was a thriving community, and the beautiful houses were homes to real people living real lives. The house that had been home to Esther Harris for decades was a fine example of simple but elegant eighteenth-century English architecture. Lavender House was two stories of warm, tawny stone, its long windows balanced along classical lines with an imposing front door. The woodwork was freshly painted white, contrasting crisply with the rich stone, while the door itself gleamed in deep French navy. Dark gray stone tiles clad the steeply pitched roof, a chimney at either end. Unlike many of the smaller, terraced houses in the village, this one was detached, and set back from the street by a neat, paved front garden which was in turn enclosed behind a low wall topped with black iron railings. Two clipped bay trees stood guard on either side of the iron gate.

Xanthe parked the cab directly outside the house and opened the door for her mother. The fog of the previous day had gone so that the village was dressed in late autumn sunshine. Even so, she was glad of the old college scarf she had tucked into her vintage tweed jacket before they set out. She made a mental note to dig out her winter coat when they got home, and next time to team her tea dress with warmer leggings.

"Ooh," said Flora, planting her crutches firmly onto the pavement and taking in her surroundings. "How very lovely. No wonder they use this place for films."

"It is fairly gorgeous," Xanthe agreed. She felt a tingle of excitement, a prickling of her scalp, and wondered briefly if it signified something special inside the house. Something that was waiting for her. The thought, after recent events, caused anxiety to knot her stomach. Shaking off the idea, she told herself it was only the normal excitement of the treasure hunt.

"Let's get started," she said. "The nephew promised he'd be here by nine. His name's Lionel. Sounded like the whole business of inheriting anything is a bit of a chore for him."

They made their way to the front door and Flora used the

key she had been sent to let them in. The hallway echoed as they stepped onto the broad boards of the floor. There were very obvious spaces where large pieces of furniture had already been removed, as well as light patches on the walls being the ghosts of the paintings that once hung there. A polished wooden staircase led up from the center of the hall, with a narrow passageway on one side toward the back of the house, and doors off right and left to the reception rooms.

Flora took her notebook from her backpack and consulted a list. "There won't be anything in here. Let's try the sitting room first. There should be a corner cabinet, a Persian rug, a chaise longue and, according to the nephew, 'a lovely fire screen.' We'll see. One man's lovely is another man's ghastly."

The screen turned out to be mediocre and the chaise too big to fit in the shop. The rug was somewhat marred by sparks from the open fire beyond it. Xanthe knelt down to inspect it more closely. It felt wonderfully soft as she ran her hand over the rich reds and blues of the pattern. As a child all such rugs had made her think of a magic carpet, and this one was no exception. She liked to think of all the children who had sat on it, perhaps playing with a favorite teddy bear, or driving a toy car along the geometric pattern at its edges. She wondered how many Christmas presents had been unwrapped on it, right there, in front of a crackling fire, and how many beloved dogs had stretched out upon it to luxuriate in the warmth from the hearth.

"It's not perfect," she told her mother, "but it's still nice. I think it would sell quite quickly."

Flora was scrutinizing the corner cabinet. "This is Victorian. Bit brown. Looks like this was used to display silver. The nephew must have already snaffled that. This is in good nick though."

"We could use it in the shop."

"Or I could rub it down and transform it with a new coat of paint. Dark wood's still pretty unfashionable. It would have a completely different feel if someone painted it . . . oh . . . mole's breath gray?"

"You're the woman to do it," said Xanthe.

Deciding they would make a low offer for the cabinet and think about the rug, they moved back through the hall and up the rather fine staircase. There were two floors of bedrooms and bathrooms. Xanthe let her mother check the ones on the first floor and took herself up the second flight to the attic rooms. She could hear the echo of her mother's crutches as she stick-stepped her way across bare floorboards.

"These rooms are pretty much empty already," she called up. "The beds might have been nice; pity not to have had a chance at those."

"We haven't room for beds, Mum," Xanthe reminded her. The smaller rooms on her floor would have originally housed the servants. The ceiling was boarded with modern insulation but still the unheated space was chilly. Xanthe could only imagine how cold the winters must have been for the maids living up in the rafters of the house. In times gone by the servants themselves served as insulation, helping to keep their employers warmer in the rooms below. Xanthe was reminded of how cold, even in autumn, her bedroom had been at Great Chalfield Manor. She thought wistfully of Jayne and wondered how her fellow kitchen maid was faring.

"Oh!" Her mother's delighted shout brought her back to the present. "A lovely escritoire! Come and have a look."

At last they went back downstairs to the dining room. As they let the door swing open, Xanthe and Flora gasped in unison. For Flora, it was the sight that greeted them that so impressed her. For Xanthe, it was the sound of a clear, high note, like the ringing of a celestial bell, that caused her to catch her breath and even throw her hands to her ears. Flora was too taken up with their find to notice her daughter's gesture. If she had seen how strongly Xanthe had reacted to the contents of the room she would have known instantly that something was singing to her. Some special object, filled with the vibrations of its own history, was calling to her. As it was, she was entirely focused on the treasures in front of her.

"Now that's what I call a collection!" she said.

The dining table and chairs had evidently been taken away, so that the main part of the room was empty. The far wall, however, had been given over entirely as a place to house the objects of Esther Harris's passion. On deep shelves, behind glass doors, sat dozens and dozens of chocolate pots. Some were copper, some fine china, some pewter, others silver. One or two were enameled. There were pots with wooden handles; pots with stirrers and pots without; pots with matching cups and saucers; pots with silver spoons and sugar bowls and tongs. There were graceful eighteenth-century porcelain examples with exquisitely painted decorations depicting flowers or finely dressed ladies. There were beaten silver pots engraved with swirling initials or coats of arms. There were sinuous pots in the art nouveau style and angular art deco ones with tiny wedgelike cups on ebony trays.

"Wow!" muttered Flora, hurrying forward to scan the shelves, taking in the range and beauty of what they had found.

Beyond the briefest of glances, Xanthe barely saw the true extent of the collection. She was irresistibly drawn to a single pot. She stepped forward, placing her hand on the glass, submitting to that unmistakable song, giving in to her gift. From anyone else this particular pot might not have earned a second glance. It had no elaborate rococo curls, nor was it fashioned from translucent French porcelain. This pot was made of copper, burnished to a deep shine over hundreds of years, dented in places, its simple shape and plain wooden handle suggesting that it had been made not for show but for function. Similar in size and shape to a modern coffeepot, the chocolatiere differed in one or two crucial details. The handle was set at right angles to the slender gooseneck spout. This was to allow the pot to be gently swirled as it was poured, the better to mix the grainy chocolate with the hot milk. The wooden half of the handle was shaped to fit the palm of the hand and to protect it from the heat of the pot. The lid had a hinged finial, which lifted to reveal a vital hole. Xanthe had seen such pots before and knew that a stirring stick, or "molinet" as it was known by aficionados, would be lowered into the liquid so that it could be stirred before pouring, to blend the mixture and keep it from separating, making sure that the chocolate was evenly distributed.

Xanthe closed her eyes. The glass beneath her hand seemed to vibrate. Above the keening note she could hear something else: a rumbling. What was that? Wheels, perhaps? Over a rough road, maybe? And something more. Water. Not the trickle of a brook or the rough sound of a rocky river, but a low thrum, suggesting a surge of deep, fast-flowing water. She waited for a vision, for a glimpse of what the pot was trying to show her, but nothing came.

Flora's voice reached her despite her dreamlike state. "Some of these are really special. Look, Meissen, Limoges . . . lovely bit of chinoiserie going on there. And those two have to be Viennese. Good grief! This lot must be worth a small fortune. Way out of our budget, I'm afraid. . . . Xanthe?" After a moment her daughter turned and Flora realized Xanthe's attention had been entirely taken by the single, unassuming pot. "Xanthe, love, have you found something?"

Xanthe opened her eyes and looked at her mother, her face confirming what Flora had already worked out.

At that moment they heard the front door open.

"Hello? Anyone about? Mrs. Westlake?" called a breezy male voice from the hallway.

Xanthe and Flora exchanged anxious glances. Both knew the price of the collection would be way beyond their means. And both knew that Xanthe absolutely had to have that copper pot.

"In here," Flora sang out as casually as she was able.

Esther Harris's nephew, middle-aged and middle management by the look of him, came striding into the room, hand outstretched in greeting, confidently accommodating Flora's need to adjust her hold on her crutches so that she could shake it.

"Lionel Harris. You got the key to work then? Well done. The front door can be a bit tricky. Poor old house needs some work. Apart from the outside, which the Trust insist is kept up, my aunt was inclined to let things slide. I see you've found her coffeepots. Can't think why she had such a fondness for the things. Don't recall her ever even drinking the stuff. But there it is, each to their own. I suppose one or two of the prettier ones have their charm."

Xanthe forced herself out of her reverie, shook the man's hand, and tried to avoid her mother's gaze. Lionel had revealed so much in such a short time it was difficult to process it. First, it was obvious to Xanthe, he had not known his aunt well. If he had he would surely have discovered what her collection really consisted of. Second, and here was the dilemma she knew Flora would be facing at precisely the same moment, he evidently had no idea how valuable the collection was. It was possible they could get a real bargain and turn a sizeable profit. But that would mean hiding the truth from him to strike a good deal. Xanthe could imagine many dealers she knew rubbing their hands together at the prospect of such a transaction. Less scrupulous members of the antique trade considered it no more than sound business, and if the seller was too lazy or too naive to find out the true value of what he had then that was his problem.

Flora, on the other hand, would never stoop to such low practices.

And yet, Xanthe could not walk away from that pot. Their only hope was that he might be prepared to split the collection.

Xanthe smiled. "Miss Harris must have been collecting for a long time."

The nephew shrugged. "My father and she weren't close. She hardly ever visited."

"And you don't want to keep any of these for yourself?" she asked.

Lionel Harris gave a dry bark of a laugh. "My wife said she won't give them house room. Mind you, that's not to say they don't have a value," he added, letting the thought sit there, waiting, presumably, for an offer.

Xanthe heard her mother tut under her breath. However much she prided herself on being a levelheaded businesswoman, to hear a lifetime of collecting reduced to nothing more than money, and to have so much craftsmanship and beauty reduced to a figure, would not sit well with her.

Xanthe nodded. "You're right," she said, knowing it was what the man wanted to hear, "some of them are quite sought after. And of course there is always a price to be had for silver." She let him enjoy his moment and then went on. "Problem is, a collection of this size, well, nobody's got room for it. We'd have difficulty shifting so many pots to the same person. And, to be honest, we don't have enough storage space for all of them. Ours is a small shop."

"I'm not surprised," said Lionel. "Business rates in Marl-borough are a nightmare. How about you just choose the ones you think you could sell? I can let the charity shop take what you don't want."

Flora's mouth fell open at this. Xanthe knew they couldn't let him give away objects that could be worth tens of thousands of pounds without knowing their value. But if they talked the pieces up too much he might realize what he had and not let them have any. Xanthe thought quickly. It was true that the collection as a whole could be worth a great deal, but it was also a fact that few collectors existed who would be interested. Getting him to split it up might not be doing him out of what he could get, but they had to at least alert him to the real value.

"There are one or two that we're interested in. They'd fit with our stock, you see. Your best bet for the others would be to put them in an auction."

"Really? Would it be worth the bother?"

"Oh yes," Flora insisted. "We can let you have the number of a good auctioneer. He'll see they go into the right sale. You might be surprised how well they do."

"All right, sounds like a plan," he said. "Which ones do you want?"

Xanthe and Flora both waited, just for a moment, deter-mined not to show any real eagerness, wary of seeming too enthusiastic.

Flora waved a stick at the shelves. "I'm quite taken with that flowery set with the cups and saucers. I think they might be Aus-trian. That silver one is Georgian and lovely, but a bit pricey for us, I should imagine. Art nouveau is always popular, so we could make you an offer for those two over there. And the one with the Chinese dragon, I like that. Xanthe, anything take your fancy?"

Xanthe's pulse began to race. The ringing in her ears grew

louder. "Oh, you know me, Mum, I like the rustic stuff," she said, pointing at the copper pot. To her it felt so important, so filled with powerful history, she found it impossible to believe that Lionel Harris wouldn't be able to see how special it was.

"What, that funny old thing with the dents?" he asked. "I suppose you know what young people want. How much for those five then? Sorry to press you, but I've a lunch meeting in Salisbury, and there's the rest of the house to get round yet."

Xanthe didn't trust herself to handle the deal. Flora did her best to sound nonchalant.

"Well, if you throw in the little corner cabinet in the sitting room I think we could go to 3,000 pounds."

To his credit, Esther's nephew did a fair job of hiding his surprise. Even so, Xanthe saw a fleeting expression of delight cross his face. He cleared his throat and strode up to the shelves, studying the pots as if, suddenly, he knew what he was talking about.

"Three thousand, you say? Hmmm."

They waited. The sound of a church bell ringing drifted in through the thin glass of the window.

"Of course pretty china will always find a buyer," he said, looking hard at the set Flora wanted. "How about we make it three and a half?" he asked at last.

Xanthe tensed. Her mother's choices were sound enough, but it was still a niche market. And yet again she was asking her to spend money they scarcely had to buy something she wouldn't want to part with, at least not for some time.

Flora made a show of considering the offer, appearing to do some mental calculations. "Well, that is rather more than I'd like to pay, we do have our markup to consider. . . ." When Lionel didn't budge she smiled. "Tell you what, throw in the Persian rug and you've got yourself a deal."

An hour later, the rest of the house toured with no great finds, Xanthe tucked the bubble-wrapped copper chocolate pot safely into the back of the taxi, swaddling it in the rug, her hands trembling ever so slightly as she did so.

"Soon have you home," she whispered to the strange treasure. "And then you can tell me your story. Promise." At the same time she promised herself that whatever it revealed to her, there would be no more jaunts to the past. Not this time. It was just too dangerous.

She helped her mother into the passenger's seat, handing her some of her painkillers and a bottle of water. The village had woken up properly now, and even so late in the year there were tourists eagerly taking selfies in front of the stunning cottages. Not for the first time, Xanthe wondered at the power of such prettiness to draw people in. It wasn't simply the charming look of the place, of course she knew that; it was the presentation of an ideal. Chocolate box. A rural idyll. Harking back to a time long gone, when lives were simpler and the sun shone constantly. Except that, as Xanthe had found out for herself, lives were often far from simple, and the winters were just as bitter, the cold just as deadly. She climbed in behind the steering wheel and they set off for Marlborough.